Maisey Yates is [...] of over one hund[...] writing strong, ha[...] or multigeneratio[...] lost in fictional worlds. An avid knitter with a dangerous yarn addiction and an aversion to housework, Maisey lives with her husband and three kids in rural Oregon. Check out her website, maiseyyates.com or find her on Facebook.

Lucy Ellis has four loves in life: books, expensive lingerie, vintage films and big, gorgeous men who have to duck going through doorways. Weaving aspects of them into her fiction is the best part of being a romance writer. Lucy lives in a small cottage in the foothills outside Melbourne.

Pippa Roscoe lives in Norfolk near her family and makes daily promises that this is the day she will leave the computer and take a long walk in the countryside. She can't remember a time when she wasn't dreaming of gorgeous alpha males and misunderstood heroines. Totally her mother's fault of course – she gave Pippa her first romance at the age of seven! She is inconceivably happy that she gets to share those daydreams with you! @PippaRoscoe pipparoscoe.com

Foreign Affairs

Foreign Affairs: Argentinean Awakenings

MAISEY YATES

LUCY ELLIS

PIPPA ROSCOE

MILLS & BOON

First Published in Great Britain 2023
By Mills & Boon, an imprint of HarperCollins*Publishers*
1 London Bridge Street, London, SE1 9GF

www.harpercollins.co.uk

HarperCollins*Publishers*
Macken House, 39/40 Mayor Street Upper,
Dublin 1, D01 C9W8, Ireland

FOREIGN AFFAIRS: ARGENTINEAN AWAKENINGS © 2023
Harlequin Enterprises ULC.

The Argentine's Price © 2011 Maisey Yates
Kept at the Argentine's Command © 2016 Lucy Ellis
A Ring to Take His Revenge © 2018 Pippa Roscoe

ISBN: 978-0-263-31870-8

MIX
Paper | Supporting
responsible forestry
FSC™ C007454
www.fsc.org

This book is produced from independently certified FSC™ paper to ensure responsible forest management.

For more information visit: www.harpercollins.co.uk/green

Printed and Bound in Spain using 100% Renewable electricity at CPI Black Print, Barcelona

THE ARGENTINE'S PRICE

MAISEY YATES

For my brother, Kyle.

My partner in crime from the beginning. Long may it continue. And for Lisa, fellow caffeine consumption queen and brain-stormer extraordinaire.

CHAPTER ONE

"YOU'RE buying up my company's stock. Why?" Vanessa clutched her silver purse tightly in her hand and tried to ignore the heat and anger curling in her stomach as she addressed the tall man in black. Lazaro Marino. Her first love. Her first kiss. Her first heartbreak and, apparently, the man who was attempting a hostile takeover of her family's company.

Lazaro's dark eyes flicked over her and he handed his glass of champagne to the slender blonde standing on his left. It was clear from his dismissive manner that he saw the woman as little more than a cup-holder in a designer gown. Well, Vanessa imagined she was a little more than that to him, in his bed at least.

Her cheeks burned, the images in her head instant and graphic. How did he do that? Thirty seconds in his presence and he had her mind in the bedroom.

She stared just past Lazaro, at the painting on the wall behind him, in order to avoid those dark, all-too-knowing eyes of his. She could feel his gaze on her, warming her, turning her blood to fire in her veins. Instant. All-consuming. Still. After all this time. It threw her right back to the summer she was sixteen, when mornings had been all about the hope that he would be there, working on the grounds of the estate. So that she could sit and simply look at him, the boy she wasn't even permitted to talk to.

The boy who ultimately inspired her to break the rules, rules that had been sacrosanct before that.

It was inconvenient that the boy had become a man who still had the power to make her pulse race. Even when he was only a picture in a magazine, looking at him was a full-on sensory experience. In person...in person he made her feel as if her skin was too tight for her body.

"Ms. Pickett." He inclined his head, a lock of obsidian hair falling forward with the motion. Not an accident, she was sure of that. He had that look about him. That sort of hot, can't-be-bothered-to-get-too-slick look. It gave the impression he'd gotten out of bed, combed his fingers through his thick black hair and thrown on a thousand-dollar suit.

And for some reason it was devilishly sexy. Probably because it was easy to imagine what he might have been doing in that bed, what activities might have prevented him from having adequate time to get ready...

She blinked furiously, redirecting her thoughts. She was not going down that rabbit trail again. She wasn't some naive sixteen-year-old anymore, imagining that the fluttering in her stomach was anything more than the first stirrings of lust, imagining that a kiss meant love. No, she wasn't that girl anymore, and Lazaro Marino didn't have any power over her.

She had power. And she would remind him of that.

"Please," she said, turning on her CEO voice. "Call me Vanessa. We are old friends after all."

"Old friends?" He chuckled, a dark, rich sound that made her blood heat. "I had not thought of us as such. But if you insist, Vanessa it is then." His accent had smoothed in the twelve years since she'd seen him, but he still said her name as he always had, his tongue caressing the syllables, drawing them out, making her own name sound impossibly sexy.

Age looked good on him. At thirty, he was even more attractive than he'd been at eighteen. His jaw a bit more square, his shoulders broader. His nose was different, slightly crooked, the imperfection adding to his mystique rather than detracting from his otherwise perfect face. She wondered if he'd broken it in a fight. It wasn't impossible. The Lazaro she'd known had been hotheaded, passionate in every conceivable way. And there had been many times when she'd wondered what it might be like to have all that passion directed at her—and one wonderful occasion when it had been. When he'd made her feel that she was the only woman, the most important thing in his world. Lazaro could lie more effectively with a kiss than most men could with a thousand words.

Vanessa tightened her grip on her purse and took a step back, fighting the rising tide of heat and anger that burned in her stomach, trying to keep herself calm. Unaffected. At least in appearance. "Do you think we could talk?"

"Not here to socialize?" he asked, one black eyebrow quirked.

"I'm here to talk to you, and it's not a social call."

A small smile tipped up the corners of his mouth. "I'm certain you donated to the charity on your way in. Or was that not on your list of priorities tonight?"

Vanessa bit the inside of her cheek, fighting to maintain composure. Taking the glass of champagne out of Lazaro's human cup-holder's hand and throwing the contents of it onto his very expensive suit might be satisfying, but it wasn't what she was here for.

Still, there was no way she was going to allow him to pretend that he was somehow a philanthropic marvel and she was a snobby rich bimbo who walked into a charity event for the company and the liquor and didn't bother to leave a dime.

"I wrote a check as I walked in. You can ask up front if you like."

"Generous of you."

"We need to talk. Without an audience." She flicked a glance at the group he was with. A lot of beautiful socialites, some of whom she recognized, not the sort of women she'd ever been permitted to associate with. Money did not mean class, as her father had always said, and that meant certain people had always been patently off limits to her.

Lazaro among them. Although, for one, heady week, she had defied that command.

"This way, *querida*." He put his hand on her lower back and she cursed the low cut of the gown she was wearing as his palm made contact with her skin. His fingers were calloused, rough from labor still, even after years of white-collar work.

She remembered how those hands had caressed her face, her body. They had been rough then, strong and hot. So very hot. She shivered slightly, thankful that her body chose the moment they stepped out into the chill, Boston air before the reaction hit. At least this way she could blame it on the weather.

The art museum's grand terrace was lit up by paper lanterns strung overhead. A few couples were secluded in dark corners, talking with their heads pressed together, or not talking, enjoying the feeling of seclusion.

Of course, there was no seclusion. There were reporters, there were other people. This was the sort of event her father wouldn't want her to come within a mile of. Discretion was the cornerstone of her father's value system. And of hers.

But she was here. She had to be. She had to talk to Lazaro. As far as Pickett Industries was concerned it was possibly a matter of life and death. She couldn't imagine he had any kind of altruistic motive for purchasing Pickett's shares. In fact, she was certain he didn't.

"You had a question for me?" he asked, leaning against the stone railing.

She turned to him, her face schooled into a neutral expression. "Why are you buying up all of my stocks?"

The corner of his mouth curved upward. "I'm surprised that you realized it so soon."

"Suddenly all of my shareholders are selling to three different corporations, all of whom have one name in common—Marino. I'm not stupid, Lazaro."

"Perhaps I underestimated you." He looked at her, as if waiting for her to be angry or indignant or something. She wouldn't give him the satisfaction.

She pushed down a surge of anger. "I don't care whether you underestimated me. I don't care what you think about me. I care about Pickett and it is in my best interest to try and understand why someone is trying to get to a point where they own equal shares with me and my family."

He paused for a moment, his smile widening, a cruel smile, void of humor, but just as devastating as it had always been. "Do you not appreciate the irony?"

"What irony is that?"

"That *I* can own my share of Pickett Industries. That a storied icon of a company can be passed into the hands of new money with such ease. The American dream, isn't it?"

She looked at his eyes, the glitter in them filled with emotion so dark and deep that she felt it reach into her and pull the air from her lungs. And that was when she realized that it was very likely she'd wandered into a trap. In that moment she wanted, more than anything, to turn and walk away. To leave Lazaro as nothing more than a vivid, unsatisfied memory.

But she couldn't. This was her responsibility. Her mess to clean up. There was no one else.

It's up to you now, Vanessa. Without you, everything crumbles.

Her father's words echoed in her head, filled her, pushed her forward.

"So…this is for your own amusement, then? Something to satisfy your twisted sense of irony?" she asked.

He chuckled, a dark sound laced with bitter undertones. "I don't have time to do things simply to amuse myself, Vanessa. I didn't get where I am by operating that way. My business was not handed to me on a silver platter."

And there was no doubt he found himself superior to her because of that. Fine, he could disdain her for having it easy if he wanted. Pickett wasn't really a silver platter to her. More like silver handcuffs with keys she couldn't access. But she'd willingly accepted the burden. Had done it for her family. For her father, and most of all for Thomas. Because her brother would have carried on Pickett's legacy gladly. He would have made it a success. He would have done it with dignity and kindness, as he had done everything else.

"Then why?" she asked.

"Pickett is dying, Vanessa, I know you know that. Your profits have dropped off in the past three years, so much so that you're now firmly in the red."

Her standard response, the one she'd been placating the shareholders with, rolled off her tongue with ease. "These things happen. It goes in cycles. Production has slowed with the economy as it is, and a lot of our clients are now getting their auto parts manufactured out of the country."

"The problem isn't simply the economy. You are stuck in the past. Times have changed and Pickett Industries has not."

"If Pickett really is dying some kind of slow, painful corporate death, why are you interested in investing your money in it?"

"The opportunity presented itself. I am a man who makes the most of all available opportunities."

Vanessa's stomach tightened as his eyes locked on hers,

the meaning of his words seeming layered in the dim light, almost erotic.

She needed to get out more. She really did. As it was, the four walls of her office were so familiar, her situation was beginning to seem desperate. But that was how it was when one was at the helm of a dying corporation. Lucky, lucky her.

And Lazaro Marino saw it as an opportunity. Heaven help her.

"And what do you intend to do with this *opportunity*?"

"I could put pressure on the board to vote you out of your position."

Vanessa felt as though a bucket of icy water had been thrown in her face. Shock froze her in place, keeping her expression unaltered despite the rolling wave of fear that was surging through her. "Why would you do that?"

"Because you are in over your head, Vanessa. The company has been in decline ever since you were appointed. It is in the best interest of the shareholders to have someone in charge who knows what they're doing."

"I've been working on my game plan."

"For three years? I'm surprised your father hasn't stepped back in and taken control again."

She stiffened. "He can't. When I was appointed CEO he signed an agreement, something the board wanted done to prevent…problems." When her father was in a good mood, he was happy with what she was doing and when he wasn't… well, she wouldn't put it past him to try to oust her himself. No one on the board had wanted the employees, or the shareholders, living with that kind of instability.

Of course, if she didn't turn things around soon that would be the least of anyone's problems.

Vanessa had a degree in business, but a prodigy she was not. She knew it. But she stuck with Pickett out of duty, loyalty to her family, the driving need to make her father happy. How could she do anything else?

Thomas had lived and breathed Pickett, even in high school. Thomas, her handsome brother with the easy smile who had always had time for her, who had shown her warmth and affection, who had remembered her birthday. Who had been the only one able to make their father smile.

And with him gone, she was all her father had left to make sure the company, the family, continued. She couldn't let Thomas's dream die. She couldn't force her father to lose the only thing in the world that truly mattered to him. She couldn't stand to fail at the only thing that made her matter in his eyes.

She couldn't be the one to see it all end, couldn't be the cause of that. She'd let go of vague, half-imagined dreams in order to keep Pickett alive already. She couldn't lose it now. She couldn't see someone else in the position her father had always wanted reserved for someone in their family.

Her great-grandfather had built the business up using family money, and it had been passed down to Vanessa's grandfather, and then to her father. It would have gone on to Thomas next.

The memory of that day was always there, sharp and vivid down to the way the rug in her father's office had made her bare feet itch, to the way her stomach had ached, so intensely she'd been convinced she would die too. Just like her brother.

It's up to you now, Vanessa. Without you, everything crumbles. Everything I've worked for, everything Thomas dreamed of.

She'd been thirteen. All of her brother's responsibilities had been passed on to her that night, the weight of her family's legacy. She'd be damned if she failed.

"It's difficult to compete now that the market has changed. So many things are being done overseas now because there's cheaper labor and lower taxes. It's a hard position for us to be in, but we're committed to keeping the factory here, to keeping the jobs here."

"Idealistic. Not necessarily practical."

He was right, and the worst thing was, she knew it. Had known it from the moment she'd taken her position in the big corporate office. She was fighting a losing battle, and she had been for three long years.

But she didn't want to move the factory, didn't want to eliminate all those jobs. Most of the employees had been with the company for more than twenty years and she couldn't fathom taking that from them. They were her friends in some ways. Her responsibility.

Of course, if the company ceased to exist, the point was moot.

"Maybe not, but I don't have any better ideas right now." It galled to have to say that to him. To be put in the position of having to admit to deficiencies she was far too familiar with.

"As your principal shareholder, I'm not very pleased to hear that."

She narrowed her eyes. "What do you want from me, Lazaro?"

"From you? Nothing. But I very much enjoy the fact that the fate of Pickett is now resting with me."

"Maybe a better question for you is whether this is business or personal."

"It is business. But it is also an interesting quirk of fate, isn't it? Your father once held my future, my mother's future, in his hands. He paid her miserable wages to do work that was so beneath any of you. To keep house and be treated very much as the help. And now I could buy your father ten times over. I have bought the portions of the business that were available."

"So you just intend to lord over us with all that newfound power?"

"As your father has done to others?"

Vanessa bit the inside of her cheek. She knew her father, knew he was difficult at best. But he was all she had, her only family. The most important things to him were their family name, the tradition of the company and their standing in the community. He needed to know that he would always have his place as a pillar of the city, his favorite chair and cigars in his country club.

She wouldn't be the one to lose that for him. Not now.

"I won't say he's been perfect, but he's an old man, he… Pickett means the world to him." And he—they—had lost too much already: Thomas, Vanessa's mother. They couldn't lose any more. It was up to her to make sure that they didn't.

Lazaro looked at Vanessa, her dark brown eyes cool and unreadable, her full lips settled into a slight frown, a berry gloss adding shine to her sexy mouth. She looked every bit what she was. Rich and upper-class, her silver gown hugging her curves without being over the top, the neckline high, the only skin on display the elegant line of her back. Restraint, dignity. That was how the Picketts were. In public at least.

He'd seen a different side to Vanessa Pickett twelve years ago. A side of her that was branded into him, under his skin.

He redirected his thoughts. "What's more important, Vanessa? The bottom line or tradition?"

To Michael Pickett, it was probably tradition. The blood in his veins was as blue as it came. He'd married old money and his daughter was the perfect aristocratic specimen, designed to keep the family name in a position of honor, to keep the family legacy going strong. Likely meant to marry a man of equal stock. That was what mattered to men like him. Not hard work, certainly not any sort of integrity. Just the pres-

ervation of an image and a way of life that was as outdated
as his business practices.

When the opportunity to buy the shares had come up,
Lazaro hadn't been able to turn it down. He hadn't been seeking any kind of poetic justice, but passing the chance up had
been impossible when it had landed in his lap.

"I... Of course profit is the most important thing but we—
my family—*is* Pickett Industries. We're the soul of the company, the reason it's lasted as long as it has. Without us, it
wouldn't be the same."

"Of course it wouldn't be the same. It would be new, modern. Which your father is most definitely not. And you are
running things based on systems put into place by him some
thirty years ago. It's outdated in the extreme."

Her throat convulsed and a muscle ticked in her cheek. Her
delicate hands clung tightly to her purse, the tendons standing out, the effort it took to maintain composure evident. "I
don't know what else to do," she said, her voice flat.

He could see the admission cost her. He wasn't surprised
by it, though. Vanessa had never seemed the CEO type. At
sixteen she'd been sweet—at least he had seen her that way
at first. She'd liked to swim in the pool in her family home's
massive backyard. The image of her lying in a lounge chair
in her electric-pink bikini was burned into his brain, a wa-
termark that colored his view of things more often than he
cared to admit.

She'd been intrigued by him from the start, the kid who
mowed her daddy's lawn. He'd sensed her attraction right
away, her hungry looks open, obvious. He imagined it had
been some form of rebellion for her. To be attracted to not
just a poor boy, but an immigrant, one who was so far removed from the long, storied lineage of the Pickett family it
was nearly laughable.

The fact that she'd managed to burrow beneath his skin,

that the thought of her had made his heart race faster, that he'd looked forward to weeding the flower beds so that he could catch sight of the princess in her tower was even more laughable.

He'd been a fool. That air of sweetness and light had been the perfect way to capture his attention, the kindness she'd shown to him so rare he'd lapped it up like a man dying of thirst. But she'd only been toying with him. And she'd made that clear the evening she rejected him. Later that same night, as a bonus prize to go with the rejection, he'd woken up face-down in an alley, his nose broken along with any of his naive notions of a romance between him and Vanessa, as one of Pickett's hired henchmen warned him to keep away from the precious heiress.

It had been the beginning of rock bottom, both for him and his mother. He at least had crawled his way to the top. His mother had never had the chance. He curled his hands into fists, fought against the blinding rage that always came when he thought of his mother. Of how needlessly she'd suffered.

He chose instead to focus on how far he'd come, how much power he held. Of course, even now, with all of his billions in the bank, he wouldn't be considered good enough for the hallowed Vanessa Pickett. He could have any woman he desired, and had spent many years doing exactly that with women whose names and faces he could no longer remember. But Vanessa was burned into his consciousness. A face he couldn't forget. Kisses he could still remember in explicit detail when far more recent, far more erotic events had faded from his memory.

All the events surrounding her were forever in his mind, etched so deeply, they would never fade. It had shown him that as long as he stayed where he was in life he could be made a victim—a victim of those with money and power, who could hire a group of men to beat up an eighteen-year-old boy, who could get a single mother evicted from her small apartment, get her thrown out onto the streets with no job and no hope of getting a job. He'd vowed never to be a victim again. Never allow anyone to have power over him.

The money he had earned—more than he had ever imagined when he'd started out. But the power, the absolute power that came with admittance into the highest echelons of society—that eluded him. He could not purchase it. It wasn't that simple.

To most on the outside, it would seem he had reached the top, but that was an illusion. What escaped him still was what Vanessa had, what her father had and what they would continue to have even if Pickett Industries went completely bankrupt. A blue bloodline. Family connections that could be traced back to America's first settlers. Not a lineage that began in a hovel in Argentina with an unwed mother and a father whose true identity was a mystery.

He clenched his teeth, fighting against the onslaught of memories brought on by Vanessa's appearance. "Pickett is fixable. And I know exactly what to do to fix it."

Her brown eyes narrowed into slits. "You do?"

"Of course I do. I've made my fortune by turning dying corporations around, you know that, I'm sure."

"Given the constant profiles *Forbes* does on you I'd have to be blind to miss it."

"I can fix the mess," he said, a new idea turning over in his head now, one that made his adrenaline spike and his pulse race.

"By appointing someone new."

"Or not."

"Feeling charitable all of the sudden? I don't buy that, not when you were just dangling the mythical sword over my head."

His heart rate quickened. Right in front of him was the key, dressed in a deceptively sexy silver gown, her dark brown hair swept up into a respectable bun. She was the final step, the way for him to make his entrance into the last part of society that remained locked to him. The way for him to grasp the ultimate power that continued to elude him.

Money was power, but connections combined with money would make his status absolute. It ate at him that there was still a place in society he was barred from. That there were still things outside his control. This was his chance to rise above all that.

And as an added bonus, he would get to see the look on Michael Pickett's face when he took possession of everything the man had always tried so hard to keep in his control. Pickett Industries *and* his only daughter. This was a way to exact revenge on the man who had made Lazaro and his mother unemployable within the circles they'd always worked, the man responsible for their nights on the street in the unforgiving Boston winter. The man responsible for his mother growing weaker and weaker until the strongest woman he had ever known had faded away.

He had watched his mother die in a homeless shelter, without possessions, without dignity.

He bit down hard, his teeth grinding together, the pressure satisfying, helping him keep control over the anger and adrenaline building inside him. He hadn't got where he was by letting opportunities pass him by. He took chances. He made snap decisions with a cool head. It was the secret to his success.

And Vanessa would be the key to his ultimate achievement.

A high-society bride would give him admittance into American aristocracy. He had considered it before, had already considered the advantage of marrying an old-money

name to add weight to his own fortune, to improve his status. But every time he thought of marriage, every time he
thought of finding a society princess, he couldn't stop himself from picturing Vanessa in her pink bikini. Couldn't erase
the memory of stolen kisses in a guesthouse late at night.

Because of that, he'd never entertained the idea of marriage for very long at a time. But now…the idea of Vanessa
as his high-society bride seemed too golden to let pass by. It
was a chance to have all his needs fulfilled: his need to reach
the top, his need for her.

Vanessa, soft and bare beneath him, over him. Touching
him, kissing him. Satisfying him.

Desire, hot and destructive, rushed through him at the
thought of the chance to have her, to be able finally to satisfy the lust he'd carried with him through every affair, that
had plagued him every sleepless night. In that instant, the
flood of lust drove out every other thought. Everything was
reduced to its most basic principle.

See. Want. Have.

He wanted Vanessa. He had spent the past twelve years
with a gnawing sense of unfulfilled desire for justice and for
the woman who haunted his dreams.

And he would have her now.

"I'll help you, Vanessa," he said, keeping his eyes locked
on hers, "on one condition."

She tilted her chin up, revealing the long, elegant line of
her neck. Tender skin he could easily imagine kissing, tasting. "Name your price."

He took a step toward her, cupped her chin between his
thumb and forefinger and was shocked by the bolt of electricity that arced between them. She still had power over his
body. But judging by the faint color in her cheeks, the tremble in her lips, he had power too.

"Marriage."

CHAPTER TWO

"Are you insane?" she hissed, looking over her shoulder, checking to see if they were drawing stares. If her father ever heard about her meeting tonight with Lazaro Marino he would very likely explode, just before taking back control of the company, tearing the contract to shreds and dismissing her as a complete and utter failure, both as CEO and his daughter.

"Not in the least," Lazaro said.

Vanessa took a step away from him, her heart thundering in her ears. "I'm serious, Lazaro. Did you by any chance suffer a head injury in the past twelve years? Because while you were never the most sophisticated man I've ever met, you seemed lucid then, at least."

"I'm perfectly lucid," he said dryly. "Don't pretend that you're a stranger to the concept of a marriage of convenience."

Of course she wasn't. There was a reason that every boyfriend she'd ever had had been introduced to her by her father. That there was usually a folder with the man's name stamped on it somewhere in her father's office. The man she ended up with had to be from the right family, with the right reputation. The right credentials.

But she'd never wanted that. A part of her, a part that she kept guarded, locked away so that no one else would ever see, was still that romantic sixteen-year-old girl who believed in love. Who wanted to be loved for who she was, not for her bank balance or for the shape of her body.

Of course, as far as her father was concerned, none of that mattered. Craig Freeman loomed in her future, the man her father had found worthy, the man with the right connections. That part of her life had been selected for her, as her job had been. As so many things in her life were.

Craig had been pinpointed as proper husband material before she'd been old enough to drive.

She'd managed to avoid marriage thanks to college and the demands of running Pickett. Before that, she had worked in most of the positions at Pickett so she could learn the ins and outs of everything, so she hadn't had time to get married. Or even to have a date.

Recently she hadn't had much time to do anything short of commuting to and from her office while taking antacids in hopes of easing the constant burn of stress in her chest.

"Of course I'm familiar with the concept, but that doesn't mean I have a desire to take part in one," she said crisply. That much was true. Marriage of any sort had never seemed like a real problem; it had always been safe in the gauzy future, not something she'd directly addressed. "And I really don't want to marry you." That part she added for good measure, and then wished she hadn't.

"Since when is any of this about want? Do you think I want to get married? To tie myself to one woman forever? Necessity. I've known for a long time that I needed to make a good marriage in order to move freely in all social circles. I hadn't considered you before, but now I see that you'll be perfect. Consider yourself a walking, talking invitation into high society."

Vanessa bit her tongue. "You're sure you didn't sustain a head injury, Lazaro?"

"Quite."

"Because I don't remember you being this much of a bastard either."

"Time changes people, Vanessa. As I'm sure you know. You aren't who you used to be either, are you?"

"No," she said.

Except maybe she was. Being so near Lazaro now made her feel things she'd thought she'd left behind long ago, things she only let herself dwell on when she was alone, in the privacy of her room, in a painfully large and empty bed. Then she let herself dream—about a man who could share not just her bed, but her life. Her love.

But as soon as dawn broke through the curtains, reality returned, and it only hit harder the minute she walked into her office each morning to confront a failing company and her family's heritage slipping through her fingertips because she couldn't figure out how to fix the mess Pickett Industries was in.

And then there was the marriage her father already had planned for her. A marriage to a man she hardly knew, a man she hadn't bothered to get to know, because she'd never been able to face the idea.

When she'd seen Lazaro for the first time, at sixteen, she'd discovered how badly she wanted love, and she'd let herself dream. A mistake. She'd fallen for him on sight, had thought he was special. Unique. But she knew the truth now. Lazaro wasn't unique. He wanted everything he could get. Money. Power. And if he had to use her to get it, he would.

His dark eyes were intent on hers, eyes that used to have a glimmer of humor in them. It was easy to imagine it there. Easy to imagine the boy he'd been. The inky black sky and the outline of the city faded and she was back there, in the summer, twelve years earlier.

* * *

"You aren't really supposed to talk to me." Vanessa looked over her shoulder to make sure her father wasn't watching. Just an instinctive check, because he was at the office, where he always was.

Lazaro smiled, teeth bright white against his bronze skin. Her heart started to beat faster. "Why is that?"

"Because I… Aren't you on the clock or something?"

He looked around the immaculate yard, then back at her, dark eyes locked on hers. It made her stomach tighten. Having him so close…she felt jittery, nervous. But she'd been watching him all summer, had been nurturing her crush on him until it had grown into something more. She lived for him to glance her way, for him to watch her while she lounged by the pool. She longed to see the interest in those beautiful eyes of his.

"I don't get paid hourly," he said, flashing her a grin that made her stomach do somersaults. "I'm done anyway."

"Oh…" she trailed off, all the words in her head jumbled.

"I'll stay until my mother's ready to leave for the day."

Vanessa suddenly felt too exposed in her bikini. She'd picked it partly to draw his attention, but now, with him standing so close, she felt acutely aware of how much skin was on display. She'd never really tried to draw attention to herself using her body, because she hadn't been ready for a man to take her up on the offer.

But Lazaro was different. He made her feel different.

They talked for the rest of the afternoon. About school, how different his inner-city public school was compared to her private all-girls school. But it turned out they liked the same foods, the same music, even though she had to hide hers from her father. She loved hearing how he talked about his mother, how proud he was of her. Vanessa told him how much she missed her mother.

They talked every day that week, sneaking around the

property, evading watchful eyes, and by the end of it, Vanessa was certain she was in love. She also knew that if her father ever found out, Lazaro and his mother wouldn't have jobs anymore and she would be grounded for the rest of her life.

Because while most of the world had modernized, Michael Pickett had not. He very much believed in a class system and in socializing only with those who shared your designated position. She wasn't naive enough to think that her father's heart would soften if she explained that she was really, truly in love with Lazaro.

She was already giving up so much in order to take on the responsibilities of Pickett Industries, already sacrificing so many dreams to major in business when she went to college and spend her life behind a desk, just as her father had done.

Surely that should count for something.

Yes, she and Lazaro had a gulf between them as far as money went. As far as prominence in society went, the gulf was even wider, impossible to bridge. But Vanessa didn't care. She couldn't care. When he looked at her, designer fashions, upscale parties and any feeling of being part of the elite faded completely. The world was reduced to her and Lazaro. There was nothing more.

And that was why risking serious consequences to see him was more than worth it.

It made her wonder what it would be like if it were only the two of them. If she had to leave it all behind for him... she would.

"Meet me tonight. Where no one can see," Lazaro said.

They were hidden in an alcove behind the guesthouse and it was doubtful that they could be seen, but there was always a risk. A bigger risk for him than for her, she knew.

"Okay." She didn't hesitate because she wanted more time with him, craved more time. She wanted to have him hold her hand. To kiss her. To tell her he loved her as she loved him. "Meet me here, at the guesthouse. I can get a key."

She spent the rest of the afternoon trying to decide what to wear, changing her clothes a hundred times. It felt like a first date. She was. Sort of. She'd never been on a date, had never kissed anyone. At her age, she felt like an oddity. Most of her friends at school had done a lot more than that.

But her father kept her on a tight leash, and boys were not something that was supposed to concern her at this stage of her life. Too bad for her father, since he couldn't control her thoughts, and boys had been among her biggest concerns for the past four years.

None of her crushes or interests mattered though, not really. There was a boy, a man really, six years her senior, that her father had his eye on for her—Craig Freeman. His family had all the right connections, the proper bloodline. And the thought of being married off to him someday made her feel like one of her father's broodmares.

She pushed the thought to one side. Craig was far in the future. He was on the West Coast building his name, and as far as she was concerned, having the entire expanse of the country between them was perfect.

And tonight, maybe she would just pretend he didn't exist. Maybe…maybe after tonight she would find the courage to tell her father that she didn't want Craig. At all. Ever.

She looked at the clock and then back at the full-length mirror. Her skirt was too short and her shirt was too tight. That's what her father would say. But she wasn't dressing for her father's approval.

Tonight, only Lazaro's approval mattered.

She left her bedroom light on and closed the door. Her father was at his country club and the odds of him coming home before midnight were slim. Still, she wasn't taking chances.

She slipped quietly through the house and out the door, across the lawn.

When she got down to the guesthouse, Lazaro was there, waiting for her. Relief and happiness flooded through her. "You came."

He smiled that wonderful, knee-weakening smile. "Of course."

She unlocked the door and led him inside. "We can't turn on any lights," she whispered. "Someone might see."

"That's fine." Lazaro took her hand, the shock of his skin against hers making her body jolt. "We don't need lights."

He tugged her gently to him and wrapped his arm around her waist, placed his other hand on the back of her head and tangled his fingers in her hair. She was glad she'd left it down.

He leaned in, his lips feather-light on hers. Everything around her stopped for a moment, time, her heart, everything, as he increased the pressure of his mouth on hers. She closed her eyes, just standing there, letting the sensation of being kissed by Lazaro wash over her.

When the tip of his tongue slid over her lower lip, her mouth parted in shock and he took advantage, stroking his tongue over hers. She wrapped her arms around his neck, boldness surging through her, a desire to make him feel the way she did, hold him captive to sensation, just as she was.

It was nothing like her friends had said. They said it was awkward. Bumping noses and teeth. She'd always heard that a lot of guys were sloppy kissers. But Lazaro was perfect. And there was nothing awkward about it.

And she was so glad she wasn't experiencing this moment with insipid, pale Craig Freeman. He looked as though he would probably be a sloppy kisser. She shoved the thought to one side, firmly planting her mind in the moment.

Lazaro took her hand in his, tugged it lightly as he took a step toward the hallway.

"What?" she asked, feeling dizzy, dazed, her body and soul focused on when he would kiss her again, caress her again.

"Looking for some place more comfortable."

She nodded and followed, her heart pounding in her throat; the only rooms back here were bedrooms, and she really didn't think she was ready for anything that might happen in a bedroom. But Lazaro was… He was different from anyone she'd ever known. She trusted him to go slow. To be what she needed.

He opened a door and looked inside, pushed it open and laced his fingers through hers again, drawing her in with him. She paused in the doorway, looking at the big bed. Her heart thundered hard—nerves, emotion, hormones threatening to wash her away in a powerful tide. He couldn't want to…they'd barely kissed.

He pulled her to him, his hand caressing her cheek. "Just kiss me," he whispered.

Yes. When she kissed him, everything else faded away. Just kissing.

He led her to the bed, his dark eyes serious on hers. She leaned in and kissed him again. He smelled clean. Not fussy and coated in cologne like the guys that went to the country club, but like soap and skin. Like Lazaro.

She'd never wanted anything, anyone, more in her life. She just wanted to stay with him forever, in the guesthouse, away from rules and propriety and all the things she was supposed to want. None of them mattered now. Only Lazaro mattered.

He sat on the bed and she sat with him, accepting a hungry kiss, his hands sliding over her back, down her waist, gripping her hips as he kissed her. Deeply. Passionately. Every thought fled her mind. Everything but how good it felt to have him touch her, kiss her, almost devour her as though she was the most decadent dessert he'd ever had.

She didn't even realize she was falling until she felt the

soft mattress beneath her back, and Lazaro's hard frame over her. She tangled her fingers in his thick dark hair, her thighs parting slightly to make room for him.

Her heart felt as though it was overflowing with emotion, with love. She had to tell him. Had to tell him how much she loved him. How she wanted him forever. No matter what her father thought, or what anyone said. The words hovered on her lips, but she couldn't find the courage to say them.

He knew though. He had to know. She wouldn't be here with him if she didn't love him.

He pushed her shirt up just enough to expose her stomach, the calloused skin of his fingertips pleasantly rough against her tender flesh. She arched into his touch and he took advantage, kissing her exposed neck.

The longing that overtook her was so big, beyond the physical, a deep emotional well that opened up inside her, desperate to be filled, so desperate for all of the attention that was being directed at her.

She was always lonely. Since Thomas had died the void in her life had been vast, her isolation in her own home devastating.

At least it had been until Lazaro. He brought the light back. He held the possibility of a future that wasn't filled with Pickett Industries.

When his hands moved higher, cupping her, she simply enjoyed his touch, tried to push all of the worries out of her mind and simply live in the moment.

He pulled away from her and stood. "What are you doing?" she asked.

"Condom," he said, his chest rising and falling with hard, labored breaths as he reached into his pocket.

A wave of shock rolled over her, making her ears buzz, her throat tight. "I… No," she said, scrambling to sit up. She'd just had her first kiss, anything more was impossible to fathom. "No."

She was torn then, torn because in so many ways she wanted him. Wanted to take advantage of being alone with him, of having all of his intensity focused on her. Part of her wanted to make love with him. To take every step possible to make him hers.

But she wasn't ready. She wanted love before there were condoms involved. She needed the words. She just did.

And if anyone found out she'd had her first kiss and her first time on the same night, in her father's guesthouse? She cringed at the thought.

"What would people think?" The words tumbled out before she had a chance to turn them over.

His eyes darkened, his mouth pressing into a tight line. A muscle jumped in his cheek. "I don't know, *querida*." The Spanish endearment sounded like a curse. "They might not think anything of it. I assumed you had arrangements with all of the gardeners."

His words were like gunfire, shocking and devastating. Harsh in the small, quiet space. "I…"

"You certainly aren't the only one of my clients' daughters I've gotten into bed."

Insults, angry words, curses she'd never spoken out loud before, all swirled in her head, but her throat was too tight for her to speak. And in his eyes, she could see her pain mirrored, raw and achingly sad.

He just looked at her for a moment, and she wished she had the courage to say something. But she just wanted to curl in on herself and hold the hurt to her heart.

"I think we're done here then." He turned and walked out, and she just sat and watched him go.

She wanted to go after him. To explain what she'd meant,

because she was certain her words had hurt him in some way. To scream at him for making her hurt.

You'll see him again tomorrow. You can fix it then.

Except she'd been wrong about that. He'd walked out and he'd never come back. All he'd wanted from her was sex. That had been her introduction to relationships. Not exactly sterling. It was a memory, an experience she couldn't free herself from.

And more often than not her mind chose to focus not on the fight, but on the way his mouth had felt moving over hers. The slide of his tongue, his hands on her skin.

Worse than that were the times when she thought about what she'd been willing to do for him. She'd been ready to leave everything behind—her father, Pickett Industries— for him. That had been a moment in time when her future had seemed fluid rather than set in stone, and sometimes she dreamed of what it would be like to have options. To have the unknown stretching before her in a good way, and not in a failing-company, heartburn-causing kind of way.

Her mind was wicked. And treacherous.

Tonight was the first time she'd seen Lazaro in person since he'd left her sitting on the bed in her father's guest-house, although she'd revisited that night a thousand times every time she saw a picture of him, heard him discussed at cocktail parties. The bad boy made good. She'd never been able to truly escape him. Though she'd tried.

She'd only tracked him down now because the ghost of make-out sessions past was trying to stage a hostile takeover of her business—her life. Otherwise, she never would have sought him out again. Ever.

"The way I see it, Vanessa, you have very little choice in the matter if you want Pickett to survive."

"No," she said, "I don't see marriage as a formal business transaction."

"Now, I find that hard to believe."

"Really?"

He nodded. "Are you saying your father has nothing to do with the man you'll marry?" He watched as the light in her dark eyes dimmed. "Are you saying you get to choose?"

She shook her head. "Not... It's complicated."

"Not really."

"I can't," Vanessa said, keeping her voice hard, commanding. The voice she used during board meetings and to men who assumed she couldn't handle being in charge.

"You're already promised to someone, aren't you? Someone with the appropriate bloodlines?" His lip curled into a sneer. "Waiting for one of those golden boys to bail you out?"

"You know my father, he doesn't leave loose ends. Of course there's someone in his plans." The admittance was strange because no one, herself included, had ever voiced it. But no one had ever had to say anything. It was understood. It was as ingrained in her as which fork to use for the salad.

"Do you love him?"

"No." She didn't love Craig Freeman, or even know him, by her own design. She'd taken pains to avoid him, in fact. That hadn't been too hard since he'd been across the country for the majority of their tentative arrangement. He seemed about as interested in the whole thing as she was.

And that was another reason she'd never broached the subject with her father.

"Then why do you have an issue with a business-oriented marriage where I'm concerned?"

Because Craig Freeman could be put off. He was unchallenging. He was a nonentity. In some ways, it had been easier knowing that he was in the not-too-distant future. It took the pressure off her finding Mr. Right when she hardly had enough time to put on lipstick in the morning. Craig didn't make her heart race or her body burn. Lazaro Marino did. And *he* would not be put off by anyone.

Vanessa sucked in a sharp breath. "Before this goes any further, I need to know what this is about."

"Why is it that I can't get business deals with your father's cronies? Why is it that their businesses languish, and yet they sit in their clubs sipping brandy and smoking cigars, ignoring the downfall, rather than pursuing help?"

"Because they're a bunch of stubborn old men who are set in their ways," she said. "Their business models are outdated, just as you've accused Pickett's of being."

"Perhaps. And also because I am not worthy in their eyes. They would rather watch their companies crumble than ask someone like me, with my dirty blood, for help."

"That's ridiculous," she said, even though she knew it was true. Those men would never stoop to taking a consultation from someone so far beneath them in station. That exclusivity was the source of their power, and they weren't about to let it go, no matter how modernized the rest of the world had become.

"It's not. We both know that."

"And you think marrying me will fix that for you?"

He chuckled. "I'm sure the son-in-law of Michael Pickett would be due some respect."

"If my father didn't disown me for marrying you instead of the golden boy he's selected for me," she said.

"Would he?"

She paused for a moment, honestly wondering if he would. She'd been ready to take the chance twelve years ago. More than ready to carve a new life for herself and Lazaro, to leave it all behind.

That dream had ended quickly. Maddeningly, it tantalized

her sometimes when she was in bed, on the edge between sleep and wakefulness. Stupid subconscious.

Finally, she shook her head. "No. He wouldn't. He has too much invested in me. And I own more stock than he does at this point. He can't vote me out of my position, which would mean that if he did disown me he would be separating himself from the company, and he won't do that."

"But if there is no company?" he asked.

If there was no company, her father would never speak to her again. Her life, everything she had worked for for so long, would be meaningless. She would have nothing but her big, empty town house—if she could even afford to keep it—with her big, empty bedroom and her big, empty bed. The thought made her sick, made her stomach physically cramp.

"It's not an option," she said. She refused to think about it. Refused to entertain the idea.

Her relationship with her father was complicated. It wasn't a happy, hugging sort of relationship, but he was all that she had, her only family. He was the one constant in her world. He had always cared for her, he had set her path in front of her and he had paid for her schooling to make sure his goals were met.

And she'd done all she could to earn his approval, done what she could to help fill the void Thomas had left behind. The Pickett heir—the real Pickett heir—hadn't lived to graduate from high school.

It was up to her now. It wasn't a responsibility she could simply shake off or ignore.

"And can you risk that, Vanessa?"

"No." She choked on the word.

"Then marry me."

"It's crazy, you know that, right?"

"More so than the arrangement you already have?"

"Yes," she fired back, brown eyes blazing.

Lazaro's gut tightened. Of course she would feel that way. He was beneath her. He had been a toy to her twelve years ago. Good enough to flirt with, to tease, but nothing more.

What would people think? The look of horror on her face, the incredulity in her voice, was crystal clear in his mind, as though she had spoken it only a moment ago, instead of what amounted to a lifetime ago.

He was the housekeeper's son, and she was the princess of the castle. Years later, now that he had billions to his name and a reputation as one of the world's savviest business minds, she still believed herself above him.

Even as the anger coursed through him, he wanted her. Wanted her with the same burning desire he'd had for her when they were teenagers. Yes, he wanted the vital connections marrying her would provide. But at the moment, more than anything, he wanted her body. He wanted to finish what he had started twelve years ago. He wanted Vanessa, naked, willing, in his bed, crying out his name. His and no other man's. He wanted to brand her as she had done to him with those kisses years ago.

Vanessa's lips on his, her delicate hands skimming over his skin—everything narrowed down to that. The broader goal was lost. There was nothing beyond lust. Simple, pure lust that had been with him since the first moment he'd seen her. A lust that had never released its hold on him. The need to satisfy it was suddenly driving, imperative.

He closed his hands into fists, took in a deep breath.

As much as he wanted that, he had to remember what his real goal was. There would be plenty of time to seduce Vanessa once they were married. It was about business now, and the rest would come later. Business, and dealing with Michael Pickett.

What sweet justice it would be, marrying Vanessa. Having her replace her hallowed last name with his.

How wonderful it would be to see Michael Pickett's face when he discovered his only daughter would be marrying the man he had had beaten in a back alley for daring to touch his beloved princess. For daring to sully her with his hands. A laborer's hands. An immigrant's hands.

Lazaro curled his fingers, forming fists.

The other man's fate—the fate of his much-loved business and that of his only child—was now Lazaro's to decide.

Just as his fate and his mother's fate, had once been Michael Pickett's to decide. And what a decision he'd made. He'd had them evicted. Had made sure they couldn't find work in Boston and that what little they'd had was lost to them.

Now the older man would know what it was like to feel desperate, to have to depend on the whims of someone else. What it was like to have his power stripped from him.

Men like him didn't deserve such absolute power.

"I'm offering you a very simple solution, Vanessa."

"Oh, yes, simple. In what world is marriage the simple solution?"

"In *this* world. Alliances are made by advantageous marriages, it happens every single day. You admitted it is already in your future."

"Nothing was finalized. I believe marriage should be about love."

She looked so sincere when she said it, brown eyes liquid in the dim light. What would Vanessa Pickett know about love? No more than he did.

"Romanticizing an institution has always seemed pointless to me."

Vanessa swallowed hard, her heart thundering, the pulse in her neck fluttering. "You don't seem the type to romanticize anything."

She knew that about him. Had known it the moment kissing had turned into more and he'd produced a condom rather than words of love. Ironic that her very first marriage proposal was from him, twelve years after she'd been hoping to hear it. Of course, there was still no mention of love.

She'd been a romantic then, with all of her heart and not just a piece of it. And she'd learned, at Lazaro's hands, that blind naïveté didn't protect you from cold reality.

And what she had now was cold reality at its finest. A dying business, one that was under her control, the very real danger of losing that control. Worse, of losing the entire company to bankruptcy along with any respect she'd managed to gain from her father. She would be the one to destroy a family legacy that had stood for one hundred years. She was so close to losing absolutely everything, having nothing but a cold, arranged marriage waiting for her when the dust settled.

She also had an out in the form of Lazaro Marino. A deal with the devil, and it would only cost her soul. Well, maybe that was an exaggeration. But from where she was standing, it must look a lot that way. A dark, handsome devil, sure, but the devil nonetheless. And it was truly an exchange of one marriage of convenience for another.

Of course, for better or for worse, the arrangement with Lazaro would never be cold.

No. Impossible. She looked at him, broad shoulders, thickly muscled chest, trim waist and hips. He had a body most women would pay money to get their hands on, and the face of a fallen angel. Perfectly handsome, but with that hint of danger provided by his slightly bent nose and dark stubble. Stubble that would feel rough against her hands, her cheek…

"It isn't as though we would marry immediately," he said, his deep voice breaking through her fantasy.

"We wouldn't?" A stupid response, as though she'd agreed to something when she hadn't done any such thing.

"No. It takes time to plan a wedding. Especially of the calibre I have in mind."

"Oh, you've thought about this?" For some reason that made her stomach tighten.

"Not in a specific sense. But there are certain things expected from a society wedding." His lips curved up into a smile. A smile that lacked humor and warmth. It made her shiver.

She'd never wanted a huge wedding. She'd seen that circus one too many times. Had been a part of it for family friends. Those weddings were impersonal, affairs for the guests and not for the couple, and she'd always found them disingenuous. Although, she was certain, the choice would have been taken from her when the time came with Craig. A big, three ring circus of a wedding, befitting the alliance between the Picketts and the Freemans. The thought made her slightly dizzy. She hadn't given a lot of thought to that eventual union, but all this wedding talk was forcing it to the forefront, making her face something she'd been dutifully ignoring for years.

It had been a foolish thing, keeping that corner of her heart reserved for romantic fantasy. There had never been a hope for that in her future. Never. Lazaro's appearance didn't alter that, it just altered the groom. Craig, with his pale, angelic looks, was after her for the connections she would provide, and Lazaro, dark and dangerous, wanted the same. Neither man offered her love. Lazaro, at least, would help her hold on to Pickett Industries.

"And what do you intend to do with me until the wedding?"

He smiled again, and this time it touched his eyes, lighting a spark in their depths. Heat. She knew the look. She'd been on the receiving end of it before. And it was no less devastating to her at twenty-eight than it had been to her at sixteen.

He extended his hand, his open palm cupping her cheek, and heat spread through her, making her knees feel shaky, her breasts heavy. How long had it been since she'd been so close to a man? And how long had it been since one had made her feel like this? The very few times she'd come into contact with Craig she hadn't felt even the slightest twinge of electricity.

"I'll spend that time seducing my future wife," he said, his voice husky, the remnants of his accent clinging to the syllables, making each word sound like a sensual caress.

She swallowed, her throat suddenly tight and dry as though it had been lined with sandpaper. He was talking about seduction. Sex. It took her right back to that moment, the moment when he'd made it clear that sex was on his agenda for the night, his hand in his pocket, reaching for a condom. She'd been tempted then too, but…she'd loved him then. Or something. She'd been sixteen and sixteen-year-old girls were given to the dramatic when it came to matters of the heart.

That romantic part of herself had always hoped against hope that the man she gave her body to would be a man who loved her desperately, a man she felt the same way about.

It wasn't that that made her want to hold back from Lazaro though. It was the fact that he seemed to command some sort of power over her body, that he could get her hot just by looking at her. He robbed her of all the steely control no other man had ever been able to crack.

That was scarier than anything. That was something she had to master because she was not allowing him to have that kind of hold over her. Not when he already had so much power.

"I'm not just going to jump into bed with you. I don't even know you."

"Sometimes that adds to the fun, Vanessa."

The way he said it, his rich, accented voice caressing the words, made her almost believe it. Made her wonder if love was overrated. "That's not how I see things, Lazaro," she said, her throat so constricted she could hardly force the words out.

"Relax. The courtship will be for the benefit of the media and my future clients. What better than a grand love story to keep everyone fascinated?"

"I don't know if any of my father's friends are old romantics."

"Perhaps not. But the more genuine it looks, the better. It's essential that it look real."

"I don't know…"

"What is it you don't know, Vanessa? Whether you want to embrace success or failure?"

"Why does it have to be marriage?" she asked. "Why can't…"

"Why can't I simply hand you the solution? Why can't I give you the knowledge and help that Pickett Industries cannot afford? Because that's what your father, your family would do for others?"

"That isn't…"

"Nothing in life is free, Vanessa. Nothing."

"I know that," she said, her voice fading. She did know it. She knew the cost of duty over desire better than he realized. Pickett Industries wasn't her dream; Craig Freeman had never been her dream. But running the company, marrying Craig, were what she was supposed to do. This was her duty to her father, to Thomas's memory. And duty was something she'd embraced rather than turning away from. It had taken strength to do that, to deny whatever else she might want in order to preserve her father's respect for her. In order to preserve the Pickett family legacy.

"These are my terms, you can take them or leave them."

Vanessa felt as though the world had just rocked beneath her feet. But it hadn't; the paper lanterns above her head were still steady, the people around them were still talking, unaware that her life was crumbling around her, that everything she had always believed about herself lay in ashes before her.

She'd never thought she would stoop so low. Had never thought she would be the one willing to do whatever it took for the sake of money and power. And maybe if it were only money and power she wouldn't. Regardless of what Lazaro said, this did seem different from the friendly, family-made arrangement she had with Craig. This seemed mercenary. It seemed… It felt in some ways that she was selling herself. Her body.

But this was her reputation. It was all she had worked for. It was her relationship with the only family she had. If she didn't have that, she would have nothing. Breaking the unofficial engagement with Craig was one thing, losing Pickett, letting it fall into someone else's hands…that her father would never forgive her for. And she would never forgive herself.

She couldn't face that. And it was time to step up. To do what she'd been doing all her life—make the choice that would best benefit her family legacy and all of the employees who depended on her family for their paychecks.

"I'll take them." Her words sounded flat and harsh in the silent night air.

"A very wise choice, Vanessa." Lazaro's expression didn't change, his eyes remained flat and dark, latent heat smoldering there, his square jaw still set firmly. But she could feel a change in him, a subtle shift in the energy radiating from him. It resonated in her, caused a response she couldn't ignore or deny.

She looked at the cool, hard man standing in front of her. To him, this was business. Another way for him to climb to the top. She just had to see it the same way. She couldn't afford to involve her heart.

"I didn't have much of a choice, did I?" she asked.

"Not one that had a better outcome. And you're a smart woman. You know that the end result is all that matters."

She wanted to be that woman. She tried to be that woman. Because that was the woman who was going to pull Pickett out of the red.

"Pickett Industries is all that matters," she said slowly, feeling the virtual shackles tightening on her wrists even as she spoke the words.

CHAPTER THREE

SURREAL didn't even begin to describe it. Waking up and re-alizing she had consented to marry Lazaro Marino the night before was surreal on an epic scale worthy of Salvador Dali. Given the state of things, she wouldn't have been shocked to see her clock melt off the wall.

But, as surreal as it was, it was her new reality. Nonetheless she couldn't make it feel real. She felt as if she was in a fog that not even driving to work through Boston's harrowing traffic could shake her out of. And when she sat down at her desk it didn't get any better.

It was early, the sun rising pink against the skyline of the city. Vanessa picked up her smartphone and snapped a picture. It was muted, nothing like it would have been if it had been done with an actual camera, something she'd never bothered to buy for herself. It wasn't that she couldn't afford one, but she didn't have time to indulge in any hobby that didn't di-rectly benefit her company.

She would have even less time as CEO of Pickett Industries and fiancée to Lazaro Marino. She looked at her left hand. It was bare, no engagement ring. But there would be one, she had no doubt about that. Lazaro was a man of details and a detail like that wouldn't be overlooked.

She leaned forward and rested her forehead on the cool wood of her desk. How had she gotten so deep into a life that she didn't want? She closed her eyes and took in a deep breath, trying to halt the tears that were starting to form.

She'd made her choice. Long before Lazaro had walked back into her life, she'd made her choice to do what she had to do to keep Pickett Industries in the family. She'd gone to college and majored in business so she could see that that happened, and that she did the best job she could. She'd chosen to put everything personal on hold in order to keep the business afloat.

It was just a part of her duty to Pickett. It felt like more though.

A strange bubble of exhilaration filled her chest because suddenly her future was different. The man standing at the altar in her mind was no longer Craig Freeman; it was the one man who had inspired a kind of reckless abandon in her. The one man who'd made her want to break the rules.

By marrying him, she was both toeing the line and rebelling against it.

That was liberating in some ways, terrifying in others. And what she really wanted to do—hide under her desk until the storm blew over—was impossible because she had to keep it together. She was the CEO of Pickett. She couldn't question her decisions, and she couldn't hide from the hard stuff.

The choice was made. There was no going back. She was committed.

"And possibly in need of being committed, since you're clearly certifiable," she mumbled into the emptiness of her office.

There was the small matter of telling her father that she would not be following his "advice" and pursuing a marriage with Craig. And that Lazaro was the one she was choosing instead. His wrath would be monumental. But she was between a serious rock and a hard place, and the broken marriage agreement, such as it was, would be much more forgivable than the loss of the family legacy.

A sharp knock on her office door had her lifting her head quickly, smoothing her hair. "Yes?"

The door swung open and her heart dropped into her stomach. Whether it had been twelve years or twelve hours, Lazaro still had all the power to make her body hot and achy, to make her lips tingle with the desire to feel his kiss.

"Good morning," he said, coming in without waiting for her permission. She doubted he ever waited for permission to do anything.

"Not especially. What brings you here?"

"I couldn't stay away from my beautiful fiancée," he said, his blinding smile making her stomach curl tightly.

Her stupid, traitorous heart leapt back into her chest and started thundering madly, despite the dry humor in his tone. She cleared her throat. "Right. Why are you here?"

"Because there are details we need to work out."

"Right. Details," she said, her voice hollow.

"There will be a prenup."

"I would hope so," she said, fighting to keep her tone neutral while nerves tightened her throat.

She didn't know if she could go through with it. Marry him. Live with him. Sleep with him. Let her whole life get tangled up in Lazaro.

Speak now, or forever hold your peace.

She looked at him, at the hardened line of his jaw, the glint of steel in his dark eyes. It was too late. If she went back now, he would take everything from her. Everything that made her Vanessa Pickett.

The words stuck in her tightened throat.

"I'm not counting on a lifetime of wedded bliss," he said, his voice dry.

"You aren't?"

"Hardly. But what I am expecting is that you will stand beside me with all the duty and conviction of a politician's wife."

"What exactly does that mean?" she asked, feeling dizzy all of a sudden, fighting to convey only cool composure.

"During a political scandal, no matter how vile, the politician's wife always stands beside her husband because it is about more than marriage. It is her job. This marriage will be your job."

"Planning on creating a vile scandal, are you?" She treated him to her deadliest glare. He seemed entirely unaffected.

"Not in the least. But my point is that no matter what, your commitment to our union must outweigh the circumstances. If at some point we are leading separate lives it is of no concern to me, so long as appearances show a united couple."

She'd been wrong about him being the friendlier option to her arrangement with Craig. As little as marriage with Craig had been truly discussed, she'd assumed he would at least try to be a husband to her. Lazaro wasn't promising that. Not even close.

"Does that mean that even if you cheat on me I have to stay with you?"

"As I will stay with you," he said, his voice hard. "The union, the legal marriage, is what I need. I cannot project thirty years into the future, but I will ensure that you are still with me."

Vanessa was having a hard time breathing. It was as though he'd turned over her solid wood desk and placed it on her chest. Thirty years. This wasn't a temporary arrangement. He was talking about the rest of her life. Shackled to this man.

She tried to imagine turning away again. Imagined telling him the deal was off, and he could take his shares and the entirety of Pickett Industries to hell with him for all she cared.

But she couldn't. The words wouldn't come. They wouldn't even form in her brain in a cohesive manner. The idea of Lazaro losing his hold on her didn't open up a wide arena of possibilities for her life, rather, it showed just how narrow her scope of options truly was. Without Lazaro, the company crumbled. Without the company she had no job, no relationship with her father.

She'd promised her father, the week that Thomas died, that she wouldn't fail him, and she'd set out to make sure she didn't from that day on. She'd dropped out of the photography club she'd been in at school, started doing some basic business courses instead. Done whatever she could to ensure she didn't let her father down.

In her mind, she was a Pickett. She was a loyal daughter. She was the CEO of Pickett Industries. Without that…she didn't know who she was beyond that. And without Lazaro's help, she wouldn't be any of those things. Of course, it was his interference that forced her to choose. But without him, there might not be any choice at all other than to watch Pickett slowly sink beneath the waves of debt, another casualty of a shifting business landscape.

And while this might not have been her first choice for how her life would end up, it was the right thing. At least this way, she would keep the business going. She would have children who would eventually take over.

Her stomach cramped at the thought. Yes, she'd planned on having children someday, but if she said yes they would be Lazaro's children. The room suddenly seemed much too small, Lazaro's presence in it far too big.

Another thought, small and insidious, reminded her of that moment of pure exhilaration when she'd realized that she had changed her future. That she had diverged from the path so carefully laid out for her.

If she said no now, it was back to that path. Everything would stay the same. The thought was suffocating.

She shook her head. "I don't want that."

"What is it you don't want?"

"You have to be faithful to me, Lazaro," she said, her throat tight. The entire conversation made her body feel hot, restless and edgy. She knew that she would be sleeping with Lazaro, and just the thought made her feel charged with adrenaline.

But the sex would be a purely physical act, with legal paperwork to make it all legitimate. There would be no feelings. No love. She didn't even have to ask him about that. The hardness in his dark eyes answered that question.

Fair enough, since she couldn't imagine falling in love with the cold man standing before her. It was shocking enough that her body seemed to respond to him. But she didn't want to share him either. There were a host of reasons why that thought didn't sit well with her, her health being foremost among them. Another being pure, possessive jealousy. But what woman would want to share her husband? None. Love or not.

"You have to give me that at least," she said. "If we have children…I assume you want children?"

"I need them."

He was talking in terms of producing heirs, and in that sense, she needed them too. It felt wrong to think of them that way, when it never had before. She'd always been confident that she would love her children, so it had never mattered if that was part of the incentive for marriage. But now, knowing Lazaro felt the same way made her see just how cold it was. Made her worry that he wouldn't ever see the children as anything more than vessels for his legacy.

Like your father?

She shook the thought off and continued, "If we have children, I think they need to know they can aspire for better than a marriage filled with lies and infidelity."

"I will honor the vows I speak," he said, clenching his jaw tightly.

"Good. Then I'll honor mine. And even if we're a miserable, distant, sexless couple, I will stay with you."

"Inspiring."

"Why should it be?" she asked. "This is a cold, mercenary agreement. I'm not pretending it's anything other than that. I don't want or expect you to fall in love with me, but respect would be nice. I consider knowing that the person you're sleeping with isn't out sleeping with other people to be a great sign of respect."

"Then you will be faithful to me," he said, his voice hard.

"I said I would be."

"And you will not deny me when I come to your bed."

Vanessa put her hand on her stomach, trying to calm the butterflies that were staging a riot inside of her. "After the wedding."

He nodded once, his eyes trained on her face. "After the wedding."

"My father isn't going to like this. I have to… Well, there's the arrangement I mentioned. And his family will be—"

"You are *engaged* to this other man?"

She held up her ringless left hand. "No. But there was an understanding."

"Your father will be grateful to you if he finds out the circumstances surrounding the union."

"No."

"You don't want him to know?"

She shook her head. "No. I can't…I don't want him to know how far things have fallen…how…how bad things have gotten."

"He will have to know what I'm bringing into the union,"

Lazaro said, dark eyes glittering. "I want him to know that I intend to revamp Pickett. I want him to know that I am saving it. That I've done what he could not. If you want to take credit for meeting me while pursuing my help, it is of no concern to me. But I want him to know that I was the one to pull this dying, outdated company into a new life in the modern era." His voice was hard, uncompromising. He knew what it would do to her father to have to accept help, let alone to have to accept help from someone he believed to be beneath him, and Lazaro was relishing it.

Vanessa had never been able to believe what her father said about some people being better than others thanks to their bloodlines. She'd seen too many cruel, horrible people in her social class. People who wasted their money and used those around them with no thought to anyone but themselves. Believing that those people were somehow better than the rest of humanity was depressing.

And when she'd been sixteen, her emotions had been held captive by a boy her father considered to be lower than them. A boy who had grown into the man standing before her.

Looking at him, she felt her chest get tight, pride swelling within her. It shocked her. But she was, she realized, proud of what Lazaro had become, professionally at least.

"Showing you have the real power?" she asked softly.

"Money *is* the real power, Vanessa. Money is how I got into this position, how I managed to purchase Pickett's shares."

"Then why do you care about the rest of it? Why do you need me at all?"

He raised a dark eyebrow. "Because I can have you."

Her stomach tightened. "The proof of how far you've come?" she asked, voice dry.

"Perhaps. But it has very little to do with anyone else's perception. I want every door open to me. I have earned it. Money, I have—I want the social power as well."

Lazaro's blood burned in his veins, adrenaline spiking through him. He wanted everything. To be at the top of absolutely everything. To sit as a social equal with the man who had had him beaten for daring to touch his precious daughter.

And to make Vanessa his. To finally to satisfy his desire for her.

"The old-money society, the American aristocracy, it's as outdated as your father's business model," he said.

"And you'll tear down centuries of it all by yourself, Lazaro?"

"I don't want to tear it down," he said, his voice rough, his accent taking over his words. "I want in."

She looked away, turning her focus out her office window and onto the Boston skyline. "And it frustrates you that you can't do it without help."

Lazaro bit down hard, a muscle in his jaw jumping. "None of this is done out of necessity, Vanessa. It is a bonus. You wouldn't know about the necessities in life, not when your biggest concern is staying employed in a multi-million-dollar position you're not qualified to do. You could walk away and there would be no great tragedy to either of us."

She just sat, frozen behind her desk, dark eyes wide, her mouth pressed into a firm line. She wouldn't walk away. She was too married to the tradition, to the lineage of her family, just as her father had been.

What will people think?

He wondered if she'd had a share in his broken nose if, after refusing him, she had told her father all about how the low-class housekeeper's son had made an attempt to touch her with his filthy, laborer's hands.

He wondered if Vanessa shared culpability for putting his mother and him out on the streets.

That had been the worst part about all of it. As he'd spat blood out onto the grimy pavement in the alley after being beaten by Michael Pickett's men, after he'd been warned never to set foot on the Pickett estate again, been warned that if he so much as looked at Vanessa again, the consequences might be fatal, the very worst part had been wondering if Vanessa had been complicit in it. If she might have wanted her father to make sure she was rid of him.

His mother had lost her job. He'd lost his job. They'd lost their home and his mother had paid the price with her health. Ultimately with her life.

But now he knew that whatever part Vanessa had played in what had happened, she had never intended it. She was thoughtless, but she wasn't evil.

That moment, when he'd been lying in the alley, had been the lowest of his life. But it had been then, jobless, broken and bleeding, that he had vowed to ensure no one else ever held power over him like that again. He would never allow anyone but himself to hold his fate in his hands.

That goal had consumed him, had propelled him from the gutter to the boardroom, had made him millions.

That Vanessa would be the key to unlock the final door, to allow him into the last segment of society where he was still unwelcome, was poetic justice.

He didn't hate her. He had no desire to hurt her or exact revenge on her. But he no longer cared for her. His body still ached for her, that was all.

Michael Pickett, on the other hand, deserved hell on earth and in the hereafter. Taking Vanessa, making her his own, wrenching her from her father's control…the satisfaction in that was endless. The man had been willing to commit murder if necessary to keep Lazaro away from his daughter, and now there would be nothing he could do to prevent him from claiming Vanessa.

"You know I can't walk away. You might not see it as a necessity, Lazaro. But this is my whole life." She met his gaze, her dark eyes glittering. "And I don't think you'll walk away either. You need me, too."

"Do I?"

"Yes, you do."

His gut burned. "You or any other society princess."

"We both know this is about more than that."

Why bother to deny it? "True. It is rather satisfying, the idea of marrying into the family whose floors my mother wasn't good enough to clean."

"What do you mean by that?" she asked, well-groomed eyebrows drawn together.

"I mean, your father fired my mother. We ended up on the streets. So yes, I suppose there is something especially satisfying about it being you."

There was no triumph in her eyes, only shock, sadness. For him? For his mother? It was far too late for that.

"I didn't know."

"Did you think we went on an extended holiday?"

"I didn't know," she repeated, her voice low.

He shrugged. "We'll start with dating, of course."

"What?"

"We need to be seen together, prior to the actual engagement."

Vanessa tried to ignore the knot in her stomach. She didn't know his mother had been fired. She wondered if that had been when he'd disappeared. If that was why he'd never come back after their disastrous almost night together.

She didn't want to ask. Didn't want to let him know she still thought about it. That it still mattered.

She cleared her throat. "And you want us to…date?"

"Of course. I intend to seduce my fiancée with all of the skill that I possess."

He took her hand in his and bent over it, pressing firm, hot lips to her skin. The gesture was light, gentlemanly even. Not even a little bit erotic. At least it shouldn't have been. But it was. It pushed all of her thoughts and concerns right out of her head and caused a riot of sensation through her system, made her entire body weak and energized at the same time. Made her breasts feel heavy as a pulse started to beat at the apex of her thighs.

She hadn't felt this way, not with this level of intensity, since the last time Lazaro had taken her in his arms when she'd been a completely inexperienced sixteen-year-old. And she hated that she still responded this way to him now. He was the man who was holding her future hostage and that she would melt under his touch with absolutely no resistance was appalling.

She pulled her hand back and pressed her palm to her chest, feeling her heart rage against her breastbone. "No seduction required," she said tightly. "You can seduce the media, I don't really care, but not me. I'll do my 'wifely duty' once we're married, but until then, you can keep your lips to yourself."

He tightened his jaw, his eyes dark, glittering. Angry. "Don't worry, princess, I won't defile you in any way."

A stab of regret hit her. For a moment, she wondered if she'd hurt him. But the moment passed quickly. Lazaro Marino didn't do feelings. And the last time she'd turned down his advances he'd walked out of her life. All he saw her as was a body. Well, now he saw her as more than that. A body and a stepping stone on his way to the top.

It wouldn't hurt him to wait.

"One thing you need to know, Vanessa. With me, sex will never feel like duty. I guarantee it." His eyes were hot on her, making her body temperature rise along with her heart rate. His words were an invitation to sin a saint could hardly resist.

Sign me up for sainthood then, because I'm not going there.
She would do what she had to do. She would make this

deal work for both of them, but she wasn't going to fall under his spell. She'd done it once, and she had no intention of ever succumbing to his wicked, deceptive charms again.

"Anything else?" she asked stiffly.

"You and I have a date tomorrow night."

CHAPTER FOUR

"Of course you picked Chev's," Vanessa murmured as Lazaro helped her from the limo.

She wasn't happy about it, that was clear. It was written all over that beautiful face of hers, her dark eyes glittering with barely suppressed anger.

"Of course," he said, drawing her to him, wrapping his arm around her slender waist.

It was a cool evening, the cobblestone sidewalk wet from rain that had fallen earlier. But Vanessa's arms were bare, her legs barely covered by the sheer veil of her nylons, killer black heels added to the look, making his mind spin with fantasies that couldn't possibly be legal at this sort of establishment.

Everything about her look was designed to entice. To torment. The formfitting, silken dress she was wearing acted as a flimsy barrier between his hands and her soft, smooth skin. He knew it was soft and smooth. He remembered, in explicit detail, how she had felt beneath his fingertips.

He slid his hand around to her lower back, the deep blue fabric catching on some of the rough patches on his hand, still calloused from so many years of labor. For a moment, his world reduced to Vanessa, to the tease she presented. It would be so easy to tear the gown from her body so that he could touch her, could see just what it would be like to feel her bare skin beneath the palm of his hand.

"This is going to get back to my father in a couple of hours. If it even takes that long."

He felt her tense, the idea of her father seeing them together clearly not something she wanted to think about.

"He won't like to hear about it?"

She shot him a sideways glance. "What do you think?"

He could imagine what Vanessa's father would think. Vividly. Almost like a blow to his face. "He'll learn to deal with it."

"I doubt it."

"Easier to handle than having you deposed as head of Pickett. Or having to file for bankruptcy."

"Possibly," she said, teeth gritted.

Lazaro didn't wait for the host. He opened the door for Vanessa and ushered her into the small, intimate dining room.

"Your usual table, Mr. Marino?" The host approached them and gestured toward the back of the restaurant.

"We'll sit somewhere up front," Lazaro said.

The other man nodded. "Excellent, come with me."

Vanessa turned and gave Lazaro a look that could have frozen fire.

He leaned in, allowing a moment, just a moment, to enjoy her scent. Light. Feminine. The same as it had been twelve years ago. He moved his lips near her ear, brushing her thick, glossy hair back. "The better for us to be seen, my dear," he whispered.

He felt a shudder go through her body. Attraction. Need. The kind that lived so strong in him. She wanted him. Good to know. He didn't want a martyr in his bed. He wanted her hot, begging for him.

"Great," she said, acid corroding the word.

She still didn't want to be seen with him. She was still worried about what people would think. Rage poured into the well of lust that had opened up in him, mixing, mingling, each making the other more potent.

He bypassed the host again and pulled the velvet chair out for Vanessa. She sat, her body held stiffly, her face stony.

Lazaro turned to the host. "Bring whatever you think is best."

"Of course, Mr. Marino."

Lazaro took his seat across from Vanessa. Her facial expression hadn't changed, her bright pink lips set into a firm line, her white-tipped fingernails drumming on the table. He put his hand over hers and halted the motion, curling his fingers around hers.

"You could at least try to look like you're enjoying yourself. Hell, you could actually enjoy yourself, I promise not to tell."

The corner of her mouth twitched. "Sorry if I'm not finding this whole sudden forced-marriage thing all that amusing."

"You use the word *force,* Vanessa, and yet I am not forcing you into anything. There is no way for me to do so. You made the choice, you agreed to it."

"Strong-arm tactics were involved," she said, raising a glass of red wine to her lips.

"Maybe. But you could walk away."

"I can't," she said, balling her hand into a fist beneath his before pulling it back and setting it in her lap.

"Status is so important to you?"

"What about you? That's why you're marrying me."

It was much harder to remember the logical reason behind the union when she was so close to him. Much easier to remember the visceral, base reasons for it. Revenge. Lust.

"Essentially," he said. "But I'm not acting like a victim. I need something, you can help me with it. It's the same for you. So we can use each other, go forward, obtain our goals.

If you want to drag yourself around like a martyr for a few months that's your prerogative."

"That's… I'm not doing that."

"You are. You made the choice."

"So own it?"

He shrugged. "Or make a new choice. Walk away now, Vanessa. I'm not going to force you to stay."

Vanessa met Lazaro's eyes, forced herself not to look away. He was right. It was so easy to blame him. To make all of this his fault somehow. And, well, him buying up all the stocks *was* his fault, but the position she was in wasn't. And agreeing to the marriage had been her choice.

She swallowed, uncomfortable with the revelation. It was more palatable to have it be Lazaro's fault and his alone. To feel as though she'd been forced into it all. It was harder to accept that she'd agreed to it because she couldn't take the thought of failing.

She forced a smile. "You're right."

"It didn't even choke you to say it," he said, his voice laced with dark humor.

"I may not say it again," she said. "But in this instance, you are. I made the choice. I'm not walking away."

She'd chosen this path a long time ago, and while this thing with Lazaro was a diversion, the road would end in the same place. She wasn't turning back now just because things had gotten harder. Picketts didn't quit. She didn't quit. She would see it through.

A server came to the table and set a plate in front of each of them. A whitefish fillet and spring vegetables. Very elegant and perfectly cooked. Exactly what she needed to take her focus off Lazaro for a few moments. But not even a divine lemon sauce could keep her from being aware of him. He was just so very there. So present. Close. And he made her tremble inside. Made her remember what it was like to be kissed with the kind of passion normally reserved for books rather than real life.

She set her fork down and put her hands in her lap.

"Now what?" she asked, looking around the restaurant.

She saw Claire Morgan in the corner, eyeing them both with interest. Claire was a major gossip, had been in high school and still was. And Vanessa was willing to bet that she was holding her phone beneath the table frantically texting people to find out if they knew why Vanessa Pickett was at a restaurant with famed billionaire Lazaro Marino.

"Now we wait for Claire to spread the word?" Vanessa asked, looking back at Lazaro.

Lazaro shrugged. "Her, or anyone else interested in why the two of us might be together. They'll wonder what we're saying." He leaned in slightly and Vanessa fought the urge to jump back, away from him, away from the danger he presented.

He was appealing. Much too appealing. He made her thoughts tangle, and she didn't want him to have that kind of power. If she was going to follow through and marry him, she was going to do it on her terms. That meant not allowing him to reduce her to a mass of quivering female longing just by looking at her.

"Your friend over there is watching us." He looked in Claire's direction. "And there's a table of women in the back corner that have been watching us since we came in."

Probably watching Lazaro, anyway. He was the kind of man that a woman really had to stop and admire. He was everything a man should be. Strong, exuding confidence and a kind of masculine grace. He was also drop-dead sexy, and that certainly didn't hurt his cause.

"They're probably creating our conversation for us," he continued, his voice husky, inviting. It made her want to lean in toward him. To draw closer. "Probably imagining me telling you how beautiful you look. That your lips look far more edible than any dessert they might have here. That your dress, as beautiful as it is, is a crime because it covers up all of your beautiful skin. That I want to spend an hour removing it, teasing you, teasing myself."

Vanessa was held in thrall by his words, her heart pounding in her head. He reached across the table and brushed his hand over her cheek, his thumb skimming her bottom lip. Her lips suddenly felt dry and she slicked her tongue over them quickly. She could taste him. The slight, lingering flavor of him. Just a tease. Enough to make her wish it were more.

"They probably think I'm telling you that I want to take you to my bed and spend hours kissing and tasting every inch of your beautiful body." He leaned back again, a wicked smile spreading over his face. "They have vivid imaginations."

Vanessa blinked. "Oh." She cleared her throat. "They're thinking all of that, huh?" Her face was burning-hot, and she was sure her cheeks were bright pink, a perk of having pale skin.

My kingdom for a little sexual sophistication.

"Probably texting it too."

Vanessa grimaced and picked her fork up again. "I sort of thought as much."

"And by the end of the night it will be common knowledge that you and I are seeing each other."

"At least professionally," she said stiffly. Anything to try and bring back some of her sanity. Because Lazaro Marino had the maddening ability to melt her defenses and she really had to…unmelt them.

"I doubt anyone here thinks this is a professional meeting."

"Why is that?"

"Because you do not look at me the way a woman looks

at an associate. At least I hope you don't look at your associates this way."

"What way?"

A small smile curved his lips. "Did you enjoy dinner?"

"The food, yes." She was almost grateful he didn't answer the question. Because in her head she was doing a really good job of disguising her recurring attraction for him. In reality, she probably wasn't.

She'd rather not have her bubble burst. Her pride had taken enough kicks in the shins in the past couple of days.

"Dessert?" he asked.

That word made a series of erotic images flash through her mind—images of him, his mouth, his hands on her body. Images of the kind of dessert she could only imagine. Heat flooded her face again, making her scalp prickle.

"No, thank you," she said, her throat tight.

The server stopped by the table again, dropping off the check. Lazaro handed the man cash, hardly blinking at the triple-digit cost of the meal. Vanessa normally wouldn't have given it a thought either, but being with Lazaro made her conscious of the cost. There was a time when he hadn't had anything. A time when the cost of this meal would have exceeded his weekly income.

Time certainly did change things.

Lazaro stood from the table, and she kept her focus on a spot of sauce on her plate. Anything to keep from looking at him again. She wanted to, though. Another visual tour of Lazaro was very high on her body's to-do list. But sensible Vanessa wasn't going to indulge in that, because she really didn't want him to know that he held such strong appeal for her. It was a matter of pride if nothing else.

A flash of movement pulled her focus away from the plate just in time for her to see Lazaro's very nice-looking hands drop a very generous tip onto the table. She looked up then.

"That's a nice tip."

He shrugged and extended his hand to her. She looked at Claire, who was pretending to pay attention to her date, but who had one eye on them, then accepted his offered hand as she stood.

"Waiting tables is a thankless job," Lazaro said. "I like to add a thank-you."

"Oh." She dropped her hand to her side and flexed her fingers, trying to erase the impression of his touch.

Lazaro didn't really seem like a generous tipper. He didn't seem generous at all. He'd smashed his way back into her life with all the destructive power of a tornado, and that, combined with his callous treatment of her all those years ago, the insults he'd hurled at her, made it hard for her to attach humanity to him.

He leaned in, his dark eyes glittering. "I've been there, Vanessa. Name the grunt job and I've had it. I escaped it. A lot of people in this position never will. They'll work hard forever just to barely pay the bills. I haven't forgotten what that feels like."

"I...I hadn't thought of it like that." Vanessa had never known what it was like to worry about basic necessities. She'd never even had to worry about the frills in life. A new car at sixteen, vacations to exotic places, a luxury town house as a gift for her eighteenth birthday.

Even now, with Pickett Industries facing bankruptcy, her own position in life wasn't jeopardized in that way. She wouldn't have to worry about being homeless, keeping her car. She'd never had that worry.

Lazaro had.

"Of course you hadn't," he said, his tone dismissive.

She put her hand on his forearm and was shocked by the flash of heat that raced through her. She jerked her hand away. "What does that mean?"

"It means I wouldn't have expected you to have such a far-reaching thought."

"Are you calling me a snob?"

"Do you believe you aren't one, Vanessa?"

The chill in his tone shocked her. The condemnation and anger. "I'm not."

"Because you write checks to charities?"

"No, because…I'm not." She'd never bought into the idea that money or status added to someone's worth, but she did have to admit to herself that she didn't often think too far out of the scope of her own reality either.

She hadn't looked down on Lazaro for being poor. For doing maintenance on the estate to earn money. But neither had she imagined him working toward other things, being unsatisfied, having financial needs that weren't really met by his position. It seemed silly now. Shortsighted.

Lazaro grasped her chin between his thumb and forefinger and tilted her face up, forcing her to meet his gaze. "They're waiting for me to kiss you now," he said, his tone soft again.

"Who?" she asked, her heart dropping into her stomach.

"Our audience."

She licked her lips, the breath shuddering from her body. Her stomach tightened in anticipation.

She swallowed. "Are you going to?"

He dipped his head slightly and her heart felt as though it was going into free fall. "No."

He put his arm around her waist and drew her near to his body, his palm warm and enticing on her waist, his fingers stroking her gently.

"Why not?" she asked. "I mean…we're putting on a… show."

"I'm not going to kiss you, because this is more than just a date." He raised his hand and brushed her hair behind her ear, his eyes locked with hers.

She wanted to laugh, because really, it wasn't a date at all. Parts of her seemed to be forgetting that, her knees certainly had. They were weak now, trembling a little bit. But just because her body seemed to have forgotten didn't mean her mind had.

This wasn't a date. They barely knew each other. She had the sense that Lazaro didn't like her very much, and considering all he'd done to her in the past few weeks, she really shouldn't like him either.

"I'm not going to kiss you because you're my future wife. And I'm showing my respect for you. Discretion," he said softly.

Oh yes, discretion was law as far as her father was concerned. And anyone present who knew her would know that.

"G-good," she said, allowing him to lead her out of the restaurant and into the cool night air. His limousine was waiting for them, idling at the curb.

He opened the door for her and helped her inside, his manners those of a perfect gentleman, the earlier tension absent now.

Vanessa leaned her head back on the seat.

It wasn't a date. They didn't have a real relationship. But they were going to get married. And for one, crazy moment she'd really wished that he was going to kiss her.

Of course, the truth was that even though she'd only seen him in pictures, part of her had been longing to be kissed by Lazaro for twelve long years.

But he held so much power over her. Her professional life, the life of her family's legacy was in his hands. She wasn't going to give him power over her body too. When they were married, she would deal with it.

But for now she had to keep her control. She couldn't forget that this relationship was as mercenary as they came.

And when Lazaro touched her it was too easy to forget. She could never let herself forget.

CHAPTER FIVE

"I HOPE you aren't busy today."

Vanessa jumped and dropped the pen she was holding into the cup of tea on her desk. She looked up and saw Lazaro standing in the doorway of her office.

She looked down into her tea then back up at tall, dark and handsome intruder. "In some cultures it's considered rude to sneak up on people."

"I didn't sneak. You were deep in thought, or something like that." He walked in and put both of his hands on the back of the chair that was positioned in front of her desk. "I wanted to talk to you about your plans for Pickett. Being your principal shareholder, it's very much a vested interest of mine."

"I thought you were going to impart your wisdom to me. That is what you do, right?"

"Yes, that is what I do. Do you know why I'm so good at consulting, Vanessa? Why I make more than any of the CEOs I give consultations to?"

"Why?" she asked, her tone dry.

"Because I'm not stuck in the past. I have no loyalty to tradition or convention. I know how to increase profit, and I'm equipped to see new ways of doing things because the old style of business means nothing to me."

Vanessa gritted her teeth. "Well, tradition means a lot to me. To my father."

"And that's probably the source of most of your problems."

"It's probably also why we've lasted as long as we have," she said stiffly.

"Until now. Now you need change. I'm bringing it. I've been over the expense reports from the past five years, and you might be interested in knowing that there was a sharp decline in sales and production the year before you took over. So it isn't all your fault."

Vanessa bit her lower lip, forcing herself to hold back a string of colorful and inventive expletives. "I know that. I told you changing markets have…"

"Made it difficult to compete. The fact is, Vanessa, if you want to keep the bulk of your production in the U.S. you won't be able to compete. But you can change what you're offering."

"Change what, exactly?"

"The future is in environmental sustainability. Responsible waste-disposal practices, using recycled materials. You might not be able to offer the cheapest product, but you can offer the safest, the most ethical."

"It would require some fairly aggressive campaigning." She started looking around the desk for a pen.

"In your teacup."

She felt the blush creep up her neck and over her cheeks. "I'll just get a new one." She opened her desk drawer and rummaged until she found a non-soggy pen.

"It would require some changes to the factory, to materials, to a lot of things actually. And it will cost."

"I'm not exactly swimming in resources."

"You could take a loan from your future husband."

Lazaro watched as Vanessa's cheeks flushed with angry color. "No."

"We have an agreement, Vanessa. I intend to honor it."

And he intended to let Michael Pickett know just how

much control he was assuming of his assets. That he didn't have just his daughter, but that he'd played the part of savior for the venerable Pickett family business.

"I am not getting myself into that much debt. Not with you."

"Not a loan, an exchange. A fair one, I think."

"Hardly. I feel like you're…buying me." She spat out the last words as though they were distasteful.

"Do you want to back out?"

She snapped her mouth shut, tightened her jaw. "I don't…"

"Because if you do, make no mistake, I don't make idle threats. I will push the board to appoint a new CEO of Pickett, Vanessa."

She curled her fingers around the pen she was holding, angry color spreading from her cheeks down to her collarbone. "Are you always going to hold your power over my head? For the rest of our lives? Because that might be the one thing I just can't deal with."

A stab of regret hit him hard in the chest. Making threats wasn't really his style. But something about the Pickett family, about the whole situation, brought things out in him that were normally dormant. Rage, a reminder of what it was to feel truly helpless, to feel as though his life wasn't really his own, but belonged to those with power over him.

"You don't have to worry about that, Vanessa, provided you don't back out of our agreement."

"I won't," she said tightly.

She looked at him, her dark eyes hard, her lush lips thinned into a tight line. He wanted to kiss her until her lips softened, until she was as desperate as he was. Until she begged.

Later. There would be time later. He wasn't about to let her manipulate him with his desire, even if she was doing it unknowingly. And he was certain she didn't know. She didn't give him any coy looks, no knowing smiles or flutters of her thick, dark lashes.

She blushed easily, her skin turning pink with nerves, embarrassment or anger. Her reactions seemed honest. He wasn't used to dealing with people who possessed Vanessa's straightforward manner. He was used to games, had gotten very good at playing them, at holding his cards close to his chest. Vanessa stripped that ability from him. She brought things to the surface, emotions, he wasn't used to dealing with. He wasn't about to allow her that sort of control. She'd turned him into a blind fool twelve years ago, a stupid boy who'd let the Pickett heiress walk all over him.

He was past that now. He would not be manipulated.

"You're right, *querida*, you won't. Because if you do, I will seize control of everything. I have that power."

"I believe it," she said, her words clipped. "But right now you're in my office. So I think the power might be in my favor."

Pride, unexpected and unwanted, made his chest expand. Pride and a strong measure of lust. He liked it better when she stood up to him. Liked it better when he saw a spark set fire to her dark brown eyes. It made his blood run faster, having her challenge him.

"Going to call security on me?" he asked.

"Do I have to?" She pursed her lips and cocked her hip to the side.

"Only if you can't handle me yourself."

"I'm more than capable. I'm not a little girl."

No, she wasn't. Not even close. His heart thundered heavily in his chest, the desire, the need to reach out and touch her almost overwhelming. But he couldn't afford to feel anything. Not now. Not when he was so close.

He forced his thoughts back on his goal, on his reason for being there. "Good. Busy tonight?"

She crossed her arms beneath her breasts. "I don't know. Am I? Do I have a choice?"

Annoyance surged through him. "Do you think I'm taking total control of your life?"

"I don't know what you expect from a little wife," her words taunting, arousing, infuriating.

His heart thundered hard in his chest. She was making him out to be some kind of a tyrant. She was making him feel like one. He didn't like it, he didn't want her to see him that way, and he had no idea why he should care. When she hadn't seen him as the enemy, she'd seen him as beneath her.

He rounded the desk and she stood, hands on her round, shapely hips, a deadly glitter in her eyes.

"I expect you to attend events on my arm," he said. "I expect to use your connections to make advantageous business deals. And I expect this." He hooked his arm around her waist and drew her to him.

She was breathing hard, her breasts rising and falling against his chest. He realized he was breathing hard too. To hell with fighting it. She was his now, no longer off limits to him.

See. Want. Have.

He put his hand on her face, cupped her cheek, touched her soft lower lip with his thumb. "I want this," he said, his voice sounding rough, strained, even to his own ears.

He dipped his head and kissed her. Her lips parted beneath his. He wasn't certain whether it was in shock or supplication, but he wasn't going to stop and analyze it either.

She would be his now. Finally. His. All the longing, the lust that he'd carried around with him for so many years, aching and unsatisfied no matter how many women had warmed his bed since…

She tasted the same. Just as he remembered. So utterly unique, unforgettable. The only woman who had ever made him lose his head, the only woman who had ever rejected him. The only woman whose memory lingered after years of separation. Most women were a vague impression after a few days. Not Vanessa. She had stayed vivid and powerful in his mind.

And it had only been a shadow of the reality.

Actually kissing her, the velvety slide of her tongue against his, the soft sigh of satisfaction she made against his lips, her fingers curling around the fabric of his shirt as she held on to him, anchoring him to her, that was better than anything in his memory. It made his blood run like liquid fire through his veins, made his body pulse with need, made him hard and aching with the necessity of burying himself inside her.

She stole any semblance of control with the softness of her lips.

He slid his hand around the indent of her waist, the curve of her hip. She had changed physically. Her curves were softer, more womanly. More enticing. He'd been a boy twelve years ago, but he was a man now. And she was all woman.

Vanessa felt empowered by his passion, his anger. He was trying to show her that he had the power, but in one intense rush, she realized that she was the one who held it, because his hands, sifting through her hair, were unsteady, his body was hard with arousal. For her. Because of her.

He deepened the kiss and she took his bottom lip between her teeth, nipping the tender skin, showing him that she wasn't going to be passive, in this or anything else, needing badly to stake a claim on him, as he was doing to her.

A growl rumbled in his chest and he took a step, backing her into her desk. She heard her pencil holder fall onto the floor, its contents scattering. She didn't care.

There was nothing. Nothing but this. This battle of wills

and the all-consuming passion that was taking over her mind, her body.

His fingers crept beneath the edge of her top and she was arched into him, powerless to do anything else. And that sudden loss of control, that concession to his power, made a jolt of reality slap her in the face.

She'd promised herself she wasn't going to let him have this control. She shouldn't feel the way she did, as if she would die if she didn't have him. Inside of her. Now. On the floor, the desk, wherever.

She couldn't afford to give him this part of her, to let him have dominion over her body. He would never love her, and if she gave in to this…she would be vulnerable. She couldn't allow that.

Maybe you can't have love, but you can have this.

Amazing, all-consuming lust.

No. It would never just be that. Not for her. Lazaro was more to her than just a hard body. And she would never be anything more to him than a simple means of feeding his sex drive.

She let go of him and pulled away, her heart thundering in her ears.

He flicked a dismissive glance in her direction, seemingly unaffected by what had just happened between them. Totally unfair, since her world had had another dramatic shift on its axis.

"I can see it won't be a problem," he said.

"What?" she asked, still feeling thick and muddled from the arousal that was crowding all the good, useful information out of her brain and leaving room only for the screaming want that was pounding through her.

"The attraction between us is very strong. That part of our marriage will not be a problem."

As far as physical attraction went, no, it wouldn't be. But

it would be everything she'd never wanted and then some. A man using her because she was convenient. Because she had status. Because she had things he wanted, not because she was who he wanted.

That he was attracted to her didn't make her feel all that special. Yes, Lazaro was a sex god with looks that could not be denied, but men tended to like sex from whoever would give it to them. And after that display he was probably feeling pretty positive that getting it would be easy.

"I have work to do," she said, sinking back into her chair.

"I'll leave you to it then. Are we on for tonight?"

"What are we doing?" she asked, her eyes wandering to the pen still resting in her teacup.

"It's a surprise."

Vanessa watched him walk out of the room and her only thought was that she didn't think she could take another surprise from Lazaro.

Lazaro touched the velvet box in his coat pocket and cursed the flash of adrenaline that raced through him. It *was* adrenaline; it certainly wasn't nerves. He didn't do nerves. He did decisive action. He didn't question, he moved forward with confidence. Always.

That was how he'd worked his way up from the ground level of the massive corporation he'd eventually built up with his ideas on how to reinvent the place. It was how he'd built a career, a name for himself. How he'd netted billions in the bank.

He took advantage of every resource and did what had to be done. As he was doing now.

It was extremely fortuitous that one of the art museum's head curators happened to be on a par with Vanessa's father as far as social clout went. And even more fortuitous that she was a gossip.

It meant that she would tell anyone who was even half-interested that Lazaro Marino had paid to have the museum empty this evening so that he could ask the woman in his life a very important question.

In Vanessa's circle, media exposure was seen as vulgar, common. Anyone could earn that kind of notoriety. The First Families and those like them saw class as something you were born with, not something you could acquire. And anyone who wasn't born with it was somehow less.

The way to spread the word was through careless discretion, nothing half so common as an actual write-up in a newspaper.

He curled his fingers around the ring box and leaned against the terrace railing. Vanessa was due to arrive soon, another detail carefully coordinated with a trail that would be easy to follow.

He heard high heels on marble and looked up. Vanessa was walking toward him, the expression on her face mutinous. She had dressed for the occasion, though, as he'd requested. Red silk this time, hugging her curves. Her lips were painted to match her dress and her dark hair was pulled back into a neat bun. He wished she'd left it down. He enjoyed the feel of the silken strands sliding through his fingers.

He tightened his hold on the ring box. This was what it was about. The ring. Taking his place in the world. The truth was, he didn't give a damn about what anyone in high society thought of him. But he wouldn't be seen as beneath anyone, as some sort of trash from the *barrio* they could despise and lord their power over. He wouldn't be beneath anyone. And Vanessa was the key.

"What is this?" she asked, looking around the terrace. It was lit by a string of paper lanterns that hung low overhead, just as it had been the night they'd met at the charity event.

"You didn't guess?"

"I wouldn't dare try to guess at the inner workings of your mind," she said, walking to the railing and resting her forearms on the top of it, leaning over, keeping her eyes fixed on the garden.

He moved so that he was standing next to her and pulled the ring box out of his pocket and placed it on the top of the stone railing. "I thought this was an ideal place to make our arrangement official."

She turned her head sharply, her eyes wide. Then she looked down at the ring box.

"Are you going to look at it?" he asked.

"I...so this is your proposal?" Her eyebrows winged halfway up her forehead, her expression one of pure incredulity.

"I think I proposed already," he said stiffly.

"Well, but...no, because now there's a ring." She didn't touch the ring box, she just looked at it.

"And most women at this point would be looking at the ring."

"Why all this?" she asked, ignoring his statement. "The museum and the lights?"

"Because I had to speak to quite a few people to arrange this romantic gesture."

She nodded slowly. "And they'll tell other people."

"Yes. Your social class is just small enough that word travels to everyone in it very quickly."

She frowned. "Right."

"I'm sorry, did you want something more public?"

She shrugged. "No."

Anger surged in him, anger and something else that he couldn't quite identify. "You're disappointed?"

"I'm not disappointed. That implies I had an expectation about this moment and, truly, for all I knew, you were going to courier me a ring at my office. But I did have expectations of this moment as far as my life goes."

"And this doesn't meet your standards?" he asked, his stomach tightening.

"Not really."

"You might want to look at the rock before you declare the effort subpar, *querida*," he said, conscious of the fact that his accent had thickened with his building anger.

He popped the top on the box and pushed it closer to her. She looked down and her eyes widened. Not a big surprise. Five carats would have that effect on someone like her.

"I hope that's fitting of a woman of your status."

Vanessa looked down at the ring, glittering beneath the lantern light. The large, square diamond set into a band of white gold with an intricate, antique-style weave was nestled in cream silk, looking as if it had been made just for her.

There was so much about the moment that seemed made just for her. An empty art museum, a gorgeous man and a marriage proposal. If it had been a real marriage proposal—real in the sense that there was love behind it and not just mercenary business dealings—he would have gotten down on one knee. They would have walked through the museum and talked about their future. They would have felt like the only two people in the world.

If they had never parted, if she had stopped him from leaving that night, maybe it would be real.

Her heart squeezed in her chest and she squelched the thought. It didn't matter. This was reality. And in reality, he'd shoved the ring in her direction and barely looked at her. He hadn't even asked the question, and it all just hung between them, awkward and unspoken. Painful. Because this was like some nightmare version of a fantasy she might have created for herself.

"It's lovely." She reached out and touched it, hesitant to pick it up, to put it on, because the ring made it all seem real. And final.

And because part of her wanted so badly to wear Lazaro's ring, so very badly. And that was embarrassing, humiliating. She didn't really want the Lazaro that had come back into her life with all the finesse of a jackhammer. She wanted the man she used to imagine he was. The man he never had been.

"Don't you like it, *querida?*" he asked.

"I love it. It's beautiful. Perfect."

"You seem giddy," he said, his expression flat.

"I love it," she said, teeth gritted.

"Put it on."

Anger surged through her, pummeling her tender heart. "That's your job, isn't it?"

She held her hand out, determined not to be the one to fasten her own diamond handcuffs. He took her hand in his, the heat of his skin on hers sending prickles of electricity through her body, making it nearly impossible for her to cling to the anger that was anchoring her to the balcony, reminding her that this was nothing more than a farce.

He took the ring out of the box and it caught the light. Such a beautiful sign of eternal bondage. She closed her eyes while he pushed it onto her fourth finger. It fit perfectly, and it was more disturbing than anything that it fit. That it somehow seemed right.

She pulled her hand back and brushed her palm down over her skirt, trying to ease the fiery, tingling sensation that was spreading from her fingertips to her wrist.

"How big is it?" Her own voice, the mercenary tone, cooled her off quickly. Reminded her that this was a transaction. Nothing more. Because she had to do something to stop her heart from pounding faster. To keep herself from thinking of all the what-ifs.

"Does it matter?" he asked, his voice as cold as the sick weight in her stomach.

"I've heard size matters."

A muscle in his jaw jumped. "Big enough to satisfy you."

She swallowed hard, the need to get the upper hand fueling her, choosing her words for her. "I'm not sure about that."

"The purebred could do better?"

She looked at the ring again. It was beautiful. Perfect. "Possibly." The lie stuck in her throat.

He jerked back, as though she'd struck him. He looked, just for a moment, like the boy he'd been the night she'd rejected him. Then any vulnerability was gone, replaced with an expression that was as hard as granite.

"I think," he said, "it's time we went and had a talk with your father."

CHAPTER SIX

"I've already heard your news, Vanessa. I've been down at the club this morning."

Vanessa fought the urge to hang her head and stare at the toes of her ruby-red shoes. Something happened to her when her father used that tone, that flat, disappointed tone that let her know she'd somehow made a mess of things. She felt like a child again. Small and desperately inadequate, trying to live up to an ideal that had been placed just out of her reach, an ideal she was falling so short of it was nearly laughable.

Michael Pickett wasn't a large man; he wasn't young anymore. His voice was thin now, wispy. He couldn't yell. He didn't need to. What he could do with a small hint of disapproval in his voice couldn't be underestimated.

Vanessa swallowed. "Well, it was…unexpected." She looked down at the rug, a floral-print rug, the same one that had been in place in her father's office since she could remember. Everything was the same at the Pickett estate. Nothing ever changed. The house was like a relic, surrounded by the modern world but not really a part of it. Like the owner of the estate himself.

"And what of your obligations to Craig Freeman? Do they mean nothing?"

"I want to marry Lazaro," she said. "I don't want to marry Craig." That, in the very strictest sense, was the truth. In spite of the fact that things had been stilted between the two of them since the previous night's engagement, he was still the better option.

"Since when is life about what you want?" he said, his voice soft, and deadlier for it.

"I…"

"Don't be stupid, Vanessa. This man is beneath you."

She could sense the moment Lazaro's control slipped its leash. The moment he was no longer playing his part.

"You had better damn well watch what you say to my fiancée," Lazaro said, his voice hard, dangerous, each word rougher, less civilized, as though a veneer was slowly being stripped away, revealing the true man. Dangerous. Feral. As far from the polished, old-money setting as it was possible to be.

Lazaro had been silent for most of the meeting, letting Vanessa do the talking. But the silence was broken now. "Vanessa was handed a crippled corporation, and with the remains that you gave to her she's fashioning something that can survive the new market, the modern sensibility, something no one else on your staff, including you, had the creativity to do."

She waited for him to say exactly why they were getting married. That he was the one saving the company from a slow corporate death. But he didn't.

Her father curled his hands into fists. "I'm not taking orders from a man whose mother used to scrub my floors."

She felt Lazaro stiffen next to her. "But maybe you will take orders from the man who is now the principal shareholder of Pickett Industries. Interesting thing about going public, Mr. Pickett…the public can buy pieces of your company. And I've bought quite a few pieces for myself."

"Having money does not make you an equal with my family," her father said. "Money doesn't buy class."

"But money does buy stock."

"Vanessa." Her father leveled his cold gray eyes on her. "Did you know about this?"

"Yes." Vanessa cleared her throat and tilted her chin up, fighting the urge to look back down at the carpet. She wasn't going to look down anymore. "He's my fiancé. So it will still be all in the family, won't it?"

She felt a thrill of excitement race through her, a surge of adrenaline that chased away any intimidation or fear.

"You do not have my blessing on this." Michael Pickett stood from behind the desk, and suddenly Vanessa saw her father clearly for the first time. How he controlled her. How hard he tried to exert his will over her.

"I didn't come here to get your blessing." She bit out the words. "Just to tell you what was going to happen. What do you want?" she asked him. "Do you want the company to succeed? Because, trust me, right now we need Lazaro for that. Accept him, welcome him, and we stand a chance at some success."

"Are you threatening me?"

"No. I'm telling you how it is. This is reality." Her heart was pounding hard, blood roaring through her ears. She felt dizzy.

"We'll be in touch," Lazaro said, wrapping his arm around her waist and leading her from the room. He closed the heavy oak door behind them, the sound echoing in the expansive corridor of the old house.

"Thank you," Vanessa said quietly when they were back on the paved circular drive in front of her childhood home.

"For?"

"For saying that stuff. For making it sound like some of the good ideas were mine." She expelled the breath she didn't realize she'd been holding. "I don't think any of them were."

Lazaro opened the passenger door of his dark blue sports

car and she sank inside, letting the soft leather seats absorb some of her tension.

He rounded the car and slid into the driver's seat, putting the key into the ignition and turning the engine on.

When they were on the maple-lined highway, headed back into Boston, Lazaro flicked her a glance. "Why exactly do you work so hard to please him?"

"I…" She looked out the window and focused on the trees, watching them blur into a steady stream of color. "He's all I have. My mother died when I was four. And my brother died when I was thirteen. Thomas was going to take over the company. He was brilliant. He would have done an amazing job. But without him…there was only me." She turned to face him. "It's up to me, Lazaro. I can't be the one that fails."

"Do you love what you do?"

"Do you?"

He laughed. "I love the money that it brings in. And yes, I like solving problems. Fixing things. Making them run better."

"I don't love what I do. I have to take antacids when I get up in the morning," she said. She'd never said that out loud to anyone. She'd never even fully admitted to herself that she was unhappy, that she didn't like what she was doing. She was the CEO of a much-lauded company and saying she would rather do almost anything else seemed ridiculous. But it was true.

It was also too late. Her course had been set since she was thirteen. She knew there were plenty of people who would have walked away. People who would have pursued the life they wanted. But there was such a weight on her, a burden of responsibility. She couldn't turn her back on it.

If not for her father, then for Thomas's memory.

"And before you ask why I do it," she said, "I'll just tell you. Because how could I be the one to put an end to a legacy?

How could I let it be my fault? Because Pickett Industries has to keep going, for my eventual children as much as for my father and for the memory of my brother. I do it because it's the right thing to do."

She took her phone out of her pocket and fiddled with the touch screen, moving icons around with her thumb. "My father will accept the marriage because he has no other choice. But the bluster was kind of a necessity for him. It's how he is."

"I know," Lazaro said, his voice hard, his grip tight on the wheel.

Vanessa looked down at the ring on her finger and turned the phone camera on, snapping a picture of the diamond glittering in the late-afternoon sunlight.

"What would you do if you could do something else?" Lazaro asked.

She smiled. "I would take pictures."

"Of what?"

She leaned her head back against the seat and let the soft leather ease away some of her tension. "Everything."

"You might find the time to do that someday. Maybe not of everything, but...of some things."

She forced the corners of her mouth up into a smile. "Maybe. Maybe when all of this gets sorted out, and things settle down in the company I'll have time."

"You will."

"No one else knows that," she said, realizing it as she spoke the words.

"That can only be a good thing. Shouldn't a husband know things about his wife no one else knows?"

Heat made her skin prickle. "I suppose so." That made her think of sexy things. Erotic things. Things that made her lips tingle with the memory of his kiss. "But it isn't like we're going to have a real marriage."

"What will be unreal about it?" he asked.

Only the very core of the union. But of course, he didn't seem overly concerned with that detail. "Well, we don't love each other."

"No." Something about the way he said it, so matter of fact, so logical, made her chest ache. Maybe because there had been a time when she'd loved him, so much, with everything she had. It seemed like yesterday and another lifetime all at once.

She put her sunglasses on, all the better to avoid his eyes. "So that's the part that makes it seem…not real."

"You didn't love that purebred you were supposed to marry."

His choice of words made her snort. "No. I barely knew him. But I didn't really… I tried not to think about it."

"This is no different."

It was different. It was different because, with Lazaro, she wanted things. Things no other man had ever made her want. At sixteen, loving him had made her feel that the whole world was open to her. As if she could do anything. Be anyone. Not just Vanessa Pickett of the Picketts of Boston.

He made her feel like that now. It was dangerous and stupid.

"I suppose it's not."

She looked at his profile. Strong. Masculine. Angry. She'd said something wrong again and she had no idea what.

"Is there any way you can take time away from the office?" he asked, effectively changing the subject.

"For how long?"

"A week. I've been doing some consulting work with a corporation in Argentina and I have to make a physical appearance this week."

"And why do you want to take me?" she asked.

"What better way to celebrate our engagement?"

"I'm not just going to jump into bed with you. We already established that," she said, sounding prim even to herself.

"I remember. Vividly. Although you certainly do a good impression of a woman who wants to do some jumping when I kiss you."

"Kissing isn't sex," she said coldly. "You've always seemed to get the two confused."

"I assure you, Vanessa, I'm not confused about any part of sex. And a kiss is not sex, I'm well aware. Not even close."

"So don't equate one kiss with me being ready to sleep with you." He'd certainly made that assumption the first time she'd kissed him. "I'm not ready. I don't sleep with men I don't know. And if that's the point of the trip..."

"It will look nice if I take my fiancée on a celebratory vacation. If you're going to be a harpy you can stay here."

She thought of the two options for her week. Staring at the four walls of her office again, or escaping to Argentina for seven days. Even if it was with Lazaro, option two was the winner. She wanted to escape. Just go for a while. Leave reality behind.

"I'll go."

"*Bien.* You and I can...get to know each other."

Buenos Aires was electric. There was energy in everything, motion and lights and heat. Vanessa had never seen anything like it. She'd traveled quite a bit before she'd graduated from high school, but they'd been trips with her father, trips that had begun at airports in air-conditioned limousines and ended up at cloistered resort properties.

She'd never truly gotten to enjoy the culture of the country she'd been visiting. And she'd never realized how sad that was until now. Had never realized what she'd been missing.

She wished she could capture it forever. The curves of the buildings, the brick on the street, the sun-washed blue sky.

"You grew up here?" She turned to Lazaro, who was sitting next to her in the back seat of the limo, engrossed in something on his smartphone.

"We left when I was thirteen," he said, not bothering to spare her a glance.

"It's beautiful."

"Sure. If you don't go down to where I used to live. But every city has its slums."

Vanessa's stomach tightened. "And that's where you're from?"

"Does that bother you, *princesa*?"

"No. Yes. Only in the sense that I don't like to think of you…of anyone, living like that."

"It's reality," he said, his voice rough.

"I know." She did. But it was sort of a hollow, half-realized knowledge.

"It's where I'm from. I hope it doesn't cause you too much despair to have a husband who comes from nothing. As your father is so fond of saying, class can't be bought."

"I've never cared, Lazaro. Never."

"That isn't how I remember it."

"How do you remember it? Because I remember risking my father's wrath to speak to you whenever I got the chance, and I don't think I ever treated you like a second-class citizen. In fact, I pretty much remember my entire sixteen-year-old world revolving around you."

The limo pulled up the curb in front of a stretch of tall, white, connected buildings. "My penthouse is here," Lazaro said.

"Good."

"Good?"

"I like it," she said, opening her own door and getting out without waiting for Lazaro.

She liked it, and she was glad to be done with the conversation. She didn't want to talk about what an idiot she'd been for him back in her angsty teenage days. And she really didn't want him guessing just how close she was to being an idiot for him now.

Lazaro Marino was as hard as concrete and just as loving. The last thing she wanted was to cultivate feelings for him. She'd had her heart broken by him before. Granted, at sixteen, everything felt fatal, and she was sure that whatever it was she'd felt for him was more infatuation than anything else. But still, she had no desire to relive it.

This time, she did have Lazaro in her future. And a lifetime of living with him and loving him while he saw her as nothing more than a possession would be worse than a relationship with no emotions at all.

So she was aiming for cool and distant. She could do that. She had plenty of practice being treated with cool distance; she ought to be able to dish a little bit out.

Lazaro got out of the limo and opened the trunk, retrieving their bags without waiting for the driver or for aid from one of the apartment building's employees.

She couldn't help but admire the grace in his movements, the easy strength. Even angry—and he was angry with her, that much was obvious—he was the single most gorgeous man she'd ever seen. Deep bronze skin, square jaw—which he was clenching tightly. He always did that when he was annoyed with her.

"You're going to get TMJ," she blurted, following him into the building.

"Que?"

"TMJ. You can get it from grinding your teeth. There was a girl at school who had to wear a mouth guard to stop her from doing it."

A smile curved his lips and a ridiculous, happy, fluttering

sensation assaulted her. "Perhaps you should just endeavor to be less of a cause of stress."

She huffed out a laugh. "I stress *you* out, Lazaro? *Really?*"

He stopped walking and turned to face her, the look on his face intense. And for a second, she forgot that breathing was important. Because nothing seemed more important, more compelling, than what was happening between herself and Lazaro.

"Maybe *stress* is the wrong word."

Vanessa leaned back slightly and her shoulders connected with the wall. "It is?"

"But I am having trouble sleeping."

"Why is that?"

"Because every night since you came to me at the museum I have stayed awake. Wanting you. In my arms. In my bed."

The need to kiss him again was unbearable. It was hard to remember why she was fighting her attraction for him, especially when sleeping with him was inevitable.

A thrill shot through her system when she realized that fully, for the first time. It was a matter of *when*, not *if*, and having it suddenly seem real made the distance between Lazaro and herself seem that much smaller.

He released his hold on one of the bags and let it drop to the carpeted floor of the lobby area. He brushed his thumb over her lower lip, an action that was becoming familiar to her. Maybe *familiar* was the wrong word, because each time he touched her like that it made her knees weaken.

She flicked the tip of her tongue to his finger, curiosity and desire mixing together to create a potent temptation she couldn't resist. His body shuddered, the movement running through every strong inch of him. She leaned her head back against the wall, pulling away from him. But he was still close. So close it wouldn't take a very big action for him to close the distance between them and take her in his arms. To kiss her again as he'd done in her office. As he'd done in the guesthouse.

"Oh, yes, Vanessa, I very much look forward to getting to know you better this week." He picked up the suitcase again and turned away from her, the spell that had descended over her breaking.

He was playing with her. Teasing her. Proving that at any moment he could call up that desire in her that was so strong, so close to the surface.

If he kept behaving like that, it wouldn't be hard to keep her emotional distance from him. Not hard at all.

CHAPTER SEVEN

"What's this?"

Lazaro flicked her an uninterested look from his position at the sleek penthouse bar. "I had some things sent ahead for you."

A lot of things. Dresses, a swimsuit…the large armoire had been stocked with items, as had the freestanding vanity in the massive bathroom that was just off her expansive bedroom. But that wasn't what caught her eye. "This," she said again, picking up a black camera bag that was positioned in the middle of the sumptuous four-poster bed, almost afraid to open it.

She peered through the open door of her bedroom and out into the spacious living area.

Lazaro waved his hand in a dismissive manner. "You mentioned you liked taking pictures."

Her heart thundered hard in her head, and she felt dizzy. Overwhelmed. She ran her fingers along the edge of the bag. It was very high-quality heavy canvas sewn with thick nylon thread.

She grasped the zipper and pulled it open. Her hands shook as she pulled the camera out. It wasn't just a camera. It was lenses and filters and just about every other accessory she could think of. Much more than she would ever need to take pictures as a hobby.

She walked out of her room and into the living room, stepping up the marble steps into the bar area.

She felt short of breath as she turned the camera over in her hands, her fingers sliding over the slick black casing. Her body felt strange, hollow.

"Lazaro, why…why did you do this for me?"

He moved around to the other side of the bar, drink in hand. "Why not? You said you liked to take pictures. You were doing it with your phone and I thought you might want a real camera. Especially as I knew you would want pictures of Buenos Aires."

"I do… I was…I was so wishing I could capture it all forever while we were driving from the airport and…you knew."

He shrugged. "It isn't a big deal. Money is nothing to me."

"This is more than money."

"It's not," he said, his focus on the city skyline beyond the large window that extended the length of the living area.

"But I just don't understand why you went to the trouble to…"

"You're going to be my wife, Vanessa," he said, cutting her off. "I don't want you to be miserable. Do you think I mean to keep you as my captive and make you pay penance for the rest of your life? I have no interest in that."

"I hadn't really given it a lot of thought."

That he intended to make her happy was an entirely foreign concept. It wasn't that she'd imagined he wanted her to be miserable, it was just that she didn't think he'd cared one way or the other.

"Really?" he asked, his tone dry.

"I've just been trying to get through the day-to-day stuff. Not only since you decided to play a little game of Russian roulette with my life, before that too. I've just been trying to get by."

"I have a lot of experience in just trying to get by," he said slowly.

"It's not fun."

"No, it's not." He looked at her, his dark eyes veiling his emotions, but she felt that his eyes were able to see into her, to read her thoughts. "It begs the question, why do you choose to do it?"

"I don't. Not really."

"You do."

"Fine, maybe. I choose to do it because as I said before, it isn't just me. It's my family. It's the inheritance for all my— our children."

"You could take an inactive role."

"It's not the same."

"No, it would save you all that money you spend on ant-acids," he said, his voice flat.

"It doesn't come naturally to me, I'll admit that. I took all the classes, I got really good grades, in fact, but a classroom isn't the real world. I don't have that extra thing that takes someone from good to great."

He took a long sip of his drink and walked back to the bar, putting both of his hands flat on the marble surface. "You might not have it for business, but that doesn't mean you don't have it."

That was a revelation—but one she couldn't accept. One she'd been trained not to accept. "It doesn't really matter if I can't do the one thing that would matter."

"Is it all that matters?"

"You can ask me that? Does your success matter, Lazaro? And is it enough? Or are you still after more?"

"I think you know the answer to that."

"Exactly. You aren't happy because there's still that one thing. This is my thing, this is what I have to do. What I have to get right."

He nodded once. "Good for you. I wouldn't have thought you'd have this kind of determination."

That stung a little bit. "Because you knew me for a few weeks when I was sixteen?"

"It made an impression," he said dryly.

"Yay, me," she said, turning the camera over in her hands, suddenly fighting back a hot flood of tears. She cleared her throat. "Thank you for this. Really."

"You can bring it when we go out tonight."

"We're going out?"

"I thought you might want to see some of the city."

She nodded. "I do. I very much do."

"Great. I have to stop by Paolo Cruz's office and give him a rundown of what we're discussing at the board meeting to-morrow, but when I get back, we'll go and have dinner."

Dinner with Lazaro in Buenos Aires and a gift. A personal gift. Proof that he'd listened to her. That he wanted her to be happy.

The emotion thing kept getting trickier. Lucky her.

Vanessa on a normal day was enough to light his blood on fire and make his libido kick into high gear. Vanessa dressed to kill in a tight black dress with a low V-neckline and a slit in the skirt that revealed one toned, gorgeous thigh when she walked was almost too much.

Already, the past few days in Buenos Aires had tested him, his body now so hot that an ice-cold shower at night did noth-ing to cool the fire that raged beneath his skin. A fire only Vanessa could dampen.

But he had not gone to her. He would not let her see that she had that power over him. It was a power she had always had. He'd been bewitched by her body, her spirit, from the moment he'd met her. It galled him that she still had him under her spell.

After three days, no, more like twelve years of resisting, right now he ached to pull her into his arms, the need so strong he thought he couldn't resist it without the pain becoming crippling. His body throbbed with the need to have her. To feel those slim, perfect legs wrapped around his waist as he drowned himself in the pleasure only she could offer.

Tonight, she'd left her hair down, rich brown waves cascading over her shoulders, partially concealing the round swell of her breasts that the daring neckline of her dress did not.

She brought something out in him, something he didn't recognize. A need, a desire, a totally primal lust that defied anything he'd ever experienced before.

They'd shared a kiss. A simple kiss. Yet she'd burrowed her way inside him as no woman, not a long-term girlfriend or one-night lover, ever had. He wished this need was tied to vengeance. That he could explain. But it was separate from the issues with her father. Even if all of the events of the past sometimes tangled in his memory, the parts with Vanessa, the memories of her lips touching his, burned bright in his mind, washed everything else away. When he thought of her mouth, of her hands on his body, there was nothing else.

It was desire. That was all. Even if it was desire such as he'd never known. And he would have a lifetime to indulge that desire. To take the edge off it so that it no longer dominated his thoughts.

Her wicked red lips curved into a smile and all of his blood rushed south of his belt. "I didn't overdress, did I?"

She was absolutely overdressed. Anything covering those luscious curves was a crime as far as he was concerned. "Not at all," he said

"Are you ready then?"

"Si." Images of them together, limbs entwined, moans of pleasure issuing from those plump red lips had him hard and shaking. He didn't want dinner. He wanted her, wanted her

body pressed against his. He felt a smile curve his lips. "I think that, in honor of your dress, we need to go somewhere different than I originally had in mind."

Even at night the streets of Buenos Aires were alive. People were still walking around, laughing, talking, eating. Heat and moisture clung to the air, to Vanessa's skin, as they walked down the crowded sidewalk.

Lazaro was completely at ease in his surroundings. Passersby stopped and looked at him, and Vanessa couldn't blame them. In his black suit and open-collared shirt, he was absolute masculine perfection. He demanded to be stared at.

He didn't seem to notice, or care, that he drew attention from every woman they passed. He didn't return any of the hungry, open stares. His eyes were on her. And it was making her blood feel hot.

"Where are we going?" she asked. It was a long shot, but talking might break up some of the tension that was building inside her.

"Right here." He took her hand in his, lacing their fingers together, and led her into a small, narrow doorway. The outside of the building had seemed the same as every building they'd passed—white brick with rounded edges showing its age. But the interior didn't match the old-world feel of the streets outside.

Inside was open and clean, with pared-down, square furniture and a large bar area surrounded by plush seating. Pendant lighting hung low at different lengths, made to look like floating candles suspended in space.

There was plenty of room to move, but everything was arranged so that it felt close, intimate. There was a band playing, and couples were on the dance floors, wrapped around each other, dancing in a rhythm so sensual that it made Vanessa feel as though she was intruding on something by witnessing it.

"Would you like a drink?" Lazaro gestured to the bar.

"I... No." Her body already felt giddy, her thoughts light and fuzzy. She didn't want to add anything to her system that might encourage the feelings.

"Dance with me," he said, touching her hand, the sensation of his skin against hers lighting a fire that burned from her fingertips to her chest, settling around her heart. "And don't tell me you can't dance, because I'm sure a woman of your...status will have had dance lessons from the time she learned to walk."

"I don't dance like this," she said, flicking a glance back at the dance floor.

"This is how I dance," he said, taking her hand and drawing her to him. "And since I'm your future husband, you should learn to dance with me, don't you think?"

"We're going to tango at our wedding?" she asked, a short laugh escaping her lips as she imagined the seductive dance with the super-traditional Pickett estate serving as a backdrop.

"It would give people something to talk about."

"We already are something to talk about, Lazaro."

"I suppose we are," he said, dark eyes glittering in the dim light of the club. He looked different here. More dangerous. The polish of sophistication he'd cultivated seemed to have worn thin in the past few hours. This was the man she'd known twelve years ago.

Rough around the edges. Utterly deadly to her senses.

"Dance with me," he said again. Not a question, a demand. One she couldn't refuse.

She allowed him to lead her to the dance floor, her heart thundering so loudly she was certain people around her would be able to hear it, even over the steady beat of the music. But here, no one looked at them, not even at Lazaro. Every couple was totally enthralled with each other, with the movements of their partner.

Lazaro wrapped one arm around her waist and brought her up against his chest, his other hand clasping hers. "Follow my lead."

She knew she didn't look like the elegant women dancing around her, but with Lazaro leading, his movements strong and sure, she felt like one of them. She could feel his heart beating hard against her chest, strong and steady, and her steps began to match his, her body moving in rhythm with the beat of his heart.

The music closed in around them, making her feel as if they were alone, everyone else fading into murky, shadowy impressions. Nothing else mattered but Lazaro, the weight of his hand on her waist, the intensity in his eyes as he looked at her.

The strains of the violin wound through Vanessa's body, filled her, joined the arousal that had been building inside her since the moment she'd walked back into Lazaro's life, making her feel too full. But also more alive than she'd ever felt before.

Lazaro slid his hand down to the curve of her hip, down lower, edging beneath the daring split in the skirt of her dress. His hand connected with the very top of her stocking, the place where nylon ended and bare flesh began. He curled his fingers in and lifted her leg, curving it around his. It was part of the dance, nothing more sensual than anyone else was doing. And yet it made her feel dizzy with desire, held captive to it, waiting to see what he would do next. Where he would touch her next.

He pulled her closer to him and the hard length of his erection pressed against her stomach. She dug her fingers into his shoulder, bit down on her lip, trying to keep back the sound of pleasure that was trying to escape.

This was real. Sexual. Raw. It stirred primal hunger in her, a sense of feminine power.

He moved his hand from her thigh, back to her hip, his grip tightening. He pulled into his body and she melted against him. It was all part of the dance.

And yet it wasn't.

He pressed his face against hers, the stubble that had grown in since that morning abrading her cheek, the slight prickle of pain combining with her mounting arousal, making her feel as if she was drowning in sensation.

"Come with me," he whispered, his voice rough.

He was leading. She was following. This felt like part of the dance too.

And yet it wasn't.

He brought her into a small alcove just off the dance floor, partly secluded with swaths of fabric that cascaded from the ceiling to the floor.

"Lazaro..." She couldn't think of anything else to say. Not when he was looking at her as though she was the only thing he could see.

He leaned in slightly and braced himself on the wall behind her, his hand resting by her head, his other arm wrapped around her waist. She was effectively trapped, and she didn't mind at all.

She tilted her head slightly, hoping that he would take the hint and kiss her. Logic and self-preservation had no place in what was happening between them now. This was about feeling, desire, the kind of passion she'd tasted once twelve years ago and had been starving for every night since then.

He kissed her and she forgot everything—everything but the graze of rough stubble on her cheeks, the velvet slide of his tongue, the firm warmth of his lips. There was nothing else.

She kissed him back with everything she had, all of the pent-up desire that had lain dormant in her for so long. Desire for him.

He cupped her cheek for a moment before sliding his hand through her hair, weaving his fingers into the thick curls. He held her like that, anchored to him, his kiss giving and demanding at the same time. Too much and not enough.

She arched against him, needing to be closer to him, as close to him as she could possibly get. She needed his touch. His hands. Needed him.

He tilted his head and kissed the tender skin beneath her jaw, the curve of her neck, her shoulder. She shivered and he continued down, his tongue tracing the line of her collarbone. He lifted his hand and cupped her breast, teased her hardened nipple until she was panting, desperate, dying of the want that had taken over her body.

She gripped his shoulders, needing something to hold her to earth. He shifted his hand lower, palming her bottom, coupling it with a kiss to her collarbone. And then he was traveling down again, the tip of his tongue on the curve of her breast, exposed by the low neckline of her gown.

She opened her eyes for a moment and saw a flash of movement through the partly closed curtains. A reminder. Just enough to bring her back to reality.

"Lazaro, stop. We have to stop," she said, her tongue thick and clumsy, unable to form words effectively.

"No, *querida*," he whispered, kissing her throat. "Not yet."

"But…what…what will people think?"

Lazaro froze, all of the heat, the molten lust that had been roaring through his veins turning into ice.

What will people think?

He tightened his hold on her for a moment and then released her. "Don't worry, no one here will think anything, Vanessa. No one here knows that you are the Pickett heiress and I'm your housekeeper's bastard son." He spat the words from his mouth, vile words that reflected the clash of emotions raging inside him.

She shook her head and took a step toward him, her hand outstretched. "Lazaro…"

"How will you bear the humiliation of being married to a man like me?" He stepped away from her, his stomach tight with disgust. "Although my money is good enough for you. My ring—" he reached out and took her hand, lifting it so that the diamond caught the light "—seems to be good enough for you."

"Don't say that. That's not fair. I…"

"Don't say what, Vanessa? Don't tell you the truth? I'm good enough to marry, as long as I'm bailing you out and giving you a ring that ought to come with its own security detail? Good enough to screw around with in your father's guesthouse as long as no one sees you slumming it with the boy who cuts the grass?"

"Lazaro…"

"You need me," he said, his voice sounding like a growl, shocking even him. "Admit it."

"I…"

Pain tore through him, made him want retribution. "Say it."

"Or what? You'll walk away? You'll forget that *you* need *me*?" She pulled away from him. "Because no matter how much you pretend to disdain me, my father, society, you want your place at the top. And you need me to get it."

Angry brown eyes clashed with his, a tear, not one of sadness but of pure rage, spilled down her cheek. "I want to go now," she said, her voice low.

He inclined his head. "Of course, *princesa*," he said, the term not meant as one of endearment.

She turned, walking ahead of him, pushing the door open.

It was warmer outside than it was in the club, the night air heavy and clinging, weighing him down, along with what felt like a rock in his gut. She was acting as though she'd been deeply wronged—offended by his touch, most likely. Because he was so beneath her. At least in public.

He curled his hands into fists, holding them so tight the tendons in his wrists ached.

The penthouse was only a couple of blocks away and Vanessa maintained her stony silence the entire way there. Once they were inside the lobby she kept a few paces in front of him, clearly determined not to look at him or acknowledge his presence.

Anger roared to life in him, replacing the unsettling guilt that had momentarily crept in. She wouldn't have her way. Not now. He wasn't a boy anymore, at the mercy of her father's henchman. And she was no longer the princess in a tower, no longer so far above him she could dismiss him at will. She couldn't just walk away from him.

"You will have to get over your aversion to being seen with me in public, *mi amor*," he said.

She stopped mid-stride and turned to face him, her dark eyes shimmering with heat. "Do I also have to get over my aversion to being groped in public? Does it somehow offend you that I want to maintain some level of public decency?"

"You maintain a high level of private decency as well, since you do not allow me in your bed."

"You take it pretty personally when a woman says no to you. I remember that well."

"No, what I take personally is a woman thinking I'm good enough to tease, but not good enough to take to her bed."

She took a step toward him, her lips tightened into a line.

"Is that what you think that was? Me teasing you?" She shook her head. "I wasn't thinking. If I was thinking I would never have let you touch me."

"You think that's the basis for a happy marriage?"

"I think maybe the basis for a happy marriage is not pursuing the union for business purposes, but then, I'm not really an expert."

"That is a shame, as you have agreed to marry for the benefit of your company. And, as we've discussed, no one has forced you into this. And I will not be made a fool of. Not twice. Not by the same woman."

"You think I made a fool of you, Lazaro?" Her voice was barely raised above a whisper, the force of her emotions making her words tremble. "You weren't the one pressed up against the wall in a public place and...and you have the gall to be angry at me?"

He took a step toward her, softening his voice. "Is that what bothers you the most, Vanessa Pickett, that I make you lose all of that respectability that's so important to you and your family?"

"No, what bothers me is that you think nothing of...of... humiliating me like that in public. Treating me like a thing, your possession that you can put your hands on whenever you want to."

"Is that it? My touch humiliates you?"

Vanessa took a step toward him, her breasts rising and falling with each breath, her delicate hands curled into fists. Arousal and lust warred with anger for prime position inside him. His body still wanted her, was still craving her after that small taste he'd gotten back at the club.

It shamed him, how badly he wanted a woman who saw him as she did. And yet, he could not stop himself. He had been craving her for twelve years. There was nothing that could destroy the desire. Not years of separation, not other lovers, not even the anger that was rolling through him like a tidal wave.

He curved his arm around her waist and pulled her to him, his hand drifting down until it touched the rounded curve of her bottom. "I don't believe that. I think what you really hate, Vanessa, is that no matter what, no matter how much you wish you didn't, no matter how ashamed you are of it, you want me."

Her expression was tight, mutinous, her dark eyes blazing with heat and rage. She put her hands on his chest, curled her fingers around the fabric of his shirt and stretched up on her toes, her breasts brushing against him. She kissed him, her mouth hungry on his, the explosion between them making the kiss at the club seem tame, harmless.

Desire was a living entity between them, dark and dangerous, driving them, pushing them. It was like hurtling toward a cliff, knowing they would both go over the edge if they didn't stop. And yet, knowing that, neither of them stopped.

Lazaro doubted if he could.

She slipped her tongue between his lips, tasting him, teasing him, and a flood of pure lust spread through him, overtaking him. He slid his hand down and cupped her bottom, drew her hard up against his erection.

Vanessa's stomach contracted when she felt the evidence of his arousal. He still wanted her. And even though she was angry at him, she wanted him. Maybe even more because of that anger, all of her emotions mixing, the anger in her a lit match against flammable desire. She wanted him more than she wanted her next breath, and it didn't make any sense to her.

Sex, in her mind, had always been about love and roses and perfect moments. This was as far from a perfect moment as she'd ever imagined, and yet she wanted him. All of him. Every last muscular inch.

She slid her hand sideways and wedged her fingers into the gap of his buttoned-up shirt. He was all hot, hard flesh. She traced a line along his skin, the faint scrape of chest hair against her palm sending a shiver of excitement through her.

On the dance floor, she'd felt as if a part of herself had been unlocked, releasing a desire for more of life than she'd been living. It had been a taste of freedom, and now she was starving for it.

She always thought things through. She planned and rationalized and made sure she was making the right decisions for everyone involved, the right decision for her family name.

But now she wanted Lazaro. And it wasn't about the company, or the marriage or anything beyond the desire to find pleasure in the man who aroused her beyond words.

"Let's go upstairs," she said, her voice breathy and unfamiliar, her words echoing in the empty lobby.

He looked down at her, his jaw tight, a muscle ticking in his cheek. Every hard line of his body was locked and tense, and she could feel his heart raging beneath her palm. He wanted her every bit as much as she wanted him.

The knowledge sent a shot of pure giddiness through her, a kind of power she'd never fully understood before.

"I don't like to be teased," he said, his voice rough, his accent more pronounced.

"I'm not teasing." She held his gaze, tried to keep her hands, her legs, from trembling. Her voice at least was steady. She was deadly serious.

"Tell me what you want." He lowered his head, his lips hovering above hers.

"You," she whispered, the word torn from her.

"More," he ground out. "Tell me more."

Her heart thundered hard, her cheeks hot. "I want…" She swallowed. This wasn't the time to be timid. There was no room for lies, for self-protection. "I want you. Your hands, your mouth, your…" A shudder of desire racked her body. "I want to make love with you. Tonight."

CHAPTER EIGHT

FINALLY. Tonight she would be his. At last he would take the edge off of the burning desire that had plagued his sleep since the day he'd first seen Vanessa Pickett.

He growled low in his throat and pulled her to him, kissing her, tasting her, his body on fire with the need to push her up against the wall and take her then and there. It would be so easy to slide that dress up over her hips and have her that way, so easy and so tempting.

He pulled away from her and pushed the button on the wall to bring the elevator down. He wanted her, desperately. But he knew she didn't want a public display. And it mattered. Because when she'd spoken of humiliation, it had been genuine.

His stomach was a tight ball of pain. Her humiliation might simply be because it was him and not some purebred show boy her father had selected for her.

But then, Vanessa's relationships had never been news- or gossip-worthy, and he had a feeling she was simply private. The intense desire to protect that part of her, to protect *her*, shocked him.

Even if her humiliation was centered around being caught with him, he found he didn't want to make her feel that way.

The lift doors opened and he took her hand and led her

inside, hitting the button immediately, unwilling to wait any longer than absolutely necessary.

She looked at him, her cheeks flushed pink, her lips bright and swollen from kissing him. He cared about her not being humiliated because he wanted her filled with nothing but desire. He wanted her mind blank of everything but the need for him to be inside her, because when he was touching her, that was how he felt, and he wanted her to feel the same.

This moment wasn't about revenge. It was about satisfying a need that had gnawed at him for the past twelve years.

As soon as the elevator doors opened into the vast living area of the penthouse he took her in his arms again, and she came willingly, her soft, delicate hands sliding over his chest, his back. Her lips were hot and soft against his neck.

Vanessa didn't think. She just felt. Nothing else mattered. Nothing. She was determined not to let it matter.

She just wanted to feel. She wanted Lazaro. And she was going to have him. There were so many things in life she'd denied herself, so many things she'd wanted that she'd walked away from because of propriety. Lazaro was one of them.

Not now.

This was her moment. All hers. It was only about desire and want and satisfying the ache inside her, filling the cavernous void that had seemed to grow with each passing year.

She'd spent so long drifting. Walking down a path simply because she'd gone too far to turn back. But she didn't really feel alive. She felt heartburn and angst and stress. But there had to be more than that.

This was more. This was different. And it was hers.

He was hers.

She slid her hands up his chest, his muscles tightening beneath her palms, his chest rising sharply with his quick intake of breath. He'd accused her of teasing him. Maybe she had teased him, but no more than she'd teased herself. She was haunted by her memories of him, of what might have been.

No more what-ifs. No more teasing.

The first step was always the hardest. Her fingers trembled as she slid the top button on his shirt through the buttonhole. The next one was easier, desire taking over and banishing nerves and doubts.

She flattened her hands on his bare chest, felt his heartbeat, strong and fast. She pushed his shirt from his shoulders and let it fall to the floor. He didn't move, he only stood in front of her, a bronzed god of masculine perfection, each muscle perfectly cut and defined. The way the light worked with his physique, adding even more extreme definition to his body, made her want to capture it on film. Forever. For her.

Her fingertips skimmed down his torso, over his washboard-flat stomach and down to his belt buckle. She sucked in a breath and worked the belt loose, letting it fall open. She felt driven now to uncover him, to see him, all of him. She had wondered, for so many years she had wondered, and now she didn't think she could wait another second to see the body her mind had woven fantasies around since she was sixteen.

She pushed his pants and underwear down his hips in one jerky movement, and he kicked them to the side, his eyes never leaving hers. He made no move toward her, he simply stood, naked, completely aroused, in the middle of his living room.

His confidence boosted hers. He wanted this. He wanted her. For once, she wasn't going to worry about possible inadequacy.

She moved her hands down, not quite touching him intimately. He closed his eyes and put his hand over hers, guiding her toward his erection. Her stomach tightened, nerves making a guest appearance now.

She took a breath and placed her hand over his hard shaft. He was hot steel beneath her palm, the hard length of him speaking of his desire for her. She felt her internal muscles tighten as she explored him, nerves fleeing, unable to exist alongside the need that was filling her now.

She squeezed him gently, then again with more strength, increased boldness, when a raw sound of pleasure escaped his lips. His civility was all gone now. Lost in desire, his custom suit on the floor, he was just a man. And he called to everything feminine inside her, made her ache with the need to have him.

"You are overdressed now, I think, *querida*," he said, his voice raw.

She felt the slide of the zipper, a rush of cool air on her back, and then her dress was pooled at her feet. She was still wearing her high heels and a barely there bra and panty set. She should have felt silly, or embarrassed or something. But she didn't.

Because she saw the hunger in his eyes. Saw the need that reflected her own.

And she felt powerful. Powerful and turned on.

"Kiss me," she said, reaching for him.

"Un momento." He unclasped her bra and discarded it. "Beautiful."

He cupped her breast, sliding his thumb over her nipple. She sucked in a breath and watched his dark hand cover her pale flesh. He leaned in and kissed her neck, then lower still, drawing one tightened bud into his mouth, teasing it with the tip of his tongue.

"Laz…" She gripped his head and held him to her, hoping that he would keep her from sliding to the floor.

He lowered himself to his knees, his lips skimming over her ribs, her stomach. He pushed her panties down her legs, baring her to him. She closed her eyes then and just felt. He kissed her thigh, his hands moving down her legs, unfastening the buckle on one of her shoes. He moved his thumb over her ankle as he removed her high heel, the contact on a totally unerotic point on her body sending sparks of sensation skittering through her.

He did the same with her other shoe, tossing it to the side along with the rest of her clothes.

"Sit down," he said, his voice rough but steady.

She looked behind her and saw the plush velvet couch. She'd forgotten where she was for a moment. Everything had gone fuzzy around the edges, everything except for Lazaro.

She lowered herself to the couch, unsure why she was doing it, only knowing that, in this instance, obeying Lazaro was going to be the most rewarding course of action. She didn't know how she knew, only that she did.

"I have dreamed of this. Of you," he said, on his knees before her. "Of how you would look. Of how you would taste."

He pressed a kiss to her inner thigh, his hands moving to grip her hips and draw her to the edge of the couch.

Her entire body was trembling, inside and out, desire and curiosity defeating any of the embarrassment she should be feeling. Because this wasn't about propriety. This was about need. And she needed Lazaro.

She wove her fingers through his hair as he continued kissing her, higher, until he hit the spot that was aching for his touch. He slid his tongue over her, the friction sending heat and flame through her body.

She could feel something building in her, could feel the onset of her climax, so close. So close. He released his grip on her hips and pushed one finger inside her, the rhythm of his penetration working in time with the flick of his tongue over the bundle of nerves at the apex of her thighs.

The tension that had been building, low and tight, released, pleasure rolling through her in pulsing waves.

When she came back to herself, Lazaro had joined her on the couch, his hands moving over her curves, caressing every inch of her body. He leaned in and kissed her lips. "Good?" he asked.

She nodded, her voice lost to her.

He shifted positions so that he was over her, and she parted her thighs for him, making room. The head of his erection pressed against her and she held her breath for a moment, waiting, for pain or satisfaction or completion, whatever it would bring.

He cursed sharply and got up from the couch, crossing to his discarded pants.

"What?" she asked, feeling dizzy.

"Condom." He fished a packet from his wallet and tore it open, making quick work of rolling it on.

They'd stopped at the condom point once before. But she had no intention of stopping him now. She couldn't stop. She had to have him. All of him. For her. For him. Because they both needed it. She did.

She shook with her need to have him. Only him.

Her heart jolted when he moved to her, not from virginal nerves, but because she understood why there hadn't been another man. It had been so easy to blame it on circumstances. To believe it was because of the specter of her almost-fiancé.

It was because of Lazaro. Because she wanted him. Because she'd been waiting for him. So stupid. So dangerously foolish. But she'd had a taste of true passion in his arms, and no one else had ever aroused anything remotely as intense.

Why take less?

And tonight, Lazaro wasn't offering less than what she'd felt before. It was more. So much more than she remembered.

"Thank you," she said, her teeth chattering slightly as a wave of emotion washed through her, making her shake inside.

"For?"

"For remembering. The condom. I think I would have forgotten."

She was glad he'd thought of it, because she hadn't. There was so much happening and she couldn't think straight. Marriage or not, she wasn't ready for a baby. Not when everything at Pickett was so unstable.

She pushed that thought to the side and focused on Lazaro. Nothing else mattered. Not now.

She wrapped her arms around his neck and kissed him as he moved back into the position he'd been in, poised to take possession of her body. She kissed him as he thrust into her, focusing only on the pleasure he was giving her with the erotic glide of his tongue, ignoring the vague, tearing pain.

It passed quickly at least, her body adjusting to him, welcoming him. He put his hand on her thigh and urged her to wrap her leg around his, as she'd done on the dance floor. The move opened her up to him, made each of his thrusts stimulate her inside and out.

Pleasure built inside her again, lower, deeper, more intense. He kissed her neck, her collarbone, lowering his head so that he could take one of her nipples into his mouth, his thumb gliding over the other one.

She arched against him, meeting his thrusts, letting his hands, his body, his touch, block out everything. Everything but the climax she was working toward, everything but the pleasure that was threatening to overtake her, body and soul.

His thrusts came faster, harder, his control slipping. He moved his hands to her hips, his fingers digging into her skin. She slid her tongue over the line of his jaw and she felt every muscle in his body shake, then seize as a harsh groan

scaped his lips. His pleasure—seeing it, feeling him pulse
nside her—pushed her over the edge and she was lost in her
own sensation, in the ecstasy that drowned out everything
else, every thought, every worry.

She wrapped her arms around his neck, holding on to him,
holding him to her. For the moment, nothing else mattered. It
was only Vanessa and Lazaro, and everything else was just
peripheral. For now, this was the reality, and everything else
was the fantasy. Distant and fuzzy. Unimportant.

Lazaro shifted and extricated himself from her arms,
standing and walking into the bathroom. She watched him
walk the whole way, dazed, sated and enjoying the view.

Her eyes started to flutter closed, a drugging sleepiness
overtaking her, making her limbs feel heavy, pleasantly numb.

Lazaro walked back in, his expression blank. "Vanessa…"

"Don't," she mumbled, sleep slurring her words. "I prom-
se, we can fight in the morning, but right now, can we just…
sleep?"

He returned to the couch, settling beside her and draw-
ng her into his arms. She put her head on his chest, his heart
thundering beneath her cheek. Tomorrow would be reality.
For now, she was going to enjoy the fantasy.

Lazaro watched a shaft of pink sunlight catch one of the windows on a building outside, throwing its reflection into the
living room of the penthouse, illuminating Vanessa's perfect body.

He had built fantasies around the idea of what her body
might look like, of the way her face would look when he
brought her to the peak of pleasure. Of what her silken flesh
would feel like beneath his fingers.

He had convinced himself that there was no way she, any
woman, could live up to what he had made Vanessa in his
mind. A fantasy spun in the mind of an eighteen-year-old,

left to grow, had to be beyond reality. Beyond what was possible.

But Vanessa had surpassed a mere fantasy last night. She had been perfection, a taste of heaven and light and a kind of soul-deep satiation he had never believed existed.

He could not have conjured up something more, something better.

She was complete female perfection. Every curve. Every dip and swell. Skin like cream; plump, pink-tipped breasts that made his stomach tighten with desire. Everything about her—touch, taste, sight and scent—satisfied him in a way that was utterly foreign.

But, incredibly, coupled with that bone-deep satisfaction was a need for more that made him ache.

She stirred against him, her nipples brushing his chest, the contact lighting a fire in his blood. He moved his hand over the curve of her hip and she made a soft sound of pleasure and arched into him.

He dropped a kiss onto her bare shoulder and her eyes popped open. She rolled slightly and slid off the couch onto the floor, cursing before standing, her cheeks bright pink.

"Where are my clothes?" she asked, her voice rusty from disuse.

"Around," he said, pushing himself into a sitting position.

"Could you not look at me for a second please?"

"I've seen it, Vanessa. More than seen."

"Please," she said again.

He looked out the window, all his concentration taken by the effort it took to pull his focus away from her perfect body.

"You act as though you haven't had a morning after before," he said.

The telling silence made his stomach tighten, and he couldn't keep himself from looking back at her. She was standing there, clutching her dress to her chest, biting her lip.

"You haven't?" he asked.

She huffed out a breath, shifted her weight to one side, one bare hip looking more rounded, more prominent. "How many women have you slept with?"

"Excuse me?"

Her dark eyebrows shot upward. "Rude question, isn't it?"

"Odd," he said. "And pointless."

"Then I don't suppose I have to answer either."

His heartbeat quickened. It really shouldn't matter, and yet, he found it did. Because he wanted her to be his. His alone. The idea that no other man had ever been with her like that sent a rush of pure, unenlightened testosterone through him. His. In every way possible.

"I don't know," he said, disgust filling him as he spoke the words.

"You don't know if I have to answer the question?"

"I don't know how many women I've slept with," he bit out.

She frowned. "Oh."

He hadn't anticipated this. That his vast experience could cause him shame. He didn't brag about his luck with women, but inevitably, if there was an article about him written anywhere, his reputation with the opposite sex was mentioned. It had always earned him a certain measure of respect.

It wasn't respect on Vanessa's face. It was disappointment. It passed quickly, her expression neutral again, her eyes focused on a spot just past him.

Even though it was a fleeting impression of disappointment, it left a hollow feeling in his chest.

"I answered," he said.

She met his eyes. "Then no, I haven't had a morning after before."

"How is that possible, Vanessa? I didn't pick you out as a virgin when you were sixteen."

"But I was. Well, obviously I was then, since last night I still was."

"Why?"

"Why don't you know how many women you've slept with?" she countered, clutching her clothes more tightly against her.

Because I was trying to forget you. He held back the stark, honest thought that filled his mind.

He shrugged and stood. "Because I'm a man, Vanessa. Once I made money, women were readily available and I took advantage."

She stood, her focus on an undefined spot on the carpet. He didn't like the look on her face. She sighed heavily and then lifted her face, meeting his eyes. "We're trading, are we?" He nodded in confirmation. "Because, in addition to the fact that my father is a professional at chasing men out of my life, I wanted…someone to want me. Not my father's money. Or my status. Or… I just hadn't found that." She averted her gaze.

"I didn't care about your money or your status."

"You just wanted sex?"

Her words bit into him. He shrugged. "I was eighteen. There isn't much more a horny teenage boy wants. Not only that, I was experienced, too much for my age. It's what we did. I think it was part of what made being so poor bearable. Taking advantage of those few moments of oblivion. It's how I related to women, so, yes, it was what I wanted."

"But it's not all you want now. Now you want my connections too."

"Things have changed."

She nodded slightly. "Can you turn around again? I don't want to have to back out of the room."

"Why did you decide to sleep with me last night?"

Her lips flattened into a line. "When I figure that out I'll get back to you."

Lazaro turned his back and faced the view, letting her walk out without an audience. He tried to ignore the odd, crushing weight that was pressing down on his chest.

CHAPTER NINE

"WHERE have you been?"

Vanessa walked back into the penthouse after a day spent in careful avoidance of Lazaro, exhausted, feet aching.

Lazaro was standing at the bar, palms rested flat on the black marble surface, his dark eyes filled with intensity. She'd spent the afternoon taking photographs of Buenos Aires, deliberately not thinking about the night before and generally having a very relaxing day.

Well, the relaxation was clearly about to end.

"Out," she said.

"Out where?" he said, his voice low, deadly.

"It's not really your business is it?" She felt compelled to put distance between them, to exert some kind of control in a situation where she really didn't have any.

"It is my business," he said.

"No, Lazaro, it's my business." She started to walk toward her bedroom.

"You're mine, Vanessa, that means I have a right to know how you spend your time."

She turned sharply. "I do not belong to you. And I never will. A marriage license isn't a deed of ownership."

He slammed his palm on the top of the bar. "That is not what I meant."

Anger fired through her. "It is, though, isn't it? You want

me to be this sparkly possession that you can show off. The proof of how far you've come. A chance to give the world the finger. Well, great. But you had to make sure that I had no other options open to get me to agree to marry you. I had no other choice. Don't forget that."

She walked straight ahead to the balcony, tears, hot and angry, blurring the lights of the city. She slammed the sliding door behind her and leaned against the railing, pressing her palms hard against her eyes, trying to stop herself from dissolving, trying to keep from making a total idiot of herself.

She couldn't let him affect her like this. Because he was dangerously close to being right in some ways. It wasn't that she truly believed he had any ownership of her, but power... she was letting him have all kinds of power over her emotions. And as long as she did, he would always be the one in control, because she didn't have a hold over him. He might like her body, but that was sex, and with nothing other than lust behind it, it would be temporary.

And what would happen then? She would be left behind, the faux-political wife committed to standing at her husband's side no matter what he'd done. No matter how broken she was inside.

And if she let him, he could destroy her.

She gritted her teeth. She didn't know why it was Lazaro. Why was he the only one who brought this out in her? She only knew that he was.

She closed her eyes and pictured a day twelve years earlier, the hot summer sun warming her skin, a boy with a smile that seemed to be meant only for her.

It hadn't been true then. Yet part of her still clung to the ridiculous fantasy. The part of her that had been waiting for him...

It was why she'd slept with him. She'd told him she didn't

know why, and that had been a lie. He was the only man she'd ever really wanted.

And part of her…part of her believed he had to feel the same way. She housed some serious delusion inside herself.

"I didn't force you into bed last night. It had nothing to do with our agreement or blackmail or the future of Pickett."

She turned around and saw Lazaro striding toward her, his expression cold with black fury.

"I didn't get in your bed. That was your couch," she said tightly.

"I didn't force you to have sex with me." he said. "You wanted it."

She couldn't deny it. She wished she could. Wished she were capable of lying on that level, to his face, without remorse. But she couldn't. She'd told him last night that she wanted him. She had directed the evening activities once they'd left the club.

"You want *me*," he said, his eyes never leaving hers, coal-black and intense, glittering in the dim light. "Say it."

She swallowed hard and turned away from him, her eyes focused on the skyline.

She felt him approach, her body responding to his, her breasts getting heavy, the pulse between her thighs pounding hard. The empty ache threatening to swallow her. She wanted him, again, during a fight. She didn't know herself. Didn't know what it was he did to her.

Only that he sparked a fire in her that no one else ever had. And it wasn't just about sex or lust or desire. It was so much more. He showed her how lacking her life was. Being with him, near him, seeing the steps he'd taken to change his life, made her so acutely aware of how little she'd done. Of how hollow all of her so-called achievements were. She'd had it all handed to her and she'd still messed up.

All her thoughts evaporated when Lazaro put his hand on

the curve of her waist, swept her hair to one side, exposing her neck to the warm night breeze. "Tell me you want me," he said, a raw note in his voice now, showing a crack in his iron control.

And she realized that he needed to hear it. That her words hadn't glanced off his thick armor, but that they'd struck a blow. She'd imagined that he was invincible—a man with so much power, the freedom to do what he wanted. A man who lived without restriction.

But he wasn't. She flashed back to that moment in the club and saw his anger for what it was. She had hurt him. She had rejected him.

He slid his hand up, cupped her breast, the thin barrier of her dress providing no protection from the sensual assault. He pinched her nipple lightly between his thumb and forefinger and tugged.

Her head fell back, and he took advantage, kissing her neck as he continued to tease her body.

"You want me, Vanessa," he said, not a question this time. "Me."

"Yes," she whispered.

"And it's not about money or what I can do for Pickett right now, is it?"

She shook her head, biting her lip to hold back the whimper of pleasure that was climbing her throat. She felt her dress give as he slid the zipper down, exposing her back. His hand drifted over the line of her spine, the light touch sending heavy waves of arousal through her.

She relaxed her shoulders and let her dress fall, the warm, heavy breeze kissing her bare skin, a completely foreign sensation. But no one would be able to see them. Even if someone might be able to, she wasn't certain she could bring herself to care.

Lazaro moved his hands over her stomach, his touch firm, warm, so sexy it made her knees weak.

"No, it's not about anything but…" She sucked in a sharp breath when he covered her breasts with one of his hands and pressed against her stomach with the other, drawing her more tightly against him, bringing his erection into firm contact with her bottom. "But how much I want you," she choked out.

He kissed her neck, her shoulder, and a tremor wracked her body, longing making her weak. But there was a fire smoldering in her stomach, a need for more. For more than simple lust. She'd confessed to wanting him, apart from their marriage arrangement and everything else.

She needed him to do the same.

She wiggled out of his grasp and turned to face him, her back against the balcony railing, her breasts pressed tightly against his chest. "Tell me you want me too."

He rocked against her, the hard length of him pressing into her stomach. "Doesn't it feel like I want you?"

"Tell me you want *me*, right now. Me. Not my status. Not my connections." She slid her hand down his chest, past his belt, pressing her palm over his erection. "Tell me," she said again.

His eyes were dark, nearly black with passion, his jaw locked tight, tension holding his body taut, every muscle rock-hard. "I want you."

"My name," she said, the words coming out broken. "I need you to say it."

"I want you, Vanessa."

She let out a gust of air. "Lazaro."

He captured her lips with his, his kiss hungry, devouring, and she returned it, sliding her tongue over his, taking his bottom lip lightly between her teeth and tugging. He growled and scooped her up in his arms.

"We're making it to bed this time," he said, striding into the penthouse and heading into his room.

She'd avoided his room since they'd arrived in Argentina, and not by accident. Just seeing that big bed pushed her desire up to another level. Of course, now her fantasies were strengthened by the memory of what it was like to be with him, to have him inside her, his steady rhythm taking her to the heights of ecstasy.

He set her down in the center of the bed and she shivered.

"Cold?"

She shook her head.

"Nervous?" he asked.

"I am, a little bit." It didn't seem like the place for self-preservation. In this moment at least, honesty seemed imperative.

He made quick work of the buttons on his shirt, shrugging it off and casting it to the floor. Vanessa could only stare at all the sculpted, masculine perfection before her. She'd been with him once, but it didn't mean it wasn't intimidating. He was perfect, experienced and fantastic in bed. She wasn't sure she was offering him an even trade.

"I just..." She got up on her knees and inched to the edge of the bed, putting her hand flat against his stomach, his muscles shifting beneath her palm. "I don't know if I can compete with the memory of...more women than you can remember."

He encircled her wrist with his hand and pulled her gently to him, kissing her on the lips. "There's a reason I don't remember. They didn't matter. They aren't here in bed with us. When I look at you, you're all I can see."

For now, she would accept his words. She wouldn't think too far into them. She refused to wonder if he'd felt the same about all of them at the time, only to have his desire for them fade as time went on, and to have memories of them fade completely later.

She pushed that thought aside because she didn't want to think of it now. Even if it was stupid and dangerous, she wanted to believe him.

He discarded the rest of his clothes and joined her on the bed, kissing her, putting his hand on the curve of her hip and dragging her panties down her legs. She kicked her shoes off and shoved them off the bed with her foot, anxious to have all of the barriers removed.

And when he took her in his arms, every inch of his body pressed against hers, she closed her eyes and inhaled his scent, tears forming in her eyes because he was everything she'd fantasized and more. He had been perfect the first night, but that had been frantic, and the main event had been so new it had been hard to focus on the finer points of what it meant to be intimate with a man. With Lazaro.

Her fingertips blazed a trail over his bicep, his skin smooth, hot, his muscles hard beneath. She skimmed her hands over his hair-roughened chest, flat abs, down to his hardened shaft. She kissed his mouth, catching the harsh sound of pleasure that rose in his throat as she explored his body.

He moved his hand down between her thighs and she stilled her movements then, luxuriating in the response he could call from her body. Orgasm built in her, quick and intense, ripples of sensation making her internal muscles tighten.

"I love watching your face when you come," he whispered.

She laughed, her throat tight with emotion. "I can't think of anything when you do that."

"Then I'm doing something right."

Yes, he was. It was something that reached down into her, something that surpassed her body and went straight for her soul.

He pulled away from her for a moment and opened the drawer to the bedside table, retrieving a condom.

And then he was in her, filling her, the friction so delicious it surpassed the climax she'd just experienced. She gave herself up to the sensation washing through her body, to the building pleasure that was blocking out everything else.

Her orgasm broke over her like a wave, spinning her in the tide, making her feel weightless. For a moment there was nothing more than her and Lazaro. Nothing more than what he was making her feel.

Dimly, she was aware of him coming with a harsh groan, his body braced hard against her as he kissed her fiercely.

Afterward, she lay with her hand on his chest, his fingers sifting through her hair, their legs tangled together.

Vanessa drew back and looked at him, running her fingers over his stubble-roughened jaw, tracing his brow, his high cheekbones. "You look different," she said, languor slurring her speech slightly. "But the same too."

"I do?"

"Mmm-hmm. You're older, in a good way, and your nose…" She touched the bump on the bridge of his nose. "What happened?"

"I broke it."

"I figured as much."

He rolled onto his back, away from her. "You said the other day that your father was very good at running interference when he doesn't approve of the men you're associating with. I carry permanent proof of that."

CHAPTER TEN

VANESSA felt as if all the air had been sucked out of her body. Because the meaning in Lazaro's words was stunningly, sickeningly clear.

She didn't know how it could be true, but she knew it was. Without knowing details, she knew. Because it explained everything. The animosity that rolled off Lazaro like a physical force when he spoke about her family, her father. She'd simply thought he was angry. Angry at life, angry in general.

That wasn't it. She'd been wrong. He was angry at her family. At her.

"What happened?" she asked.

She didn't want to know. She wanted to cover her ears and hide under the covers. But that wasn't an option. She had to know.

"Tell me, Vanessa. Did you ever question why I never came back to your father's estate? Why you never saw me again? Where my mother went?"

"I… Of course I did." And she'd made it all about herself. Because, of course, Lazaro had never come back because she'd refused to sleep with him. But she was a fool. A shallow idiot who had never been able to see past herself.

"What was your conclusion?" he asked, his voice soft.

"I thought you didn't want to see me anymore because I wouldn't put out," she said. She wished she could protect herself and lie, but in bed with Lazaro, nothing between them, there couldn't be any lies. No matter how much she wanted to lie to him. No matter how much she wished he'd lie to her.

"Amazing that it seems neither of us knew each other at all."

"What do you mean?"

"I thought you turned me down because I was good enough to play with, but not good enough to sleep with."

"That wasn't it at all. I was… You were my first kiss and I wasn't ready to go from first kiss to bed in five minutes time."

"I said things then that I should not have said," he said. "I thought you were playing a game with me."

"The same game you thought I was playing in the club?" She didn't need a hint of affirmation and she didn't get one. "It wasn't a game. I was worried about…what people would think if they saw me behaving that way."

"With me?"

"With anyone. But…you do make me lose control, Lazaro, and it scares me sometimes."

Silence settled between them and she knew it was up to her to ask again. Even though it had been derailed and she'd been given an out. There was no simple out. They had to wade through the mess of the past if they were ever going to go forward. It was that simple.

She took a shuddering breath. "What did my father do to you?"

"Not your father personally. He would never have gotten his hands dirty that way. He has people on hand to take care of life's more unsavory problems."

"You were an unsavory problem?"

"Of the worst sort. I had my sights set on his daughter's virtue." Vanessa felt every line in Lazaro's body tense, could sense the scarcely harnessed aggression that was flowing through him. She wanted to soothe him, and she honestly didn't know how.

"What did they do?"

"After I left the guesthouse that night I was upset. I went into town. I was followed. I don't know that you need details, but I woke up facedown in the alley and, at the time, a broken nose was the least of my problems."

"They beat you?" She scrambled out of the bed, her breath coming hard, fast. "My father had you beaten?"

"You didn't know, then," he said, his voice flat.

"No." She put her hand on her stomach, trying to quell the nausea that was rising in her. "You thought I knew? You thought that I…"

"Your father puts on a convincing front of civility, Vanessa. At the time I thought it was possible you did the same."

"I would never…"

"I know. I had let go of the idea of you being involved a long time ago."

She was relieved to hear him say that, even if that was selfish.

"I told you we were fired from the estate, but there was more," Lazaro continued. "Your father made sure no one else would hire us either. We were evicted from our apartment. Usually, we had a shelter to sleep in, but sometimes we ended up sleeping outside. My mother's health did not do well in those conditions."

For the third time since Lazaro had come back into her life, she felt the ground shift beneath her feet.

"I knew…" Her voice cracked. "I knew my father was a hard man, I knew he was controlling, but I didn't know…I didn't know he'd gone that far. I had a… There was a man I was interested in at Pickett when I was first hired on and my father was adamant about me not seeing him because he was just an employee. I did what he asked. I didn't want to be with anyone he didn't approve of. I just didn't imagine he would ever do something like... Something so horrible."

She felt like her world was falling away, shattering into tiny little pieces, fragile and in danger of being scattered by the wind.

She had protected her father's legacy at the expense of everything. Her dreams. She could hardly remember her dreams anymore because she'd shoved them to the side with ruthless efficiency when she was thirteen years old in order to fulfill the demands of the most important man in her life.

And that man was a coward. A criminal.

She believed Lazaro's words. She felt the truth of them all the way down to her soul. She was sick with the truth of it spreading through her like poison, undeniable and deadly.

"I survived, Vanessa," he said, his voice hard. "More than. And I don't want your wide-eyed pity."

"I don't pity you," she said.

She didn't. It was impossible to pity a man like Lazaro. He was too strong, the pride that radiated from him forbidding anything as debasing as pity.

But she felt betrayed. Betrayed by the man who shared her blood, the man whose legacy she had fought so hard to preserve. The man who had brought so much destruction into the lives of other people for the sake of his vision for the future.

It made her feel tainted. Made everything in her, her ambition, her *blood,* feel dirty. That blood that was supposed to be so important, that was supposed to define her...she hated it now.

"It is done, Vanessa. The only thing I regret is that my mother lived out her last days in discomfort, rather than in the lifestyle she deserved. But it was the defining moment in my life." The gleam in his eyes was deadly, cold and devoid of anything tender. "It was the moment when I realized that

I would stop at nothing to make it to the top where I could crush men like your father beneath my heel."

It was the venom in his voice, not aggressive or blatant, woven into every syllable, touching every word, that shocked her the most. The hatred that was there.

She had been a fool. She had imagined that Lazaro's quest was about vanity, but it was about something so much deeper. She had thought herself a trophy to him, but that was so far removed from the truth it was laughable.

She was his avenue to vengeance. He was using her, a fact she'd known from the beginning, but what she hadn't realized was exactly what she was being used for.

He would use her not only to bring him to the top, but to mock her father's efforts. To show him that he now owned everything that her father had tried to keep from him. That he, Lazaro, had won.

Even as the realization crashed through her, she could understand it, but she didn't want to be Lazaro's pawn. Or his queen, as the case may be.

And yet, she wasn't certain she had a choice because everything felt tangled now, complicated beyond fixing.

She couldn't feel nothing for this man who made love to her with such explosive, sweet passion. She couldn't shut off what she felt for her first lover, the man she had fallen for at sixteen. As clichéd as it was, she felt connected to him now. As though he were a part of her.

If she were really honest with herself, the connection wasn't new. Having their bodies joined was just a physical manifestation of what had been from the beginning. He'd been in her from the start.

It was why she had always kept an eye on his career when he'd started getting media attention. Why she'd silently cheered for his success even while she hurt inside over not sharing it with him.

It was why part of her wanted to cheer for his success now in this, his quest for vengeance and justice.

And part of her wanted to scream at him and ask him why he'd dragged her into everything. Or more to the point, why he'd made her care. Why he looked at her as though he wanted to devour her. Why he kissed her as though he were sampling some rare, exquisite wine. How he could make her feel this way when she knew he had to hate her.

Why couldn't he just be a jerk? Why couldn't she simply see him as he was: a man set on using her for his own ends?

But it wasn't so simple that it could be reduced to anything that easy to understand. There was nothing simple about it.

There was nothing simple about the massive knot of emotion that was filling her chest, making it hard to breathe. There was nothing easy about the thick tension that hung in the air. Sexual. Emotional.

"Come back to bed," Lazaro said, pulling back the covers.

"I should maybe go—"

"You're coming to bed. With me. You need to sleep, we're going to be flying out tomorrow."

And because she was exhausted, and because she ached to be in his arms, she climbed back into the bed.

He drew her close to his body, his hands moving over her curves, soothing her, making her brain fuzzy and her body sleepy.

Her last thought before drifting off was, how did a man with so much anger in him, a man who was only using her, make her feel more wanted, more desired, than anyone else in her life ever had?

Reality set in quickly back in Boston. Lazaro was busy, and Vanessa had a mountain of paperwork on her desk, thanks to the remaining fossils Pickett Industries had accounts with who had never heard of sending documents via email.

Her office was her home away from home again, and her personal life was back to being nonexistent. She doubted it had ever really existed. Lazaro was some unholy mash-up of her personal and professional life, not to mention her new-found sex life, which she was missing after a few nights alone in her big, cold bed.

She would see him tonight though. After work he was taking her to a big gala that was historically reserved for a very select group. The Pickett name was always on the list and, since word of their engagement had spread and Lazaro was now becoming a part of that legacy, he had secured an invitation too.

She was serving her purpose at least—bringing Lazaro into the hallowed institutions of the American aristocracy. Into a cornerstone of which she was about to put a big crack.

Her phone buzzed and she hit the intercom button. "Yes?"

"Ms. Pickett, your father is here to see you."

Vanessa swallowed hard. "Send him in."

Her father strode into the room, his expression dark. Dangerous. His gray eyebrows were locked together in a show of disapproval. "You've been on vacation?"

"I took some time off with my new fiancé," she said, striving to keep her tone light.

"Can you afford time off?"

"I have to do my part to ensure my marriage is successful."

"That isn't what you called me here to say though, is it, Vanessa?"

"No," she said slowly, standing from her chair, planting both palms firmly on her desk. She hoped the gesture conveyed confidence, because what she was really doing was trying to keep her knees from buckling. "I know what you did to Lazaro."

Her father didn't flinch. "I thought you might."

"You're a cold-blooded bastard," she said, through clenched teeth.

"I did it for you, Vanessa, so we could avoid a situation like this—you marrying so patently beneath your station."

"My station? Because Lazaro wasn't born into money he's somehow beneath me? Beneath you? Lazaro is a better man than you will ever be, and you have to keep men like him shut out because he has something you don't. He's brilliant, he solves problems. He even knows how to fix this disaster you and I are standing in."

Michael Pickett looked at her, his eyes—eyes she'd always imagined looking like her own—stared back at her, cold and dead. "Did you call me in here for the sole purpose of hearing your impassioned little speech or did you have a point?"

"I had a point," she said. "You will make sure Lazaro is welcomed into high society with your blessing. Because if you don't, I will let this place crumble. Hell, I'll tear it apart myself. Brick by brick."

"Insolent, ungrateful…"

"I don't think you understand the reality here. Lazaro and myself combined own the majority of this company. You don't have the power here. Not even close. Lazaro and some of our board members have close professional relationships and his influence carries a lot of weight."

"You would dismantle your family legacy? The one meant for your brother? The one he would have seen flourish?"

"For the man I love? In a heartbeat."

They were the truest words she'd ever spoken. She didn't realize it until she spoke them. She loved Lazaro. She would move heaven and earth for him. She would stand up to Michael Pickett for him. She *had* stood up to Michael Pickett. She would do it again, ten times over.

"Lazaro isn't a boy that you can have beaten and left for dead in an alley, not anymore." She took a breath. "And I'm not a little girl. I won't simply do as I'm told without looking into what's really going on. Lazaro isn't just going away," she said, watching her father's face for a hint of what he was thinking, whether he was going to explode.

Silence hung between them, the only sound Vanessa's thundering heart in her ears.

Her father's face remained set in stone. "Of course he will be welcomed," he said, his tone cold. "He's my future son-in-law."

"Yes," she said, over the blood roaring in her ears. "He is."

She watched her father leave and felt a pleasant numbness spread from the pain in her fingertips to the pain in her chest, blocking it out. She'd done what she had to do. She wouldn't allow her father to have any kind of victory, not in Lazaro's life, not in hers. Not now that she knew who he really was. Who she had been protecting, helping for so many years.

Her secretary buzzed her again. "Yes?" Her voice was shaking now, the adrenaline seeping from her system and leaving her weak, drained.

"Mr. Marino has sent a limo."

"And is Mr. Marino in said limo?"

"Not that I saw."

A spike of disappointment pierced the blessed numbness. A limo, but not the man himself. Well, that was life with rich, important men, she was well aware. As long as she served her purpose, things went smoothly. But she wouldn't be getting any excess attention.

"I'll be right down."

CHAPTER ELEVEN

LAZARO's heart squeezed tight when Vanessa walked into the main living area of his Beacon Hill penthouse.

She was dressed in her business clothes, wide-legged slacks and spiky heels combined with a dark fitted jacket and a brightly colored top underneath. Her dark hair was swept back into a low ponytail and the gloss on her lips was a sedate rose, perfect for board meetings. And, apparently, for making his blood pump hot and fast.

But then, there was never a time when his desire for Vanessa seemed to cool, no matter what she was wearing—or not wearing.

He had missed her over the past few days. He had hoped the separation might help him regain some of his control. But now that she was here, he was on fire with lust. A response that was as instant as it was beyond his control.

"I didn't bring my dress with me," she said, shifting her weight, her eyes scanning the room, careful not to land on him for too long. "I didn't realize you wanted me to meet you here."

"I bought you a dress."

Then she did look at him. "You bought me a dress? For tonight? I have one. I had what I was going to wear planned out."

"You won't need it," he said.

He'd seen the dress at a shop in Buenos Aires when they'd been there, and he'd instantly envisioned Vanessa wearing it. He'd contacted the designer and ordered the dress in a color and size he thought would suit Vanessa and had had it shipped back to Boston just for the gala.

It was the kind of thing she should have. Something made just for her. Something nice and expensive. She deserved everything he could give.

"But you didn't ask me."

"It was a surprise."

That earned him stony silence and a censorious look from her dark brown eyes. "Show me," she said, after a pause.

He led her through the main living area of the house and up the open staircase to the loft floor that overlooked the open kitchen, living- and dining-room portions of the penthouse. He opened the door to his bedroom and ushered her inside.

He noticed, for the first time, how Spartan everything was. How masculine. Vanessa looked so pale and delicate in these surroundings, out of place. The black-and-gray design scheme, the stark angled lines, didn't suit her at all.

That his room was a wholly masculine domain had never mattered before. He didn't bring women into his home. It was much too personal. Vanessa was the first woman he'd brought into his bedroom. And the first person he'd brought into the house for a very long time. Entertaining at home wasn't high on his agenda.

Vanessa walked over to the bed where the dress was draped across the black comforter, the red silk shocking against the dark background. There were gold shoes beside it, high heels with delicate ankle straps that he knew would draw attention to her slender legs.

She frowned as she examined the offering and his gut tightened.

"I don't know that it's a red sort of event," she said crisply.

He locked his teeth together, then loosened them, the stupid thing she'd said about TMJ ringing in his ears. "That's why you should wear it."

"So I'll stand out?"

"So everyone will look at us."

"And that's a good thing?"

Frustration boiled inside him. "Yes. I want everyone to see us there. To know I'm with you."

She frowned again. "I see."

"There's a wrap to wear over it. It will be cold tonight." As if that fixed his intent somehow.

"Okay."

Vanessa watched Lazaro stalk from the room, his annoyance with her a palpable presence that lingered long after he left.

She examined the dress spread out on his bed and the black cashmere wrap that was folded next to it. It was such an intimate thing, and yet he had presented it in a way that was anything but. The gesture spoke clearly of what she was to him, the part he expected her to play tonight. She was his accessory for the evening and he hadn't trusted her to dress accordingly. He had to go to extraordinary lengths to ensure that she was exactly as she should be. So that people would look at them.

So that he could use her as a status symbol.

Her stomach lurched.

Was he any different than her father?

Yes.

Yes, he was different. He would never have anyone harmed, would never do anything so reprehensible. But as far as his feelings for her? She was a thing. A possession.

You are mine.

His. His status symbol in red.

She picked the dress up by the spaghetti straps and held

it in front of her, the delicate fabric swishing as she lifted it. This was what she'd signed on for. Trophy wife, agreeable accessory who did as she was told in public, who put on a good front so that Lazaro could move freely in the upper levels of society.

It was what she'd signed on for, and now it seemed unbearable.

She didn't know if she had the strength to walk away, even if she wanted to. But she didn't know if she had the strength to stay, either. To stay and fulfill, in her husband's mind, the same thing that Beacon Hill property did. Nothing more than status.

She slowly took her clothes off, hands shaking as she folded her top and slacks and set them on the bed. She picked up the red dress and held it in front of her naked body, looking at herself in the mirror.

She picked the dress up and pulled it on, contorting her arm so that she could pull the zipper into place. It was daring, sexy in an overt way.

She picked the wrap up and draped it around her shoulders. It went a long way toward making the dress more respectable. She flung it back on the bed. If he wanted a show, she'd give the people a show. And if he didn't like it, that was too bad.

The gala was crowded with glittering men and women, the majority of them in black. Vanessa knew she stood out like a very vulgar sore thumb. For the first time in her life she wasn't dressed appropriately for the gathering. It wasn't a very good feeling.

But when she'd come out of the bedroom, Lazaro's eyes had lit with hungry flames, his expression telling her just how much he approved—until she'd told him she was going without the handy cover he'd given her. Since they'd arrived at the party he'd had his hand on her, on her back, her waist, his manner possessive.

She sighed and took a glass of champagne from a passing waiter. If his goal was to have them be the center of attention, his mission was well and truly accomplished. She was maybe being a little more obvious than he'd intended, but she hadn't been about to just cater to his wishes. If she'd had another dress at her disposal at his penthouse, she would have simply gone with that.

She tried to let the stares slide off her, tried not to worry about them.

Of course, it might not have been her the other guests were staring at. The women could just as easily be staring at Lazaro and not at her at all. In his custom-made black suit he looked a cut above every other man present. His olive skin was complemented perfectly by his red tie, and the suit showed the shape of his fabulous physique. It certainly made her want to undo every button and see the man beneath. She was sure she wasn't the only one with that thought.

Lazaro worked the room, his natural charisma on display tonight, charisma she had been pulled in by at the age of sixteen when he'd flashed her that killer smile of his for the first time.

She was so proud of him. Of all he had become. And she was merely his invitation to the event. She gripped the stem of her glass more tightly.

"Lazaro." A man Vanessa recognized from some gatherings at the Pickett estate stepped forward to shake Lazaro's hand. "I've been wanting to have a talk with you about some of the things going on at Garrison Limited."

"Have you?" Lazaro asked.

"Yes, I… Well, times being what they are, I thought you might want to come and give me a consultation on what I can do to keep up with the changing market."

"You can call my secretary and arrange an appointment."

"I will, I will. But…would you like to come and meet my business partner?"

Vanessa could sense Lazaro tensing beside her, could feel the annoyance radiating from him like a physical force.

"Of course," he said, ever the diplomat. "Hold this, please, Vanessa." He placed his champagne flute in her hand and walked away with the other man.

Vanessa's stomach sank into her toes as a similar scene flashed through her mind. The night at the art museum. Lazaro had been with a woman then. Vanessa had dubbed her a human cup-holder at the time.

She looked at her hand, at the full glass of champagne, the condensation running down the sides as the bubbles floated up to the surface. She set it down on the nearest table and leaned against the wall, dizzy with anger and hurt.

She wasn't different. She was the same as every other woman he'd ever been with.

No, even worse, she *was* different. He was stuck with her if he wanted to make it to the top, because of her name, her connections, things that were beyond her control. Things that couldn't be bought or negotiated for. If he could have done it any other way, he would have.

She was sure of that now.

It struck her now, just how foolish she was. That she'd imagined he could care for her when he carried so much anger toward her family, anger she couldn't even blame him for.

But, as sorry as she was for the sins of her father, they weren't her sins. They never had been. Her only crime had been loving him, wanting more from him than he could give. And she had committed it again twelve years on.

Because she loved him. And all she would ever be to him was status. A symbol of thoroughly meted-out vengeance. A trophy. He had never pretended otherwise. She was a fool.

He would never love her for who she was. Only for what she could do for him. And if she couldn't do anything for him anymore he would discard her without a backward glance. There was no doubt in her mind.

Could she handle another lifetime of that? Her father had only ever used her. He had held Thomas's memory, her love for her late brother, over her head to get her to do what she was told. He had played her like a master all of her life.

And Lazaro would have even more power. Because he had her heart.

"No," she whispered the word.

She had always defined herself by her last name. By the family legacy. But she had found more to herself in Buenos Aires. In Lazaro's arms. There was more to her than the preservation of a business. More to her than becoming a status symbol for her husband.

And she knew for a fact that she couldn't stay with him and take the crumbs of his affection. She deserved more. She deserved what everyone else had. Freedom. Choices.

Her heart expanded, even as it cracked inside her. She had the freedom to make choices, to follow the path she wanted to go down. She always had had.

She was making a choice now. For herself.

She looked at Lazaro, engrossed in his conversation, and then at the glass of champagne she'd set on the table.

Then she turned and walked out of the ballroom. Out of the building.

She called her driver. "I need to be picked up."

"Vanessa?" The voice on the other side of her door was frantic. Familiar.

She opened it and her heart jumped when she saw Lazaro, still dressed in his suit, his tie untied and draped over his shoulders, his jacket open, the top few buttons of his shirt undone.

"Where did you go?" he asked, his voice soft.

"I left."

"So I gathered, when I searched every last room in the building and didn't find you. I thought that something had happened to you."

The bleakness in his eyes, in his tone, spoke the truth of it.

Lazaro looked at her standing there, arms folded beneath her breasts, her dress, the dress she'd gone out of her way to tantalize him with, long discarded, and not by him as he'd fantasized. She was wearing blue pajama pants and a gray long-sleeved top, her makeup scrubbed off, leaving her face pink.

When he looked closer, he could tell it was not pink from being scrubbed. Her eyes were rimmed in red and there were shimmering tracks on her cheeks.

"Did something happen?" he asked, stepping into her home, not bothering to wait for an invitation. "Did someone hurt you?" He swore then and there that whoever it was would wish that Lazaro had been merciful and simply killed him. Because he would ruin the man. No one would ever harm Vanessa. Ever. She would want for nothing, not while she was his woman. His wife.

When he'd realized she wasn't at the gala, that she was gone…he'd imagined every horrible scenario possible, all of it flashing through his mind's eye at a rapid pace as panic flooded his body.

He'd stared into his future, one without her, black and empty, stretching before him. Blank nothing. The terror of it had been beyond anything he'd ever imagined.

But she was home in her pajamas. Safe.

"No. Yes."

"What happened?"

"I realized something."

"What was that?" he asked, his heart thundering, his body still high from the rush of adrenaline that had been propelling him since he'd realized she was gone.

Her brows locked together, her expression fierce and sad and completely stunning. "I can't marry you. More than that, I don't want to marry you."

The meaning of her words became clear slowly, and along with the meaning, a searing, tearing pain started deep in his chest, growing as her words resonated in him until it was a blinding, overwhelming ache that overtook him, immobilized his limbs, made his heart feel as if it had been removed and discarded.

"We have a deal." He managed to force the words out.

"We can work something else out. I don't want to do this," she said.

"Why is that, Vanessa? Because you didn't like the stares you were getting tonight, being with me? The man from the gutter? Or was it that the damn dress wasn't good enough for you? Do you need a bigger ring, is that it?"

"Lazaro…"

"Enough," he cut her off, unable to bear hearing her reasoning. Unable to be told how much he was wanting in her eyes. How beneath her he was. *Dios,* it choked him, made him feel as though his chest was caving in.

Desperation clawed at him, a black hole that threatened to take him down. He couldn't lose her. Not again. "You *will* marry me."

She shook her head. "I don't need to be in charge of Pickett anymore. I don't care about my father's legacy."

"And what about the employees? Their jobs?" If there was a problem, he would solve it. He always left himself the means to do so. If Vanessa thought otherwise, then she'd thoroughly underestimated him.

"Of course I care, but they'll still have jobs even if you replace me as CEO."

"Not if there is no more company."

She took a step back, her hands on her chest. "What are you saying?"

"I've bought more shares."

He'd never stopped acquiring them. When the opportunity presented, he had taken advantage. Leverage was valuable, and he had gone after all the leverage he could get himself. He was glad he had now. Because she was intent on backing out, and he couldn't allow it.

Her eyes widened, her lip curling into a snarl. "When?"

"I never stopped buying them. The company was going down, and there were people eager to get out and get what they could. I'm now the majority shareholder by a very large margin, and I'm sure that, given that the recovery of Pickett is still in its fledgling stage and not one-hundred-percent viable, the board would be open to the idea of liquidating and distributing assets."

"But all those people…some of them have been with Pickett for more than twenty years and there is no comparable place for them to work, not for all of them, or even half of them, not here."

"It's your choice, Vanessa. It's on your head if they lose their jobs." Lazaro turned and walked back out into the frigid night, his body wracked with pain, guilt spreading through him like a sickness.

He couldn't lose her. He needed time to think.

He *needed* her.

Vanessa moved to the door, her heart in her throat. Before, he might not have loved her, but now it looked as if he hated her. She put a hand to her stomach and tried to ease the nausea, tried to ease the pain that was flowing freely through her body.

She had thought, for a few fleeting moments, that she would sell her house and go somewhere else. Cut ties from her family. Be Vanessa, just Vanessa and not The Pickett Family with all of the expectations and baggage.

She could study photography, as she'd dreamed of doing when she was younger.

But the bottom had fallen out of that fantasy when she'd realized that when she pictured starting over, Lazaro was in the background, his warmth and encouragement spurring her on.

And then even that little fantasy had been crushed by the force of his anger when he'd shown up at her door tonight.

She thought of all the people who would lose their jobs. Hundreds of them. Family men and women, some of them with no other job experience.

Boiling anger churned in her stomach, anger that he would do this to so many people. That he could keep doing this to her. "Why can't you just leave me alone?" she whispered.

It would be so much simpler if he would. If she could excise him, her feelings for him, from her life. And yet, it seemed impossible. Twelve years apart hadn't managed to accomplish it.

She couldn't let him do it. Couldn't let him destroy the lives of her workers. The legacy that belonged to her family, her future children.

"Lazaro." She stepped outside, arms crossed over her chest as she jogged after him. "Lazaro."

He turned, his expression unreadable in the dim light provided by the street lamps. "I'll marry you," she said.

Lazaro studied her expression, the hard glitter in her dark eyes, the deep sadness peering out beneath her rage. He felt no triumph in that moment, no sense of victory. Only the need to hold her in his arms and the knowledge that, at the moment, she would not allow it.

"I'm going to get in touch with a wedding coordinator tomorrow," he said. "We'll have the wedding as soon as possible."

She nodded slowly. "I'll do whatever I have to."

He had her. She was his. She had agreed to marry him.

And he felt as if he had truly lost her.

CHAPTER TWELVE

"As soon as possible" turned out to be two weeks. And they had gone by in a blur of motion and anguish and tiny bouts of happiness that had given way to stark slaps from reality.

Vanessa sort of hated reality. She liked the cocoon of her fantasies. The ones that seemed to have been left behind in Buenos Aires.

The wedding day seemed too bright. The sun shone a little bit too much, the sound of birds and traffic was too loud. It was too clear. And she couldn't hide from it.

Vanessa shifted her bouquet from one hand to the other. Orchids. And they were gorgeous. So was her dress, a flowing, fitted white gown that skimmed her curves and flattered her figure. It was elegant, sophisticated and without an ounce of princess, which suited her perfectly.

It was all romantic and dreamy, at odds with the prenuptial agreement she'd signed earlier in the week that kept her assets and her future husband's firmly separated and had custody agreements for hypothetical children and punishments for infidelities. That had been one of the week's low points.

One of the high points was booking St. John's on short notice, a lovely, historic cathedral with stained glass and high arched ceilings. Everything was just how she would have wanted it if she'd had years to plan.

Well, had she had her choice her groom would have seen

her as a person and not a commodity. He would have loved her. As she loved him. Still. In spite of the ugliness that had passed between them. Lazaro Marino had a piece of her. He always had had.

It was because she saw the man beneath the trappings. She saw the boy he used to be. The boy with the easy smile. The boy who had had a straight nose before her father had sent his henchman to break him and to steal that perfection. To steal his smile.

If Lazaro was hard, full of anger, so much of it was on her father's shoulders.

That was just one of the many reasons she was walking down the aisle alone today. She already felt like a thing, an asset. She wasn't about to let her father "give her away" to Lazaro.

She sucked in a deep breath and walked through the double doors and into the sanctuary, her heart pounding hard in her chest.

She looked up at Lazaro's face, and, for a moment, everything, everyone receded. The clarity was gone, and things were fuzzy around the edges again. For a moment, she thought she saw something soften in him, thought she saw a return of the heat in his eyes—not just the heat, but something tender, an emotion she'd never seen on his face before. An emotion she would only ever see there in dreams.

And then it was gone, replaced with that hardened resolve, that flat, unreadable mask that Lazaro wore to keep her, and everyone else, out.

His voice was measured, controlled as he spoke vows she knew he didn't mean. Her voice cracked, wavered, because she meant every word. And she wished that she didn't.

The priest pronounced them man and wife, and gave them the invitation to kiss. She hadn't touched Lazaro in over two weeks, not any kind of contact. Her heart fluttered as she

ooked at him, and this time she knew, the heat wasn't imagined.

He swept her hair over her shoulder and cupped her cheek,
his thumb brushing her skin gently as he studied her face.

And she realized he was waiting for her. It was her move.
Her decision.

She angled her head and leaned into him, touching her lips
to his tentatively. His hold on her tightened and he wrapped
his arm around her waist, drawing her to him. She clutched
his shoulders tightly, kissing him with every ounce of passion
pent up inside of her, and all of the anger and the love and
the sadness. Because if he was marrying her, he was getting
all of it.

She wasn't just a passive thing to add to his collection.
She was a woman. A person. She was Vanessa. He might be
able to force her into marriage, but he couldn't change who
she was.

He kissed her back, matching her emotion, her passion,
making her dizzy with it.

When they parted, they were both breathing heavily.
Vanessa felt her cheeks heat, because during that kiss, the
crowd of people witnessing their sacred vows had very much
faded away, and now they were in crystal clear focus.

Lazaro leaned in to the priest and said, loud enough for
everyone to hear, "I'm a very lucky man."

That broke some of the tension and brought laughter from
even their stuffiest witnesses. It made Vanessa's cheeks heat
further. Made her body ache with the longing to have more
of him. To do more. To make love with him.

Tonight was their wedding night, and it seemed as though
that was what should happen. It was the only thing that felt
right. They were back on civil footing, but after the way
things had happened…she wasn't sure. She wasn't sure about
anything.

As they walked back down the aisle, applause filling the sanctuary, Vanessa fought back tears and an overwhelming ache of loneliness she was afraid would never go away.

"I've had all of your things moved in already," Lazaro said when they reached his penthouse. "Your clothing and personal items are in the room next to mine."

"Oh. And my furniture?"

"Still at your home. We can hold on to your house as long as you like. Rent it out or keep it vacant. Although, we don't need two homes in the city."

"Right." She walked further into the main area of the house, feeling disoriented—a stranger in a strange land. And this was supposed to be her home. But there was nothing of her in it.

It was cold and clean, with sparse furnishings and a lot of brushed metal giving it a sterile, unlived-in feeling. It was top of the line, no question, everything in it of the highest quality money could buy. But it wasn't her.

Her town house was plush and luxurious, furnished with her father's money. But it still had a homey feel. It was a place she was glad to be in at the end of the day. A place that made her feel warm. Lazaro's penthouse felt like her office. And it kind of gave her heartburn, which made it even more like her office.

"I guess you did it, Lazaro," she said.

"I did what?"

"You have everything. You're rich, the richest man in Boston, possibly in the United States. You're the principal shareholder of Pickett Industries and you have me, your ticket into high society. I guess there's nothing left for you to go after."

He looked at her, his dark eyes assessing. "There's always something more, Vanessa."

"What?"

"There's always work to do," he said, shrugging.

"I see." That made it all even worse. She was just a means to one end. For Lazaro there would never be rest. Never be satisfaction with what he had.

"Speaking of, I have some work to do. We can have dinner later."

Vanessa nodded, more than ready to go to her room and sleep off the stress of the day. The stress of the past month.

She walked through the house, feeling a sense of disconnection so strong that she thought she might crumble beneath it. She'd cut ties with her father. She and Lazaro seemed to have lost whatever connection they had found in Buenos Aires.

She blinked and looked around again. No, her surroundings weren't really to her taste. And yes, she and Lazaro weren't engaged in the love affair of the century, not emotionally anyway. But they had passion. And she had options.

She had let other people make her decisions for far too long. She had seen herself as honorable, continuing her family's legacy, doing her duty, being the kind of daughter, the kind of person everyone should be. So self-sacrificing.

She laughed into the empty room. She wasn't any of that. She was a coward. Too afraid to make her own decisions and step out on her own. So she'd let other people do it for her. Her father. And then, following down that same path, Lazaro. And then, of course, if she was unhappy it was somehow down to someone else. And that made her what? A long-suffering martyr doing her duty?

No. She shook her head and sat down on the couch. She'd made this choice. And she'd hidden behind all kinds of reasons, but the fact remained that she'd made the choice. Just as she'd chosen to put aside her dreams and go to school for business. Just as she'd chosen to give up photography for a life behind a desk.

She had no one to blame. And no one to fix it for her now but herself.

Lazaro's housekeeper had decided that the newlyweds needed a nice, intimate dinner prepared for them before she went home for the evening. Which was how Vanessa found herself sitting opposite her stoic husband, searching for conversation so they weren't trapped in uncomfortable silence.

"I want to step down from my position at Pickett," she said. Those weren't the words she'd been searching for, but it was the truth. It was her heart. And it was too late to call them back now. "I want to keep my ownership, my stock, but I don't want an active role in the company."

"You want to take up lunching?" he asked, looking up from his dinner plate, one dark brow raised.

"Photography," she said. "I want to take some classes. I want to pursue it as a career."

"Then you should," he said. That simple. That easy.

"Really?"

"I told you in Buenos Aires, I want you to be happy."

"I thought all bets might be off on that."

"Why is that?"

"Since...you know. Since things haven't been overly amicable between us for the past couple of weeks," she said studying her plate of pasta.

"I want them to be."

"Well, you forced me to marry you, so...the odds of that are low."

This time she was certain what she saw in his eyes was hurt. A brief flash of it, a tiny glimpse past the stone wall he built over his emotions.

She lifted her glass of wine and touched it to her lips, then set it down without taking a drink. "I don't have to tell you how it happened. I'm sure you remember," she said, her voice cracking.

"I don't want you to be miserable, Vanessa."

"Am I supposed to be happy? You could have fooled me. Was any of this ever about happiness? Mine or yours?"

He didn't speak, he simply toyed with the stem of his wineglass, his dark eyes glittering in the candlelight. A nice touch from his housekeeper, meant to give them a romantic atmosphere. What a sad farce it was.

"This has always been about business," he said, taking his hand away from the glass and curling it into a fist.

"And revenge."

"Yes, that too. I had never planned on seeking revenge…"

"But the temptation was too great. I get that. I just don't think I like being in the middle of it. But I've told my father that he isn't to bar your entrance into the inner circles of society in any way. He's to roll out the red carpet for you."

"And how did you get him to agree to that?"

Vanessa looked down at her food again, unable to meet his searching gaze. "I threatened him. You would have been proud. I actually used the same threat you used on me. I told him we would dismantle Pickett Industries, brick by brick if necessary. Because what he did to you, what he's done to me all of my life, it's not right."

"How do you feel now that you've stood up to him?"

She sighed heavily and spun her glass in a slow circle on the table. "I felt free. For about ten minutes." She looked at Lazaro again, then down at the diamond engagement ring and the thick platinum band next to it. "I'm tired. I think I'll go to bed."

She stood from the table, expecting him to stop her, to kiss her, demand she join him in bed on their wedding night. He did none of those things. He hardly flicked her a glance.

"Good night."

Her throat tightened. "Good night."

Vanessa felt empty. The bed felt empty. Everything did. She rolled onto her back and stared at the unfamiliar ceiling. No tiles to count. It was smooth and glossy, just like the rest of the house.

She wondered if Lazaro was in bed. If he was asleep.

It was their wedding night and it didn't seem right for them to sleep separately. But then, they were married and it didn't seem right for there to be this…distance between them.

She was the one who'd tried to back out of the agreement. She was the one who'd created the distance between them— to protect herself because she was afraid of her feelings for Lazaro. They were so strong, woven through her being, like roots of one plant overtaking the roots of another beneath the surface of the ground. Impossible to extricate either without destroying the delicate flower involved.

She loved him. All he had been, all he had become. The man with so much determination and brilliance. The man who was still hurting beneath it all. She sensed that hurt, mostly because she kept coming close to the wounds. She had a knack for saying the wrong things, things that brought those little flashes of pain into his eyes.

He didn't feel like he was enough. She knew it now, recognized it, because it was what she felt about herself. Lazaro had married her for status, she had done it for Pickett. And none of it was that clean or simple now. Because if all of the external things were stripped away, Lazaro was the man she would want.

It was all the *things*, they were the deterrent now, not the draw.

She wanted just him. She wanted to forget. To let go of all

of the pain and just feel alive. Feel what only he could make her feel.

She slid out of bed and padded over to the door, and out onto the mezzanine floor that overlooked the living area, the windows that stretched from the floor to the ceiling showing the lights of Boston shining in the inky night.

The city, at least, was home, even if the house didn't feel like it.

She knocked on Lazaro's bedroom door.

"Vanessa?" She heard his accented voice, sleepy and muffled through the bedroom door.

She pushed open the door and crossed to his bed, standing at the side of it. "I couldn't sleep. And it's our wedding night, and frankly, I didn't imagine I would be spending my wedding night alone."

"You said you were tired, was I meant to break down your door and demand you make love with me?" He was lying in the bed, a blanket pulled up over his lap, revealing his bare chest.

She tried to keep her eyes on his face and not glued to his amazing body. But it was hard. "No. But I...I don't want to be alone."

"Neither do I." He drew back the covers and she slipped in beside him, her heart hammering.

She placed her hand delicately on his chest, excitement and arousal firing through her. "I missed you," she said. "I missed this."

This was the man she loved. Here, in bed, it brought him back. There was nothing else now. No revenge. No company. No status. It was everything he'd made her feel from the beginning, before so many things had gotten in the way.

"I did too," he said, brushing her hair away from her face, trailing his fingertips down over her shoulder to her hand. He lifted it to his lips and kissed the sensitive skin of her palm.

Her heart ached. It was tempting to wonder what might have been. Where they would be now if they had never parted. Maybe poor. In an apartment somewhere with him mowing lawns and her taking wedding pictures. With children. Without all of the anger and the trappings of life that they seemed so tangled up in.

With love.

She closed her eyes, fought the tears that were mounting. She wasn't living in a fantasy. Right now, this was her reality, and she meant to feel all of it.

He pressed his lips to hers, his kiss urgent, his hands roaming over her curves, slow and firm, his movements sure and expert. "I will never tire of this," he said against her lips. "Of you."

Her heart burned in her chest, pain lancing her. He *would* tire of her. She was a status symbol, the ultimate I-told-you-so. He had been told he couldn't have her, and Lazaro wasn't a man who liked to be told no. Beyond that, there was nothing unique about her. He'd wanted to select a society bride and she had been available, and had come with the added perk of vengeance.

She believed him when he said he hadn't been planning revenge for the entirety of the past twelve years, but she also knew that she served to satisfy a wrong that had been committed against him. And in his place, she wasn't entirely certain she wouldn't have done the same thing.

She blocked out the thoughts that were flooding her mind, increasing the flow of pain to her chest. She focused only on Lazaro's hands, his lips, all the amazing things he could make her body feel. She ignored the pain gushing from her heart with every beat.

"It's convenient that you don't wear pajamas to bed," she said, sliding her hand over his washboard-flat abs and down to where he was hard and ready for her.

He tilted his head back, and even in the dark, she could see his expression, one of pure pleasure. It filled her with feminine pride to know she had the power to make him feel that way.

"More than convenient," he said, his voice strained.

"I want to try something."

She moved down his body, flicked her tongue over the head of his erection.

Air hissed hard through his teeth and he wove his fingers through her hair, holding on to her tightly while she explored him, taking pleasure in giving him pleasure.

His thighs were tight beneath her hands, his muscles starting to shake as she took him fully into her mouth.

"Vanessa, someday we'll do it this way...but now...now I need you."

The words were broken, strained, and she understood exactly what he meant, because she needed him too. She'd been without him for too long, aching and lonely. To the outside world, she was only the part that she played. But Lazaro knew the woman beneath.

Having one person in the world who knew, truly knew, what she wanted, what made her happy, had made her wonder how she'd ever lived without that. And being without him had been so isolating. She'd felt cut off from everyone, even more than she normally did. She'd felt trapped inside of herself.

She'd been squeezed into a box all of her life, trying so hard to be who she was supposed to be. Not now. Not with him.

Here and now, she was free.

She pushed herself up and positioned herself over him, leaning in to kiss his lips, her palms on his chest, his heart raging beneath them. He was watching her, not giving instruction, just watching and waiting. And she knew that she was in control now.

She smiled and changed her position slightly, bringing the head of his erection against the entrance to her body, slick and so very ready for him. He helped her by guiding himself to the right place and she sank onto him slowly, sighing as he filled her completely.

She locked eyes with him as she moved over him, finding her rhythm slowly, awkwardly at first. Lazaro gripped her hips and urged her on, his words alternating between sweet and explicit, encouraging her.

She could feel her climax building within her, could feel it building with each thrust, could feel, as Lazaro's muscles tensed and shook, that he was close too.

He thrust up into her and pushed her over the edge, her orgasm moving through her like a crescendo, building as it flowed through her body.

"Lazaro." She gripped his shoulders hard, her nails digging into his skin.

He groaned harshly as he found his own pleasure and Vanessa collapsed against him, her cheek resting on his sweat-slicked chest, his heart pounding hard beneath her ear, evidence of what she'd done to him. To them.

She wished she knew what it had meant to him. What he felt. It was frightening, being connected with someone physically and feeling so blocked out emotionally. Feeling alone.

Her eyes filled with tears and one escaped, sliding down her nose and onto Lazaro's chest. He tightened his hold on her and kissed her hair.

Vanessa closed her eyes, trying to focus on the sweet languor that was making her limbs feel heavy, that was bringing her closer to sleep.

Anything to dull the ache in her chest.

CHAPTER THIRTEEN

LAZARO couldn't erase the impression of the tear on his chest; it was as though it had burned into his skin, through to his heart. He felt weighted down by it, by the unhappiness it represented. Vanessa's unhappiness.

In the days since, she'd spent every night in his bed, making love to him with an abandon that blew his mind each and every time. The passion between them was explosive, but afterwards she seemed to retreat, to fold in on herself and move away from him. He hadn't seen her tears since, but he wondered if they were still there.

He had never thought it possible, but he wanted to hold her after they made love. He wanted to ask what she was thinking. To tell her his thoughts, to pour himself out to her. He had never felt that need, had never understood it.

But he needed it with Vanessa. Needed to find some way to feel close to her. To make her happy. He could make her happy. He could give her everything she desired. He *would* make her happy.

He would do whatever it took. He would buy her her own studio, her own gallery to display her work. Take her to any location she wanted to photograph. Whatever she could possibly want to have, he could buy for her. Money was no object.

She'd been enjoying her classes, and had been cutting back

on hours at Pickett while the board worked on finding a replacement they could all agree upon. In some ways, she was more relaxed than he'd seen her. But sometimes...sometimes he saw a deep sadness in her eyes that tore at his gut. And with that pain came a sense of helplessness. He had given her everything he knew to give, and he didn't know another way to make her happy.

He pushed the thought to the side and headed upstairs, hoping he could entice Vanessa into bed for the afternoon. Or, if not that, maybe entice a smile from her.

Her bedroom door was partway opened and he let himself in. Vanessa was sitting at her computer, leaning in, examining images on the screen.

"Did you get some good shots?" he asked.

"I did." She turned to face him and he felt as if he'd been punched in the chest. Her smile made him weak and as though he could move the earth if he had to, all at once. "We're doing a mini exhibition at the end of the class. A lot of the technical things I knew already, but I love the way the teacher talks about melding art and technique. It's all so fascinating."

"You love it," he said, looking at the way her eyes caught fire when she spoke. He would chase the happiness he saw in her eyes now. Would give her whatever she needed to made her smile like that.

"I really do." The light in her eyes turned impish. "Hey, we're supposed to do live subjects this week."

"I have a friend who has a dog. He might be willing to help."

The corners of her mouth turned up. "No, I want to take your picture."

"Wanting and having are two very different things."

"Lazaro, please?" The look of sweet supplication on her face undid him entirely. He couldn't say no to her, not when the idea made her so...happy. She truly looked happy now,

ot because she was smiling, but because of what he saw re-
lecting in her eyes. He hadn't seen her look that way since
Buenos Aires.

"Where?" he asked, indulging her because there was nothing else he could do.

"The bed."

"No, Vanessa."

She walked to him and pressed a kiss to his cheek, her fingers working at the buttons on his shirt. The flood of desire
was instant, unstoppable.

"I just want you to look relaxed," she said. "You always
look relaxed in the morning, right when you wake up."

"There are other times I look relaxed."

She laughed. "No, there really aren't."

She gripped the lapels of his shirt and tugged and he went
willingly, allowing her to bring him down onto the bed. He
gripped her hips and held her to him, kissing her, tasting her.
Just being with her. She was happy with him. She wasn't acting as though he was her jailer.

Aren't you?

He gritted his teeth and banished the thought, focusing
instead on the slide of her tongue, the scent of her body, the
way her hands moved over him.

She pulled away from him and got off the bed, going to her
desk for her camera. She clicked off a succession of shots.

"What is it you want me to do?" A male model he was not.

"Just look at me."

How could he do anything else? With her glossy brown
curls loose and mussed, her cheeks flushed with the same
arousal that was pounding through him. Those lips, full and
pink, and her body…so perfect. Made for him.

She stopped and lowered the camera, looking at the screen,
her lips parting. "Wow. Can you…can you look away now?"

He did, tearing his focus from her one of the harder things

he'd ever attempted. He heard the click of the shutter an
turned back to her.

"Come here," he said.

He didn't have to ask twice. She came willingly, camer
in hand. He took it from her and used the viewfinder scree
on the back, taking a picture of her. "Fair is fair," he said.

She smiled, one corner of her mouth turning up higher tha
the other. It made her look wicked and very, very tempting
He took the shot, capturing it forever. The look that spoke c
her desire, and all the naughty things she was thinking of.

"I think you're done now," she said, kissing his neck.

"With the camera, yes. With you? Not nearly."

His heart pounded fiercely as he lifted her shirt over he
head, exposing her breasts to his gaze. She was so beautifu
everything he had ever desired and so much more. Thing
he had never known to want.

He shrugged his shirt off the rest of the way and mad
quick work of the rest of his clothes. He always wanted t
spend hours touching and tasting her, to lavish her with ever
sort of pleasure his mind could conjure up. But when h
started uncovering her body, inch by delicious inch, impa
tience seemed to overtake him.

He tugged her jeans and her delicate, barely-there pantie
down her thighs and tossed them to the floor. "Now I'd lik
the camera back," he said.

Pink color suffused her cheeks. "No way."

"Someday."

She shook her head and he leaned in and captured her lips
pulling her up so that she was sitting on his lap, her thigh
draped over his. He pressed a kiss to her throat, her breasts
his hands moving over her elegant curves, her waist, her hips

"I want to capture this perfection forever," he said.

He urged her up, positioning himself at the entrance of he
body, and she accepted, took him in on a sigh of pleasure.

He watched her face as she moved over him, the way her lips parted, the way a heavy flush of color spread over her skin as she neared her climax. How she squeezed her eyes tight, and grabbed his shoulders as her orgasm started to take her. Every detail seemed important. Every nuance of who she was and what gave her pleasure.

He wanted to give her everything, to be everything she needed.

And then he was too caught in the grip of his own pleasure to think of anything else. He let himself go over the edge, let his release steal everything from his mind, let it break through the walls surrounding his heart so that he felt everything, truly felt it.

Sex had always been something he'd enjoyed at a distance, pleasure he'd let his body take while his emotions stayed unaffected.

Not now. Not with Vanessa. Never with her. From the first moment she had put a crack in his defenses, and this time, the walls crumbled down. He felt raw, exposed, naked and vulnerable to the kind of pain that intense emotion promised to bring.

And yet, he couldn't stop the flow, wouldn't if he had the power.

He held her after, her silken hair spread over his chest, her breath hot against his neck as she slept off the post lovemaking lethargy.

He knew how to bring her pleasure. He could make her happy.

Except he would always be the man who'd had to buy her to make her his wife. Who'd had to threaten her down the aisle. She was here for what he had, not who he was. And he was a fool to have believed otherwise, even for a moment.

The pain he'd cleared a path for began to flood him. Overtake him.

She was growing now, changing what she did, who she was. And he had clipped her wings. He was everything he had always despised. A man who used people. A man who treated everyone like steps, there to be trod upon as he made his way to the top.

But she was his wife. He tightened his grip on her. She was his. He needed her, like air.

He loved her.

Vanessa noticed a change in Lazaro after their afternoon photo session. He seemed distant. Cold. The only time he warmed for her was in bed at night, and then he was on fire. The flames of their passion were enough to consume both of them for a moment, to make the reality of their situation fade away.

She was a bought bride, no more important than any of the other signs of status that were evident in Lazaro's home: a home with the right view in the right neighborhood, some high-end art on the wall and a wife with the right bloodline.

She was no more important than any of it. And it killed her. She wanted to be special to someone, and she truly never had been. Her father had seen her as a last-resort way to continue his dynasty, her ex-almost-fiancé had seen her as a great acquisition in a merger of families, and Lazaro...well, she was his ticket to the top. The checkmate to her father. Revenge and power in one move.

She didn't care about Craig Freeman's feelings—or lack thereof—for her, and there was no point in wishing her father would suddenly gain the ability to see people as anything other than pawns to be moved around at his every whim.

But Lazaro...she wanted him to love her. Her. Not what she could give him. Not as an addition to his almighty empire.

He was the only one who truly mattered, and every day

he slipped further and further away from her. He was closing himself off to her, his guard never slipping, his eyes never betraying what he was thinking or feeling.

And even though he held her every night while she slept, she felt alone.

She took a deep breath and walked out of her bedroom, fastening her earring and pushing her foot the rest of the way into her high-heeled shoe. She wasn't going to be passive anymore. She understood the things that were holding Lazaro back. At least, she hoped she did. She prayed she did.

Because if she was wrong, it would only end in devastation. Hers specifically.

She pulled her phone out of her pocket and dashed off a quick text to Lazaro. Specific instructions on where he was supposed to meet her tonight, because she wanted to show him and she knew it was going to take more than sweet words spoken in private to undo all of the hurt that was inside him. It might even take more than she had planned.

But she was willing to try.

She pressed Send and grabbed her coat, covering her daring dress with the sedate, gray wool outerwear.

Now she just had to hope her husband followed her instructions. She smiled slightly at the thought. If there was one thing Lazaro didn't do, it was follow orders.

She needed him to tonight though. Because tonight, she was going to reveal her heart to him. There was a time for self-protection, and this wasn't it. Lazaro had given her the strength to find out who she really was.

And he was going to have to deal with the consequences of that newfound strength.

Lazaro wasn't sure what to expect when he walked into the smoky, downtown club. A rare experience, although, with Vanessa rare experiences seemed to be getting more and more common. She surprised him. Challenged him. Turned him on and made his heart pound faster.

She was like no other woman, no other person he'd ever known.

He shut off his line of thinking and scanned the dense crowd for his wife. His wife. The thought still made his chest feel tight. Made his stomach ache with longing because while he had her, he would never truly have her.

She had not married him because of any great love for him. She didn't stay with him out of a desire to. He was making her stay.

Then he saw her, weaving through the tightly packed bodies. She was wearing a shockingly brief dress, black and tight, revealing the killer curves of her body. Possessiveness coursed through his veins. Possessiveness and pride. She was his wife, and she was the most beautiful woman in the room.

Not only that, she was the smartest, the bravest, the most artistic. She was everything.

She smiled at him and his heart began to pound, hard, heavy and fast in his chest. He sucked in a sharp breath and tried to regain control. He had let his defenses drop and he'd spent the better part of the past two weeks trying to rebuild them, trying to hold Vanessa at a distance when he knew it was a futile effort. She was in him. Entwined with him. In his blood, flowing through him, keeping his heart beating.

She wrapped her arms around his neck and kissed him in greeting, in front of everyone in the club, passionately and shamelessly.

When they parted, she smiled. "Dance with me." Not a request, but an order he didn't want to refuse.

"Like in Buenos Aires," she whispered when they were on the dance floor.

He pulled her to him, one hand clasping hers, the other planted firmly on her lower back. "Here? But people will see."

"I'm glad," she said. "I'm proud to be seen with you."

His heart expanded inside him, making everything in him feel tight, as though he might burst with the feelings that were taking over his body. He swallowed hard. "I feel the same way."

She didn't dance with precise skill, but she put everything into it, the freedom she'd found in life that he'd watched grow in her over the past weeks. When she smiled now it came from deep within her, a light that radiated from the inside out.

And yet the smile could not be for him. He had forced her into marriage, had treated her the same way her father had always done.

His heart seized in his chest. When the opportunity had presented itself, he had become so consumed with the undoing of Michael Pickett that, in the process, he'd become him. He had taken Vanessa, a vibrant force of life and beauty and tried to bend her to his will. To make her fulfill his needs, without thinking of hers.

And, just as she'd done with her father, she was doing her duty. Doing what she knew she had to do, the honorable thing. Bile rose in his throat when he thought of the soft sighs she made in bed, the way she gripped his shoulders. Was that duty to her? The only way to preserve the company she loved?

She leaned in, her lips grazing his ear. "I was doing research on some really interesting ways we can bring energy-efficient manufacturing techniques into Pickett. I was also thinking we might try and do something about the packaging? I know that you consulted for someone who makes boxes and containers out of recycled materials."

He pulled back from her, his heart thundering in his chest. "Is that why you asked me here?"

She moved her hands over his shoulders. "Of course not. But we haven't really talked in a few days and I had the idea earlier. I think with a little more money invested we can see some huge returns. You really did have a fantastic idea on how to resurrect the company."

Lazaro felt as though he'd been punched in the stomach. Every doubt that had ever gnawed at the back of his mind roared to the forefront. Of course this was about Pickett. She had married him to save it, to keep people she cared for employed. He had been a fool to think that any part of their relationship, their marriage, had been separate from that.

He had forced her into it. He had no right to stand in judgment of her. She hadn't lied to him. He was the one who'd asked her to be his wife, who'd wanted her in his bed. He had created the deception for the world, but he was the one who had fallen prey to it.

A sharp pain stabbed at him, ripped through his chest. It was real, physical pain unlike any he'd ever known. He pulled away from her, stumbling back a step before righting himself. He took a breath and concentrated on shielding himself, his emotions. He had lied to himself, pretending any part of what they shared had been real. It could not be. How could she ever care for a man like him? Why would she?

"Lazaro?"

He ignored her and turned, walking off the dance floor, away from the throbbing beat of the music and the heavy crush of people, out into the crisp air. He shook his head, trying to clear it, trying to find the man he'd been before Vanessa had walked back into his life. The man who thrived on emotionless dealings, success without any personal ties.

The man who had ruthlessly pursued what he wanted with single-minded determination. The man who had been willing to do whatever it took to reach his goals.

"Lazaro?"

He turned and saw Vanessa standing a foot away, her arms crossed in an attempt to keep warm. She'd left her coat inside, nothing but her insubstantial dress between her and the increasingly cold night.

"What was this, Vanessa?" he bit out. "Were you trying to make a fool of me? Trying to use your body to talk me into investing more money in Pickett?"

He wished she would say yes. That she would prove herself to be the woman he'd imagined her to be in the beginning. That she would do something to abolish the feelings he had for her.

Her eyes widened. "What?"

"Why did you want to go out tonight?"

"Because I…I wanted to dance with you." She looked at him, her eyes glistening in the moonlight. "Because I missed you."

"I've been with you every day."

She shook her head, dark hair swirling around her shoulders. "No, you haven't been. You've been gone. You've gone somewhere I can't reach you, and I want you back."

"I'm not quite sure what you mean, Vanessa. I've complied with my part of the deal, and I haven't made you unhappy. I'm paying for your photography courses." He shrugged, trying to look casual even as his throat tightened. "I can only assume you're upset about not having a chance to hit me up for more money for your company."

"You know what I mean. You aren't stupid, Lazaro. Don't pretend to be now."

"What exactly do you mean by that?"

"Don't pretend everything is fine when it isn't," she said.

"Everything is fine, Vanessa. As long as things continue going as we agreed. Pickett Industries will keep improving, and the employees will keep their jobs. And I'll have what I want.

"Status and some kind of sick sense of justice?"

His stomach churned and he had to force the next words out. "There was never anything else."

"Never?"

"No," he ground out, the lie acrid in his mouth.

He would not humble himself before her, would not admit that she had breached his heart, as no one else had ever done. He wouldn't confess his feelings to a woman who must hate him. A woman who had every right to.

And he couldn't be the man who held her captive anymore. He had forced her to marry him, and all his pretending it had been her choice was rubbish and he knew it. He knew her, he knew where her priorities lay, that she loved her employees. That she was too good, too loyal to let the company crumble if there was anything she could do to solve the problem.

He had practically forced her hand to sign the marriage license. He hated himself for it now.

You had to make sure that I had no other options open to get me to agree to marry you. I had no other choice. Don't forget that.

He hadn't. Not for a moment. It had been there, in the back of his mind while he had fooled himself into thinking that she could grow to care for him.

For the man who had forced her to the altar. Not likely.

"I have what I want now, Vanessa," he said, the words scraping his throat raw. "I've been invited to go to your father's country club. I have potential business connections made with several people who had never considered dealing with me prior to our marriage."

He watched the color drain from her face. "And?"

"And I think the marriage is unnecessary at this point in time."

She blinked rapidly. "Unnecessary?"

"I have what I want," he repeated, the lie bitter on his

tongue. "I see no point in continuing with the charade. I think we should divorce."

She stumbled back, her hand on her stomach, her dark eyebrows locked together, her eyes shimmering. "You...*you bastard*. You dragged me to the altar, you forced me into this farce of a marriage and for what? So you could divorce me less than a month later? Are you going to use this as an excuse to destroy my father's company too? Your last laugh against the Pickett family?"

Her words, the anger, only reinforced the rightness of what he was doing. She was too loyal to Pickett Industries to initiate it herself, but the simple truth was that she was more put out by what he'd put her through than the actual dissolution of the marriage.

And he couldn't force her to stay with him anymore. He had been wrong to do it. Selfish beyond measure. A man he hated.

"It would be poetic, no?"

"No." She shook head. "Lazaro, I love you."

He felt as though he'd been punched in the gut. She was offering him words of love, words he was so far from deserving. Words she could not mean. Words he *knew* she didn't mean. She was trying to protect Pickett. Because hadn't she already proved she would do anything to save her family's legacy? Hadn't she married him? Made love to him? Why not a little lie, three little words, words that might make him change his mind.

They could not be true. He was beyond the point of being a man anyone could love. Least of all Vanessa.

"Don't, Vanessa," he bit out.

"I do."

"No," he roared the words, not caring if they drew stares. "I do not want your love." He denied the need even as his heart wept. The desire to believe her was so strong it was nearly overpowering. He shook with it.

Worse than never hearing the words at all was having them used against him.

"And you don't want me," she said, her tone flat. "Was this your plan all along? To cast me aside and destroy my company? After you talked me into stepping down as CEO, of course."

"No," he said. "I'm not out to destroy Pickett, and I don't need you to try and manipulate me to get me to change my mind. You kept your end. I will keep mine," he said. "I will continue to be active in Pickett, in its improvement. But I do not see the marriage as a necessity at this point."

"So—" she swallowed and he saw the tendons in her throat working, as though it were hard for her to do "—you want a divorce?"

"I think we should," he said. But he didn't want a divorce. He wanted to cling to her forever, force her to stay with him. Make her want him. Failing that, he wanted things to go back to the way they were. He wanted the walls back up around his heart. He wanted anything but to be standing on the sidewalk in downtown Boston offering Vanessa her freedom while his heart was torn to pieces with each and every syllable out of his mouth.

He wanted to cling to her last, desperate lie. Her greatest attempt at saving Pickett. He wanted to claim it as truth and hold it inside him. He wanted to take her love and let it heal the raw wounds in him.

But those words weren't about feeling. And there was no way for him to be certain of the truth of them. Not as long as he held the fate of her beloved company over her head.

He wanted anything but a divorce. Anything but this moment. But he couldn't force her to be with him anymore. It was emptier than being without her.

"Okay," she said softly.

He had to grit his teeth to fight against the anguish that was tearing at him. "I knew you would be grateful for the out."

She nodded. "I'm going home."

"I don't think I will."

She shook her head. "My home. My town house."

His stomach tightened, tense with the strength it took to keep from crumbling under the agony that was overtaking every inch of his body. It was like death, worse than being beaten in an alley.

"I will have your things sent over in the morning."

"I won't be there."

He nodded curtly. "It's for the best."

She bit her bottom lip. "Goodbye, Lazaro."

He couldn't force a goodbye from his lips. He simply turned and walked away, wishing he could dull the pain by being angry with her, by making this her fault.

He couldn't. And the absence of anger only left him with a raw, searing pain that threatened to destroy him from the inside out.

Lazaro's penthouse was empty when he returned. As he had expected. Had he truly fantasized that Vanessa would have come back to him? He had destroyed any chance of that. He had made it swift and final.

He had been truthful though about one thing. He was guaranteed an in at her father's club, entry into that last exclusive grouping of people. Access to new clients. A kind of forced respect. It was all likely due to the fancy bit of threatening Vanessa had done on his behalf.

He poured himself three fingers of Scotch and walked out onto the balcony, letting the cool night air numb some of his pain, hoping the alcohol would take care of the rest.

The view he had was worth millions. It represented a physical manifestation of all of the work he'd done over the past decade. He was at the top now. He was the richest man in Boston, a world-famous consultant. There was nowhere else for him to go. Every door was open, everything he'd ever been barred from available to him now. The world was at his feet.

Suddenly, the emptiness of it all threatened to consume him.

There was no sense of triumph. No feeling of accomplishment. He had chased this moment for the entirety of his adult life—the moment when he would overlook the city, a man apart. The man at the top. The man no one could ever hold any power over, ever again. The man who had won.

He was there now, finally, after all the years of pushing for it. And there was nothing. Only a dark, blank void. The sweetness of victory turned to ash in his mouth.

In that moment, he would give it all away to be the boy who mowed the lawn, the boy who had earned a genuine smile from the one girl who held his heart. To grow into a man who deserved a woman like Vanessa.

But there was no going back. He had gained the entire world and lost the only thing that had ever had any meaning.

CHAPTER FOURTEEN

TRUE to his word, Lazaro had had all of her things delivered the day after he asked for the divorce. Vanessa left them packed, stepping over them when she came home from her photography class, digging through them when she needed something.

He had only ever wanted her for what she could give him, and then he'd gotten it, and he'd had no use for her. And she had done exactly what she'd promised herself she wouldn't do. She'd fallen deeply and irrevocably in love with him.

She felt bruised inside. It hurt to breathe. To eat. Just *being* hurt.

She wished that she could just turn her feelings off, quick and clean like shutting off a water main. But it wasn't that simple, not even close.

There was more to Lazaro than mindless acquisitions and status. She knew there was. She'd seen it. A man consumed only by a desire for *things* never would have cared that she had to take antacids to get through her day at work. He never would have encouraged her to work on her photography or bought her a camera.

He would never have made love to her as Lazaro did—with skill and tenderness, passion and heat. Always ensuring her pleasure came before his.

He had brought her out of her stagnant life. She felt as

though he'd opened her eyes to living. To feeling. He had given her so much—the strength to chase her own desires.

She wiped a tear off her cheek, frustrated that she was still crying four days after he'd rejected her love. Unsure if she would ever stop.

No one else had ever really seen *her* before. She was afraid no one else ever would.

But I see me now.

She took a deep breath. At least she knew what she wanted now. No more living behind the four walls of her office, no more pouring everything she had into something that she didn't love to do.

She'd found her own life. Her own path. And she'd lost her heart in the process.

But at least she was alive now. Truly living, making her own choices and living with the consequences, rather than hiding behind honor and duty. Cowering in fear of making choices and mistakes and playing the martyr instead of taking responsibility for things.

Still, right now, her newfound self was consumed with heartbreak that felt nearly fatal at the moment.

"This too shall pass. I hope," she said into her empty living room.

At least this time she'd told him she loved him. Back all those years ago in the guesthouse, the words had hovered on her lips, and she wondered if things would have changed if she had just spoken them. If he had said he loved her too, or if the honesty would have at least made them talk. Made them understand each other.

Yes, he had rejected her love. But she'd offered it. She'd tried.

There was a sharp knock on her front door, followed by a rich, familiar voice. "Vanessa?"

Her heart stopped beating for a moment before racing forward, tripping over itself. She swallowed hard and went to the door, opening it but keeping the shield of the wood between her and her soon-to-be-ex-husband. If there was nothing between them she might just cast her pride aside completely and fall into his arms.

"Lazaro…I…didn't expect you."

"I have something for you."

Her heart sank into her stomach and she opened the door wider, allowing him in. "Divorce papers? Do you want to sit down?" She gestured to her blue Victorian love seat.

"If you want them, and no."

"If I want them?"

"I brought divorce papers. But…that is not all."

She looked at him, really looked at him. He looked like she did. Tired, sick, tormented. His cheekbones looked sharper, the grooves that bracketed his mouth deeper. His black hair was disheveled, as though he'd been running his fingers through it.

"What else?" she asked, her throat tightening.

He cleared his throat, raising his hand and running it through his hair, just as she'd envisioned him doing. His hand shook as he lowered it. "I have to tell you this. I…I spent every moment since that day I woke up facedown in the alley working my way up. I swore I would never stop until I reached the top. And I did. I reached it, Vanessa."

"I remember," she said, her voice cracking. "You asked for a divorce ten seconds after telling me this the first time."

"Yes, I found it, all I was looking for. And then I found out the big hole that's been inside me for all of my life was still there." His voice broke. "I fixed nothing. I accomplished nothing. Because I was at the top, and I was alone. I used you as a stepping stone. I *used* you. I forced you to marry me. It's unforgivable."

Vanessa watched Lazaro's expression contort, his eyes filled with bleak torment. "Laz…"

"Don't, Vanessa. Don't excuse me," he ground out. "I don't deserve it." He drew his hand over his face. "When I was eighteen I had more than I do at this moment, because you smiled at me as though I meant something to you, and now when you look at me…there is no light. And you left me."

"You asked me to."

"I was a fool. I wanted to run after you the moment you turned away from me, and I did not. I couldn't."

Vanessa felt her heart fold in. "I thought…I thought you only wanted to be with me because of what I could give you and then…and then you asked for a divorce when you had what you wanted…" Her voice broke. "I needed so much to have someone love me. Me and not my name, not what I could do for them. *Me.* And you didn't. You were just like everyone else." The words were torn from her, her pride be damned.

He took a step forward and extended his hand, his fingers trembling as he cupped her cheek, ran his thumb over her lower lip. He let his hand fall back to his side. "I'm sorry I made you feel that way. I'm sorry I was such a fool. I didn't realize, Vanessa. I thought I couldn't be whole until I had all the money, all the status. All the power. I thought that when I was certain I would never be weak or helpless again, everything would be perfect. But I had it all. I've had it all since the moment I put that ring on your finger, but I am not whole. I'm in pieces. More now than I ever have been. I became a man I despise to gain the power and wealth that I craved. But I lost my soul. I lost my heart."

He reached into the pocket of his jacket and took out a stack of papers. "I'm hoping that this will help me get it back." He took her hand in his and lifted it, then he put the documents in her upturned palm. "This is everything I own. All of the shares for Pickett. All of my money. The title to the penthouse…all of my houses. It's yours, Vanessa. Because it means nothing if I don't have you. Without you, I have nothing, I am nothing. This isn't just some empty gesture. If you want me to leave, I will. And I'll leave you with everything I've acquired in the past twelve years. This is what I hurt you for, all of the things that I have defined myself by, and I would trade it all to have you in my arms again."

Vanessa stared down at the papers in her hand. "There are no divorce papers?" she asked, the words sounding hollow, inane.

"They're in there too. Whatever you want. But if you take me, it is only me. You can have it all without me. Money, power. Pickett will be safe. I'll have no hold over you."

"But…this is everything you have."

He shook his head. "It's nothing. I thought it was everything, Vanessa, I truly believed it. Do you know how frightening it was? To achieve my goal and realize that it was nothing more than vain emptiness? That I was more unhappy than I had ever been?"

He moved to her, cupped her cheek. "I do love you for what you can give me. Happiness. Hope. Satisfaction. Things I have chased all my life and found nowhere. Nowhere but with you. I love you, Vanessa Pickett. Everything about you. I have from the first moment I saw you, in your bright pink bikini, and I will love you until I take my last breath."

He pressed his forehead against hers. "I come to you with nothing. I am just a man who loves you."

She put the stack of papers on her hall table and wrapped her arms around his neck, her cheeks wet with tears. "I love you too."

He pulled back, his dark eyes searching hers. "How?"

"Same as you. I always have. I always will."

"What I said the other night…I was afraid you were only telling me you loved me so that you could secure Pickett's future. I didn't want that. And I didn't want to hold you to an arrangement that I had forced you into."

"I meant it then, I mean it now. With everything or with nothing, sickness or in health, I love you, Lazaro Marino. You. Not your position or your bank balance. Everything you are, everything you will be." She kissed him, pouring all of her love into him. When they parted, they were both short of breath. "And I don't want anything from you but you," she said, looking down at the documents on the table. "I really, really don't want the divorce papers."

"I'm very glad to hear you say that," he whispered, his voice rough.

She touched his face. "It's easy to be angry for so many years lost. So many years when we could have been together."

"I don't know if I could have been the man you deserved then, Vanessa. I wasn't the man you deserved twenty-four hours ago. I'm not sure if I am now."

"You are. You're the man I need. You push me. You make me stronger. You've shown me who I am."

"That's what you've done for me, Vanessa. I'm stronger, better, because I have you." He kissed her lightly and she sighed, happiness filling her. "I've turned down your father's offer to join his club," he said, the corners of his mouth lifting.

"You don't have to do that."

"I do. I don't want to do business with men like that. It's not worth any amount of money or prestige." He looked at her, his eyes unveiled, the love in them clear and true. "I don't need it. I love you, Vanessa Pickett. Not for your last name, not for your connections. For all of my days."

She smiled, her heart so full she thought it might burst. All of the pain flooded from her, washed away by Lazaro's love, the love they shared, leaving everything in her feeling clean. New. Complete for the first time.

"I'm glad you aren't too attached to my last name," she said. "Because I'm going to have it changed. Vanessa Marino suits me better. You're my family now. I want everyone to know how proud I am to be your wife."

"Vanessa Marino," he repeated. "I am honored."

She touched his cheek. "The honor is all mine."

EPILOGUE

THE past three years had been the best of Vanessa's life. She felt as though all the time spent apart from Lazaro was slowly being restored, as though wounds were truly healing, the past no longer something filled with hurt and regret.

She took a deep breath and looked around the gallery, at the people looking at her photographs. It was her first real exhibition. She hadn't been confident enough in her skills to have one right away, and she'd wanted to earn the right to have one, not simply have it handed to her because of her maiden name or her husband's position in the community.

The picture that drew the biggest crowd was the one that was still her favorite. Lazaro, in their bed, looking at her with so much desire in his eyes that it made her burn to see it even now.

She walked over to the photo, drawn to it still.

"That's a man in love." It came from one of the women gazing at the print.

Vanessa smiled.

Lazaro came to stand beside her, his arm around her waist. "Yes, it is." He leaned in and kissed her neck. "I'm still in love with you, too."

"I know," she said.

"Sure of yourself," he said, smiling at her.

"Sure of you," she said.

He'd never given her reason to doubt. He showed her his love every day in a thousand different ways. He loved her as she was, in all her moods.

He kissed her again. "Have I mentioned how very proud I am of you?"

"About a hundred times, but tell me again."

"I'm proud of you," he whispered, pulling her close. "Of everything you've accomplished. Of everything you are."

Vanessa blinked back tears and leaned into his embrace, love filling her. "The feeling is one-hundred-percent mutual."

* * * * *

KEPT AT THE ARGENTINE'S COMMAND

LUCY ELLIS

For my dear dad, who is 80 this year.
May he see many more stories to come.

CHAPTER ONE

ALEJANDRO NOTICED HER on boarding because she was easily
the sweetest view on offer: a drop of honey on a dull day.

A slightly built girl, sitting with her long slender legs
crossed at the knee, her head was bent as she read, causing
her mop of artfully arranged blue-black curls, cut short at
the back and longer towards the front, to topple forward
around her face. She wore the highly feminised clothes of
an earlier era in a way he recognised was a fashion statement.

As he made his way down the aisle towards his seat she
lifted her eyes from her e-reader and they locked with his.

Those curls, he discovered, framed delicate features.
She had a short upturned nose, big dark brown eyes and a
mouth like a red rosebud. Her eyes widened, but there was
nothing inviting in the way she looked at him. In fact her
gaze dropped skittishly away. She reminded him of one of
his fillies at home on the *estancia*, toeing the ground for
some attention and then shying away.

He didn't mind shy—he could work with it fine.

Sure enough, her gaze swung upwards again, back for
another look, a little bolder this time, and her lavish rosebud of a mouth quivered with the beginnings of a smile.

He returned her smile—the barest tilt of his mouth,
because he was out of practice with the gesture. She responded by blushing and ducking her eyes back to the little screen.

He was hooked.

He was also barely in his seat before she gestured for
assistance from a flight attendant. He watched in bemused
interest as for the next twenty minutes Brown Eyes kept

the cabin crew on their toes with a steady stream of what appeared to be trivial requests. Glasses of water, a cushion, a blanket… It was only when she began whispering furiously to the by now harassed female flight attendant that the points she'd scored with him for being pretty to look at flew out of the window.

'No, I really *cannot* move!' Her raised voice—demanding and shrill, despite the sexy French accent—had Alejandro putting down his tablet.

When the flustered flight attendant came up the aisle he leaned out and asked what the problem was.

'An elderly gentleman is finding it difficult to make the trip to the facilities, sir,' she explained, 'and we were hoping to relocate him to a closer seat.'

She didn't mention the intransigent Brown Eyes. But she was hard to miss.

Alejandro grabbed his jacket and reached up to the overhead locker.

'Not a problem,' he said, flashing the flight attendant a smile. She blushed.

Re-seated further towards the rear of the plane, he reopened his tablet, forgot about the brunette and gave his attention to the screen.

The morning papers on his tablet didn't offer much encouragement about his destination.

When one of Russia's richest oligarchs tied the knot with a sprightly red-haired ex-showgirl in a Scottish castle it was news, and from what Alejandro had heard from the groom himself the press had already set up shop in the surrounding town and area for long-lens shots of the 'who's who' guest list.

Being one of the 'who's who' himself, he'd decided not to make a splash entering the country. In Alejandro's opinion, if you didn't want the attention, you shouldn't act as if you were somebody who needed it. Which meant he was flying commercial and driving the four-hour trip from Edinburgh to the coast a day early. The route would reportedly take him through some picturesque countryside, and he intended to cruise into Dunlosie under the radar.

Still, the hullaballoo he was surely headed for didn't inspire encouragement that this was going to be anything other than a weekend to endure.

Impatiently Alejandro tossed aside his tablet and angled his wide-shouldered frame out of his seat. He'd never been able to sit still for long.

And that was when a little cough sounded to his left and he looked down.

It was Brown Eyes.

She'd taken a few trips up and down the aisle to the 'facilities'. Either she had a little bladder problem or, more likely, she was looking for some attention.

He surveyed her coolly. Possibly not the attention she wanted.

With each trip up the aisle her step had become more rolling and he suspected she was a little drunk.

She was also considerably tall for a woman. He took a look down and found the culprits: a pair of very high-heeled turquoise shoes, ridiculously encumbered by ribbons that frothed around her trim ankles.

She in turn was gazing up at him, all brown eyes and carefully cultivated curls. Irritatingly, she was as pretty as ever.

'Pardon, m'sieur.'

Her voice sounded a little slurred. Definitely drinking.

Unimpressed, he murmured, 'Maybe you should go easy on the free liquor, *señorita*, and do us all a favour.'

She blinked. *'Pardonnez-moi?'*

'You heard me.'

For a moment she seemed to be utterly lost for words. Then she screwed up her nose and stamped her foot.

It took a great deal of his self-control not to smile.

'Why don't you move out of the way instead of bullying

people?' she demanded, her French accent doing an excellent job on the precise English she used.

He ran his gaze insolently from the top of her shiny curls to the ribbons cascading over her pointy shoes and back to everything in between.

The in between was rather sweetly distributed...

She backed up a bit, but he wasn't letting her get away scot-free.

'You're quite a piece of work, aren't you, *chica*?' he drawled.

'I beg your pardon?'

'There are fourteen people in First Class today,' he spelt out. 'Your name isn't written on the plane and the cabin crew aren't your personal galley slaves. How about cutting us all some slack?'

Her eyes fell away from his. 'I don't know what you're talking about,' she mumbled. 'Now, move, why don't you?'

It was all he needed. 'Make me.'

Her chin came up and her rosebud of a mouth dropped open.

He was slightly surprised himself. He didn't, as a rule, hassle women. Especially silly little girls who needed to grow up.

For a moment he thought those big brown eyes were going to fill with ready tears. She certainly seemed on the brink of something.

So he moved.

Just.

She made a very French *'ouf'* sound of disapproval, averted her face and stalked back to her seat. Once more in charge of herself. Self-interest on two legs.

Only then she ruined it with an almost furtive look back over her shoulder, as if to make sure he wasn't following her.

The first finger of doubt touched his shoulder.

He'd made a few hard conclusions drawn from not much.

But life had taught him to pay attention to what people told you by their actions, not their words.

She had barely reached her seat when he heard her give a soft cry.

Alejandro turned—fast.

'*Non*, leave those things alone!'

He relaxed, a little surprised at his own reflexes when he didn't even like the woman. She was back to making everyone's life a misery.

She followed this up with a hushed volley of what sounded like furious French, but she was speaking so fast it was hard to tell. And all of it was directed at the poor steward, who was tidying up the clutter she had accumulated around her.

Heads emerged into the aisle.

Alejandro swung back into his seat and checked his phone. He was done with her.

There was a message from the groom.

Change in plans. Do me a favour and pick up a bridesmaid on your way in. Answers to Lulu Lachaille. Exiting Flight 338 at Gate Four. She's precious cargo. If you lose her, Gigi will cut off my balls and call off the wedding.

Alejandro briefly considered texting back *no*, even as he kissed his peaceful drive goodbye. Weddings were his worst nightmare. Spending four hours in a car with a chatty little bridesmaid didn't exactly float his boat.

Although the bridal party was bound to be stocked with leggy showgirls, so it might not be that bad...

Dios.

He stuck his head out into the aisle, only to find that the French Miss was leaning out too.

She had the open, hopeful expression of a cartoon princess awaiting aid from one of her magical creatures.

Then she saw him, and her expression darkened and her eyes diminished to dark cat-like slits.

As if on cue a flight attendant appeared at her side, with still water and what appeared to be some form of medication.

A headache? It just got better and better.

He flipped open the attachment Khaled had sent him, but a part of him already knew what he was going to see.

He didn't know whether to laugh or groan.

A dark-eyed angel gazed seriously up at him from the screen.

She was really quite something.

He angled a resigned glance down the aisle. The only problem was—she was also *her*.

CHAPTER TWO

MAKE ME?

Trotting across the plane's bridge, Lulu fumed. It was at the forefront of her mind to make a complaint to the airline.

Women should be free to fly the skies unmolested by hulking great brutes who thought they occupied the high moral ground.

Although she guessed he *did*.

She guessed he didn't think much of her because she hadn't given up her seat.

Lulu's heart plummeted.

She'd seen the looks on the other passengers' faces and knew they all felt the same way, but what could she have done?

The cabin crew had been apprised of her condition and had been considerate with all of her requests. Only one of them clearly hadn't got the memo regarding her flying issues, and when she'd been asked to move to another seat her feet had turned to lead.

Just the idea of shifting everything, when she'd created a safe little space for herself around her seat, had been too overwhelming. She might as well have been asked to leap from the plane!

By the time she was waiting at the luggage carousel Lulu was no longer fuming but feeling utterly wretched.

What kind of a person didn't give up their seat to a sick, elderly man?

Perhaps she should have heeded her mother's advice and brought someone with her? Lulu worried. Then none of this would have happened.

But how was she to have anything like a normal life if

she always had to take people along with her? She was a full-grown woman—not an invalid! She could do better than this. She stood up straighter. She could try harder...

She *was* trying harder.

Ever since she had tried to break up her best friend's relationship six months ago she'd been actively trying to do better.

She'd found a different therapist from the one her parents had arranged and got a proper diagnosis. At least she knew now that her actions with Gigi had been motivated by separation anxiety and were a symptom of her illness.

But it would have been too easy to use her condition as an excuse for her behaviour—lying to bring Gigi back home just so she could feel safer, and in the process trying to steal her best friend's joy with a man who'd proved to be the best thing that had ever happened to her. Who *did* something like that? A boxed-in, desperate person, that was who—and she didn't want to be that person any more.

That was why she was in the process of turning her entire life upside down.

She had signed up for a course in costume design and she now had ambitions for a life beyond the cabaret.

It had been that single act which had given her the necessary self-confidence to imagine she could undertake this flight on her own.

But all her preparations for taking the flight hadn't factored in a big, macho stranger, cornering her in the aisle on her way back from the facilities, where most of the contents of her stomach had gone down the toilet.

'A piece of work', he'd called her. As if she were defective—something she'd worked hard with her therapist to convince herself she wasn't.

Lulu realised her hand was shaking as she pointed out her luggage to the nice airport attendant who had volunteered to help her.

That was something that man from the plane could have been—helpful rather than being horrible to her.

Oh, forget him, she told herself briskly. *He's probably forgotten all about you!*

To be honest, as she made her way out into Arrivals with her stick-and-stop trolley, she was feeling a bit desperate, and was looking forward to seeing her fellow bridesmaids, Susie and Trixie. They at least would provide a buffer against the rest of the world.

Right now Lulu didn't think she could face anything more challenging.

Only ten minutes later she was still scanning the crowd anxiously and wondering if she was even going to get to the castle before Gigi said *I do*.

She had her phone out to track down the other girls when she was nudged by a new influx of people streaming around her and jostled backwards into a warm, hard body. Incredibly hard. Masculine, judging by the size, the solidity and the weight of the strong hands that settled around her shoulders to steady her.

He said something and Lulu froze.

She recognised that voice.

Dieu, it was the bully from the plane.

Run—run!

But her legs had gone to water. As much as she reminded herself that hostile men didn't scare her any more—she had rights…she was protected under the law—she still felt incredibly vulnerable. And she hated that feeling. She was trying so hard to be strong.

Which didn't explain why she'd fastened her gaze on his wide sensual mouth, noticing the shadow along his jaw where he'd clearly shaved this morning and would probably need to shave again later. He was *very* masculine.

Lulu reminded herself that she didn't like masculine men. She didn't like the way they pushed and shoved and shouldered their way through the world and got away with things through intimidation. They made her nervous. Only this man didn't exactly make her nervous—he made her something else.

It was the *something else* she was struggling with now, even knowing what a bully he was.

He was also gorgeously tall and broad-shouldered, with a stunning face—all cheekbones and sensuous mouth and golden-brown eyes that looked magnetic against the olive tint of his skin.

His tousled chestnut-brown hair was so thick and silky-looking her fingers just itched to touch it. She made fists of her hands.

She didn't like him, and he was looking at her as if he didn't like her very much either.

Good, it was mutual. The not liking, that was.

So what if he looked like…? Well, he looked like Gary Cooper. In his rakish early career, when he'd picked up and slept with every starlet who wasn't nailed down.

Not Gregory Peck, though. Gregory Peck was reliable and stalwart and…*decent*. He would never insult a woman.

Stop staring at him. Stop comparing him to Golden Age Hollywood movie stars.

'*Buenas tardes, señorita,*' he said, in a voice that made him sound as if he was making an indecent proposal to her. 'I believe you're looking for me.'

Lulu automatically repressed the responsive curl of smoke in her lower belly raised by the sound of his deep and sexy Spanish accent.

No, no, *no*—he would be lighting no fires in *her* valley.

She drew herself up. 'I certainly am not.'

Alejandro was tempted to shrug and walk away, and let the little *princesita* discover the hard way that he wasn't trying to pick her up. But in the end he had a duty to perform for a friend and she was it.

She continued to regard him as if he would spring at her, so he extended his hand.

'Alejandro du Crozier.'

She looked at his hand as if he'd pulled a gun on her.

'Please leave me alone,' she said, a touch furtively, and turned a rigid shoulder on him.

'I'm not trying to pick you up, *señorita*.' He tried again with what he considered was remarkable patience.

Her narrow back told him what she thought about *that* claim.

'You clearly didn't get the message. *Lulu*,' he added dryly.

The use of her name had the intended effect. She peered at him cautiously over her shoulder, reminding Alejandro absurdly of a timid creature sticking its head out of a hole.

'H-how do you know my name?'

He folded his arms.

'I'm your ride,' he said flatly.

'My *ride*?'

As soon as she said it Lulu felt herself go red.

She didn't have a dirty mind—truly she didn't. She was always the last one to get the blue jokes that ran like quicksilver around the dressing room before shows at L'Oiseau Bleu, the Parisian cabaret where she danced in the chorus, but right now something seemed to have gone wrong with her. It had something to do with the way he looked at her— as if he knew exactly how she looked in her underwear.

Earlier he'd looked at her as if she was a bug he'd wanted to squash. Better to think about being the bug.

To her embarrassment she stepped back and almost tripped over her hand luggage. His hand shot out and grasped her elbow, saving her from a fall.

'Careful, *bella*,' he said, his warm breath brushing the top of her ear.

Her knees went to jelly.

She tried to tug herself free, confused. 'Will you let me pass?'

'*Señorita,*' he said, holding her in place, 'I am Alejandro du Crozier, and I will be driving you to the wedding.'

Her eyes flew to his. He knew about the wedding? That meant he was a guest too.

'But Susie and Trixie are driving me to the wedding.' As soon as she said it she realised those plans had possibly changed.

'I know nothing of these women. I only know of you.' His expression said that this wasn't making his day.

Which was fine, Lulu decided. That made two of them. She gave another tug and he let go.

'I don't make a habit of going off with strange men, Mr—Mr—'

He pulled out his phone and held it up in front of her. She peered at the message on the screen and then looked at him in mute astonishment.

'*Khaled* sent you?'

He gave that question the look it deserved. But he didn't have to stand so close, did he? And he didn't have to look at her mouth as if there was something about it that interested him. She most definitely didn't have *anything* to interest him.

Weirdly, her heart was hammering.

His amber eyes, lushly lashed, met hers with a splintering intensity.

'Unless you're interested in walking, *chica*, I suggest you come with me now.'

He didn't give her a chance to object. He was walking away. He clearly expected her to follow him.

Lulu stared after him.

He was the rudest man.

She found herself struggling one-handed with her stick-and-stop trolley, her hand luggage banging painfully against her leg.

She most certainly was *not* travelling with him in a car for three or four hours.

She would find a taxi.

She would entrust her person and her luggage to a man she had *paid* to do the task—not one who thought he was doing her a big favour.

Money was a woman's greatest ally and protection. She knew it to be so. Without money her mother had been unable to escape her violent father.

Even now, with her mother blissfully married to another man, Lulu pushed her to keep her own bank account and manage her own money. Money gave you options. Lulu lifted her chin. Right now her own personal bank account gave her the ability to pay her way to Dunlosie Castle.

But when she emerged from the building it was into an overcast Edinburgh day. There was a light rain falling and Lulu stopped to retrieve her umbrella, opening it against the elements and peering about. She spotted the cab rank but there was a queue.

All right, sometimes those options a woman had weren't optimal, but there was no help for it.

She pushed resolutely in that direction, aware that her pretty harlequin seamed stockings were receiving tiny splashes of dirty water with each step from the washback beneath the wheels of her trolley. The fact that she felt depleted from withstanding her own anxieties in the air for the last couple of hours wasn't helping. Lulu wanted nothing more than to be warm and comfortable inside a car, with her shoes off, watching this bad weather through a windscreen.

Maybe she'd been a little hasty…

Which was when she saw the lovingly restored red vintage Jaguar.

The passenger side window came rolling down.

'Get in,' he instructed.

CHAPTER THREE

LULU KNEW SHE had a decision to make.

She lifted her umbrella to take another look at the queue. Then she looked at her 'ride'.

Hot and sexy and far too full of himself—and he had looked at her as if she was a bug.

Her pride pushed to the fore. She was *not* climbing into a car with a man who didn't even have the decency to open the door for her. And what about her luggage?

Lulu was tempted in that moment to phone her parents, who would be arriving at the castle tonight. But how would that look? And she couldn't lean on Gigi this weekend of all weekends.

She gasped as another splash of muddy water, this time from passing pedestrians, hit her shoes and saw the mud now attached to her sadly limp blue ribbons. Her pride wavered.

Dieu, she knew she'd regret this.

She grabbed her trolley and pushed it towards the back end of the car.

It was really completely unfair, but frankly she'd be a fool if she passed this up.

She stood there. In the rain. Waiting.

He took his time.

Lulu narrowed her eyes on his languid stroll around to the boot, all shoulders and confident attitude, looking infinitely rugged and male and capable.

But she knew differently. Knew how a sturdy exterior could mask all kinds of weaknesses and flaws.

She'd bet this man had plenty. For one thing, he didn't like women. The things he'd said to her on the plane…

The way he'd curled his lip at her shoes… She'd seen the way he'd looked at them. He had no idea how secure these shoes made her feel. She stamped one of them, because he was making her wait deliberately.

'Open the boot, would you?'

He looked her up and down. She wasn't going to apologise for her rudeness. He needed to know she was onto him.

All the same, she took a shuffling step backwards.

She drew herself up, happily over six feet in her shoes, but still gallingly forced to tip up her chin to look him in the eye.

With a half-smile, as if he knew what she was doing, he unlocked the boot, and Lulu was mollified—and a little relieved—when without a word he began hauling her luggage inside.

He handled the matching powder-blue cases as if they weighed nothing. The problem was he was tossing them into the boot as if he was shifting hay bales.

Lulu made a sound of dismay, but from the look he gave her she was a little afraid he might haul her in there too if she said something.

It was only when he looked about to launch her carpet bag after the cases that she jumped and threw herself bodily in front of him to prevent certain shattering.

'*Doux Jésus*, stop!'

He held off, but the look on his face told her he was unimpressed—which was pretty rich, given he was the one destroying her property!

'It contains the crystal I've brought as a wedding gift. For Gigi—and Khaled,' she added, grudgingly.

'Crystal?'

'Goblets…tableware. Crystal.'

He continued to stare at her, as if she'd announced she was giving them a horse and cart.

Lulu inhaled a breath. She held out her arms. 'Give that to me.'

He complied, but she wasn't expecting him to step right up to her. She was suddenly more aware of him than ever, and inhaled his aftershave—something woodsy that mingled with the scent of his own skin. It was attractively male in a way she wasn't used to.

Confused and flustered, Lulu looked up.

She encountered his firm chin and the sensuous line of his mouth, which only made her feel more unsettled.

He had a faint frown on his face and she suspected she mirrored it.

She turned her back on him to lodge the bag carefully between two cases to prevent it being bounced around.

Rude, ignorant, appalling, macho jerk.

He waited until she'd stepped back to lower the boot. She waited patiently by the passenger door with her umbrella. But he abruptly headed for the driver's side of the car.

'The "macho jerk" wants you to get in the car,' he said flatly as he yanked open his door.

Lulu realised two things in that moment. One, she'd spoken her thoughts aloud, and, two, he wasn't going to open her door.

Given he had all her luggage now locked up inside his car, she didn't have much choice, but she cursed herself for her weakness. She should have waited for a cab.

As if to remind her why she'd made her choice, the rain began to pelt harder.

Why is this happening to me?

She closed her umbrella and opened the door herself.

'Try not to drip on the upholstery,' he shot at her as she lodged her furled umbrella at her feet.

Distinctly queasy with the added tension, Lulu looked around in desperation. Where did he expect her to put it?

'Here.' He took it from her hand and laid it on the coat he'd tossed on the back seat.

Alejandro then turned back to discover that instead of

buckling herself in she had shoved the door open further, so that the rain had begun to slant in.

His temper snapped. 'Close that damn door!'

She looked for a moment as if she was going to jump right out of the car.

And then she leaned forward and began to dry retch miserably into the gutter.

He wrenched open his door and cut around the car to find her bent double.

He hunkered down. The face she lifted was bone-white. This she couldn't fake. She clearly wasn't well, and he suspected he'd got some things wrong. He produced a handkerchief to blot her mouth and soak up the tears that were sliding down her cheeks.

If she'd been hoping for some sympathy it was effective. The big glistening eyes, the silent tears, how fragile she suddenly looked beneath her showy outfit—as if she was trying to shrink into invisibility within it…

He put his hands around her shoulders to help her back into the car and out of the rain, but her response took him off guard. Her arms shot out and she instantly had them wrapped around his neck as tenaciously as a strangling vine.

He was enveloped in the scent of her, and he wondered for a second if this was her clumsy attempt at a pass. Only the feel of her rapid heartbeat told him she was scared. It was like holding a small nervous bird to his chest—as if what she was feeling was too big for her slight body. And yet what had she to be scared of?

She was overwrought—that was all, he told himself, and possibly a little the worse for wear from her in-flight tippling.

A better question was how had he come to be the only man in Scotland who was saddled with the job of delivering a vodka-wilted bridesmaid to their shared destination?

It had to be vodka, because he couldn't smell any alcohol on her. All he smelt were those cottage violets—and something warmer and real that was just *her.*

He tentatively rubbed her back, as he would one of the young kids on the *estancia* who had taken a fall from a horse and had the wind knocked out of them, and tried to ignore the fact that she was an incredibly appealing full-grown female with her breasts pushed up against his chest.

'I don't think I'll be sick again,' she confided miserably.

She hadn't actually done anything other than spit up a little bile, but he didn't doubt her suffering. She looked more miserable than a human being should.

'Please don't tell anybody about this,' she said in a muffled voice against his neck.

It was a strange request, but she was obviously serious about it.

He cleared his throat. 'Come on, let's strap you in. Are you all right to travel?'

She nodded, allowing him to help her.

He went around to the boot to grab a bottle of water from the chiller. He yanked the screw lid off for her and when he offered it to her she took a few grateful sips.

'Okay now?' he asked gruffly.

'I'm sorry,' she said huskily, swallowing deeply and refusing to meet his eyes. 'It won't happen again.'

He drove the keys into the ignition.

'Do you want to stop for coffee? Get something in your stomach?'

She shuddered. 'I can't think of anything worse.'

'It might sober you up.'

Her eyes flashed his way in confusion. 'I *am* sober.'

He gave her an old-fashioned look.

'I am not drunk. I have not been drinking.'

'You can deny it if you want, *querida.* It doesn't change the fact you were stumbling all over that flight, your words were a little slurry and you've just been sick.'

She looked at him in horror, her knuckles white around

the bottle. 'I wasn't— That's you— I mean, nobody else thought that—'

Lulu tried to control her shaking because it wasn't helping her case.

'Maybe I should just find a taxi,' she said, deeply humiliated, and distressed as she sloshed some of the water on her skirt. Although getting out of this car was the last thing she felt up to doing. 'This isn't working for me and it's clearly not working for you.'

'Look,' he said, keeping the car idling while he took the bottle from her hands, lidded it and tossed it onto the back seat. 'In my experience nobody likes to be confronted with their behaviour while under the influence. You had a few drinks on the flight…they didn't agree with you. I'm not judging.'

'Yes, you *are* judging,' she burst out unhappily. 'And nobody thought I was drunk.'

'No, probably not—they were too busy thinking what a pain in the arse you were to fly with.'

Her chin wobbled. 'Do you get something out of insulting me?'

'*Sí*, it takes the edge off.'

She stared at him. He'd silenced her. Good. The truth was she still looked very pale, and he didn't want to argue with her any more.

'If you must know,' she said, clearly unable or unwilling to let this go, 'I had some analgesics on the plane on an empty stomach and they disagreed with me. They're to blame.'

Alejandro was ready to dismiss this out of hand, only then he remembered the medication he'd seen delivered to her.

'Well, that was stupid,' he said.

He ignored the wounded look on her face. She could save it. He'd been manipulated by women who made this one look like a rank amateur. Besides, he wasn't playing

Sir Galahad to her fair maiden. Been there, done that—had the divorce papers to prove it. The problem was she was already getting to him.

He swung the car out into the traffic. 'Almost as stupid as not giving up your seat on the flight,' he reiterated.

Lulu realised she was cornered. How on earth did she answer *that*?

'It's not your business,' she muttered, looking away.

There was no way she could tell him that whatever had been in her stomach had ended up in the plane toilet, because that was going to lead to more questions.

Questions with answers that had nothing whatsoever to do with him.

It was her private business. Her mother had drummed that into her years ago.

'If you weren't drunk there's nowhere to hide, *querida*. I'm sorry you're not feeling well. But you behaved like a spoilt brat. Forgive me if I choose to treat you like one.'

Lulu wanted to die of shame.

'You're an awful man,' she muttered, 'I hope we have nothing to do with each other this weekend at the castle.'

'Sweetheart, you took the words out of my mouth.'

CHAPTER FOUR

THEY STOPPED TO fuel up the car after a couple of hours on the road. Lulu wound down her window and saw a newspaper headline behind the glass of the service station window: *Celebrity Wedding. Oligarch Brings in Private Army of Security.*

It was a little daunting to realise she was heading into all that.

The other daunting reality was striding back towards the car. His superbly fit and powerful frame was gloved in an understated but clearly expensive set of dark trousers and a navy shirt. *Like a man who went on secret missions with the armed forces and climbed walls without ropes, just using his weapon of a body as all the equipment he required.*

Lulu looked away.

Ah, *oui*, this was her new little problem. She had discovered now she felt physically better that she was responding to that Latin machismo thing some women went a little silly over. She might not have a boyfriend as such, but she did have hormones.

She really needed to make a big effort to curb her imagination.

People were looking his way as he approached the car. So maybe she wasn't the only one. She had to admit he had the impervious aura of confidence that belonged to someone for whom the small stuff of life was taken care of. She imagined Alejandro du Crozier rarely fuelled up his own car, although he'd taken care of it easily enough.

She had watched him do it through the side mirror—watched him sticking the petrol gun into the tank. There was something about a man's broad forearm, a chunk of watch, a powerful wrist and a strong hand gripping the nozzle that put all sorts of erotic images into a woman's head.

Admittedly they were images mostly gleaned from books she'd read. Her personal notebook of erotic experiences was fairly limited.

Alejandro tossed a wrapped sandwich onto her lap as he eased in beside her and turned the engine over.

'Ham salad. It's not much, but it should tide you over until we reach Dunlosie.'

Lulu wondered if this was him thawing towards her. Whatever it was, it was a thoughtful gesture. 'Thank you,' she said uncertainly, and busied herself with unwrapping her sandwich.

She could feel his eyes on her.

'Would you like half?' she offered.

Alejandro had bought the sandwich with an eye to her turning up her pert little nose at plastic-wrapped food. His preconceptions took a solid hit.

'I had a king's breakfast,' he said shortly. 'Eat up.'

Lulu gave an internal sigh. So much for the thaw.

Half an hour up the road, Alejandro flipped his phone onto speaker.

A male voice began to speak in Spanish, and Alejandro replied in the same language.

Lulu found herself transfixed by the deep, mellifluous quality of his voice as he spoke his own language. Then a Scot's voice came on the line.

'We're pleased to have you here in Edinburgh, Mr du Crozier. Congratulations on captaining South America to that win in Palermo. It warms a Scotsman's heart to see the English floundering on a field.'

Lulu's head snapped around at that. *What was this?*

Alejandro chuckled. 'No problem at all,' he said easily in his smooth, deep voice. 'It was a good match.'

Lulu felt as if she'd had the rug pulled out from under

her. Where had *this* come from? The smile, the ease, the charm?

'We will be sending our principal to you tomorrow, at your convenience and we'll give you an aerial viewing of the property. Will it be just you, Mr du Crozier?'

'Possibly one other.' Alejandro glanced her way. 'Two o'clock looks good.'

As he ended the call Lulu told herself not to make any enquiries—she would only look nosey.

'I'm looking at property while I'm here,' he said, his eyes on the road. 'I'm thinking of investing in a golf course. It's on a picturesque strip of land along the coast near Dunlosie.'

He didn't look like a golfer. Although she suspected those broad shoulders and strong arms could hit a golf ball to the moon and back.

'Do you play golf professionally?' she ventured. When he raised an eyebrow she added hurriedly, so that she didn't look stupid, 'That man said something about you captaining a team?'

He smiled slightly. 'Polo. I captained South America.' He was watching her as if gauging her reaction. 'It received some press coverage.'

Vaguely his name stirred a memory. She rather thought she ought to know it.

'I have a little fame, Lulu.'

He must have read her frown.

'Ah, *oui*.'

She tried not to look curious or impressed, or as if she cared. He was smiling to himself, and she wanted to tell him she didn't care if he was famous, or who he knew. It wasn't as if she was angling to spend any time with him when they reached the castle. She wasn't *interested* in him. He was just transport.

She leaned forward and rummaged in her bag.

It was almost a relief to have her phone in her hand and

something to concentrate on other than the magnetism of the man beside her.

He flicked on the sound system.

'Is that necessary?'

Alejandro spared her a glance. 'It passes the time.'

'I'm trying to do some work.'

'Games on your phone?'

'Wedding plans. See.' She held it up but he kept his eye on the wet road.

'Isn't that the bride and groom's prerogative?'

'I'm maid of honour,' she said proudly. 'I have responsibilities.'

Alejandro thumped the wheel with the heel of his hand.

'What's wrong?' she demanded.

'Santa Maria,' he said under his breath, and after a moment began to chuckle.

'What's so funny?'

When he kept laughing her expression took on a look of bafflement, and for a moment she looked very young and decidedly adorable.

He didn't want her to look adorable. He took another look. Definitely adorable. No wonder she had entitlement issues. He doubted there was a man alive who could resist those big brown eyes or her air of fragility.

It would bother him. If he was considering taking this anywhere. But since the day he had learned he'd inherited everything, in the form of the *estancia* and all the debts his father had collected, and gained nothing but his mother's endless demands for more money, his wife's desire for freedom and the everlasting dissatisfaction of his disinherited sisters he'd carried around the feeling that he'd let them all down.

Fragile women required a lot more than he was able to give.

'I want to know why you're laughing at me,' she insisted.

'I'm going to kill him.'

'Kill who? What are you talking about?'

'Fate. The universe. Khaled Kitaev.'

'You're not making any sense.'

'I'm *padrino de boda, querida.*'

She had a blank look on her face that made him want to spin this out a little longer, because watching her lose a little of that tight composure was almost worth the hassle.

He relented and filled her in. 'Best man.'

She dropped her device and it slithered through her satin skirt and thumped at her feet.

'You *can't* be!'

'I am.'

'But we don't like each other.' She clamped her mouth shut, as if she couldn't believe that had just slipped out.

No, maybe not, but he'd just discovered he *did* like her. She might be spoiled and self-centred, but he lived in a world where most women fell at his feet.

Lulu Lachaille would fall, if he applied the right pressure here and there, but she wasn't going to trip herself up.

She might just be what he was looking for this weekend after all.

Distraction from the spectacle that was a wedding, where everybody mouthed belief in fidelity and love ever after but nobody in his world practised it.

Although he had to admit Khaled and Gigi did seem to be that rarest of unions—a couple who genuinely liked one another.

And he liked Gigi's little friend, with her pretty curls and her rosebud pout and her French girl's way of looking as if she was bored and it was his job to entertain her.

'I wouldn't say I don't like you,' he said, checking out her pretty knees, just visible under the froth of her netted underskirt. Her hands went there immediately, smoothing it down.

'Not in that way,' she said crossly. 'I don't want you to

like me that way at all. I mean in a *platonic* sense. In a maid of honour and best man *duty* sense.'

'Now I'm a duty? Careful, *querida*, you'll damage my ego.'

'I doubt that,' she said repressively.

He grinned.

She looked decidedly flummoxed.

'You'll need to make an effort, then,' she blurted out almost defensively.

'I intend to.'

Lulu tried to ignore the fact that she felt hot all over. Was he *flirting* with her?

'I'm serious. You'll have to be polite to me so people don't notice anything's wrong.'

But something *is* wrong, thought Lulu, checking him out surreptitiously. Why did he have that sexy half-smile sitting at the corner of his mouth? He kept looking at her and she didn't want him to look at her. It made her feel most unlike herself.

'The best man has duties with the maid of honour,' she persevered staunchly, feeling as if she was drowning in something and holding on to talk of the wedding as a life buoy.

'*Sí*, I believe he does.'

Not those kind of duties. The thought just appeared in her head. It should have embarrassed her, and her heart was racing crazily, but a big part of her was actually enjoying the attention.

Alejandro du Crozier was flirting with her and she wasn't diving for the nearest manhole to escape.

Probably because she knew she wouldn't be seeing him again after this weekend.

It wasn't as if he was going to ask her out. This was just a straightforward few hours in a car together, and then there was the weekend… Maybe it would be okay just to

pretend for a few hours that she was normal and he was…
interested?

That was when the car gave a bit of a lurch, and the
sound of rubber dragging on the road had Lulu gripping
her seat.

Alejandro said something filthy in Spanish even as he
braked, and all the heat that had been building between
them dissipated with the reality of the car coming to a stop
at the side of the road.

Lulu forgot how much she'd been enjoying herself as
her old friend panic set in and she looked around wildly.
'What's going on? Why are we stopping?'

There was no way she was getting out *here*, in the middle of nowhere!

'It's a flat. The back left tyre is shot.'

At least it wasn't electrical. Lulu slumped a little in her
seat. She could stay where she was, safe and sound, and
it wouldn't take too long. She could manage this. But she
needed to dial down the panic. She cast about for something
to pin her focus to in the car and remembered her phone.

In the silence that followed she glanced up, only to find
he was watching her. She really didn't want him to notice
how nervous she was. 'Well, fix it,' she said defensively,
before returning her attention to the screen.

Fix it?

Alejandro cut the engine and eased back in his seat to
take a good look at what exactly he had on his hands.

One hundred and thirty pounds, at a guess, of Paris-bred
entitlement—and he damn well wasn't her mechanic. His
gaze dwelt on her soft, petulant mouth. Although there was
something he wouldn't mind fixing.

He reached across, plucked her phone from her hands
and tossed it onto the back seat.

Time to take the edge off his distracting sexual interest in her.

Lulu gave him a puzzled look. He'd sort that out for her too.

He leaned in.

Her eyes widened, her breath came short, but she didn't exactly push him away as he slid his fingers through the astonishingly silky weight of curls behind her head and fitted his mouth with practised ease to hers.

Her muffled yelp gave him the opportunity to invade her warm mouth. He had planned to make this quick. He didn't linger where he wasn't wanted. Only Lulu wasn't struggling, and she made no attempt to push him away. Instead her hands unfolded over his shoulders and then, almost tentatively, she was kissing him back.

He let her.

This wasn't about proving a point any more.

Her hand stroked gently against his shoulder as she moved her mouth sensuously against his.

She was seducing him. And it was working. His body was suddenly as hard as a pick axe.

Which was inconvenient, given neither of them could do anything about it right now, in a broken-down car on the side of a quiet Scottish road.

Sí, not one of his smarter moves.

He began to think about leaping into ice holes in Reykjavik, of losing to a lesser team, about the very real possibility that a photo of him making out like a teenager with this girl might all too easily end up on the internet.

But what *should* have killed his desire stone-dead was the wave of tenderness that came over him as she drew away and hid her face in his neck in a gesture of embarrassment that oddly, crazily, had a rush of male protectiveness surging up from nowhere.

He found himself stroking the back of her neck, the urge to be affectionate with her amazingly strong.

Fragile, he told himself again. *She's fragile.*

Lulu was aware that Alejandro was moving away from

her and she had nowhere to hide. One minute she'd been trying to control her panic, the next she'd been tipped into something she hadn't had a lot of in her twenty-three years—the feel, the scent, the excitement of a man kissing her. And not just *any* man. *This* man. This very masculine man, who knew exactly what he was doing.

Her heart had slammed against her chest as his mouth had slid against hers. It had been the most invigorating experience of her life.

She waited for him to say something, because for the life of her she had nothing. Zero.

'All fixed now,' he said, dropping the words into her lap as if he'd tossed her his hotel room key.

It wasn't his words but the deliberation with which he wielded them that had her gaze flying to meet his. And then his meaning became clear.

Fixed? Lulu floundered with the concept. He'd done it on purpose? He hadn't been carried away like her at all?

Mon Dieu, what a little fool she was.

Her heart was still galloping like a wild horse, and now it picked up pace for all the wrong reasons.

She was aware of him watching her from beneath hooded eyes…aware that he now knew a great deal more about her than he had minutes ago. More than any man knew, to her deep embarrassment. And he'd set her up. He'd done it to humiliate her.

Her hand shot out but he caught it before she found her target. 'No slapping, *mi belleza*.'

Alejandro watched the struggle on her face and, as much as he welcomed the status quo between them being lodged once more in place, he knew he'd acted like a bastard.

And that was when he heard it. The rumble.

His attention moved across to the side rear-vision mirror and he saw what was coming.

Lulu wrenched her wrist out of his hold and wiped her

mouth with the back of her hand to give him the message. 'You're *never* to do that again.'

'Fine.' He kept his eye on what was coming.

'There's a name for men who force themselves on unwilling women.' She addressed him directly, unbuckling her belt.

That had his attention.

'I didn't use any force, *querida*.' He was frowning at her. 'You were with me the whole way. It's called chemistry.'

'I know what it's called.' She opened her door.

'Where the hell are you going?' he growled, not liking her spin on this.

'Somewhere far away from *you*.' Which was when she gave a shriek and slammed the door shut again.

Around them a sea of black-faced sheep surged, like something out of a biblical plague. The car rocked slightly with the force.

'I probably should have mentioned that,' Alejandro drawled, winding down his window. 'We've got company.'

CHAPTER FIVE

I'M GOING TO DIE.

Lulu went stiff as a board as all around her the road just seemed to fill up with sheep.

'Welcome to Scotland,' said Alejandro, propping one arm casually on the door, as if floating in a sea of sheep happened regularly in Argentina.

A whimper had buried itself at the base of her throat, and she just knew that if she opened her mouth it would come out and humiliate her. But, really, how much worse could it get?

She had to speak. To make something happen.

'Drive, why don't you?' she hissed at him a little desperately.

'Where?' He gestured at the woolly tide. 'This is Scotland, *chica*. Here we give way to sheep.'

Lulu didn't know if this was true or just more of him tormenting her. She suspected a little of both.

'Besides,' he added, 'the back tyre's shot.'

Forget the tyre! *She* was shot. Her mouth pulsed from his kiss and her body felt oddly light, but that might be shock setting in. Because those big, woolly mammoths with their black faces were turning her tummy to cold liquid and her pulse was going so fast she thought she might pass out.

This was worse than a two-hour flight from Paris to Edinburgh, or letting a man she had only known for a few hours at most plant a kiss on her.

This was her worst nightmare.

Because she couldn't escape. And the knowledge that she was only inches away from a full meltdown in front of this man was probably the only thing keeping her upright and frozen in her seat.

She knew she should never have got in this car with him.

She had no more control over her anxieties than she'd possessed this morning before the flight, when she'd knelt over the porcelain bowl at home in her flat and lost her breakfast.

Dieu, what if she was sick again? In this car? He wouldn't be kind. There wasn't a kind bone in his body.

There was a click, and Lulu realised he'd opened his door.

'What are you doing?' she almost shrieked.

He looked surprised by her vehemence. 'I'm going to have a word with the farmer,' he said mildly. 'It's a damn sight better than sitting here. Come on.'

'No!' She clutched hold of his arm.

'Or we could stay here and neck like a couple of teen-agers,' he said dryly.

Lulu let him go in a flash, and discovered she really was between a rock and a hard place.

'Come on,' he said more patiently. 'Stretch your legs.'

Lulu flailed around for a reason not to—any reason. 'I don't like sheep. They're smelly, and—' she cast about for something…anything '—and I'll wreck my shoes.'

He gave her a look that in all honesty she knew her comments deserved and her toes curled under inside said shoes. The last of the confident, take-on-the-world Lulu died inside her. The Lulu who had sprung to life in his arms and kissed him back barely had time to take flight. She was back to being useless.

What made it worse was that he shrugged, as if it didn't matter to him either way, which she guessed it didn't.

'Suit yourself, *chica*.' He swung open his door and Lulu realised he was serious.

He was also back to calling her *chica*.

Lulu watched in tense dismay as he took off in easy

strides down the road, all shoulders and masculine confidence, shouting out something to the two men driving the sheep. Obviously magic words, given they waited for him and then stood around conversing with him like old friends.

She sat forward, her nose almost to the glass, wondering what on earth they had to say to one another that was causing such a friendly, animated discussion. When he spoke to *her* all he did was rile her and growl. Or kiss her. Lulu hesitantly touched her mouth and swore she could still feel tingling.

A loud, long bleat sounded over her right shoulder and Lulu almost shot through the roof, any thoughts of kissing him shattering into a thousand pieces.

To her relief he came strolling back to the car. He leaned in.

'Some of the connections are probably loose, I could fix it but it might happen again. Tell you what, I'll give road assistance a call and organize another car. There's a pub just down the road. We can wander down and wait for them there.'

Lulu knew this was the moment a normal, sensible woman would confess her problem. She would explain why there was no way she could get out, due to her difficulties, and they would come up with a solution together.

Only there wasn't really a solution, was there? And right now she wasn't a sensible woman. She was in the grip of a building panic attack.

Lulu heard herself say, 'I have no intention of going anywhere.'

He straightened up, and for a long, awful moment Lulu thought he was going to turn around and leave her here.

Please don't abandon me.

The words were forced up from deep inside her, where a small frightened girl was still cowering.

Then she realised he was walking away, and an awful

cold feeling began to invade her limbs, only for him to stop at the front of the car.

'Pop the hood,' he called to her.

Lulu scrambled to obey him, jamming her middle with the gearstick but hardly noticing. He would never know how grateful she was that he wasn't going anywhere, and she knew she was safe as long as she stayed in the car.

All she needed now was to keep her adrenal glands from overshooting the mark.

She fumbled in her bag for her handkerchief, soaked in lavender, peppermint and rosemary oil, and held it to her nose with one hand as she attached the earbuds to her mp3 player and pushed them into her ears with the other.

She shut her eyes and willed the meditation track she'd been listening to throughout the flight to drop her back into her own little world, where nothing could harm her.

Alejandro checked the connections and then opened the back door to grab a hand towel from the storage space under the front seat.

The little French princess was plugged into her music, a handkerchief at her nose to block out the odour of the sheep…the farmer…of anything that offended her delicate sensibilities. Which probably included him.

There's a name for men who force themselves on unwilling women.

Bull.

He shut the rear door with a slam.

Lulu pulled the earbuds out and looked around with a start. She transferred her attention to the raised bonnet.

Which was when it occurred to her that he was at the wrong end of the car.

The sheep appeared to have moved on. Carefully she edged open the door and, when it felt safe, stepped out onto the road. Nothing happened. The ground didn't tilt under her, and there was nothing but the smell of fresh grass and sheep manure and peat. She inhaled. It wasn't bad.

Alejandro saw the flash of turquoise skirts disappear to the rear of the car. The boot came up.

He lowered the bonnet and came around to find Lulu wrestling the spare tyre out of the wheel well.

'Should I ask what you're doing?'

She ignored him, yanking at the tyre with both hands, moving it to the rim of the boot and then bouncing it onto the ground.

With a little lift of her chin she rolled it around to lean it against the side of the car.

'I suppose a better question is do you *know* what you're doing?' he asked, his voice taking on a note of real amusement.

In answer, she retrieved the canvas bag tucked to the side of the wheel well, untied it and produced the wheel brace like a trophy, together with the jack and jack handle, which she laid out on the ground.

Alejandro gave her a grudging nod of respect and Lulu felt a small surge of confidence.

There was very little she had to thank her deadbeat dad for, but the fact that she could change a tyre, fix a leaky tap and unclog the drains in a bathroom were all down to a childhood when she hadn't had a choice. Maman hadn't been able to afford help—they'd had to do everything themselves.

'You might want to take those shoes off first, *querida*,' he suggested.

She gave that the disdainful look that comment deserved. 'I'm an ex-ballerina. After *pointes* four-inch heels are nothing.'

Still, it was a bit of a wrestle to get the hubcap off and keep her balance, so he might have had a point, but once she had it free she used the wheel brace to loosen the nuts. She crouched down in a puff of satin and tulle underskirts and positioned the jack under the car.

She was aware that Alejandro was leaning over her for a

closer look. Determined to do a good job, she began turning the jack handle and the car lifted with a slow creak.

When the wheel was clear of the ground she clasped it on either side and pulled.

The weight of it had her staggering backwards, and she gave an *'ouf'* as Alejandro caught and steadied her.

Lulu had the oddest sensation that she would have liked to stay there, with his big solid body sheltering her and his hands sending all sorts of messages to parts of her she had grown used to ignoring.

'That's enough,' said in his deep voice. 'I'll finish this.'

For a moment Lulu had an altogether different image in her mind from the one she beheld as he let her go, stepped in and lifted the spare tyre with enviable ease, swiftly replacing all the wheel nuts with the brace and winding the jack in a reverse position to lower the car to the ground.

He's turned me into a nymphomaniac, she thought. Who knew what he did to women who already liked sex?

He tightened the nuts and shoved the hubcap back into place, replaced the old wheel in the boot, along with the tools, and slammed down the lid.

Lulu had her hand out.

'Give me the keys,' she said.

Alejandro knew where this was going, but it was no skin off his nose. He handed them over.

She marched around to the driver's seat, casting him a pointed look over the roof of the car. 'Well, get in.'

He grinned and eased his muscled frame in beside her.

Violets. The scent was hot in his nostrils now. They flared appreciably.

She didn't look like the girl he'd picked up this morning. Her dark curls were ruffled in a halo around a face that was reddened either from the wind or exertion or just sheer temper. Her dark eyes shone and her skirt was sadly crumpled. There was a grease stain on her top. But, with her jacket neatly folded on the back seat, she was showing off two neat little scoops of bosom above the tight neckline of her top.

He noticed that her shoes, now caked in mud, had been discarded in the passenger footwell and she had a look of fierce concentration on her face.

She looked exactly the way she had when he'd kissed her, wild and beautiful, and it sharpened his hunger for her.

She pulled out onto the road and took off.

'You might want to watch your speed,' he observed, unable to take his eyes off her.

'You might want to tell me why you thought it was fine to leave me locked in a car in the middle of nowhere.'

'You weren't locked in, and I went to find out what we needed to know.' He eyed her stained clothing. 'What I can't work out is why you put on that little show back there about not getting out of the car—'

'None of your business.'

'When you're so clearly capable.'

She glanced at him, a little dumbfounded, then looked back at the road. He was glad she was concentrating on the road.

'Yes, I am. Capable.'

'Do you know where we're going, *querida*?'

She changed gear and pushed those wild curls out of her eyes in a defiant gesture. 'Of course I do.'

He noted the sign to Inverary as it flashed past. His gaze dropped to those twin scoops, rising and falling gently above her neckline, to the sensual pout of her lower lip above that jaunty little chin.

She looked so pleased with herself he decided not to inform her that they were going the wrong way. He was in no hurry to get to the castle, to be bored to death by talk of for ever and happy-ever-after. No... He settled back comfortably, folded his arms across his chest and pretended to close his eyes. He was going to let this run a little longer, and then, when she'd run out of steam and learned her lesson, he'd think about taking this chemistry between them to its natural conclusion.

Lulu peered out at the passing countryside. According to her map, shouldn't they be approaching the motorway by now? It was growing dark, and it was raining, and she didn't have a clue where they were.

The ribbon of road had grown narrower and it was impossible to read the signs. The headlights on the car lit up only the road ahead, making everything that lay outside it seem menacing and vaguely supernatural.

Lulu liked the countryside—in the daylight, and from the confines of a car, and preferably not stopping. But she was going to have to pull over. The fuel tank was bobbing close to empty.

She brought the car to a stop on the shoulder of the road. Then reached over and touched Alejandro's impressive shoulder.

He felt warm and reassuringly powerful beneath her hand.

He didn't stir.

She gave him a more definite push. 'Mr du Crozier.'

No response.

'Alejandro!'

Thick sable lashes lifted and his eyes gleamed speculatively over her in the same way the headlights lit up the road ahead. He was looking at her as if she were naked, which was disconcerting enough, and Lulu had a sudden, completely outrageous thought that he hadn't been sleeping at all.

'We appear to be lost,' she said unwillingly.

'You don't say?'

His voice was husky, but not with sleep. Lulu swallowed. There was something very intimate about their proximity, as if the darkness outside and the quiet within had made the space between them somehow more personal.

Lulu licked her lips. 'I don't know where we are.'

'Fortunate, isn't it,' he said in that low, taunting voice, 'that I do?'

He undid his seatbelt and opened the car door.

'*I'm* driving,' he said unnecessarily.

Lulu released the breath she hadn't known she was holding and, rather than stepping outside, scrambled nimbly over the gearbox and tucked her skirts around her in the passenger seat.

Alejandro took the wheel and swung the car back out onto the road.

'How do you know?' she demanded.

'I saw the last sign. We're just outside Inverness.'

Relief swamped her. Then she frowned. 'But you were asleep.'

'Let's just say I'm not a heavy sleeper, *querida*,' he responded with a glint in his eyes.

She knew it! Impossible man. But her heart was pounding a little, and she found herself watching him and waiting to see what he'd do next.

Alejandro had them on the motorway within ten short minutes. Lulu discovered she was feeling a little out of sorts now her adventure was over.

She tried to envisage the weekend ahead on her own, and it was so depressing that in her head she found herself shaping sentences she didn't know if she had the guts to go through with, let alone ask.

I'm on my own this weekend...you're on your own. I'm maid of honour...you're best man. Doesn't it make sense if we pair up? Maybe you could kiss me again?

And that was when a huge gust of wind buffeted the car and all the available light left in the sky dwindled to nothing and the rain came down.

Alejandro slowed them to a crawl, along with the two or three other vehicles on the road.

'Kilantree...' she read from the sign ahead under the spray of their headlights. 'One mile. Is Kilantree near Dunlosie Castle?' she asked.

'Not near enough.'

To her surprise, Alejandro eased the car into the turn-off lane.

'What are you doing?'

'It's dark, it's raining, and I don't know these roads. We won't make Dunlosie tonight.'

'What does that mean?'

Although all of a sudden she *did* know, and for the first time in years having her routine destroyed didn't bring on feelings of anxiety. Quite the contrary...

'We're spending the night here.'

CHAPTER SIX

THE DIRECTIONS THEY'D received at the pub in Kilantree's main street took them just out of town and up a long steep drive to Mrs Bailey's B&B. The place proved to be a fairly substantial cottage. The eponymous Mrs Bailey appeared in dressing gown and slippers.

'Well, now, bring the lassie in—you'll be blown away out there. How are you, m'dear? You look pale as a ghost! We've got one of those, but I'm sure it won't bother you tonight.'

'Ghost?'

Lulu's eyes sought his. She didn't look amused.

Alejandro was aware that her small hand had slipped into his.

'It brings the tourists in, no doubt?' he commented, and Mrs Bailey laughed.

'Aye, it does—but that's not to say it doesn't exist. Come up these stairs. You don't mind carrying your own luggage, do you? My husband is already in bed. He has a four a.m. start with the sheep.'

Lulu's expression said, *More sheep?*

Alejandro suppressed a smile. He had to duck at the top of the stairs. The ceilings were low and age permeated the very beams of the place.

The older woman opened a door on a bedroom so snug the double bed itself and a chest of drawers took up most of the room.

There was an unlit fireplace that their landlady began fussing with.

'We'll have you warm in no time. I'll bring ye up some dinner in a half-hour, if that suits. The bathroom is at the end of the hall and there are fresh towels.'

Lulu's mouth had fallen open. 'I am *not* sharing this room with you,' she hissed as Mrs Bailey closed the door.

He was ready for this. 'It's fine, *querida*, I trust you.'

She rolled her eyes, but he noticed her gaze was expectant. He wasn't going to be making the first move this time. He needed this to be very clearly *her* decision.

'You should have explained the situation to her.'

He folded his arms.

'There's only one bed!'

'*Sí*, it looks comfortable.'

It was her turn to fold her arms.

'I'm afraid you'll have to sleep on the floor,' she said.

They both looked at the stretch of floorboards between them.

'No,' he said.

She flushed.

'Maybe you can sleep in the chair,' she suggested, as if she was being helpful.

He raised an eyebrow. 'How about we toss a coin for it?'

She opened her mouth, and then at the expression on his face shut it.

He pulled a coin from his back pocket. 'Heads or tails?'

'Heads.'

He flipped the coin, slid his hand away. 'Tails. I'll give you a blanket.'

He could feel her eyes boring into him as he set about improving Mrs Bailey's attempt at a fire. He was half minded just to scoop her off her feet and put her mind at rest. He had no intention of sleeping alone.

'I need my things,' she said, her voice a little loud given he was right there.

He shoved one of the logs deeper into the smouldering ash.

'Are you going to do the right thing or make me go outside again?'

'I'll be a gentleman,' he said, straightening up to find her watching him owlishly, 'and get them.'

She backed up as he headed out. Timid as a dormouse.

'The little blue case will be enough,' she called after him when he was halfway down the hall. 'And don't shake it about.'

Alejandro was coming inside with the blue case he wasn't supposed to shake when he met Mrs Bailey at the bottom of the stairs.

'I'll include a bottle of brandy with your dinner, laddie. Your wife looks like she needs a little warming up.'

Alejandro nodded a brief thanks, but knew the only thing warming up Lulu would be him.

If he'd been a less confident man he might have taken pause when Lulu met him at the top of the stairs, uttered an unconvincing *'Merci beaucoup,'* snatched her suitcase and, with a suspicious look at him, as if he were a villainous seducer, fled for the bathroom at the end of the hall, slamming the door.

But confidence had never been his problem, and Alejandro grinned and went back downstairs to find out about their meal.

When he returned, carrying a wooden tray, Lulu was rummaging around in her suitcase. She looked up, her big brown eyes doing that uncertain thing again, but that was before she noticed the bottle under his arm and the two glasses wedged between his blunt fingers.

She leapt to her feet. 'That's my wedding crystal!'

'Sí.' He shrugged. 'We'll rinse them and they'll never know.'

'I'll know!'

'We can eat on the floor,' he said, ignoring her outburst, and settled the tray on the hearth. Then he took a better look at her new outfit. It was wool, full-length, and buttoned up to her neck. 'Whose grandmother did you steal that from?'

Lulu's face fell as she glanced down at her dressing gown. 'I heard that the Scottish nights are cold because of the North Sea,' she said seriously.

'The North Sea?'

'Out there.' She waved her hand vaguely at the wall.

By Alejandro's calculations she was pointing inland, or at a stretch of the Atlantic.

He didn't like her dressing gown, Lulu thought, tugging uneasily at the sleeves. But it was practical, and that was what mattered.

Lulu noticed his hair was wet from the rain, and that he'd brought the scent of the wild outdoors in on his clothes. Her senses stirred. More than stirred. He'd braved the elements for her. She shouldn't find that sexy…but she did. Her gaze went a little helplessly to the stretch of damp fabric across his upper body, the swell of muscle, the hard male bones.

'Are you going to eat?'

Lulu realised she'd just been standing there all this time, and that he'd caught her checking him out.

Flustered, she made a production of sitting down on the rug and surveying their dinner. It was stew and dumplings. The kind of food she would have been careful around if she hadn't been on a break.

'What's that?' she asked rather desperately as he uncorked the bottle.

'It's one of the bottles of burgundy I brought over for Khaled and Gigi. They won't miss one.'

Lulu held out her hand and examined the old faded label. '1945?' she said.

'It was produced at the end of World War II—I sourced a handful of bottles through Christie's.'

'You bought wine at an *auction*?'

'Why not?'

'Wasn't it a little expensive?'

He angled a speculative look her way that set all the hormones in her body aquiver. 'Just a little.'

'This feels so wasteful,' Lulu half whispered as she watched him expertly decant the blood-dark wine into goblets. 'I'm sure Mrs Bailey's stew isn't up to the standards of a forty-five burgundy.'

'Good wine improves everything,' he told her, and she knew he wasn't talking about the wine.

She found herself checking to see that none of her buttons had come undone.

Non, all accounted for. To settle her nerves Lulu concentrated on sipping her wine. It slid down like heaven, and she gave a soft sigh of approval and looked over at him— only to discover he hadn't touched his. He was watching her, and she was instantly back in the car with him, his hand at the back of her head, his mouth making all kinds of magic with hers, leaving her breathless and flustered all over again.

'So,' he said with intent, 'from ballerina to topless showgirl. How did you get there?'

Lulu glared at him. Sprawled against the post at the end of the bed, long powerful legs stretched out across the rug, bare feet idling in the firelight, he looked like every fantasy any woman could ever have. And he knew it.

Not hers, though. She wanted Gregory Peck. She wanted someone decent and reliable who would always give up his bed to a lady and would not expect her to share it—and he certainly wouldn't make assumptions about her profession.

Although she guessed half the dancers at L'Oiseau Bleu *were* topless—*nude*—there wasn't anything wrong with that; it was artistic. There was a whole heritage behind it. But Alejandro probably didn't care much about the history of things. He just liked naked women.

Which shouldn't have her gaze lingering just a little too long on the wide, sensual line of his mouth. That dark shadow was already making itself known around it and along his jaw, hinting at a heavy beard. She wondered if it would scratch a little if he kissed her again...

Lulu fanned herself. 'The fire is very warm.'

'You'll be glad of it later tonight, when the temperature plummets,' he commented.

She glanced at the bed and then met his eyes. She waited for him to volunteer to take the chair. He didn't.

Tightening her lips, she reached for her glass of wine.

'So, from completely rude man to professional polo player. How did that happen?'

He didn't even flinch. 'I was put on a horse when I was four years old and my father handed me a mallet, I didn't have much choice.'

Against her will, Lulu's sympathies were stirred. She tried to picture him at four. She failed. He was so big and testosterone-fuelled it was hard to imagine him small and vulnerable.

'Even if I hadn't been, my family has bred horses in Argentina for many generations and the sport is popular in my country. It's in the blood.'

'So you inherited everything?' she said, still annoyed about the bed.

If he behaved like a gentleman she might—*might*—consider sharing it with him. Platonically.

Although Alejandro du Crozier did not strike her as the platonic type.

He was the type to grab a woman and kiss her until she slapped him and then leave her to the mercy of a hundred black-faced sheep.

'Inherited?' He appeared to inspect the word. 'No, I earned it. Every acre, every pound of horse flesh, every match. No hand-outs,' he said, with an emphasis that made her think she'd hit a nerve. He paused, taking a mouthful of wine. 'I run a working *estancia*, Lulu,' he added, meeting her eyes, 'and I have a corporate portfolio that among other things supports our national polo team.'

'That must keep you busy.'

'You have no idea, *querida*.'

No, but she was going to. Once she started college in a month's time, coupled with a full season at L'Oiseau Bleu. That was pretty impressive on its own, although she guessed it didn't stand up to breeding horses and captaining his country in international polo matches.

'I don't know anything about polo, but it must take a lot of work—with the horses, I mean.'

'You get out of it what you put in. But, *sí*, it's all about the ponies. You're only as competitive as your mount.'

She imagined *he* was incredibly competitive. You didn't get to that level in a professional sport without it.

Weirdly, she liked it. She liked his assurance…the way he got things done. Mostly she liked talking like this with him.

For the first time it occurred to her that maybe she could have tonight for herself. The other girls weren't here to tell him that there was something wrong with her…her parents weren't here to make it abundantly clear that there was something wrong with her. She didn't even have any responsibilities to Gigi tonight.

This could be *her* night. Which meant she had to stop talking on and on about polo!

She took a big gulp of wine. 'Your parents must be proud of you.'

Alejandro shifted his long legs in front of the fire restlessly.

'They divorced when I was fifteen,' he said easily.

He was a child of divorced parents, just like her. They had something in common.

'I didn't have much to do with my father after that,' he added, swirling the contents of his glass.

'Divorce can be tough.'

He raised a sceptical eyebrow. 'My parents conducted a war of attrition, Lulu. Divorce was the day peace was declared.'

She knew exactly what he meant. But she wasn't opening up that can of worms. 'Did you stay with your mother?'

'*Sí*, we stayed with her—my sisters and I.' He took another mouthful of wine and then put down the glass. 'Before you ask, *querida*, my mother is too busy with her new husband in Rio de Janeiro to follow my career now.'

Ouch. But he looked too big and tough to really care.

'So your father put you on a horse—but why did you choose to play professionally once you grew up? You must enjoy it.'

'I'm naturally competitive.' He said it the same way someone might say their eye colour was brown. 'I've had the opportunity to play against the world's best. Why pass it up?'

He made it sound so easy. Lulu wondered what he'd say if he knew that some days she couldn't even go outside.

'I admit polo takes up a lot of the time I'd prefer to spend on the ranch, but I think it's worth it if my involvement helps popularise the sport. My ex-wife would probably disagree. Professional sport takes its toll on your personal life.'

'You've been married?'

'This surprises you?'

'It's just you don't look like the marrying kind.'

He cast a speculative look her way. 'What kind *do* I look like?'

'Busy,' she said, a little astonished by her own boldness.

'Not as busy as you imagine, *querida*,' he drawled, with a faint hint of a smile, and Lulu suddenly couldn't hear above the thundering of her pulse.

She hadn't done the prep for this. Being interested in a man, flirting, and all the while wondering what he really thought of her.

Not much, she suspected.

'We have an internationally renowned breeding pro-gramme on the *estancia*,' he went on.

Just when she thought she had the measure of him he got more impressive.

'It's how I got to know Khaled—sourcing Kabardian stock in the Caucasus a few years ago. We got tight.'

Lulu didn't want to talk about Khaled Kitaev. But she realised she'd stumbled into something she'd heard about from the other girls at the cabaret. *Talk to a man about what fascinates him and he'll think you're riveting.*

'So you're the best friend,' he said, immediately con-founding her expectation that he would only want to talk about himself.

'Pardon?'

'Of Gigi. You were flatmates? Was that the set-up?'

Disconcerted that he knew that much about her, Lulu wondered a little uneasily what else Khaled and Gigi had told him. *Nothing*, she decided. *They would have told him nothing.*

'We auditioned for the Bluebirds at the same time,' she explained self-consciously, 'and Gigi was looking for a flat. My parents had arranged one for me in a nice neighbour-hood, so she moved in.'

She glanced up at his dry chuckle.

'What is so funny? You think my parents shouldn't help pay my rent? Didn't *your* parents help you out when you got started in life?'

'My parents just got in the way, frankly, *querida*, and no, they didn't. Relax—I'm not judging.'

Lulu narrowed her eyes on the faint amusement that danced around his wide, disturbingly sensual mouth.

He *was* judging.

She wondered what he'd say if he knew that in addition to living in her beautiful flat, owned by her parents, she was driven everywhere by her mother or her stepfather's driver, and her bills were often met by her parents. It was all part of the highly stratified life put in place for her when she was eighteen, to cushion her anxieties. What would he think of her if he knew she was a walking, talking failure at the game of life?

'So it's just you in the parents-endorsed flat nowadays?'

'Yes,' she said slowly, not sure where this was going.

'Is this why you resent him?'

'Who?'

'Khaled. Gigi's done well for herself.'

A cold feeling pooled in Lulu's belly and a hot feeling flashed up through her. What did he mean? What was he implying?

'I do not resent him. Who told you that? I'm very happy for Gigi.' She was aware she had raised her voice. She never raised her voice. 'And what do you mean, she's done well for herself?'

'He's writing her some pretty big cheques.'

Lulu almost choked. 'Excuse me? Gigi is not marrying Khaled for his *money*!'

'I'm aware of that. I was talking about you.'

'Me?' she spluttered. 'I don't want Khaled's money!' She sucked in a breath. 'Do you mean am I looking for a billionaire of my own?'

'You wouldn't be the first girl.'

CHAPTER SEVEN

THE WEALTH OF cynicism in that comment left Lulu flabbergasted.

'Gigi and I weren't starring in our own version of *How to Marry a Millionaire*, if that's what you mean,' she said, trying to sound as dismissive as he did, but knowing it just came out defensively. 'We're working girls. Gigi's still working. She runs the cabaret. I *work*!'

'You're a woman who by her own admission is supported by her parents.'

Lulu went to deny it, but she couldn't, and nor could she explain her circumstances. It was so frustrating!

'You wouldn't be the first person to want what your friend's got. Maybe I'm wrong…' He shrugged.

Lulu hated him for that shrug, as if it didn't matter one way or the other. It *did* matter when you were the one being unjustly accused!

'You *are* wrong! And Khaled Kitaev has no right to talk about me to you or anyone.'

'He's hardly said a word.' Alejandro leaned back, all wide shoulders and amused speculation. 'I'd worked you out five minutes into that flight, *querida*.'

'You'd *worked me out*?' Lulu could feel herself crumbling inside like a sandcastle.

'Troublemaker.'

'What…?' The word emerged as a whisper.

All of a sudden she was convinced he knew everything about her. Gigi might not have spilled her secrets to Khaled, but somehow this man knew everything.

Did he know she'd never had a boyfriend? Probably. Did he think she was some kind of misfit freak? Probably.

Did he think it was funny, making a joke of spending the night with her?

Her confidence hit an all-time low.

Khaled had taken her best friend away and it had felt as if a large piece of her inhabited land had been annexed by a ruthless invading force because her private world was already so small. How would Alejandro like it if he was forced to question everything about his life, let alone try to start again?

But she couldn't begin to explain it to this man.

And why should she?

'What have I done to make you say those things to me?' she defended herself. 'All you've done is attack me since we met on the plane. I'm not a bad person, but I think you want me to be awful so you can take your bad mood out on me. I thought—I thought when you kissed me—'

Mon Dieu, what was she saying? Lulu scrambled to her feet, belatedly aware that there wasn't anywhere to go.

Her *derrière* hit the bed-end.

'You don't know a thing about me,' she muttered fiercely, turning her back on him, 'and I hope after this weekend we never see each other again.'

Alejandro's first instinct was to turn her in his arms and kiss her. But the last time he'd done that she'd been upset, and he'd just had his conscience slammed up against the wall.

He dated independent, self-assured women every time. Not that it always worked out. His ex-wife had independently propelled herself into other men's beds. But Lulu's words had truth to them.

Everything about her rang true.

Was he still judging other women by his relationship with his ex-wife?

Sometimes it was just about chemistry and timing. Both of which he had here. He was wasting it by twisting this girl around the knot that had been his long-ago short-lived marriage.

He looked at her rigid shoulders and it occurred to him that this was about her only defence with him.

She'd been using it all day.

He felt even more like a bully.

'Forgive me, Lulu, it's been a long day and I've unfairly taken it out on you.'

Lulu hadn't expected an apology, and she hadn't expected him to be on his feet so fast and standing behind her. She didn't want to turn around because she knew her face would be red and her mascara streaky.

More, she didn't want to turn around because she suddenly felt at a loss as to what was expected of her, and she wasn't quite sure what this tension between them was.

'Lulu?'

'I accept your apology,' she said stiffly.

There was an odd little silence, in which Lulu suffered the indignity of knowing he probably just felt sorry for her. Which was about as sexy as porridge.

'We could try to just be civil to one another, do you think?' she said in a small voice.

'Agreed. But I'm finding being civil to you taxing.'

'Why?' She looked up over her shoulder at him.

Why was he looking at her like that? He could probably hear her heart beating. Beating? It was fairly stomping, like the chorus at L'Oiseau Bleu when they were still learning new moves.

'I think you know why.' There was a faint smile on his lips but those eyes were serious, and they promised things she couldn't quite get a clear visual on. She knew only that they would probably put what they'd done in the car into the shade.

It was the unknown, and Lulu knew she was losing traction on all her firmly held beliefs about herself as she began the slide towards it. A little too fast for her...a little too soon. But everything seemed to go fast when she was around this man.

One minute she truly hated him, and the fact that he'd seen her at her most foolish made it worse.

But now she was tempted beyond belief just to step up to him, pull at his shirt and make him kiss her again.

But that wasn't going to happen now.

'I really think I should go to bed,' she said, and told herself she wasn't disappointed when he didn't argue with her.

Alejandro returned from the bathroom freshly shaven, dressed in boxer shorts and with bare feet, to find Lulu in the armchair.

He'd assumed she'd take the bed as her due. Obviously not. Her expression in the lamplight was serious, and there was something about the way she was evidently trying to find a way to make herself comfortable that he recognised in other things she'd done today. It was crazy, but he got the idea she was trying her hardest.

Alejandro looked at the bed, and then at the girl curling herself up in the chair.

Dios.

Deep down he'd known from the start that he'd have to take the chair. She'd never been going to share that bed with him.

She would sleep in the bed and he'd play footman in her fairytale, try to arrange his large frame on that armchair and get what shut-eye he could.

He'd slept in the saddle before.

He could manage a badly sprung armchair in a Scottish farmhouse.

He dumped his toiletries bag, strode over and scooped her up, blanket and all. It was a mistake, because everything suddenly felt incredibly intimate between them. The lovely weight of her, his arms around her... She felt like *his*.

She seemed to know it, because she didn't struggle.

He put her on the bed.

'What are you doing?'

'What does it look like? I'm giving you the bed.'

That was when he realised she'd shed the dressing gown. The blanket was pooled at her hips and Lulu was sitting up in the sexiest lingerie ensemble he'd ever seen.

Or maybe it was just the girl wearing it.

Some kind of vintage cream satin bra and panties trimmed in old-fashioned white lace. Later, when he was thinking with his brain again, he would wonder what it was about that white lace…

But now he was more interested in the soft pale curves poured into it.

She was delicate, and more lovely than anything he'd ever seen.

She'd also seen him. The snug boxers didn't hide much.

She looked fascinated, and it was only when the mattress gave under his weight and he got close enough to feel the warmth of her body that she seemed to realise she was only wearing her underwear. She made a wordless gesture, pulling the blanket towards her, which should have stopped him. He kissed her anyway. But not as he had kissed her in the car, with his blood up and her mouth full of snippy demands and his male ego making him want to prove a point.

His blood was up, all right, but he was looking to prove something else.

That he was good enough for her.

That she could trust him.

That she was *his*.

Tomorrow he would have to share her with everyone at the wedding, but right now she was his, and he realised that this knowledge had been growing from the moment he'd boarded that flight and set eyes on her—before everything else had intervened between them.

She pulled away first, looking at him as if she was every bit as stunned by this turn of events as he was.

'I don't know—' she began, and it was everything he didn't want to hear.

He watched her, waiting.

Lulu could see his amber eyes gleaming beneath those ridiculously long, thick sable lashes, holding all kinds of knowledge she wanted to have. He was one of the most beautiful men she'd ever seen. He made her feel so...*alive*, and he hadn't treated her like glass all day. He'd been absolutely, appallingly awful to her. Just the thought made her body ache a little more for him.

If I don't have sex with him I'll regret it for the rest of my life.

Even before she could think about doing it she was tracing the seam of his parted lips with her fingertip.

He took her hand and gently folded her fingers into a fist. 'You are not sure, *hermosa*.'

'I am.'

'I'm not looking for a relationship, and I think you are.'

Lulu weighed that up. *Non*, she knew how hard relationships were to sustain when you were trapped in your own fears, as she was. She knew she couldn't have that.

'That's not what I want.'

'No?'

Frankly, she didn't know what she wanted—other than what she was having right now. When what she'd been having for far too many years was—nothing.

'I just want something different,' she admitted.

'Different from what?'

Where did she begin? Lulu tried to find words that just wouldn't come. Everything was bound up so tightly inside her—safe and sound, she'd once thought. But she was beginning to feel like a prisoner, locked up along with her anxieties.

Alejandro watched the struggle on her face. She couldn't answer him because he suspected 'different' for her was having sex outside a relationship.

He *always* had sex outside relationships, and there was the salient difference between them.

This was going to kill him.

'You've had an exciting day, a little wine, and you don't know what you want. I don't want to be the man who takes advantage of that.'

As he spoke Lulu found herself being boxed very neatly back into the corner she'd fought so hard to get out of.

Poor invalid Lulu, whose disability always had to be taken into account.

In this case that disability appeared to be her inexperience with men.

'You'll regret this in the morning,' he assured her, as if he knew best. 'And I don't do regrets.'

She remembered what he'd told her about his parents. A war of attrition.

Her parents hadn't been at war—her mother had been a civilian casualty, with her biological father rampaging about like a one-man vigilante mob, until the day Félicienne had got up the courage to leave.

But being brave was something Lulu recognised she'd lost touch with. Somehow she'd allowed her courage to slip away, with the tide of her childhood going out and the sea of her anxieties rushing in.

Seeing the risk to her friendship with Gigi had been the catalyst to make her want to change all that.

It had taken something that big to push her out into the open.

Because of that determination to change she was sitting on this bed tonight, in the middle of the Scottish countryside, with a gorgeous, fascinating man—and he was the man she wanted.

She wasn't just someone he could put in a box labelled *'Defective'*.

He thought she'd be like glue. Sticking to him all weekend because she was so needy.

Well, she was. Needy, that was. Her whole body felt as if it had been stirred up by his kisses and there was an ache low in her pelvis. And although she knew it would go away, and also knew she would eventually fall asleep, when tomorrow came she would have lost her chance to know what it felt like to have this intimate connection with another person.

It was entirely probable, given the circumstances of her life and her condition that she was going to never have this chance again.

I don't do regrets.

Well, neither did she. Before she could chicken out Lulu rose up on her knees. In a single move she wrapped her long legs around him and looked at him fiercely.

Any arguments Alejandro had against this fell away.

He was a man, not a monk. And Lulu was… She was…

Lowering herself onto his lap, draping her slender arms over his shoulders.

'I don't want anything more than tonight,' she said, and Alejandro found himself at her mercy as her eyes dusted over the top of his bare chest as if mesmerised by him. 'Just one night—with you.'

She fitted her mouth to his inexpertly and want shuddered through his body.

He caught her face in his hands, because in a moment there wouldn't be any going back.

'Are you sure?' he made himself ask.

She smiled, a dimple winking alongside her mouth as she bent to kiss him again.

He took over then. His tongue made forays along her lower lip, into her mouth, and Lulu could feel the fire burning inside her. He was stoking it with his mouth.

Not just his mouth.

Lulu could feel him against her most intimate place, much bigger than she'd ever imagined, and hard, and his hands on her satin-covered bottom were bringing her into closer contact.

Lulu couldn't believe how aroused she was getting, or how much she wanted him. His shoulders felt like rock under her hands, but his flesh was hot and springy. He felt so alive, and for the first time she began to understand the scale of what she'd been missing. She'd only been half alive, and that didn't have much to do with sex, although that was a part of it. It was just that the fear had taken so much away from her and she'd let it.

She wasn't letting this go.

She was having this.

It was hers.

He broke their kiss to give her one last warning, 'I'm not looking for anything more than this, Lulu.'

'Bon,' she said breathlessly, ignoring everything but what she was finding with him.

Alejandro slid his hand under the satin and lace bra and found skin much softer than the satin that had encased it, and an astonishingly plump breast for such a slight girl, with a taut little nipple that seemed to furl under his touch.

Madre di Dios.

He rubbed, she whimpered, and he said a word of prayer under his breath, because this was pushing him to the brink and he hadn't even got her naked.

She was breathing in low, shallow pants that were growing more frantic. He could deal with that. He took one taut lace-covered nipple gently between his teeth and sucked. She gave an almost startled cry before he applied the same attention to the other, sliding his hand under the loose leg of her cami-knickers. She felt so soft and wet and warm and he couldn't wait.

He shoved down his boxers.

She knelt on the bed, just looking, her eyes all over him and her expression almost unbearable in its curiosity.

Then she seemed to remember herself, and reached

around to unhook her bra. But he was there before her. He could feel the subtle tension in her body as he carefully peeled down the straps and she held out her arms to let the satin and lace drop away. Her breasts were crested with raspberry-coloured nipples. She actually raised her arms again to cover herself—an act of modesty he recognised but one that didn't make sense. He witnessed a flash of uncertainty in the eyes she lifted to his, but then she set her chin and slowly took her arms away.

Alejandro was convinced he saw that chin jut out a little more.

A tenderness spread through him that somehow wasn't at odds with the lust tearing at his insides.

He ran his hands gently over her shoulders, down her arms, watching the tightening of the buds of her nipples, the way her breasts lifted slightly with the deep shuddering breath she took. She put the palms of her hands to his shoulders, ran them over his arms in a mimicking movement.

'Are we going to have sex?'

It was a crazy question, but it was one he took seriously because it was Lulu asking.

'Only if you want to.'

'Mmm. Yes. I want to.' She put her arms around his neck as he came over her. 'With *you*,' she said, looking into his eyes.

He considered asking who else? There was nobody but them in the room. But her words reminded him of how sweet she was.

Sweet and sexy and not like any other woman he'd ever been with.

'Lulu?'

'Mmm?'

'Just tonight.'

'Stop saying that.' She screwed up her nose.

She was right. This wasn't about her—it was *him*. He

was finding an intensity in this experience and as a man of experience it gave him pause.

But not enough to stop. He couldn't have stopped now if the whole damn farmhouse had collapsed around them.

Besides, she'd assured him she only wanted one night. It was his problem if it felt like something more.

He put his hands to her cami-knickers and drew them down, past her ankles, feasting his eyes on her.

She had surprisingly rounded hips, and tiny dark curls at the apex of her thighs, and her skin had clearly never seen the sun—it was like snow.

Lulu was breathing shallowly. There was something touchingly private about the way she watched him, as if trying to work out what he was thinking.

He could have told her what he was thinking—that he was the luckiest man in Scotland tonight.

Her eyes were big, her mouth wet from their kisses. Her nipples looked like bright jewels against her flushed breasts.

Her arms tightened around his neck.

'I have to tell you something,' she blurted out.

'Tell me.' He tried not to sound too gruff, because right now talking wasn't high on his agenda.

'I watch a lot of old films.'

Alejandro looked at her and wondered if lust could jam up your hearing.

'You watch old films?' he repeated huskily.

She nodded. 'There's a film… Joanne Woodward…Paul Newman. It's very good.' She moistened her lips. 'It's about a girl who tried love once but it didn't stick. So she's given up on men.'

'Good. I'll watch it some time.'

He lowered his mouth to her throat, where the skin was soft as satin. But Lulu kept talking.

'She's a semi-maiden.'

His head came up. He looked into her eyes, surprise registering. 'This is you?'

She nodded, no longer talking, just fixing those big brown eyes on him.

He wasn't completely taken off guard, but there was something about her admitting it and giving him that trustful look that made him feel incredibly protective of her.

It's a gift, he thought. *She's giving you a gift. Her trust.*

It twisted inside him painfully. Because what did he have to give her in return? Cynicism born of a deep understanding. Most people had strings attached to gifts—everyone had a motive. Nothing was ever as it seemed.

'It's worse than being one thing or the other—you're sort of stuck.' She spoke softly, tangling her fingers in the soft whorls of dark hair on his chest. 'I'm so very, very tired of being stuck, Alejandro.'

This he could understand. She wanted a little more experience—he could give it to her.

'Let's see what we can do about it, then,' he said, and slid down the bed, parted her thighs and put his mouth on her.

She gave a squeak of dismay and a husky, *'Non!'* But her body was on board and she melted under his tongue as he had known she would, until he had her twisting, panting, pinned to the mattress as he drew an orgasm from her that had her crying out into the pillow.

He considered telling her that the Baileys assumed they were married and she could yell as loud as she liked, but there was something about her restraint that was highly erotic.

He kept his mouth where she most wanted it until she subsided and then he began again, until the throbbing in his own body became unbearable and all he could concentrate on was being inside her.

He dealt with a condom and joined her on the pillow, kissed her soft, responsive mouth. She was flushed and gratifyingly dazed.

He told himself this was what he did. He worked hard, he rode like a demon, and he gave good sex. Women didn't leave his bed disappointed.

But what he was doing now wasn't a part of that. He didn't stroke a woman's hair and gaze into her eyes, a little mesmerised by the wonder he saw there as she gazed back at him, and he didn't question why he felt so good being with her.

'Are you ready?'

She nodded and kissed him and he moved carefully over her. He nudged her thighs apart with his knee and shifted between them. He was desperate to feel her around him, but as he forged forward into that soft, slick heat there wasn't a lot of room. He was big and she was small and her body wasn't giving way.

Lulu was aware of him nudging at the heart of her and she forgot to breathe. She felt so excited—she wanted this—and yet as she shifted a little and he pressed she knew it wasn't happening. Something was wrong. She froze. Frustration and humiliation joined hands and Lulu just wanted to cry. How typical of her. She couldn't even pass through this fundamental rite of passage without her body conspiring against her.

She was useless—*useless*.

'Lulu.' Alejandro steered her face with his hand so she was looking into his eyes.

'You just need to relax,' he told her, his expression making her think he must be in some degree of pain.

Relax? She didn't want to *relax*. She wanted to have sex. She'd relax when it was over. Which looked like round about now...

Oh...

She felt his index finger gently circle her little bud of nerve-endings and familiar sensation streaked through her—only it was sharper, more intense, with him lodged partway inside her. He kept up the circular motion, sipping at her lips, and Lulu soon found herself caught up in this very nice activity that was coaxing her senses towards that blissful rippling pleasure.

It was only as she softened around him and gave way, and he forged forward inside her, that she realised what he'd done. But it was only a moment's flashing thought, because his thumb continued to stroke her and her body seemed instinctively to take up the dance, drawing him into her.

He was coaxing her with husky words to wrap her legs around him, his hands remarkably gentle as he cupped her hips. It was only then that he began to move, with immense restraint, and she knew he was doing this for her. All for her. Her breath stopped in her chest at the sweetness of it.

His jaw was locked and he was studying her face with an almost unholy intensity.

'Am I hurting you?'

She shook her head.

Lulu tried to think, but all she could do was feel. She began to give herself up to the rhythm they were creating together, and as she arched against him his thrusts lengthened. She could hear herself making small sounds, until she cried out and her entire body seemed to release around him.

His rhythm quickened and he moved inside her with a fierceness he hadn't shown before, finding his own pleasure. Buried inside her, he shuddered heavily and Lulu was overcome by a sense of utter unity with him. She revelled in the sheer animal heat of their bodies wrapped around one another.

Alejandro did his best not to collapse on top of her, and when his back hit the mattress he anchored her to him. He found himself holding her—something he never did. Which was when he became aware that Lulu was hiding her face against his shoulder. He remembered the way he'd dismissed her in the car, the way she'd hidden her face as he'd said those words to her. He hadn't understood anything. He felt a blade of self-revulsion sink deep as he wondered if he'd hurt her.

'*Dulzura...*' he said, bombarded by feelings he was damn sure he didn't recognise or want. He thought he'd made it good for her.

She lifted her head, her eyes bright as stars through those silky black curls. He was a little mesmerised by them and he'd underestimated her. She didn't look unhappy at all.

'That was amazing,' she breathed. 'When can we do it again?'

CHAPTER EIGHT

LULU'S BACK HIT his forearm, between herself and the wall, and she heard something smash on the floor.

Oh, dear.

Only Alejandro was already lifting her, and with her legs locked around his waist he was filling her so absolutely all she could concentrate on was how good it felt.

She wasn't sure if a woman with as little sexual experience as she currently had should be so adventurous right off the bat, but it was hard to argue with something that felt so amazing.

Thump, thump—her shoulder nudged at the framed cross-stitch on the wall.

She whimpered, sliding her mouth against his neck as he built their pleasure.

It was all extraordinarily illuminating, if at times a little overwhelming. Nothing he did failed to bring her pleasure.

Now, as she came apart around him, her legs wound tight around his waist, the little picture fell off the wall and she didn't have it in her to care.

In the aftermath he tumbled her onto the bed and sprawled beside her, breathing heavily.

Lulu lay on her back, feeling the cool air rush over her overheated body, and wondered at this new world opening up to her.

Her body felt replete. Her heart was still pounding, but it was from excitement and exertion, not anxiety, and her mind seemed to be pumped full of happy chemicals, because all she could formulate on her face was a smile.

She turned her head and saw a look of similar satisfaction on Alejandro's face as he looked at her.

She didn't feel one bit shy.

'You must love horses,' she said.

He began to chuckle. 'Where *has* your mind gone?'

She rolled herself onto him and propped herself up on his chest, his chest hair tickling her nipples. He bent one arm behind his head the better to look at her.

'I want to know all about you,' she confessed.

Pillow talk. It wasn't something he usually did, but Alejandro found he really didn't mind.

'I'll tell you about Luna Plateada—the beautiful stallion my great-great-grandfather brought with him to Argentina in the nineteenth century.'

'Yes, please.'

'The legend goes that the bloodline of that horse is still alive in our current champion.'

'It sounds very romantic. Is it true?'

'Practical. The story enhances the price of the stock we've bred from him.'

'Still, it's a good story.'

Lulu smiled at him, all big eyes and hot, shiny cheeks. Perspiration had stuck some of her curls to her temples and cheeks. She looked as if she'd had a wild time. He stroked them back.

'Where did your great-great-grandfather come from?'

'Curiously enough—here in Scotland. His name was Alexander Crozier—he added the "du" after he became a land baron.'

'That sounds like another romantic story.'

'To tell the truth, he was most likely a swindler and a gun-for-hire. I suspect the family legend of him washing up in Buenos Aires and meeting my great-great-grandmother, being hit by a grand passion and winning her by building up a successful ranch has more to do with his ambitions. He probably fought and stole and bribed his way into a position where he could marry into one of Buenos Aires's oldest families.'

'Why do you think that?'

'Let's just say the du Croziers haven't been known for their moderation since. It had to come from somewhere, *novia.*'

'What does that mean—*"novia"*?'

'Sweetheart.'

'Oh.'

She looked adorably flushed, and the urge to stop talking and delve back into her sweet embrace had him shifting beside her.

But he knew she had to be sore, or would be sore come the morning, because he suspected she'd been a little stretchy with the truth.

He'd never been with a virgin, but he would put money on this being her first time and it made him feel responsible for her in some way—or that was as close to his feelings as he wanted to investigate.

'So when did you learn to change a tyre?' He settled back against the headboard, hooking Lulu in against him. 'You don't look like the tyre-changing type.'

'I was ten years old and we got a flat on a motorway. A man stopped and offered to show my mother how to change it. Maman isn't great with practical things, so he showed me instead.'

'Where was your father?'

Lulu had been enjoying herself, but now she felt that private part of her crouching in the corner at his question.

She opted for saying, 'He wasn't in our lives.' Which wasn't exactly the truth. Every day of her young life, even if her father had been absent, his restless, angry presence had always been felt.

'My grandfather was the one who taught me everything I needed to know,' Alejandro shared, and she got the impression he was backing off.

She relaxed against him. She didn't want to think about what was going to separate them in the morning, and besides, she was used to the idea of not involving other people in her problems.

'My father wasn't around much either—before or after the divorce,' Alejandro mused. 'And when he was it was like being hit by a cyclone of presents and energy. He would make a fuss of the girls and drag me out on some wild excursion that usually ended in someone getting hurt.'

Lulu frowned and looked up. 'He *hurt* you?'

'Fernando? No, nothing like that. He just never grew up—it was always a *Boys' Own* adventure with him. Quad bikes...fast cars when I got older. He crashed everything. I was a man at sixteen. He was—well, more of a buddy than a father.'

'What did your mother think about all this?'

'As long as he paid her bills she couldn't have cared less.'

Lulu flinched at his tone, and the urge to touch him, offer comfort, was strong in her. She hadn't had a father figure until she was fourteen, but it sounded as if Alejandro hadn't had either parent. She was so close to her own mother—perhaps too close—that it was difficult to imagine what the lack of one would feel like.

'I was the bone my parents warred with one another for. They lavished me with attention when it suited them, but when it came to the practicalities of life it was my grandfather who offered lessons.'

'But you said your father taught you to ride?'

'He put me on a saddle, smacked the horse's rump and let me fend for myself. As in riding lessons, so in life.'

He spoke without rancour, but Lulu knew enough about hiding those deepest hurts from her last year of therapy to suspect his big, tough exterior hid the boy he'd once been—longing for his father's attention and not getting it. The fact he had taken up polo professionally despite this start said a lot about his feelings for his father. She guessed it wasn't so much about wanting his father's approval as proving himself a better man.

Lulu wisely kept that observation to herself.

Alejandro ruffled the curls at her neck. He was so tactile, and she noticed he had a thing about her hair. It made her feel all squishy inside.

'Don't listen to me, *hermosa*, it's the long day talking.'

But it wasn't, and it made her feel closer to him. She watched him massage the muscle where his thigh joined his knee, stretching out his leg.

'Torn ligament a couple of months ago,' he said, following her gaze and answering her unspoken question. 'I usually patch up a lot faster than this. Must be age and fast living catching up.'

Lulu thought that if he was paying for his sins he must be like Dorian Gray—there had to be a ruined portrait somewhere—because his looks were a hymn to male beauty. He did look tired, though, and speaking about his parents had brought a seriousness into his eyes. She sensed he would not reveal any more.

She could have told him she had no intention of probing any further.

The last thing she wanted to do was rake over the coals of the long-dead bonfire that was her father's time in her life. She was too busy doing battle with spot fires—the anxieties and phobias that were its fall-out—and she knew were waiting for her tomorrow. Because they never went away.

She found her refuge in routine, and she couldn't have that this weekend.

But she was doing okay, and right now she felt better than okay. She felt something new was possible. In this room. On this night.

There hadn't been a panic attack and she knew she wouldn't have one tonight. She had never felt as safe as she did lying in his arms.

She glanced down at herself.

Lulu knew that in the real world she would feel shy,

would cover herself up, but as his gaze slid down her naked body she didn't feel anything but thrilled as his eyes darkened appreciably, and she was glad. She felt free to look at *his* body—so different from her own. He was hard where she was soft, and even her musculature after years of dance had a different, more rounded shape from the powerful planes and dips of his.

She rolled onto her side and studied the definition of his chest with her hand, gliding her fingers down over his abdomen to make sense of the ridging of muscle under the taut pull of his springy olive-toned flesh. Her hand slid down between his hairy thighs to cup him there.

Alejandro hadn't been expecting that from her. His *semimaiden*.

He drew a breath that hissed between his teeth.

She lifted her head. 'Am I hurting you?'

'No…' he choked.

'*Bon*, I'm being as gentle as I can. I know how vulnerable men are in this area.'

He made a sound—half-snort, half-groan. 'No, you don't,' he told her. 'You don't know the half of it.'

'I was once forced to use my knee here. He hit the ground like a sack of potatoes.'

'I bet,' he grunted, before the content of what she'd just said hit him. He lifted his head. 'What do you mean, you were *forced* to?'

'I had a date who got rather pushy about where he thought the evening was going.'

Alejandro examined her face for clues as to what 'pushy' meant. 'How did he react?'

'He howled like a hyena.'

'No, I mean towards *you*.'

She bit her lip. 'After the kneeing he wasn't good for much.'

'He didn't hurt you? Physically?'

She gave an abrupt shake of her head. 'Just gave me a fright. Said some horrible things.'

Her face contorted painfully and it bothered him a great deal.

He ignored all the conditioning he'd had not to offer comfort and found himself sitting up and pulling her into the shelter of his arms. She looked both startled and pleased.

'It was over a year ago—I should be over it,' she mumbled.

'Why should you be over it?'

'I don't know. It shouldn't be that important. He said I was cold and shallow and needed to loosen up. He said—' Lulu broke off to take a deep breath. 'He said some people open a gate to life and let it in, but that I had put a lock on my gate and one day it would be old and rusty and no one would want me.'

'And you believed him?'

'No. Yes. I don't know.'

'How long had you known him?'

'Several weeks. I thought we were friends.'

She pressed her lips together and he waited, because he knew there was more.

'I don't have a lot of friends.'

It was an odd thing for her to say. He couldn't imagine she found it difficult to charm anyone. She was sweet and funny and clearly loyal, going by her friendship with Gigi.

He brushed a finger under her chin and tipped it up so he could look into her eyes. 'He wasn't your friend, Lulu. I've only known you a day and I don't see a cold, shallow person.'

'You don't really know me,' she said in a small voice.

No, he guessed he didn't, and he knew he couldn't make any false promises to her. The only way he could get to know her was to see her again—and that wasn't going to happen after this weekend. He only did weekends. Besides, they'd agreed. One night.

But why? murmured a low, persuasive voice. Why not continue over this weekend? Hell, why not fly out to the Mediterranean with her? Forget the wedding.

He could imagine Lulu's response.

It was part of the reason he was so attracted to her. Any other woman of his acquaintance would fall in with his plans without a squeak.

Lulu wouldn't just squeak—she'd give him a lecture on the duties and etiquette of being best man.

So he kissed her gently and her lips clung a little, as if she were already afraid he was going to get up out of their bed and walk away.

Nothing short of an earthquake was going to drag him away from her tonight. He already knew he wasn't going to be able to fly out on Monday and forget about her.

He also knew something else. He wanted to meet the guy who'd frightened her and knocked her confidence like this. Meet him in a back alley and take his balls off.

'I do know you're beautiful and giving, and when I'm playing in the Buenos Aires Cup next month I'm going to have a hard time concentrating on my game because I'll still be thinking about you.'

It sounded like a line, and it had begun as one, but Alejandro recognised with an odd sense of having finally found something worth having that it was also true.

She smiled at him, and while she looked pleased he could see in the flicker behind those beautiful dark eyes that she'd got the message his words were supposed to convey.

Now he just needed to convince himself.

CHAPTER NINE

THE MORNING AFTER came too soon.

Last night her fears had hidden themselves away, but Lulu was well aware that the longer she lay there in that bed in broad daylight the more easily she'd begin to make them out.

They were all coming back, like crows gathering on a wire, waiting to rush in upon her in a frenzy of flapping wings and pecking beaks.

She knew her parents were going to be waiting for her. They'd take one look at Alejandro and then her mother would take him aside and spill all.

Lulu is special. Lulu needs looking after. Are you sure you're the man for the job?

He'd take one look at the set-up and head in the other direction.

It had happened before. Julien Levolier—dance class, the summer she was almost eighteen. He'd been very keen, until the little 'talk' from her mother. At least he hadn't just hopped on his Vespa and headed off to greener pastures, where the girls were lower maintenance and able to look after themselves. No, he'd taken the time to explain first that he didn't want the hassle. She'd understood. Sort of.

She sat up and let herself appreciate Alejandro's striking physical presence as he stood fully dressed by the window, his hair damp from the shower.

He wouldn't want the hassle. Who would?

She remembered a book she'd once read, in which the hero, after his first night with the heroine, had strewn the bed in red rose petals as the heroine slept, and when she woke up he'd made love to her on those crushed petals.

That wasn't this.

They were virtual strangers and it had to stay that way.

As Lulu considered these facts all the bright, unexpected lights he'd lit inside her began to go out, one by one, until she was just anxiety-ridden Lulu again, naked and suddenly cold, with her options few and regimented.

It was time to pull herself together—and, really, she had to get out of this bed and wash and put on clothes.

Feeling a little shell-shocked, despite her best intentions, she slid out of bed, opting to pull the eiderdown around her, and waddled over to join him at the window.

She didn't know the etiquette in these situations. What people did and didn't do. She couldn't even imagine what it would be like to do this so regularly you had a script for it.

He looked down at her with a smile. 'You need to get dressed, *querida*.'

Her chest felt oddly hollow. 'Alejandro, we need to talk.'

'*Sí*, we do.' He reached out and curved a hand around her neck, pressed a kiss to her astonished mouth.

Lulu melted into him and the eiderdown slid to her feet.

When he released her she was trembling.

'We really need to get a move on, *lucero*,' he smiled.

'Oh, right…yes.' She stepped away from him, trying not to be too embarrassed about her nakedness as she heaved up the eiderdown, but Alejandro fetched her robe and draped it around her instead.

It was such a lovely gesture her heart contracted.

'Alejandro, there's something I need to ask you.'

He looked amused. 'Go ahead.'

'Please don't say anything to anyone at the castle.'

He stilled. 'Say anything?'

'About last night. About us.'

'Why would I say anything?' he asked slowly.

'I don't know. It's just I don't want people to know anything happened. It's private.'

'Yes, it is private.'

She relaxed a little, moistening her suddenly dry lips. 'Then we're on the same page?'

But he was frowning at her. 'What exactly is the problem here?'

Lulu hesitated. She had known deep down it wasn't going to be that easy, but putting it into words made her feel so ineffably sad. 'It's just that we're not going to see each other beyond this weekend.' She looked at anything but him as she said it. 'I don't want people speculating about us and what happened last night.'

She took a peek at him. His expression had relaxed and he touched the underside of her chin to have her meet his eyes. 'What I said last night, Lulu, about it just being one night—I was too hasty. I want to see you again, *hermosa*... can you doubt it?'

Misery rose up to flood her as she realised he was saying the words any other woman would be thrilled by.

But that sense of incredible well-being this man had instilled in her was fast being swamped by panic.

'I can't,' she choked.

'Is there someone else?' His eyes hardened, only to grow more probing as she shook her head.

'You might have changed your mind,' she said softly, averting her eyes, 'but I haven't. I was only looking for last night.'

'Are you sure?' His voice was coaxing, as soft as hers, but about a hundred times deeper and rendered incredibly sexy by his accent.

He didn't believe her, she realised. Probably because any normal woman in her position would fling herself at him. The problem being *she* wasn't normal...

'I can't,' she said, stepping away from him. 'Please don't push, Alejandro.'

He just stood there, watching her, his arms by his side, clearly trying to work her out. Lulu wanted to tell him not to bother. It was really terribly simple—she was too much trouble. He just didn't know that yet.

'You know I will try to change your mind this weekend?' he said, in that beautiful, coaxing voice she needed to block out.

Lulu wanted to stopper his mouth. He had to stop saying these wonderful, thrilling things to her. He had to be made to see she wasn't worth the trouble.

'No, don't do that, Alejandro. Please. I don't want you touching me or acting—acting in any way towards me that might be construed as intimate.'

It had come out all wrong, and she could feel her chest growing tight as a drum as he regarded her in newly tense silence.

'My friends and family are going to be there and they'll only ask questions,' she finished, half under her breath, unable to meet his eyes.

Alejandro discovered he didn't much like being put in the interesting position of being a woman's dirty little secret. Although at least it would explain the stone lodged in his chest.

It was also a reminder to him that the moment you expected something better from a woman was the moment she let you down.

'Please don't be difficult about it,' she said.

It was the bare shoulders, he decided, and the inky curls out of control above them, and her mouth, still swollen from kissing him. That was what was rubbing him up the wrong way.

As soon as they were back in the real world this feeling of possessiveness about her would loosen and fall away. There were plenty of beautiful women out there.

'There is no difficulty, querida. I'm just surprised. You didn't seem like that kind of girl.'

'What kind of girl?' she framed uneasily.

'A woman who was looking for a one-night stand.'

A flash of real hurt glanced across her face, but she merely looked away and didn't deny it, and Alejandro discovered that all his reasonableness in this situation was gone. He wanted to destroy something.

He'd slept with a lot of women as a younger man who just wanted to score a little fame and it hadn't bothered him, because he hadn't been in it for anything other than the sex.

But inexplicably the woman who came to mind was Valentina. He could still see his ex-wife—then his very *current* wife—clutching a sheet to her breasts while her lover, his erstwhile teammate, yanked on clothes so at least he would be dressed when Alejandro knocked him out cold.

In the end he hadn't swung that punch. The guy had done him a favour—had destroyed whatever his parents' crazy marriage had left of his faith in an old-fashioned till-death-do-us-part relationship.

When he'd asked Valentina why she'd married him as they'd signed the divorce papers she'd said simply, 'You're a ten-goal player.'

He looked at Lulu now—at her closed expression, her tightly held mouth.

Was that what this was about?

He remembered how she'd been on the plane: spoilt and demanding and exactly the kind of woman he avoided like the plague. He grimly reflected on the efforts he'd made in the past with Valentina, to satisfy her endless demands for a different life while holding together the livelihoods of everyone on the *estancia*. He'd wasted two years on a woman who was empty inside and had blamed him for it. He wasn't wasting any time here.

He grabbed his bag and shoved a few things inside. 'We need to get a move on,' he repeated calmly.

Lulu watched Alejandro zip up his bag, utterly together, as if something very special *hadn't* just been smashed at their feet.

She guessed he did things like this all the time, whereas

she'd only done it once—now, with him—and it felt so strange and emotional and...*knotty*.

The problem was she couldn't explain the circumstances of her request any more than she'd been able to explain why she hadn't been able to give up her seat on the plane.

But she wanted to.

She opened her mouth to ask if he could think of another way, but what was the point? What was she going to ask of him? That he sneak into her room at night when no one would see? It was too ridiculous, and he'd just laugh at her or—worse—see her as odd and damaged. Better he think she could turn off her feelings like a tap, that last night had meant nothing to her. Because she had to let this go.

One day, when she was better, she'd be able to handle a relationship, but not now. She just wasn't ready yet. Certainly not this weekend.

'You might want to get dressed,' he said.

His expression was cool, but she couldn't blame him for it.

'Our transport's here.'

'Transport?'

She followed his gaze out of the window. And she forgot about feeling about an inch high. She forgot about feeling in the wrong. Forgot everything but the need to hold herself upright by clinging onto the windowsill.

There was a stonking great black helicopter sitting on the hill.

Leaving the bed and breakfast, Alejandro peeled off a couple of large notes to cover the picture they'd knocked off the wall and the broken lamp.

Mrs Bailey gave them a knowing look. 'Not married long, then?' she said, and Lulu wanted to die.

If she'd been a normal sort of girl it would have been funny. This morning would have been the start of something wonderful—but it wasn't.

Instead she felt all knotted up inside, and with a murmur of goodbye and thanks she hurried outside, insisting on carrying her own case.

Perhaps it was foolish to ask him what he'd said to Mrs Bailey, given the mood between them.

'Why would she think we were married?' she asked as he led the way across the gravel to dump their luggage in the car.

According to Alejandro, a staff member from the castle would be driving his car in for him. If she'd needed any indication beyond a *helicopter* that Alejandro occupied a different stratosphere from her, his casual expectation that employees would take care of things settled the issue.

He opened up the boot, grabbed her bag and dropped it in.

Lulu bit her lip to stop herself from mentioning the crystal...

'I didn't say anything, *querida*, if that's your question. I think it must have been all the noise you were making.'

With that he flashed her a challenging look, locked up the car and led the way towards their behemoth transport.

It was a short and thankfully uneventful flight before Dunlosie Castle came into view.

The place Lulu had been so anxious to reach yesterday was now the last place she wanted to be. All she wanted to do was lick her wounds in private. But at the same time she was so frustrated with herself she could scream.

She gazed out over the view of the nineteenth-century castle built around the original twelfth-century ruin on the shores of a loch, still smarting from his words.

He might be angry with her, but he didn't have to make her feel self-conscious about making the wrong sounds during sex. She couldn't help the sounds she made. Any more than she could help it that she was not going any further with him.

'As far as wedding gifts go,' he drawled, 'it's a jaw-dropper.'

She whipped her head around, because it was the first thing Alejandro had said to her since they'd boarded.

'What wedding gift?'

'Khaled gave Gigi the deeds to the castle last night.'

Lulu bit her lip and for an awful moment wondered if her best friend was going to up sticks and move here.

'Want one?'

What? Lulu didn't know how to answer that. Of course she didn't. But it was impossible to read him, so she wasn't sure if he was having a go at her again.

Well, he could believe what he liked. About her being jealous...about her wanting the things Gigi had. Even if she did.

She did.

She dragged her eyes off his hard expression.

Only they weren't the things he *thought* mattered to her.

How on earth had they been as intimate as they had been last night and yet they still seemed to know nothing but superficialities about one another?

Because you want it that way, Lulu. It's more comfortable for you.

She pushed that voice away. She couldn't help her condition.

Isn't it convenient, though, that it's there? You don't have to delve a little deeper and look at what's really going on here.

Lulu tensed, and that horribly familiar twisted feeling started up in her belly. By the time they landed the feeling was getting worse by the second.

It wasn't helped when, as they disembarked, Lulu's attention was caught by the woman who was coming towards the helipad across the lawn. The one person she really didn't want to see right now.

In her distress she almost lost her balance, but Alejandro had her and for a moment didn't seem about to let her go.

She looked up in alarm.

He had to let her go!

All she could see was the uninhibited things they'd done together last night.

And he was about to meet her mother!

Félicienne would make a fuss, and then Alejandro would know the truth about her, and she just couldn't bear that.

'Take your hands off me,' she hissed, and after a long look he let her go. She turned away from the expression on his face because it made her feel like a horrible person.

She wasn't horrible—she was just having a very bad day.

Pulling herself together, Lulu took off across the lawn, her attention fixed on her mother, who had that frantic look on her face—as if her only daughter had been off trekking down the Amazon, not taking a short flight from Paris to Edinburgh and staying overnight in a nearby village.

She could imagine Alejandro behind her, looking big and rugged and exactly the kind of man her mother would shrink from. She really, *really* didn't want them to meet, and the faster she moved the better chance she had of keeping her two worlds from colliding in the worst possible way.

Only she was shaking so hard she thought she was going to fall down.

She stumbled.

'Lulu?' Alejandro was at her elbow to steady her, but she pulled away as if he'd touched her inappropriately.

'I told you to leave me alone!' she cried, her distress making her shrill. 'What don't you understand about that? I don't *want* you!'

Alejandro's big body tensed but he let her go. 'Fine,' he said simply.

Which was when she finally lost control of her legs, wobbled and collapsed headlong in a heap in the grass.

CHAPTER TEN

'SHE'S FAKING IT,' Khaled said dismissively, pouring them both a couple of fingers of whisky.

Alejandro had been telling himself exactly the same thing, but hearing it coming from another man pulled an aggressive response out of him.

'You didn't see her,' he said grimly. 'Something's wrong.'

Khaled gave him a long look. 'Good trip, then?'

Alejandro knew he should put it aside. He didn't want to discuss Lulu and it had nothing to do with her plea for discretion. He felt protective of her, and he didn't do protective. It left you open to manipulation, and the last time that had happened he'd almost lost the *estancia*.

No, he was here to enjoy the weekend. To watch his good friend make official the relationship that had intrigued Paris since the cabaret Khaled had won in a card game had hit the headlines and a red-haired showgirl had come into his life.

Alejandro had been at that game. He might have won that hand. He might have met that showgirl. But the one who swam to mind had glossy black curls and big brown eyes and the sweetest raspberry-tipped breasts.

He rubbed at his temples. It wasn't just Lulu's body that was playing havoc with his thoughts.

No, what really bothered him was the way she had felt, flopped in his arms as he carried her inside. She'd behaved so erratically this morning...as if she'd been struggling with something he hadn't been able to see and then it had seemed to overwhelm her.

When her mother had intervened he'd felt aggravatingly powerless, and for a man who made sure he called the shots it had been an unsettling position to be in. But what right did he have to interfere? Why in the hell would he *want* to?

Lulu had made herself very clear on the subject. Besides, he knew well enough what happened when you went riding to a woman's rescue.

The tension in him deepened.

'So why aren't you down there, mopping her brow?'

Khaled appeared to be enjoying this, and Alejandro found himself wanting to hit something. Probably not a good idea if it was the groom, a day before the wedding.

'Her mother appears to have it covered.'

'Probably a good thing. Gigi wouldn't be happy with you making a move on her friend.'

Alejandro straightened up. 'Why's that?'

'Lulu's special.' Khaled sipped his whisky, looking at home in this draughty pile of stone.

'Special?' Alejandro discovered his pulse was beating hard in his ears.

'Sheltered, wrapped in cotton wool by her parents, not much idea of the real world. I doubt she's ever had a boyfriend.'

The glass he held dropped through his fingers and smashed on the stone.

Khaled raised an eyebrow. 'That answers *that* question. Man, you'd better hope Gigi doesn't find out.'

'He scooped you up and carried you inside…it was so romantic,' enthused Trixie. 'It was like something out of *Gone with the Wind*—you know, when Rhett carries Scarlett up those stairs.'

'To force himself on her,' scoffed Susie. 'Yes, really romantic.'

'Rubbish—no one forced himself on Scarlett,' Trixie shot back. 'Remember the smile she had on her face the next morning?'

Lulu wanted to die. She didn't remember Alejandro carrying her inside. She only knew where she was now, as her mother's face swam into view, and then she heard Gigi making everyone clear the room.

Fortunately that meant only Gigi heard her mother begin to cross-examine her about taking her sedatives and why she'd thought she was capable of flying alone in the first place.

The urge to scream at her mother was strong, held back by Gigi's eyes telegraphing rescue over Félicienne's narrow shoulder, and then her suggestion that the older woman might organise some tea while she and Lulu talked.

Gigi had always been able to manage her mother.

'You'll feel better when you've had a cup of tea,' Gigi said gently, for Félicienne's benefit.

The moment the door closed Lulu struggled upright.

'I'm sorry, Gigi. I'll do better.'

'What are you talking about?' Gigi took her hands. 'You're doing fine.'

'I'm supposed to be making this the best weekend of your life, and so far all I've done is cause mayhem!'

'Lu, tomorrow's going to be perfect, whatever happens. It's all good. Calm down.'

'It's your *wedding* day.'

'We said "I do" in a registry office almost six months ago. This is the cherry on top. Nothing is going to ruin this wedding.'

Gigi looked and sounded so confident it was hard not to believe her. Responsibility for running the cabaret and her life with Khaled had given her a new maturity and calm Lulu could only envy.

It just made her feel more of a mess. It threw the events of this morning into relief and brought home to her just how badly she'd handled herself.

'So what's going on with Alejandro?'

'Nothing.' She swallowed.

'He was pretty concerned, Lu, when you hit the grass.'

'Was he?' She hated the way her heart lifted. 'We didn't get on at all,' she lied. 'He made me change a car tyre.'

'He what?'

'The tyre that blew out on our car—I changed it.'

Gigi was grinning at her. 'So you showed him your skills? Nice, Lu.'

Lulu thought of what else she'd shown him and she could feel all the colour in her body meeting in her cheeks.

She was aware of Gigi watching her closely.

'So last night—?'

'We stayed in a bed and breakfast just out of town,' Lulu supplied, studying her sleeve.

'And?'

'It was surprisingly comfortable.'

'Lulu, what happened last night?'

I seduced him.

'Last night's over now,' she said briskly. 'I want to talk about the wedding.'

'Oh. My. God…' Gigi breathed. 'You *slept* with him.'

'No.' She bit her lip. 'Maybe. A little bit.'

'Lulu!'

'Stop making such a big deal of it. I *am* over twenty-one.'

'So what happens after this weekend? Are you together now?' It was impossible to miss Gigi's hopeful interest.

'No, it was just one night.' Lulu couldn't meet her best friend's eyes as she said it.

'One night? Lulu, it was your first time.'

'No, it wasn't,' she mumbled. 'I told you—I lost my virginity to Julien Levolier from dance class when we were both eighteen.'

She raised her eyes to find Gigi looking so doubtful she almost confessed the truth—she'd made it up to get the other girls off her back.

'I didn't believe you,' Gigi admitted. 'I thought you'd made it up.'

'Honestly.' Lulu fiddled with her sleeve. 'I *can* be sexually liberated, Gigi.'

'No, you can't—well, you haven't been until now. Why aren't you seeing him again?'

'It's not that sort of thing.'

Gigi's eyes narrowed. 'Is that what he said?'

'No, it's what we decided together.' Of course that wasn't strictly true either, but the truth stuck in her throat—*I was a coward... I insulted his pride... I messed up.*

Gigi was quiet for a moment. 'You don't want Alejandro to know about your panic attacks,' she said quietly.

Lulu opened her mouth to deny it, but what was the point? Gigi knew her too well. 'It's not his business.' She looked her best friend in the eye, willing her to disagree. 'It's not anyone's business but my own.'

Gigi squeezed her shoulder but was smart enough not to push. A little part of Lulu wished she would push.

Wedding talk eased them away from the difficult subject, but at length Lulu couldn't help circling back in on the thing that mattered most to her and asked, 'Did Alejandro say anything earlier? When I passed out?'

'He was pretty concerned, Lu. But Félicienne told him you had a little medical condition.'

'What?' Could it get any worse?

'You're going to have to tell him something.'

No. No, she wouldn't be telling him anything.

The other bridesmaids filled her in as they dressed for the wedding rehearsal dinner.

'He's like a polo *god*,' explained Susie. 'He's won everything, and people pay a mint to watch him play.'

'I couldn't believe it when I saw him getting out of that helicopter,' added Trixie, fanning herself. 'I knew he was coming, but in the flesh he's just so much *more*.'

'What about that footage of him taking a string of ponies into the surf on that Patagonian beach last year?' said

Susie. 'No shirt. Just muscle and horseflesh. It melted the internet.'

There was a hum of appreciation which left Lulu feeling cross.

'How would you feel if someone took a picture of you at the beach and put it on the internet so that desperate men could salivate all over it?' she grumbled.

Susie laughed. 'It's just publicity, Lu, and he'll be used to it…what with his father and all.'

'His father?'

'Ferdinand du Crozier—international playboy. He broke up a famous Hollywood actress's marriage years ago and then he was seen a week later cruising the Med with her children's nanny! All while he was married to Alejandro's mother.'

'Any publicity is good publicity,' dismissed Adele. 'Anyway, nowadays Alejandro is virtually a brand. You can buy luggage with his polo team's imprimatur on it. How do you think he bought himself a state-of-the-art helicopter?'

Lulu had assumed it was leased. It appeared she'd assumed a lot of things. She was still trying to wade through all this information and work out if it was Alejandro or his father who had seduced the nanny…

'Booooring!' sang out Susie from the bathroom. 'Who cares about what he's worth? He's a sexual athlete. I would have nailed him.'

A sexual *what*? Lulu's chest hollowed.

'Women throw themselves at him. I know he's gorgeous, but it's demeaning, don't you think?' said Trixie. 'Pushing yourself on a man…him knowing it's because he's famous?'

The other girls' gossip, which had battered her a moment before, now sent her stomach cold.

Dieu, was that how he viewed last night? Some desperate woman chasing him because he was famous?

'He dates the most beautiful women in the world—he wouldn't be interested in any of us.' Trixie sighed.

'He does have a reputation for slaying some pretty impressive names,' agreed Adele. 'His last girlfriend was the daughter of a high-profile British politician—she worked for the UN.'

The UN?

Trixie slipped an arm through Lulu's. 'You weren't feeling too crash-hot when you got here, were you, darl? How are you feeling now?'

'Better.' The other two bridesmaids were looking at her expectantly. 'I'm getting over a virus,' she trotted out, feeling wretched.

'Something happened,' she heard Trixie say as she went into the next room to change.

'Nothing happened,' came back Susie's response. 'We're talking about *Lulu*.'

Everything happened, Lulu thought, hanging her head, only it wouldn't happen again.

Dressed an hour later, with her hair drawn up in an Edwardian-style bandeau—the dress code for today was *Downton Abbey*—Lulu walked the vast corridors, went down the stairs and into the dining room, where they would be assembling in half an hour.

With each step she compounded her doubts. She'd barely kept it together after her disastrous arrival. Stumbling out of the helicopter, making it a few paces and then crumpling like cellophane.

If Alejandro hadn't already wiped his hands of her he wouldn't be looking her up after this.

What was worse was that she couldn't talk to Gigi about any of it.

Tomorrow was the Big Day.

It had to be perfect. It had to be all about the bride.

And what had she done on arrival? Set the tone for the whole weekend with her mother running to her rescue.

She understood why her *maman* was so protective. After leaning on her when she was at a young age, now Félicienne only wanted her to have the best of everything and to be safe. But her cossetting wasn't helping her overcome her anxiety. It only added to it.

And this morning she'd been so scared of what her parents might say or do, and of how Alejandro would react. So she'd insulted him and wrecked any chances of them being together at all this weekend, and then she'd leaned on Gigi and used her to handle her mother.

Nothing had changed. And nothing would ever change if she didn't face her fears.

She'd come here this weekend determined to change her life and she'd been doing so well. Last night she had moved past her fear and it had been wonderful. And yet this morning she'd fallen back into the old patterns.

Lulu pulled out the chair she'd be seated in this evening and sank onto it, resting her head in her hands. What was she going to do?

Her phone began to play its jaunty tune and, stirred from her painful thoughts, Lulu reached into her purse.

It was just a text from her mother, telling her she'd come to her room and seen she wasn't there, and she wanted to know where she was and if she was all right.

Lulu was tempted to throw the phone across the room when she sensed movement behind her.

A group of men were passing the dining room and Lulu's ears pricked up. She recognised those rich, low tones. Holding on tight to the phone she'd wanted to hurl, she edged towards the doorway and watched Alejandro, magnificent in formal evening attire that was tailored to his powerful body like a glove, as he and Khaled and several other men she didn't know vanished into the billiards room.

He looked nothing like the laid-back guy who had lowered his aviators to meet her gaze at the airport yesterday, or the generous, tender lover who had made her body known to her in ways she'd never even suspected existed last night.

Instead he looked polished, powerful and predatory. The kind of man she would have shuffled to the back of the chorus line to avoid eye contact with back in Paris, because she could never have handled him.

There was surely something dangerous about physical intimacy. It had done something to her usual reserve, shaken everything she believed in, and Lulu found herself following him down the corridor.

But she could hardly follow him into the billiards room. What would she say?

Besides, he was probably already learning from Khaled what a mess she was—all the things she couldn't do—and now he wouldn't look at her as if she fascinated him. He would look at her and see someone who was too much work.

That was when Lulu became aware that she was standing in a dark corridor just feeling sorry for herself.

If anyone had found her there how stupid she would have looked.

Sad little Lulu, scared of her own shadow and too damn gutless—as Susie would put it—to grab the things she wanted most in life. Willing to let a man think she was a shallow narcissist in order to cover up how truly pathetic her life was in truth.

Whatever had passed between them she owed him an apology—and if she couldn't tell him all of the truth, at least she could tell him *something*, so he wouldn't go away thinking the worst of her.

It was easier said than done.

An hour later she watched him making the rounds of the guests, so tall and broad-shouldered, with his tousled chestnut hair tamed and a slow half-smile making him look as if he knew a secret nobody else did. She couldn't seem to get close enough to him to engineer a casual bumping of elbows, and he had made no move to approach her at all since he entered the room.

She doubted he'd even looked her way. She, on the other hand, couldn't take her eyes off him.

Lulu fought off the memories but suddenly they were all she had moving through her mind, drawing her attention to the gentle ache that lingered from last night's unfamiliar activities.

It was her own fault they weren't together now. She'd asked for this.

A braver woman would just go up to him, draw him aside and discreetly make her apology. But all her bravery from earlier seemed to have fled in the face of all these people and his apparent indifference, and now she just felt as if the room was closing in on her.

Her skin was clammy, her hands were shaking, and to make matters worse her mother kept advancing on her with an agonised expression barely hidden behind her practised social ease.

Lulu had evaded her for some time now, by circulating like a good little bridesmaid among the wedding party members and their partners, clutching a glass of champagne she actually hadn't touched. By the time they went into dinner she was a jangled mass of nerves.

She dared another flickering glance Alejandro's way as Gigi rose to announce, just when they were on their third course, that there would be games this weekend.

Amidst the laughter and commentary she was startled when his attention came her way. It was a casual movement. His gaze just seemed to drift over her, and his eyes, when she looked at them, were dark in the candlelight.

For a fanciful moment she was reminded of a leopard, hanging deceptively lazily in the branches of a tree, every muscle in its superb killer's body seemingly at rest. But those eyes…those eyes held pure predatory intent.

Lulu watched Susie touch his arm, leaning across in all

her sexy glory and saying something that made him smile, displaying the easy charm of a man for whom attractive women did and said anything to claim his attention.

It was somewhat disconcerting to see evidence of what she knew would happen. He would move on.

Not with Susie, nor even this weekend, but with someone. And he would forget about her.

But it had never occurred to her she would have to watch other women come on to him this weekend.

The guests were handing a hat down the table, and she was so enmeshed in her thoughts she didn't pay much attention. She obediently shoved her hand in and took out a small folded piece of paper, ignoring its contents as she glared daggers at Susie across the table.

'There are four teams,' Gigi announced, 'and you'll only find the prize if you solve the clues for your team in consecutive order. There's a time limit so—go!'

Chairs scraped…couples paired off. People were taking their champagne with them. There was laughter, a shriek as a girl was swept up into her companion's arms. Lulu's heart sank. It was going to be *that* sort of game.

She could see her mother, saying something to her stepfather and another older woman, and then Félicienne began scanning the room. In a moment Lulu knew she was going to be dragged off with the middle-aged party, as if she were thirteen and not twenty-three.

She watched Susie grab a bottle and was wondering who would be drinking that with her when a hand closed around her elbow.

'Come on,' said a darkly familiar voice in her ear. 'We can win this.'

Alejandro used his big body to block the crowd and the view of her mother as he pushed her into the stream of guests heading out into the draughty hall.

'But you're purple and I'm pink,' she said, her heart hammering, knowing that wasn't the point.

He snatched the paper easily from her fingers and tore it up, along with his own, tossing it like confetti over his shoulder.

'Problem solved—now we're on the same team.'

Lulu felt hope soar up inside her and explode in a cascading spin of light like a Catherine wheel.

He kept her moving, guiding her up the stairs, the warmth of his body bracketing hers. Lulu had never felt so relieved in her life.

She couldn't help looking up at him, to make sure he was with her and it wasn't just some elaborate sensory hallucination she was having.

He pushed her ahead of him into the book-muffled quiet of what appeared to be the library and closed the doors behind them with finality.

Lulu knew he hadn't brought her here for the reason other couples were vanishing into dark corners of the castle.

This was her opportunity to apologise. Even if she couldn't explain.

'Alejandro—'

He advanced on her and Lulu found herself edging backwards, towards an old nineteenth-century desk. A thrill darted through her.

Maybe he had brought her here for exactly that reason.

'If you still want me to be your dirty little secret I'll do it,' he said, with that same ruthless focus that had so unnerved her earlier.

Embarrassingly, she experienced a liquid pull low in her pelvis and she took another backward step.

'No,' she muttered, 'it's not like that.'

'Then how is it, Lulu?'

'All I want is for you to not want me any more.'

Her bottom hit the edge of the desk. She would probably be struck down for her lies, because she did want him to want her—she wanted it desperately.

He leaned in, hot and male and crowding her. It was

highly exciting. The most exciting thing ever to happen to her apart from last night.

'Then we've got a problem.'

She wanted to tell him that, frankly, this wasn't feeling like a problem just at that moment.

'I still want you.'

Lulu made an involuntary sound, embarrassingly a little like a whimper.

His hips nudged hers and she registered that he was powerfully aroused.

'What's the problem?' he growled. 'Worried your mother's going to find out?'

Yes. Yes, she was.

'Certainly not. I'm a grown woman.'

'Then behave like one.'

And there was the challenge—and also the escape route. Because making love he wouldn't be asking questions, and she'd have this—one more time, just one. So many lonely nights stretched ahead for her. She'd have this and she'd apologise and then everything would go back to normal. Well, *her* normal.

In frustration she reached out and pulled on his shirt. A pearl button popped, and then another. Impatiently she ripped his shirt open with both hands, because sometimes life was complicated enough not to have to deal with buttons.

The sound was almost shocking.

He seemed to like the trashing of his expensive clothes, though, because in answer he lifted her back onto the desk, rucking her skirt up her thighs.

Alejandro ran his palms over them, determined not to rush this. They were as long and smooth as he remembered, and he'd been doing a *lot* of remembering. The scent of her stirred his senses: violets and woman.

She wore more cream satin—this time with shell-pink inserts falling to the tops of her thighs, where her stockings were clipped by tiny blue suspenders. Alejandro hadn't known he had a thing for old-time lingerie, but it definitely did something for him—or the woman wearing it did. He smiled at her as he slid his fingers under the satin to stroke her, because it brought back memories, and the old-fashioned cut made her easily accessible to his hand.

Lulu's chest rose and fell rapidly, a gasp spilling from her lips.

His mouth found hers and he bit down gently on her lower lip, feeling her shudder against him.

He caught her hips in his hands and angled her so that he was cradled against her pelvis. She made a little sound of helpless need and began rocking against him.

He lifted his hands to her beautiful hair but she shook her head.

'No, no—keep your hands below my shoulders,' she muttered. She was unbuckling him with shaking hands.

'Sí.' Although right now she could ask for her own damn castle and he'd promise it to her. 'Why?'

She paused to look up and said, quite seriously, 'I don't want to wreck my hair.'

Her hair? It did seem to be some sort of elaborate confection. Alejandro swallowed the laughter moving through him. It was astonishing how much lighter he felt when he was with her. Freer.

'I'm spending the night with Gigi and the other girls. I don't want them to know.'

Her expression crumpled as she appeared to realise the import of what she'd said.

Again with the secrecy, but he didn't care. All he wanted was to feel her against him again.

They could deal with this secrecy stuff later.

He unclipped her suspenders and slid her pretty vintage panties down over her ankles. He stuffed them in his back pocket and then unbuttoned himself—fast.

He slid his hand up her impossibly silken inner thigh

and found her wet and wanting, and so soft he almost disgraced himself there and then. His damn hand was shaking, and he realised Lulu was trembling too. She wanted him just as badly as he wanted her.

The musky scent of sex mingled with the aroma of old books, the leather furnishings and the subtle apricot fragrance of Lulu's hair which he wasn't supposed to touch. He remembered to grab a condom from his wallet and don it before he positioned himself against her and thrust.

Lulu bit his shoulder, and the next sound to come from her was muffled, but he knew he was finding the spot she loved because she clung to him.

'You feel like hot silk,' he told her with a groan as her long legs wrapped around him for greater purchase. 'Lulu, you're so beautiful…this is all I've been able to think about.'

'Me too.'

He arched her over the desk and pinned her hands above her head as he thrust inside her. With each movement he gazed deeply into her eyes, looking for the wonder he'd seen in her last night, and there it was, flashing like the Northern Lights.

He knew he wasn't going to last, and when he felt her contract around him he buried himself deep and followed her to oblivion.

Lulu clung to him weakly as he sat her up, and he realised every ounce of resentment and anger he had felt towards her today had evaporated completely.

He felt nothing but a deep satisfaction.

She was his.

Her gaze remained unfocussed, and he felt a surge of male pride that he could do this to her.

It had to be pride, because if it was anything else he was in trouble.

'Did I make too much noise this time?' She was serious.

Alejandro remembered what he'd said to her in anger and his conscience did something unfamiliar. It kicked.

'I love the sounds you make,' he said huskily, gently stroking the curve of her cheek.

A little smile trembled at the corners of her mouth. It was the sweetest thing.

He cleared his throat. 'How about we go on seeing one another?'

'You mean for this weekend?'

He'd never known a girl so keen to finish something before it even began. In the past she would have been exactly his type of woman. But he didn't want that this time. He wanted more.

'Let's play it by ear.' He knew her well enough now not to push her. 'I know I'm not ready to give this up just yet...' He swiped her lower lip gently with his thumb. 'That was incredible.'

'I want to,' she began, 'but—'

'Lulu,' he interrupted gently, 'stop making something simple complicated.'

Ouf! Lulu's heart sank. If only it *was* simple.

Seen from his point of view, she knew she was behaving absurdly. But the more time she spent with him the higher the likelihood he would work her out. Find out what a little freak she really was.

Still, it was only forty-eight hours...she'd just have to keep him away from her mother.

'Is that a yes?'

Alejandro watched Lulu's pensive expression grow softer and felt that unfamiliar kick to his chest. What *was* it about this girl that undid all his certainties?

'Oui,' she said, and Alejandro was astonished at the feeling that seized him—it was like scoring a goal under pressure.

Then she turned her head, as if listening for something, and froze. It took him another moment to recognise that there were voices coming down the hall.

Lulu began pulling up her bodice, covering those plump

raspberry-tipped breasts he loved, and she looked so adorably dishevelled he knew he had no intention of letting her
spend the night with a gaggle of girls.

She would spend every night of this weekend with *him*.

Alejandro was about to tell her he'd locked the door
when she pressed her hand to his mouth and with a sweet
look whispered, 'I'm so glad you'll be partnering me at the
wedding. I'll see you tomorrow.'

And with those frustrating words she slipped away.

Partnering her at the wedding?

He briefly shut his eyes. *Idiota!* This had just got complicated.

He was about to go after her—only when he looked
down to deal with the condom time stood still for the second occasion on that day.

Thoughts about negotiating with Lulu over the reality
that he already *had* a date for the wedding—someone who
was arriving tomorrow morning—evaporated.

He had a bigger problem.

It had split. The latex had split.

CHAPTER ELEVEN

As LULU DRESSED for the big day it hit her that she actually had a date for the wedding.

She hadn't thought she minded being the only bridesmaid without a partner. Clearly deep down she did.

But it was more than that. She'd taken a big step forward, and the fact that she'd come this far with Alejandro was simply astonishing to her.

Lulu did a pirouette in the middle of her room, with its tester bed and its wall hangings—staying here was definitely like living in a National Trust property.

She had a date. She had a date. Alejandro was her date!

Lulu clapped her hands together, aware that she was behaving as if she were seventeen again, and going to a concert with a boy she liked. Which had, of course, been her last real date—if you didn't count the circumspect dinners she'd had with the odd man over the years.

That last real romantic experience had fallen in a heap when she'd had a panic attack in the crowd and thought she was going to suffocate. At the time it had been terrifying. But, looking back, she remembered how light-hearted she'd been before the incident, and full of hope. She had her hope back this morning and she was proud of herself for getting this far.

Which got her thinking about how it would be if she was brave enough to take this further.

If she got up the courage to tell Alejandro the truth about herself.

He wasn't a boy—he was a grown man. Surely he could handle it?

If they went forward he would have to know. She couldn't hide it for ever.

He must want this with her—to have put up with everything and still be so passionate and determined to track her down last night.

She was feeling more certain and her heart was light as she laughed with the other girls on the steps of the chapel and then floated up the aisle, her eyes seeking out Alejandro, resplendent in a morning suit beside the groom.

Gregory Peck, eat your heart out.

All the attention in the chapel had turned to the bride, behind her, but he was still looking at her and Lulu knew she'd made the right decision to tell him.

But this was Gigi's day. She would wait until tomorrow.

There was no chance for conversation anyway. The wedding party was swept up in the taking of photographs, but Lulu was aware of him all the time. His expression was resolute. She beamed at him as they stood together beside the bride and groom.

Then, as they were released from their duties by the photographer, Lulu kissed Gigi and bravely began to make her way over to join Alejandro. She knew her actions wouldn't go unnoticed.

But he was already moving off through the crowd of guests waiting for them on the lawn, and as she watched a bright blonde girl in a beautiful yellow dress broke through and made her way over to him.

She held out her hand and he took it. The young woman was chattering to him and he had his head bent, clearly intent on everything she had to say.

'Who's that woman with Alejandro?' she asked Adele, in a voice that sounded remarkably normal, considering.

'His date,' said Adele, and then turned back to her escort.

And with that Lulu's tremulous, sweet world of possibility shattered into pieces around her.

* * *

For the first time in her life Lulu pictured herself making a scene. She would jump to her feet and upend the table, sending crystal and dishes and all the good wine and champagne flying.

She could actually feel the adrenalin pouring into her limbs in preparation. But she wouldn't do it. She wouldn't make a scene on Gigi's wedding day. She would sit here, with her stepfather to her right and her mother leaning across him to ask if she was all right, and pretend nothing was the matter.

She was an expert in pretending nothing was the matter.

So what if she'd had sex with someone else's boyfriend? It happened. She wasn't to blame. *Was* she to blame?

Lulu could feel herself withdrawing back into her shell. She'd heard the other girls talking about men they'd slept with who'd never called, or who had wives and girlfriends they'd conveniently forgotten about in the heat of the moment. She'd heard their painful stories and, yes, she'd felt a tiny bit superior, thinking that would never happen to her. But the first time she stepped out of her comfort zone—*bang.* Alejandro had taken her down like a big game hunter.

A normal woman would have known. Somehow. There must have been signs. But her social life was absurdly confined. She didn't have the experience to be able to tell. She'd believed everything he'd said to her. What kind of moron did that make her?

All her self-doubt was filling her up again. Making her feel useless. Pathetic.

But she caught herself on that downward slope to self-hatred.

No, not pathetic. Stop beating up on yourself. You've done really well this weekend. You've flown in on your own, you've been an indispensable bridesmaid, and come Monday you'll be back in Paris to start your new course at college and life will open up for you.

Only life was currently staring her in the face in the person of his date—one of those blindingly white-toothed, shiny-haired American girls—a girl who clearly hadn't worked out how two-faced her boyfriend was.

It was a relief when the speeches started. As much as she tried to drown him out, Alejandro acquitted himself spectacularly. He had the one hundred and fifty guests in the palm of his hand. His legendary charm was on display. Gigi was laughing so much she had tears running down her cheeks, and despite everything going on in her own life Lulu felt glad it was all working out so beautifully for her best friend.

Not so much for her, though. Because as Alejandro took his seat, with a significant glance her way she chose to ignore, she remembered what she had forgotten in all the inner turmoil. The wedding waltz.

As Khaled and Gigi took to the floor horror settled like stone in her belly.

Was Alejandro going to dance with that other woman?

Who would *she* dance with?

Lulu bent her head. The only wallflower maid of honour in the history of wedding receptions.

She'd possibly hit a new nadir.

But perhaps it was for the best. Lulu wasn't even sure she was going to be able to stand up.

'Lulu.'

Alejandro was beside her, extending his hand. The same hand he'd slipped between her inner thighs.

She wanted to slap it. She also wanted to grab hold of it like a lifeline.

She gripped him. Dug her nails in a little.

The moment his arm came around her his hand settled at her waist. With his other hand in hers she felt all the fury and hurt and confusion rise up inside her, making it impossible for her to speak.

Alejandro had none of those problems. 'I know you're

angry with me, Lulu, but we need to talk in private. In the library.'

Oh, yes, she could just imagine. He'd probably try to ruck her skirts up again… No—nothing doing!

She suddenly wanted to cry. Very much.

'Anything you have to say to me you can say here.' Thank God her voice only shook slightly. 'We won't be in private together ever again.'

His hand tightened at her waist and Lulu wondered, crazily, if he might pick her up and throw her over his shoulder and haul her out of there. But why would he do that? She wasn't Gigi. She wasn't intrinsically loveable. Her limitations meant she wasn't going to have a normal life.

'The condom broke.'

For a moment Lulu was too busy swimming in her self-pity to pay much attention, and when she did she didn't have a clue why he was saying this to *her*. Why had he said 'condom' in the middle of the wedding waltz?

The. Condom. Broke.

The words shot across her mind as if they'd been lit up in fireworks against a night sky.

Understanding scalded her and she stared up into his beautiful, still face. His jaw was like granite.

Now she knew why his expression had been like the Pyrenees all morning.

'How?' she breathed.

'The usual reasons…latex isn't foolproof. There's only a ninety-eight per cent success rate. We're the two per cent.'

Lulu didn't know when she'd stopped dancing. Only knew that they were standing together in the middle of the dance floor while the other couples glided around them and everything she'd taken to be fixed in her life was falling down around her.

The floor seemed to come rushing up to meet her.

'Where are you in your cycle?' He spoke calmly, but his eyes were like flint looking into hers.

'What? I—I don't know.'

'Think.'

Somewhere off to the side, where the old version of her was still standing, she didn't like his tone. But the stripped-down Lulu, grappling to understand what all this meant, was trying to figure out dates.

'Lulu?' he growled.

'I'm a dancer—my periods are all over the place.'

'Great.'

She really didn't like his tone—nor the way he was telling her this in the middle of the wedding waltz. Although she guessed he *had* given her the option to do it in private.

'One week in,' she came up with.

'That's probably the best news we can hope for. You're less likely to be fertile immediately following your period.'

'How did you become an expert on this?' Her voice had grown slightly shrill.

'An internet search and not much sleep last night,' he growled back.

Good, thought Lulu unhappily, *let him suffer.*

'What will happen now?'

'You'll need to contact me if you're pregnant.'

When she thought about last night—lying awake in the champagne-lulled heap she and Gigi had formed on one of the beds, imagining seeing him again, feeling the happiness that had been bubbling up inside her—the realisation now that the only reason he'd wanted to see her again was to check her fertility was almost too cruel for her to accept.

'What a prince you turned out to be,' she whispered, and whirled around and made her way across the hall.

People were staring. Well, let them stare. Gigi was the only one who mattered, and she was so caught up in Khaled she'd never know at this late stage in the day.

Lulu began to run when she was outside the grand hall. She knew where she was going because she had already set down her routine here. The same corridors, the same

rooms. But she found herself pressing close to the walls—
a sure sign that things were closing in on her.

It had been such a beautiful ceremony, and Gigi was so
happy. Everything had gone off splendidly—only for this
news to drop like a bombshell…

But surely she wouldn't be that unlucky?

Lulu found herself pushing open the tall, heavy doors
in front of her and entering the hushed, carpeted surrounds
of the library.

Explicit memories from last night washed over her.

'Lulu, you can't run away from this.'

She jumped, plastering a hand over her chest, until she
realised she was playing the role of a gothic heroine and
snatched it away. 'You *followed* me!' she accused.

'Of course I bloody followed you.' He strode towards
her, so powerfully masculine she couldn't help shrinking
back. 'This is important, Lulu. You can't just push this
away and pretend it hasn't happened.'

'You think I don't know that?'

Was he making a crack about what had happened at the
bed and breakfast?

She backed up against a table, gripped its edge. It only
reminded her more of what had happened in here last night.
She didn't want to think about last night.

'What sort of a man are you anyway?' She didn't give
him a chance to respond. 'Well, I know now, don't I? You
just go from one woman to the next, like a bee to a flower,
only you don't extract anything—' *except for her heart*
'—you just leave deposits.'

'What are you talking about?'

Her *heart*? Really?

Lulu stared at him, horrified. Her heart wasn't involved.
It was her feelings he'd trashed. The bastard did *not* have
her heart!

'You're just like your father. You're a…a philanderer.'

Like his father? Where had that come from? What had she heard? Read?

Alejandro's first reaction as a young man had been to punch in the face any journalist who had come at him with prurient accusations about *like father, like son*. The intervening years had seasoned his reaction down to a cool, half-amused 'no comment' response.

Hearing the accusation come out of Lulu's sweet mouth made it raw all over again.

'You know nothing about me, Lulu, and even less about my father.'

'I know that—and now you're telling me I could be pregnant by a man I'm not married to. How am I expected to react?'

'Try not screeching out the news to all the inhabitants of the castle.'

'I do *not* screech! she shouted, then looked around as if people might come pouring in to see what the fuss was about. 'What are you going to do about it?' she hissed.

Later, when he analysed the situation, Alejandro would recognise that this was the line he should never have uttered. 'I think I've done my bit.'

Lulu looked ready to haul off and punch him, but for some reason he relaxed. Alejandro discovered that with Lulu the hostility was starting to feel like foreplay.

He made the mistake of smiling at the idea.

'You think this is *funny*?'

She was almost dancing on her toes with fury—a little French tornado of outraged sensibilities.

And he felt...surprisingly calm. For the first time all day he felt good—because now they were talking everything felt a lot less fraught. He was beginning to think that if he'd forced her to talk yesterday they wouldn't be facing this problem now. Sex between them was incendiary, and it just burned the reason out of both of them.

His gaze dropped to her pelvis, where she had settled

her hands, as if trying to repel any imaginary seeding in her womb.

He frowned. It wasn't as if he'd been *trying* to impregnate her. But she was glaring at him as if he'd wilfully and wantonly planted a baby inside her. And now he was seeing other things: Lulu's slender curvy shape distended, a little person growing inside her until she was a soft, round, fecund woman, with *his* baby…somewhere in Paris.

This sudden and to his mind bizarre detour of his imagination had him doing a double-take.

He focused on the more important question. Paris was a big city. He didn't even have her address.

Dios.

How the hell had he missed all this?

Logically, he knew he could get it from Khaled. But right now this was about the two of them. He had no intention of involving other people who would by necessity come between them.

She spun away from him.

'Where the hell are you going?' he growled.

She didn't even look around as she flung over her shoulder, 'Away from *you.*'

'Oh, no, you don't, *querida.*'

He seized her by the wrist and Lulu jerked her head round, and for a moment all he saw was the true panic in her eyes. He was so puzzled by it that when she rounded on him with a raised elbow he wasn't quick enough to deflect the blow and it connected with his jaw. His head jerked back and he let her go.

'Damn!'

Pain radiated from his face and around the back of his neck, and when his vision cleared Lulu was nowhere to be seen… And then he saw her knee. Narrow and pointy and shaking. She was crouched behind the desk.

'Lulu?' he said quietly, stepping carefully around the corner so as not to frighten her.

She was huddled there, looking as shocked as he was.

'Mon Dieu!' She pressed her hands to her mouth. 'I'm sorry—I'm so sorry. I didn't mean it.'

He just offered her his hand and after a hesitation she took it.

'I hit you!' she said jerkily, shaking her head as if she needed to clear it of something. Her whole body was trembling.

'You struck out at me—there's a difference.' He wanted to comfort her but was careful not to embrace her. Something had spooked her, and he didn't like the picture it was painting.

She lifted her hand to his chin and tentatively stroked him where a red mark was already appearing. 'You'll have a bruise.'

'It's all right, Lulu.' He covered her hand and she let him.

'No, it's not. What sort of a maniac hits people?'

But she knew. Out of the past came a memory of her father catching hold of her mother, of the way he would shake her. Never a punch, never a slap, never anything that would leave a mark.

Only fingerprints, standing out on her wrist long after he had let her go.

Her mother had always pretended they didn't matter. Would rub her skin. Would hide it.

'Lulu…' She became aware that he was saying her name. Had possibly said it several times.

She looked up at him blindly.

'Lulu, what happened to you?' he asked, with a quiet intensity she'd only seen in him when they were intimate. It focused her.

'I—' She shook her head. 'I can't talk about it.'

She just couldn't, but her hands had curved over his forearms and she realised she was holding tightly on to him.

Why was she seeking comfort from the very man who'd thrown her life into such disarray?

Because...because he made her feel like a bigger person—stronger, *normal*. He made her feel like the Lulu she might one day be.

This man who'd brought another woman to the wedding.

Lulu stepped back, wiping at her eyes and her nose with the back of her wrist. It wasn't very ladylike, but it was all she had.

'Why don't you go and dance with your girlfriend and leave me alone? I'll let you know if there are...consequences.'

'Madeline is not my girlfriend,' he said decisively. 'She's my plus one.'

'Plus what?' Lulu's voice quavered.

'Madeline's an old friend. We've never been romantically involved. I promise you, Lulu. The invitation was for two, it's a high-profile wedding, and she asked if she could come with me.'

Lulu felt like a balloon that just had the air let out of it. She knew in a minute that she would feel relieved, but right now all she could do was stare at him.

'I was going to tell you last night, but you rushed off. Lulu—' He stepped towards her.

'Non!' She glared at him unhappily. 'Don't come any closer. It's never good when you come closer.'

He stopped. Then he ran a hand through his hair and seemed suddenly younger, less the cold stranger he'd been at the reception—the man who had brought another woman to Gigi's wedding and not told her. He was suddenly Alejandro again, but an Alejandro toting a great deal of baggage she hadn't known about—like the fame, and the women who apparently pursued him in droves.

'Dios,' he said. 'This is a mess.'

Lulu couldn't agree more. At least in that they were on the same page.

'We need to get you onto contraception.'

Or not!

'Excuse me? That has nothing to do with you.'

'The hell it doesn't. You could be pregnant, Lulu. If you have unprotected sex this is what happens.'

'As I never intend to have sex again in my entire life, it's no longer a problem,' said Lulu, her chin trembling, 'I was perfectly happy keeping myself to myself, and then you wrecked everything.'

He was frowning at her. He seemed to be struggling to follow her words and she wondered for a moment if her English had clotted up, as it had a habit of doing when she was overwrought.

'What do you mean, keeping yourself to yourself?'

He suddenly seem to loom over her.

'I don't want to talk about it.' Lulu pursed her lips, folded her arms and faced the other direction.

'*Dios,*' he said, almost under his breath. 'I knew you were a virgin.'

It was the last straw.

'Did you?' she snapped. 'How clever you are. Give the man a medal.'

'Lulu—'

'I was *not* a virgin,' she stated, staring at an old tapestry on the wall, in which a man in armour appeared to be poking a dragon viciously with a three-pronged weapon. She wished above all things she could be doing that to Alejandro du Crozier right now. 'I lost my virginity when I was eighteen—how many times do I have to explain this to people? I just never followed up with anyone else.'

She heard him sigh.

'Not that it's any business of *yours*,' she added. 'Any more.'

'Then why the hell did you decide to follow up with *me*?' He sounded angry again, but in a different way. He sounded as if he cared.

Lulu discovered she disliked that even more. It was just a trick. She whirled around, wishing he would ignore all her ravings and put his arms around her. But he wasn't going to do that.

'And that's the million-dollar question, isn't it?' she shouted—she never shouted, but this was a weekend of firsts. 'Why don't you call me if you ever work it out?'

He'd handled that well.

Alejandro nursed a whisky as he stood at the window of his guest room. The place was draughty, but that probably went with it being several hundred years old, and yet in shirtsleeves he wasn't feeling much except the adrenalin his brain was pumping through his body.

He couldn't put together a coherent picture of her. At every turn Lulu confounded him. She threw up walls, drew lines in the sand for him to step over, made him jump through hoops. She was his worst nightmare.

The kind of woman he'd avoided all his adult life.

A woman who needed drama.

Only she wasn't quite that either... He was missing a piece in this puzzle, and when he had it everything would fall into place.

He couldn't blot out the image of her huddling behind the desk. Hiding. He thought of the story she'd told him of being attacked and wondered if this was the fallout from that. He wanted to take that fear away, and yet he'd given up taking responsibility for other people's happiness years ago, when he knew he couldn't fit the bill.

More to the point, how the hell was he going to handle a baby?

Not that there *was* a baby. Even if Lulu was pregnant she might very well not want to go through with it, which just opened up all kinds of conflicting feelings inside him. He'd always supported a woman's right to choose, but he discovered he had strong feelings when it came to his own potential child.

Was this how his father had felt about the various children he'd fathered on the women who had become a big part of the decline of the *estancia*? Six kids who'd had to be fed, clothed and educated—along with himself and his two sisters—and the alimony for his mother had been its own drain.

But this wasn't the same at all.

He wasn't his father, following every twitching skirt.

True, he didn't ignore his healthy sex drive and live like a monk, tied to the *estancia*. Women were part of his life on the circuit. But they didn't interfere with his passion, which was for horses and winning and seeing his patrimony stand strong, as it had for several generations before his father had almost scuppered it with his extra-marital affairs and illegitimate children.

Illegitimate children. He wasn't having that either.

Alejandro steeled his resolve.

He knew deep down that he wasn't cut out to be a protector of anyone. Every time he'd tried to help his mother as a child she'd pushed him away. His brief marriage when he was barely out of his teens had hit a wall as soon as it had begun. As a grown man he'd erected a barrier to protect himself and push others away.

But he couldn't push a baby away. He couldn't ignore his own child.

He'd been raised by people who did that, and he knew how heavy a burden it was to carry the knowledge that your own parents didn't love you through life.

But at least it clarified what he had to do now. He'd solve all this by taking Lulu with him to Buenos Aires for the next few weeks. He'd put her up in a nice hotel, look after her with the best money could buy, do the test with her at the scheduled start of her period and if she was pregnant they'd work it out from there.

But he knew one thing. If Lulu *was* pregnant, he'd marry her and take the consequences.

CHAPTER TWELVE

MOST OF THE guests had departed last night, after the newly married couple had left for the Seychelles, but the rest of the wedding party was still there and he found Lulu among the other bridesmaids and some late-leaving guests in the room off the main hall, saying their farewells and organising their transport back to where they'd come from.

Madeline was long gone, with one of the groomsmen she'd been entwined with the last time he'd seen her, having a very nice time. She'd waved him off when he'd gone over to apologise for his long absence and mouthed, *I'll find my own way home*, which had freed him to focus entirely on the issue at hand: Lulu.

While everyone else was in jeans, country casual, Lulu was dressed to the nines, wearing another vintage outfit—a raspberry-red fitted dress this time, with long sleeves—and she had a bow around her neck to modestly cover the scooped bodice that made her look as if she should be in a nineteen-forties film.

It was Lulu's little waist and neatly rounded hips, rising at the back to her nicely constructed behind, that made her so damn sexy. On her feet she had clumpy black high heels from the same era, and they made her legs look ridiculously slender and long.

Her hair had been teased into a sleek up-do that had his fingers itching to muss it up. Clips glittered like fireflies in the shiny dark mass.

But when she turned around he could see she was wearing sunglasses. Indoors. In Scotland. Now *there* was a statement.

Alejandro knew he was currently standing in a trench called *bastard*, and that he'd dug it for himself.

He couldn't go any deeper, and was tempted just to haul her over his shoulder and carry her out. It did have a precedent. But drawing attention to their situation was hardly the optimum solution at the moment.

He took her aside.

'I've been doing some research. You can take a reliable test on the first day your period's due—which, according to you, puts us three weeks from today.'

He couldn't see her eyes—those bloody glasses—but the tightening of her rosebud mouth said everything.

'I want you to come to Buenos Aires with me. When the time comes we'll take the test and settle the question. Together.'

Her lips parted.

'*We'll* take the test, will we? I think it will be *me* peeing on a stick.'

Alejandro recognised that Lulu had clearly done some self-defence training overnight and knew this wasn't going to be easy.

'If it makes you feel better, *hermosa*, I'll pee in sympathy.'

She glared at him. He might not be able to see her eyes, but her mobile little mouth was doing the expressions for her.

'I'll make it good for you,' he coaxed. 'Put you up in a nice hotel…you can do some shopping. Buenos Aires is big on fashion—right up your alley.' He indicated her pretty frock.

Lulu stared at him in disbelief. She had cried on and off all night. Hence the sunglasses she wouldn't be removing. But, seeing him again this morning, she had felt her blasted heart jump up and down and she'd really hoped he might say something that would make this a little better. Then she would apologise for going off like a firecracker yesterday, and they could talk like grown-ups about how best to handle this.

Only now she'd been pulled into a corner and dictated to. No mention of *them*—it was all about this non-existent pregnancy. Because, really, how unlucky could he be?

Stuck with some girl he'd got lucky with on his drive in to Dunlosie?

He couldn't make it any clearer.

Instead of going out of his way to visit her in Paris, he wanted her to upend her life and go to Buenos Aires and not inconvenience *him*!

Did he really think she was so shallow that shopping for clothes was all she thought about?

Lulu wondered how on earth he'd got her so wrong.

Because he barely knows you. He's not even interested in getting to know you, whispered a caustic voice. *You're just the next girl in a line of girls and he can't move on from you because of a condom malfunction.*

It really wasn't making her feel special.

It was making her angry.

'Why on earth would I come to Buenos Aires?'

'Because I have to work and we have a problem.'

'You may have to work, but so do I.'

'The cabaret season's ended.' At her surprised look he added, 'Your little blonde friend was full of information last night. You're a lady of leisure for the next month.'

This provoked a choking noise.

He glanced at his watch. 'Let's get out of here.'

'No!' She folded her arms. 'I'm not going anywhere with you. I will take a test, and I'll let you know if there's anything that concerns you.'

He glowered down at her. 'What the hell's *that* supposed to mean?'

'Just what I say. I don't need you standing in the bathroom with me.'

Lulu tipped up her chin. It was certainly easier staring him down from behind the shades, and she wished she'd had them yesterday.

'I won't be bullied,' she added, 'and I won't be made to feel I don't have a choice.'

'In what way am I bullying you?'

'Going behind my back, finding out about my schedule. We don't have a relationship, Alejandro, we just have a problem. And I can deal with it.'

He gave her a long, unsettling look. All the more unsettling because, unlike her, he could hide what he was thinking. Then he seemed to make up his mind about something. His mouth curled into a tight smile that somehow held no humour and his eyes searched her face.

'You're right, Lulu, we *don't* have a relationship.'

To Lulu's astonishment her stomach dropped.

'Give me a call if we've got a problem.'

He strode away and Lulu watched him go, unable to credit the disappointment that was dropping through her at a rate of knots.

What was wrong with her? This was what she wanted, wasn't it? He was a control freak. She couldn't believe he'd been scoping out her schedule when she'd thought he was flirting with Susie!

How could he have put her through that?

Lulu blinked. Wait a moment—two nights ago there had been no reason for him to be interested in her schedule. She bit her lip. Unless he was interested in her.

'Chérie?'

Her mother had approached and was looking at her with that half-agonised expression Lulu discovered she could barely look at nowadays.

'I'm flying home today,' she heard herself say, sidling over to the window, which gave her an excellent view of anyone coming and going from this wing of the castle. 'You should stay on with Jean-Luc for the golf.'

'I rather thought you and I could fly down to London for a West End show and some shopping and then shoot home at the end of the week with Jean-Luc—that way I'll be with you if something goes awry.'

Lulu was watching Alejandro cross the courtyard. His long, easy strides were in direct contrast to her own jerking heartbeat. How could he just walk off like that? Although she guessed he *had* tried, hadn't he?

She closed her eyes momentarily, trying to block out her mother's voice telling her how well she'd done this weekend, asking why she'd make it any more difficult for herself by facing another plane journey alone.

Lulu had a sudden image of herself hiding in a hotel bathroom in London, with her mother in the next room, and her peeing on a stick.

She turned around, pecked her mother on the cheek. 'I love you, Maman, but I have made other arrangements.'

'Lulu!'

She grabbed her hand luggage and ran as fast as she could in her clumpy shoes and narrow skirt—out of the room, down the stairs, across the flagstone-laid hall, out into the courtyard.

She was on the lawn when she saw him heading for the helipad.

'Alejandro! Wait for me!'

He turned around, arms hanging loose from those broad shoulders, and Lulu had to swallow a very large lump of nerves. Because he was such a force of nature, so assured in his masculinity and determined to have his way.

Well, so was she. Determined to have her own way, that was. And she was about to take a huge leap into the unknown.

'Why did you ask Susie about my schedule the other night?' she shouted over the *whup-whup* of the blades.

'Because I wanted to date you.'

Finally he'd said the right words.

'I'm coming, then,' she announced. The wind from the

rotors was already destroying her carefully constructed up-do. 'What do you think?'

'You don't want to *know* what I think, *querida*.' His expression was wry. He gave a jerk of his head. 'Get in.'

Lulu scrambled into the chopper. Fresh nerves assaulted her, but she didn't have much choice.

They were already in the air when she thought to look down, and there on the lawn was not only her mother but Trixie and Susie too, all of them gazing skywards. Trixie was waving madly. Lulu extended her hand and waved back, feeling nothing but relief that she was leaving them and their questions behind, but as she turned to Alejandro beside her she felt a big ball of dread in her belly.

So much could go wrong.

Alejandro was looking at her as if he had her exactly where he wanted her. She guessed he did. Only she wondered where the man who had taken her so passionately on the library desk had gone, and she figured that if the idea of an unplanned pregnancy had spooked him, he needed to wait until he'd learned the truth about her.

Too much trouble. Lulu already knew that, and it was only a matter of time until he knew it too.

He'd known if he stopped pushing she would push herself—and she had, Alejandro thought with some satisfaction as they drew up in front of the Four Seasons Hotel in Buenos Aires.

They were right on schedule. He would stash her here and then he could still make his meetings across town, before taking the long drive out to the *estancia* this afternoon.

Naturally he'd keep an eye on her—maybe they could have dinner. Probably a good idea. Discuss their options. What mattered was that she was in town, within easy reach. If she was carrying his baby he wanted to know about it.

Which didn't explain his unease as he escorted her across the square. He was growing distinctly tense as they approached the hotel. Lulu kept looking at him with those big anxious eyes. He should probably explain the set-up.

'You'll be comfortable here—you'll want for nothing, *querida*. You only need to pick up the phone.'

She didn't say a word, but as they walked through the doors and into the lobby of the hotel Lulu slipped her hand into his.

It was a small gesture. No one looking on would even notice it.

Alejandro felt it like a lightning strike.

Her small fingers curled trustingly around his. His mind was back on that Edinburgh street, when she had wound her arms so tightly around his neck and her heart had beat like a trapped bird.

He halted and looked around.

'Alejandro?'

With a nod he turned and strode back the way they'd come, dragging Lulu on her clumpy heels after him.

Alejandro knew he was behaving like a madman. But her small smooth hand in his felt as if she was squeezing something vital inside him.

'What are we doing?' she asked as they stepped out into the warm afternoon and the familiar sounds of his city wrapped around them.

'Sightseeing,' he said.

'Really?'

Instead of being full of disbelief she was beaming up at him as if he'd promised her rubies, not blisters. He paid some attention to her shoes.

'Are they okay for a long walk?'

She looked a little offended. 'You forget, I'm a showgirl—I dance in heels.'

He *had* forgotten. Alejandro just couldn't imagine her up on stage in a rhinestone bikini and feathers. Unclothed, she looked as if she belonged in an eighteenth-century portrait by Goya, *La maja desnuda*.

'Where are we going?'

Her voice broke into his thoughts and he must have looked blank for a moment, because her forehead formed a tiny concertina of indecision.

'Not that we have to go anywhere,' she added. 'Unless this is like a date or something?'

A date? It was the one thing they hadn't had. He'd skipped it all in favour of deflowering her and possibly getting her pregnant. It was wince-inducing stuff.

He could picture the tabloid headlines: *Like father, like son.*

He was *not* his father's son. He had long been his own man. And the press were not going to run with this story.

His hand tightened around Lulu's.

'*Sí*, like a date, Lulu.'

A slow smile curved her mouth. 'It's your city, Mr du Crozier. Where will we go?'

He showed her the historic centre of his town, its cobbled streets with their *belle époque* architecture. He led her into El Ateneo—once a theatre, now one of the most beautiful bookshops in the world.

'I thought this might particularly interest you,' he explained, standing behind her with his hands folded behind his back. 'It was once a theatre where they danced the tango, but tastes changed in the early twentieth century. A local businessman siphoned in the funds to turn it into what you see now.'

She looked up into the domed ceiling. 'What an amazing thing to do—it's like a jewel box for books.' She looked up at him. 'I don't know what would have happened to the club if Khaled hadn't come along. I still shudder to think of the theatre coming down under a wrecking ball if anyone else had been in charge. But, between you and me, I think I would rather like L'Oiseau Bleu to become a bookshop. Only don't tell Gigi.'

'You'd be out of a job.'

'I wouldn't mind so much.' She drifted towards an aisle of books, taking down some volumes on theatre costume.

She wouldn't?

'This is what you're interested in?' he asked over her shoulder, inhaling the gorgeous violet scent of her.

Lulu nodded. 'I've always spent my free time at the theatre hanging around the costumiers. I find it fascinating.' She closed the book and he took it out of her hands to re-shelve it. She turned up her face. 'Actually, I'm starting a part-time degree in costume design.' She hesitated, then confided, 'You're the first person I've told.'

Alejandro could see how much it meant to her by the way she searched his face, as if wanting approval.

'That's amazing, Lulu.'

She smiled almost shyly back at him and he had to fight the urge not to kiss her. Then her smile faded and he wondered what she was thinking.

Lulu was trying to picture herself hugely pregnant in front of a sewing machine. She guessed it could be done—other women did it all the time. But she wouldn't be able to work. She would have to rely on…Alejandro. After all her efforts to prise herself lose from her parents she would be back where she started.

'How are you going to fit it in with your showgirl gig?'

Lulu suspected he was implying that working nights and studying during the day wouldn't really be her problem any more *if she was pregnant.*

He clearly wanted to go down that road, so she made herself smile at him and pretend nothing was the matter.

Alejandro saw the light and shadow flickering over Lulu's face. Right now he was struggling to imagine her in a revue. He'd seen the Folies Bergère, and what he remembered was sparkles and bare behinds and jiggling bare breasts.

At the time he'd appreciated it.

Thinking about Lulu that way—in front of an audience of men—just made him hot under the collar.

It also didn't fit with the private, modest girl he knew. The girl who had covered her breasts the first time he took off her bra. He blew out a breath. He really didn't need to be thinking about *that* now.

Instead he looked down at her neat little outfit, at the thirties-style wide-legged green trousers and the cute little cream blouse. She'd changed on the plane en route from Heathrow to Buenos Aires. He found it sexy, but she did also look as if she might be on her way to do the school pick-up—if she was Norma Shearer.

Putting Norma aside, thinking about Lulu as a young mother wasn't a stretch.

Not that any of that was going to happen.

'Well, I dance six nights a week, so there's time during the day when I can go to college. Just about.'

'You dance *six* nights a week?'

'Being a dancer isn't for the faint-hearted,' Lulu replied, clearly relishing proof of her hard work.

He remembered the quick assessment he'd made of her as being spoilt and helpless. He'd been so wide of the mark it made him wonder afresh at his misreading of her. He also acknowledged for the first time what a huge impact pregnancy would have on Lulu's plans.

He raked a hand through his hair. 'I'm sorry, *querida*.'

'Sorry? For what?'

'This situation we find ourselves in. I should have taken better care of you.'

To his surprise she looked slightly irritated. 'I was there too, Alejandro, if you remember, and nobody needs to take care of me. I can take care of myself.'

She turned away and trotted on those clumpy heels towards the doors of the bookshop and out into the busy street, not looking back to see if he followed.

He caught up with her.

'Can't we agree on equal responsibility for the "situation"?' she asked less heatedly as he steered her into a nearby café, where the music was hot and the food was good.

He ordered a lemonade for Lulu and a coffee for himself. 'Agreed.'

He didn't agree. They hadn't been on an equal playing field. Lulu was a rookie—he should have looked after her better.

But he watched her defensiveness fall away at his agreement and acknowledged that her independence was a point of conflict for her. He wasn't sure why. Although after seeing her mother in action with her he could make a stab in the dark at it.

He didn't know much about mother/daughter relationships. His own mother had been about as interested in the girls as a cat. He had only counted because he'd been the heir his grandfather had depended upon and the future source of his mother's income.

He watched Lulu's face as she talked earnestly about her course. It trickled through his mind that his mother might once have been like this, at the start of her modelling career, with the world before her—only to find herself a handful of years later trapped in a marriage she saw as inescapable and taking her misery out on her kids.

But Lulu talked on and on with such determination. He suspected that in the same situation as his mother she would make her own way out, bringing her children along with her.

It made him want to drag her back to the hotel and make her his again. But they weren't doing that. They were having a drink and she was sharing her hopes and dreams, and the fact that they were so simple and yet clearly so profoundly important to her stirred a protectiveness in him he hadn't felt about anyone except his sisters in many years.

He didn't see why she couldn't achieve all she wanted

to. There was no reason why she shouldn't. Except there was that slight wistfulness that crept into her voice as she talked about the various career options her course would open up. As if she might not make it.

'So what will we be doing tonight?'

She brought him back to the here and now with that question. He cleared his throat. 'I'll be working, Lulu, out on the ranch, but I'll drop by when I can.'

Her eyes flew to his and then dropped away.

'I'll organise people to take you out,' he found himself explaining. 'You won't be bored.'

Her face had frozen into a little mask of pleasant indifference. 'I'm sure I won't,' she said tightly, not looking at him.

She put down her glass and started stirring the lemonade with her candy-cane-striped straw.

Alejandro told himself it was for the best. He should be at a meeting right now. She should be back at the hotel.

It was time to wind this up.

'You don't have any luggage,' he said instead.

'No, not even a toothbrush.'

She looked tense, deliberately avoiding his gaze by pretending to watch the crowds go by on the footpath beyond the plate-glass windows. All of a sudden she noisily scraped back her chair.

'I have to go to the ladies'.'

As Lulu dried her hands at the sink she wondered what on earth she thought she was doing.

Alejandro hadn't mentioned this morning that he wasn't going to be around for the next three weeks.

Which was fine, really.

At least he wouldn't witness any of her weird behaviour. She could just sit in her hotel room…

But she wished he'd quit with the confusing messages he was sending.

He kept taking hold of her hand and making her feel like part of a couple, and he'd lulled her into a false sense of togetherness by letting her talk on and on about her plans. She'd definitely relished the opportunity, given that every time she'd seen Gigi lately the talk had always been about the wedding. But mainly it had just been nice sitting together, talking.

She shook her head. Really, he was being very careless with her feelings. Listening to her ramblings, behaving in a protective fashion, making her feel as if she was the only girl in the world. Didn't he know all the nice gestures were making it harder for her?

No wonder she hadn't looked for a sexual relationship before.

Sex made everything so much more complicated.

And it felt awful when it went wrong.

Because it *had* gone wrong. Somehow she'd misread things.

As she came out into the restaurant Alejandro's body language caused what was left of her optimism to drop to her shoes. He looked faintly bored, sprawled in the booth with his phone open while two of the waitresses were clearing their table when it only took one. She couldn't blame them. His long, lean muscular frame was on display in a T-shirt and jeans, but even dressed down he looked incredible, with his tousled chestnut hair falling over his temples.

She hadn't missed the flurry of excitement as their waitresses had recognised him, nor the way Alejandro had dealt with that recognition, erecting a little wall of cool disregard that held them all at bay.

I'm not his girlfriend, she imagined herself telling the drooling girls flitting around him, *but I might be carrying his child. We're doing a test in a few weeks. Peeing on a stick.*

Lulu's pride lifted her spine.

No, she wouldn't be spending time with him.

This wasn't about that.

Besides, it was his loss.

Alejandro shot a couple of emails across town and looked up to see Lulu making her way back towards him.

She could at least smile at him.

He'd changed his plans for her. He'd skipped a meeting this afternoon at his office a few blocks from here, hence the explanatory emails, but he was supposed to be at the *estancia* right now.

She sat down. 'I guess we can go now.'

Alejandro discovered he didn't want to go anywhere.

She wouldn't be alone, he reminded himself. It was the centre of Buenos Aires—the privileged centre. He'd organised a suite for her, he'd hand over a credit card, and with a gym and a pool and a health spa and the Recoleta district just outside, with its high-end boutiques, she wouldn't be bored.

But he knew she wouldn't use the card, and he suddenly felt a deep twist in his gut at the idea of her sitting alone in a hotel room.

She could be at this moment pregnant with his baby and he was planning to dump her in a hotel suite—like a secret he wanted to keep.

He'd be no better than his father.

That decided him—or rather her small hand creeping across the table to touch his did. He slid his fingers between hers.

'Alejandro,' she said, swallowing hard, but her eyes issued a challenge nonetheless, 'I don't want to stay in a hotel.'

'It's all right. I don't want you to either. I'm taking you home with me,' he said.

CHAPTER THIRTEEN

LULU GLANCED AT her phone again and made a face. They had been driving for several minutes down a tree-lined road through the property Alejandro's ancestors had held for centuries—called, evocatively enough, Luna Plateada, Silver Moon, after the stallion his Scots-born ancestor had brought across the seas two hundred years ago.

'It's just my mother,' she said, when he asked her what was wrong.

She hadn't even realised she was frowning.

'Maybe you should put that away,' he suggested. 'We're here.'

Lulu looked up and she knew in that moment she'd bitten off more than she could chew as she saw the villa looming up ahead. It was a colonial-style mansion that spoke of money and history.

It was also a working farm. She'd seen the horses grazing in the home paddocks, and now they drove past brick stables and various outbuildings into the courtyard.

Lulu took a steadying breath and kept her eyes down as Alejandro escorted her inside.

There was a lake behind the house. She saw this because there were glass windows everywhere and an expansive feel to the house, as if it were open to the outdoors. Moorish arches linked the entrance hall to various other rooms.

Lulu felt a vertiginous sense of dislocation, but countered it by pressing her back up against the wall as she stopped in one of the archways.

Staff came trooping past with her luggage.

'How many people live here?' she asked.

'There's eight permanent staff for the house, but they

come in daily, the gauchos who work on the *estancia*, and I keep an office manager here on the estate—he lives in one of the guest houses.'

Alejandro was frowning at her, possibly because she had stuck herself to the wall.

Edging forward just enough not to look completely foolish, Lulu told herself she would cope.

'I'll take you on a tour...'

'No! I mean... I'm tired. Can I go to my room?'

She hated how abrupt she sounded, but it was difficult to speak normally when her vocal cords felt as if they were freezing.

He frowned.

Her phone buzzed.

'Again?'

She shook her head. 'My mother worries.' She read the message.

Alejandro watched her face fall as she read the text and it had his own tension levels knotting. He knew what it was like to be on the end of a tugging string of phone calls and texts. His disaster of a mother couldn't make a decision without dragging him into it. It was probably why he only ever had relationships with women who could take care of themselves.

Lulu clearly couldn't draw that line with her mother. He told himself not to get involved.

Her pleated brow didn't change as she put the phone away.

'Do you want me to throw your phone into the lake?'

Lulu looked up in surprise and then remembered the other night, when she'd wanted to throw her phone across the room. Her mouth trembled into a reluctant smile. 'That might be a bit extreme,' she said.

How had he known?

'Your mother is a nightmare.'

Her forced smile faded. 'How can you say that? You don't even know her.'

'How many times has she rung you today?'

'We're close—I'm her only daughter.'

'I saw her in action back at the castle. She treats you like a little girl.'

'She has her reasons.'

'Your medical condition?'

Lulu's heart began to speed up.

'I'd like to go to my room right now, if that's all the same to you.' She sounded curt even to her own ears. 'It's been a long day.'

'Lulu—'

'No,' she said, her voice rising. 'This is not your business.'

To her confusion he looked as if she had slapped him, when all she'd been trying to do... What *had* she been doing? Didn't she want to change things? But it was so hard, Lulu thought as she followed him closely up the stairs, when your mind and body betrayed you at every turn.

'This is your room,' he said at the top of the stairs, opening the door for her.

'The thing is,' Lulu blurted out, 'when I was looking to push my life in a different direction I didn't factor in pregnancy.'

He leaned back against the door frame. 'It wasn't exactly on *my* radar.'

No, she guessed not.

If the latex hadn't split would she even be with him right now? It was a confrontational thought. Just because he'd come looking for her the night before last it didn't mean anything. He hadn't used any words to her that had even hinted at them pursuing anything beyond the weekend.

He raked a hand through his tousled chestnut hair, stepping closer to her as if he wanted to take things in another direction, and the masculine scent of him tugged on all those new sexual responses she had to him.

'Do you want to talk about it?'

Lulu bit her inner lip. The urge to confide was very strong. To tell him what was going on with her...to share a little of the struggle she faced on a daily basis. But, given he wasn't interested in trying a relationship with her, it was probably not a good idea.

She knew now that she'd misread everything on the eve of Gigi's wedding.

Sex was part of Alejandro's normal life—it wasn't some big deal. She didn't *have* a normal life—let alone a sex-life—and somehow in her inexperience she had made it into something it wasn't.

They were both doing the right thing: waiting for confirmation together. It was good of him to put her up in his home, but it didn't mean she should be holding him hostage to her issues.

It was the house that had thrown her. Managing the space. She couldn't share any of that with him. She couldn't share it with anyone.

Lulu had never felt more alone.

'There's nothing to talk about, is there? We don't know yet—it might all be worry for nothing.' She needed to get out of his sight before she burst into tears. 'I'm really tired, Alejandro...' She turned away. 'Let me go to bed.'

Alejandro found himself standing alone in the hall, staring at Lulu's closed bedroom door.

There wasn't anything more to say, was there?

He'd learned long ago that trying to help someone who didn't want to be helped was a dead-end road. He'd tried to help his mother, and then his sisters to launch their lives free of the *estancia*, but it had earned him nothing from the girls but requests to butt out.

He didn't open himself up like that any more. He'd offered support—Lulu didn't want it. There wasn't much more he could do.

He'd seen her face as they drove up. The way her features had frozen to mask her disappointment. He knew now he should have left her at the hotel.

She'd made it obvious she was uncomfortable here. He had vivid memories of long before his ex-wife had made it clear she hated it there—of his mother, dropping them at the house and then tearing back up the drive in a cloud of dust. But worse had been the times his grandfather had insisted she remain, when she'd closeted herself away in her rooms, from which she'd refused to emerge.

Sí, eyeing Lulu's closed door brought back many memories. None of them good.

He turned away abruptly. He didn't need reminding.

Lulu got up the next morning and ventured across the echoing parquet floors from sumptuous room to room, trying not to hear the silence or look out at the immense flatness around them, rising to low blue hills in the distance.

She felt almost unmoored in large open spaces. They were worse than being locked up in the cabin of a plane. But as long as she could establish a routine here for the next few days and have her touchstones—her room, Alejandro, knowing the people around her—she would do fine.

Only then she discovered Alejandro was gone. She stood in the kitchen with Maria Sanchez, who acted as his housekeeper, and learned that he wasn't expected back until Thursday.

Two whole days!

'He works hard,' said Maria in English, when Lulu asked if he'd said where he was going. 'I tell him his grandfather had his two brothers to help—and he didn't have the pressures of a polo team. But he does not listen. He is like his grandfather that way. He sets his mind on something and nothing will deter him.'

'You've worked for the du Croziers a long time?'

'Over thirty years.' Maria looked proud. 'I came here when Alejandro's grandfather was El Patron. It is a shame he never knew what a success his grandson has made of the *estancia*—especially after that son of his.'

'Alejandro's father?'

Maria made a face. 'Fernandez never cared for the land…never cared for the people here. His grandfather took Alejandro under his wing and sent his parents away. Good riddance, I say. Now we have the best pure-bred Criollos in the country.'

Lulu frowned. 'He sent his parents *away*?'

Maria drew herself up, clearly relishing an audience for her views. 'El Patron could see how it was tearing Alejandro and his sisters Isabella and Luciana apart, watching them fight. Fernandez was never here, but Marguerite aired their dirty laundry to anyone who would listen. People felt sorry for her, because of Fernandez and his women, but she manipulated everyone with her weakness. A real woman works. Instead she liked the easy money.'

Lulu thought of her own mother, married at eighteen with no job skills. Married to a man who had only shown his true colours when she'd had a small child and another one on the way and had been trapped.

Félicienne had remarried now, and she worked. She had her own flourishing import business. She'd never be trapped again.

'Are you his sweetheart?'

'P-pardon?' Lulu stammered.

'Alejandro doesn't bring his women here. Yet *you* are here.'

'I'm not his sweetheart…um…girlfriend.' Lulu knew she was babbling, but what did Maria mean by *his women*? 'I'm not anything.' Which was a sobering thought.

Lulu discovered that she felt even more unmoored.

'You are something,' said Maria wryly, and turned towards the oven.

Lulu moved faster, slid on oven mitts and opened the oven.

'Gracias.'

Lulu stayed in the kitchen, helping Maria prepare the food. It was easier than explaining why she didn't want to go outside.

She told herself she would venture out tomorrow. She just needed to get her bearings.

She also needed a routine for her meals—something Maria was agreeable to after all her help in her kitchen.

The three weeks stretched out interminably. There was no way she could hide her problem for that long. There would be an incident, and Alejandro would witness it, or somebody else here in the house, and they would tell him, and she would be humiliated, and—baby or no baby—he wouldn't want her.

Nobody would want to be around her. Whatever happened, he wouldn't want her when he found out.

There was a problem with his champion stallion, Chariot. According to the phone call Alejandro had got that afternoon the old boy was still limping, and he wanted to have a look at that injured fetlock himself. It was the only reason he'd walked out of a reception for the team in one of Buenos Aires's better hotels tonight and torn up the highway to home.

At least he told himself that.

By the time he was striding through the house he'd heard from Miguel Sanchez, his steward, that Señorita Lachaille had not wanted to be shown around the *estancia*. That in fact no one had seen her emerge from the house for two days. From Maria he learned that Lulu wasn't sick, but that she appeared to prefer to eat her meals in her room.

His housekeeper didn't seem to think this was a problem—which was unusual, as Maria complained about most things.

He took the stairs by threes, then stood at Lulu's door.

His door.

The guest room door.

Memories swamped him. Of sitting slumped at another door, listening to his mother crying on the other side. Of his mother sending for him to relay her complaints about the food, about the way she was being treated.

His hand hovered over the door. He wanted to thump on it, but if Lulu was exhibiting behaviour that pushed his buttons he knew he didn't have all the facts.

He knocked softly. 'Lulu?'

Nothing.

He knocked more heavily. Again nothing. He pushed it open and stepped inside.

Ten minutes later it was apparent that she wasn't in the house.

'Check the outbuildings,' he told the men he'd gathered in the courtyard.

He eyed the lake and told himself he was being overly dramatic.

He was crossing towards it when he saw the light in the high gable of the brick stables. Nobody was supposed to be in there. Chariot was in there. He'd given orders.

Lulu?

His chest was tight with adrenalin as he slipped through the half-open door, his tread light on the gravel. If it wasn't Lulu, then someone was in there illegally. There was several million euros' worth of horseflesh alone in these stalls.

It was dark and quiet, but around the corner a light shone over Chariot's stall.

He heard the light murmur of her voice. He'd have known it anywhere, even if she hadn't had that French accent, sexy and flowery with all those soft *V*s.

As Alejandro drew closer he realised she was talking to someone. He stopped.

'You have to stay there. If you come any closer I don't know what I'll do.'

Every muscle in his body tensed. Was someone threatening her?

'*Bien*, be a good horsey and let me pass. If you don't I know what happens from experience—and it's not good. You really don't want be around me when I lose it. And I *mean* lose it. No one wants to be around that.'

He stepped around the corner and looked over the stable door. Chariot was standing quietly, rocking a little from side to side, and Lulu was pressed up against the far wall, eyes huge, face white. There were traces of blood on her blouse and scratches on the fine skin just below her collarbone, which worried him, and she was cradling something to her breast.

'Lulu?'

She looked up and relief swept over her face, but she kept herself plastered against the stable wall.

'It's all right, *hermosa*,' he said in a quiet voice. 'Just stay where you are. I'm coming in to get you.'

'That would be good…' she choked.

Chariot lifted his head at Alejandro's familiar scent. 'Hello, boy…nice and easy. I'm just taking the lady with me. You've got that lovely harem and this one is mine.'

The moment he was between her and Chariot, Lulu sidled behind him and he backed her out of the stall, keeping his eye on the stallion.

Anyone else and he would have had no sympathy.

There were *signs*. Any damn fool would know enough not to enter a stallion's stall. Chariot's mood was dicey, at best, and with an injured fetlock he wasn't making friends at the moment. One of those hooves, precisely placed, could have knocked the life out of her.

But when he turned around Lulu was crouched on the ground, head bent.

He was beside her in an instant.

'Can't breathe…' she gasped.

He settled her back, only to realise she was still cradling something against her breast. He disengaged what turned out to be a newborn kitten from her hands and, at a loss as to what to do with it, slipped it into his shirt pocket. Then he returned his attention to Lulu, who had drawn her knees up. He gently encouraged her to keep her head between them while he rubbed her back in concentric circles, counting breaths for her. All the while she made wheezing sounds that sent him cold.

When her breathing was less laboured she lifted her face. 'Oh…' she said, and reached out gently to touch the head of the tiny creature hanging over the side of his pocket, its blue eyes barely open.

He was beginning to get a picture of why Lulu had been in the stall. 'I believe you two are friends?'

Lulu insisted on wobbling to her feet, with his help, and indicated the neighbouring empty stall. 'They're in here,' she said.

Sure enough there was a barn cat, with a litter of four kittens lying in a nest of fresh, fragrant hay. Lulu restored the fifth to the pile. They couldn't be more than a few hours old.

She stood looking down at them. He noticed she had colour in her face again, but the expression in the eyes she lifted to his took him off-guard. She looked almost jubilant.

'I *did* it,' she said.

'Did what?' he asked huskily. 'Rescued the kittens?'

'Managed…' She bit her lip. 'Almost.'

He gave in to his frustration with her. 'You could have been *killed*.' His voice was hoarse, as if he'd been yelling. But he never raised his voice. He'd grown up with adults for whom screaming matches had been part of a daily ritual.

Lulu made a face. 'I know. It was stupid. But I was passing and I saw the light on. I wanted—I wanted to pat the horses.'

'You wanted to *what*?'

She sank down into the hay, as if her legs weren't going to hold her, and he remembered she'd had a significant fright. Hell, he wasn't feeling so crash-hot himself. Seeing her pinned up against that wall…

'I saw the cat at the rear of his stall with her kittens and I had to get them out.'

'You mean you went in more than once?'

'Three times.'

His gaze dropped to what he could see of her chest, crisscrossed with scratches. He hunkered down and took hold of her hands, equally bloodied, pushing up the long sleeves to find her wrists red and white with raised welts.

'*Dios…*'

'I'll mend,' she said, almost impatiently, pulling her hands back.

'Woman…' he breathed, and the urge to shake her was subsumed in the need to hold her close. He dragged her in tight against him. She came.

'What made you come out here so late in the day?' he asked, holding her so that she rested against him in the hay.

'I wasn't ready until now,' she said haltingly.

'Ready for what?'

He looked at her as if she was speaking another language. Another minute of this and he was going to look at her as if she was a complete flake.

Lulu swallowed hard. She could convince herself that she had to tell him the truth now because whatever happened he was going to think she was crazy anyway. Or tell herself that he'd just rescued her and she owed him an explanation.

But right now what she really wanted was to tell him

the worst thing about herself and hope he might overlook it and see the woman beneath.

'I have an anxiety condition.'

Put like that, it sounded utterly underwhelming. But Alejandro was looking into her eyes as if what she was telling him was of the utmost importance. It gave her the courage to continue.

'It's a form of agoraphobia.'

'A fear of open spaces?'

'No—that's a common misconception. I have panic attacks if I'm in a situation where I don't think I can control the outcome. If I'm out of doors and I feel my safety is threatened it can come on... If I'm in an enclosed space and don't have access to an exit it can come on... But with me it's more of a fear of losing control. In public.'

Alejandro stroked the curls back from her eyes. 'You should have told me.'

'It's a bit tricky,' she said softly, 'telling people you're not normal.'

'It's a medical condition, Lulu, not something that's a judgement on your character.'

She lowered her eyes. 'You're not the one who can't breathe—who falls down and makes a fool of herself in public.'

'Have you?'

She hesitated. 'Once. When I was sixteen. At a concert.'

'Never again?'

She shook her head. 'But I *could*,' she said.

'And this has been going on all your life?'

'No.' This was the shameful bit. This was where everything led back to, and Lulu could feel herself closing up like a fist inside.

'When I was little we used to live with my father. He used to shout all the time, and break things and hurt my mother.'

Alejandro had a peculiar quality of stillness about him. 'Did he hurt *you*?'

'Not physically, no,' she said slowly. 'My mother protected me and the boys from that, but it was like living on top of a volcano. His rages came out of nowhere.'

'He beat your mother? You *saw* him beat your mother?'

'Only once. That was when we left. That's the thing about emotional abuse—it's not like a bruise or a cut you can look at and say, "This is what is happening." It's so subtle it plays tricks with your mind. To this day Maman still struggles with blaming herself.'

'Which is why she is so protective with you?'

'She tried to protect all of us in a difficult situation. I know she did her best.'

'But it wasn't enough.'

It wasn't a question. So she told him. She told him everything. About being reluctant to go home after school, always unsure of what she would find there. How ballet classes had been her refuge. How she would take her brothers out of their beds in the middle of the night when their father came home in a mood. How she'd learned where to hide, and how to keep it all a secret at school. After all, they were middle class...they'd lived in a nice neighbourhood, where nasty, brutish things didn't happen.

'Then we were just poor,' she said, 'which was better. Because then I could tell people my parents didn't live together and my mother had to work. It felt something like normal. But I got busier with the boys, because Maman was gone all hours. I learned how to do things around the house because Félicienne couldn't.'

'I suspect you're a useful woman to have around in a crisis, Lulu Lachaille.'

She felt a little better then.

'When did the fairytale kick in?' he asked, unable *not* to stroke the curls out of her eyes.

She looked up. 'You noticed that?'

'Your mother is married to one of France's leading for-eign policy advisors—a constitutional lawyer,' Alejandro responded dryly. 'It's a little hard to miss, Lulu.'

She laughed a little then, and for the first time all night Alejandro relaxed a little. It was good to hear. He threaded the fingers of one of his hands with hers, careful not to press against her cuts.

'Jean-Luc is so sweet. They met at work, you know. Maman got a law degree after she left my father, and she was working nights as a clerk in Jean-Luc's department when she spotted something about a caveat in a contract everyone else had missed. He came down to thank her personally—'

'And tripped over his feet and could hardly get the words out?'

Lulu's mouth rounded. 'How did you know?'

'I've seen your mother—she's breathtakingly beauti-ful. The two of you are mirror images, twenty years apart.'

'Well, yes,' said Lulu, clearly flustered, 'if you think so. Anyway, he started giving her lifts home from work, and then we got to meet him and he was so kind. I was a little afraid of grown men until he came into our lives. All I'd seen was the havoc they caused. He's been a great role model for my brothers, and he looks after Maman so beautifully.'

But no mention of *her*. Alejandro stroked her curls again. 'He must have had a seismic impact on your life?'

She nodded vigorously, as if the telling was shifting a great weight off her shoulders. She had such slender shoul-ders, thought Alejandro, hit by a tenderness he hadn't expected, and from what she was telling him it was a con-siderable weight.

'Suddenly, at fourteen, I got my own room—fit for a princess. I was sent to a good school… I could invite other girls home for the holidays. Only I didn't.' She licked her lips. 'That's when the panic attacks started.'

'*Sí*, it would have been a miracle if they hadn't.'

Her head came back and she looked at him in astonishment.

'I have good friends on active duty in the armed forces. You're describing PTSD, Lulu—it's a natural reaction to trauma.'

'That's what I've been told,' she said slowly, jolted by the realisation that he understood. It encouraged her to reveal more. 'Routine helps me. When I know what to expect I'm better able to handle things. It's why being in the chorus works for me—being part of that team, being surrounded by the other girls, doing the same thing night after night.'

'How do you get up on stage?'

'Ballet was always my refuge, but I grew too tall. My dance teacher suggested I try out as a showgirl. I wouldn't have lasted beyond the audition stage if it hadn't been for Gigi. She was trying out too and we sort of fell in together and I just stuck to her like glue. She got me through, and once it had become my routine I discovered all sorts of ways to make it work for me. I don't feel like *myself* when I'm on stage.' She eyed him covertly. 'Don't tell anyone, but sometimes I pretend to be Rita Hayworth or Miriam Hopkins and it helps.'

Alejandro had no idea who Miriam Hopkins was, but Lulu's confession had destroyed any last remnants of his pretending he wasn't involved.

'I *am* making progress,' she went on in stalwart fashion. 'I have a therapist, and we're trialling desensitisation therapy. The fact I'm even here is huge for me. When Gigi announced she was having her wedding in Scotland I saw it as my chance to make the break. I wanted to make big changes and I was willing to take risks to push my life in a different direction. That's where you came in. At the airport.'

Alejandro was suddenly seeing that entire episode from a different angle, and his own behaviour struck at him hard. 'How did you make that flight?'

'With great organisation,' she said seriously. 'I threw up twice.'

Alejandro cursed himself under his breath.

'That was why you wouldn't move seats. You couldn't.'

'I was so embarrassed.'

'And I was a Class A bastard to you on that trip.'

'No,' she said forcefully, sitting back. 'Don't you dare apologise. You treated me like a real person, Alejandro. Like a grown woman responsible for her own actions.'

'You are without doubt a grown woman, Lulu.' He plucked a piece of straw from her hair and used it as an excuse to stroke the curls out of her eyes. 'Only a grown woman could drive me as crazy as you've been doing since you stumbled into my life.'

He was looking at her as if she was amazing. As if she was something special for all the right reasons.

Lulu couldn't believe it. She wanted to cry, but then she thought of something better.

'Maybe you could treat me like a grown woman again?'

She felt confident saying it. She liked making the first move—she'd learned that the night they'd spent together in the Scottish Highlands. It gave her a feeling of womanly power as she rose up onto her knees, watching his expression as she began unbuttoning her blouse.

He could have reminded her she'd just had a panic attack.

Told her she really should be resting.

It was what her mother would have said. Even Gigi. Treating her like the invalid she wasn't.

But Alejandro didn't do any of those things.

He carefully lifted her astride him, reached around to undo her lacy white bra and gave her full tender dominion over him.

CHAPTER FOURTEEN

ALEJANDRO PUT HER on a horse the next day.

He had a small mare saddled and brought out into the home paddock, where he patiently spent time explaining what was going on in the animal's head.

'She's used to being ridden, and she likes women. I think the two of you will get on.'

Lulu stroked her neck, and when the mare swung her head around and Lulu jumped Alejandro merely tugged on the mare's mane to show her who was boss.

'She likes you.' He grinned.

Lulu stepped a little closer and tried again, rubbing her hand over the horse's flank.

'She's so beautiful.'

'Do you think you could sit on her?'

'I'll try, but I want you to take a picture with your phone—because it might be the one and only time I'm ever on a horse.'

She was nervous, but she let Alejandro give her a leg up and found herself gripping the pommel as he fitted her feet into the stirrups.

Her heart was pounding, and she'd broken into a sweat, but Alejandro stroked her thigh reassuringly.

'It's all right, girl, she won't do anything you don't like.'

'Do you mean me or the horse?'

Alejandro grinned again and gave her the reins. He took hold of the lead rope.

His eyes were serious, though, as he looked up at her. 'I won't let go, *amorcito*. I promise.'

It was a bit like standing on the deck of a boat, but Lulu found herself falling into the rhythm of the horse's gentle stroll.

'You're a natural,' Alejandro told her.

'I don't know about that. My body understands what it needs to do—it's my mind where the battle is.'

'Then we'll do this every day until your mind comes to accept it.'

'But don't you have better things to do?'

'You need routine, Lulu,' he said calmly, as if it made sense, 'so we'll make a routine for you.'

She felt a lump rise into her throat but she didn't cry.

It took several days before she was happy enough for Alejandro to let go of the leading rope. She got the mare up to a canter—and inevitably took her first spill. She was on her feet before he reached her, straightening her helmet, laughing and groaning.

The mare nudged her and Lulu stroked her neck. 'It's not your fault, girl, I got too ambitious.'

'Nothing broken?'

Alejandro had his hands all over her, checking for damage, and Lulu rather enjoyed it and put her arms around his neck.

'Nothing a bath won't fix.'

He seemed relieved she was unhurt, and slid his hands over her bottom encased in jodhpurs. 'I should probably supervise this bath…you might drown.'

'I am a notoriously bad swimmer.' She kissed him, her arms tight around his neck.

A few mornings and several falls and bruises later, in her quest to ride at least competently, Lulu awoke to hear Alejandro moving about.

She lifted her head off the pillow. It was still dark.

'Where are you going? What's happening?'

He came over to the bed and the mattress gave beside her as he sat down and bent to stroke her hair.

'It's a working day. Go back to sleep. I'll see you after breakfast.'

Lulu peered at the time glowing from the digital clock.

It was half past four. She struggled to sit up, switching on the lamp so that she could see his face.

He was fully dressed, and so beautiful her heart contracted. 'Take me with you, if I won't be in the way. I would like to see how the estate works and what you do all day.'

He stroked her bare shoulder, looked curiously into her half-asleep eyes. 'Are you sure?'

Which meant, could she cope?

Lulu sat herself up properly. 'I won't know if I don't try.' Her expression drooped. 'But I don't want to get in the way.'

A smile broke across his face. He scooped her up, bed-clothes and all.

'What are you doing?' She laughed, fighting a yawn at the same time.

'Putting you in a shower, *amorcito*. Then we're going to dress you like a gaucho.'

A very pretty gaucho, in a cotton shirt and trousers that tucked into long leather boots.

It was a long day, but then they all were—working with the horses, driving out to a horse auction some kilometres away, checking fences. Lulu remained at his side. Sometimes she stayed in the car for a while, and he didn't question her reason, but she would eventually emerge and ask questions about what he was doing.

Everywhere they went she drew stares—because he'd never brought a woman to the *estancia* after his brief early marriage, and Valentina certainly hadn't been a presence in his working life.

At the auction he stood with her on the rails, his arms either side of her.

He couldn't blame the other men for looking. Even amidst the glamorous crowd at the wedding Lulu had stood out. Her lithe height and her embracing of a timeless femininity in everything she did had made the castle a perfect setting for a girl who seemed to have one foot in the past. At a busy horse auction, amidst the dust and the gauchos, she was glorious in a stylish vintage jacket and the thirties-style cutaway pants she seemed to prefer to wear—a magical creature come among them, eyes shining, smiling radiantly and asking questions.

No one looking on would be able to tell how nervous she was.

Dios, how hadn't he noticed that about her until now? Plainly because she'd hidden it like a pro.

But she trusted him enough now to tell him her secret, and that knowledge had ramped up his possessiveness tenfold.

When she looked up at him and smiled he found he couldn't concentrate on what was going on around them. Her kiss was a sigh just below his ear, where he discovered he was ticklish, and then her head was resting against his shoulder in an attitude of trust that had another emotion thundering through him.

His arm tightened around her. Alejandro knew then that if anyone ever tried to harm her he wouldn't be responsible for his actions.

He also knew there were probably some paparazzi in this crowd. Argentina celebrated its sporting heroes. He was rarely seen with women, so he knew that if there were, his turning up at an auction with Lulu under his arm was going to cause a bit of a feeding frenzy.

It didn't matter. He'd already made his decision.

'I have to be in the States at the end of next week,' he told Lulu when she asked if his days were always this packed.

They were driving back to Luna Plateada, with the late-afternoon sun glaring off the windscreen.

'It means time away from the *estancia*, which requires me to do all I can now.'

The end of next week. They should know about her condition then. It brought Lulu up cold. She wondered if she should worry that they never talked about it. Was Alejandro avoiding the topic because he was so set against it? She wasn't exactly over the moon about the prospect of unwed motherhood at twenty-three either! Surely they should be talking about it…

'What if I'm pregnant?' she blurted out.

Alejandro lost speed.

Oui, *Lulu, start this conversation when he's driving a high-powered four-wheel drive. You'll both be killed and the problem will be most horribly solved.*

And that was when her hand slipped protectively to her belly and she realised she wasn't exactly feeling like a woman who wouldn't be going through with an unplanned pregnancy.

Alejandro changed gear, looked over at her and said calmly, 'I'll marry you.'

'You can't just say you'll marry me and leave it at that.'

Alejandro turned the steaks over, telling himself it was just a conversation.

Although he could imagine the look on the faces of quite a few of his past girlfriends on hearing this. Sheer disbelief for one thing.

'I don't want a shotgun marriage,' she said firmly.

'No one is pointing a gun at me, *querida.*'

Lulu worried at her bottom lip and said, 'Actually—'

He looked up. She was curled on one of the outdoor sofas with a lemonade, and she wore a little frown.

She was wearing some sort of print dress with a white collar that made her look as if she'd stepped out of a nineteen-thirties film. She'd tied her curls back in bunches, which was so adorable he couldn't stop looking at her.

He was yet to see her in a pair of jeans, or in anything you could call casual or unisex.

'Should I expect one of your brothers to come bursting through the door?'

'Georg and Max? No, they wouldn't care,' she said, sounding affectionate. 'They're busy with their own lives.'

Alejandro frowned. 'They *should* care. You're their sister. You're their responsibility.'

Lulu wasn't entirely sure how she felt about the term 'responsibility', but she liked it that he cared. 'Is that how you are with *your* sisters?'

He made a grunting sound and Lulu climbed to her feet and went over to him, because this was a side of him she hadn't seen before. The growly big brother.

'I don't want any kid of mine growing up where I can't see him or her every day. Children need two parents.'

She couldn't argue with him. 'What were yours like?'

'Not great. My father was a gambler—and not a clever one. He spent most of his inheritance on the gaming tables, or on women who weren't my mother.'

'I'm sorry,' said Lulu. 'That can't have been fun for you or your sisters.'

He leaned back, folding his arms, a bottle of beer in one hand. 'I always said I'd do better by my own kids.'

'What about your *maman*?'

'She was no better. She'd arrive here with us kids and lock herself in her rooms. She was always sick unless she had a party of friends with her. We hardly ever saw her.'

'That's why you're so protective of your sisters.'

Alejandro looked uncomfortable. 'My grandfather drummed it into me—*Look after the girls...see to their interests.* And I have. But that's it. I don't interfere in their lives.'

Lulu wondered at that and drew a little closer. 'What do you mean?'

'They have their lives and I have mine. We don't live in each other's pockets.'

Given that was exactly what *they'd* been doing for the last couple of weeks, Lulu felt something lodge uncomfortably at the base of her throat.

'You like your own space?' she said slowly, giving him exactly that, edging her bottom away against the table.

'It's suited me up until now.'

Lulu tried not to take that personally. 'Would you like to have more to do with your sisters?'

He swigged at the beer, looking markedly uncomfortable. 'With me in their lives things can only end in tears. I'm there if they get into trouble, but that's about it.'

'I would have loved to have had an older brother to lean on a little,' Lulu confessed. 'I always felt like a second mum to my brothers. I think your sisters are very lucky.'

Colour actually scored the high ridge of his cheekbones. 'It's my *job*.'

Lulu felt a little sliver of cold run down her spine. Was that what his *I'll marry you* notion was about? *All* it was about? He felt *responsible*?

'You don't love them? Your sisters?'

'What kind of a question is that?'

'A simple one—it's either yes or no.'

She held his gaze, knowing that this didn't have much to do with his siblings. She wanted to hear him say it. To her. Or at least she wanted to know if there was a possibility he could love *her*.

Because that was the only reason she could see to get married. She believed in romantic love—even if she'd always imagined it wasn't something that would ever happen for her.

'Of course I love them,' he said simply. 'They're my sisters.'

'Then why would you being in their lives end in tears?'

'It's complicated, Lulu.'

'Possibly...' She looked up at him expectantly.

He made a timeless male gesture of exasperation. 'I inherited the *estancia*...the girls received dowries. They both wanted a say in the ranch—I didn't think that was a good idea. Satisfied?'

'Oh, so it's a will thing?'

Alejandro looked taken aback. 'A *will thing*?'

'Like in *King Lear*—your father hung the ranch over your heads and the child who flattered him the most got it all. Although in your case you just had to be a boy.'

'My grandfather was King Lear. He disinherited my father in favour of *me*.'

Lulu realised she'd gone stomping unaware into a minefield. Alejandro looked grim.

'How did your father feel about that?' she asked, more circumspectly.

'He never spoke to me again.'

'Oh, Alejandro, that's *awful*.'

Alejandro shrugged, but the empathy in Lulu's brown eyes warmed something that had been cold inside him for a long time.

'I took control of this place at twenty, and almost lost it. My father's gambling debts had to be paid off. The girls were still at school and there were fees.'

'Your mother couldn't help?'

'She told me she'd put up with the old man for almost two decades and she wanted her share. It wasn't as if she could go out and resurrect her modelling career.'

'But couldn't she have retrained and done something else?'

Alejandro gave her an arrested look. 'She's nothing like you, Lulu. It would never have occurred to my mother to help herself—or anyone else.'

'I'm so sorry that happened to you.' Lulu was aware he'd just paid her the most enormous compliment.

She desperately wanted to wrap her arms around him, but she also didn't want to impose when he was standing there so obviously man as an island. Men did that. She'd noticed it with her brothers when they were hurting. She would wait to have her cuddle.

'It's obvious you had a lot of responsibility on your shoulders from a young age.'

He lifted those thick lashes guarding his amazing amber-brown eyes. 'From what you've said, Lulu, so did you.'

'But my mother was always there to help me.'

Alejandro acknowledged this with a slight grunt.

'My mother didn't give a damn about her kids,' he said in a low voice, chewing out the words, 'and she sure as hell didn't lift a finger to help anyone—including herself. She took her frustrations out on us. All I remember from my childhood are her threats. She'd say she wanted to leave my father—he wouldn't let her go. She'd tell me she was going to kill herself—' He ground to a halt, rolled his shoulders as if shaking it off. 'She was a nightmare,' he muttered.

'She threatened to kill herself?' Lulu tried to keep her voice even and not make a drama of this. 'Did you believe her?'

'I was a kid,' he said without inflection. 'Of course I believed her.'

'She shouldn't have put that on you. How could she do that to you and your sisters?'

'Not the girls.' His tone was flat. 'Just me.' Alejandro's hand tightened around the beer bottle and his knuckles showed white. 'I felt responsible for her, I guess. I was the one she turned to...confided in.'

'But you were a child—she should have been protecting you from all that.'

Lulu stopped, her own chest filling with cold as her own sweet, frustrating mother flared into her mind. But *her* mother had done the best she could with what she'd had. It sounded as if Alejandro's mother hadn't cared at all.

'That's right,' he said, meeting her eyes, 'and that's why I want any child of mine under my protection.'

'From me?' Lulu framed the words in a voice that suddenly sounded very far away.

He frowned and put down the bottle, his arms falling loose to his sides. 'No, Lulu, that's not what I mean.'

'It's all right,' she said faintly, backing up. 'It's not as if I haven't thought about it. How does a woman like me take care of a helpless baby?'

'The same way you've been taking care of yourself,' he said, his tone firm. 'Look at you—you're riding a horse, you've been in crowds, you're here with me now.'

Lulu tried to focus on that, but all she was seeing was herself with a tiny baby, so vulnerable and needy, and being unable to care for it.

Alejandro put his hands on her shoulders and she felt his warmth and his strength.

'You're not alone, Lulu.'

She nodded, because she knew that was what he wanted from her, but the panic she was so familiar with was stirring like a snake in the grass and she could feel herself preparing for the worst.

She grasped at the issue at hand like a drowning woman. 'What happened with your sisters?'

'They resented me inheriting the ranch, being the favourite. They were away at school when I was struggling to keep it all together.'

'You hid it from them?'

'Protected them,' he substituted.

Lulu swallowed hard. 'So you protected them but you didn't confide in them? You don't trust them?'

'I wouldn't go that far, Lulu.' His hands slid with disarming gentleness down her arms.

'But you inherited this ranch. What about them?'

'They're taken care of.' He frowned. 'Why does this bother you?'

'Because it clearly bothers *you*. Do you see them regularly?' She knew she was being incredibly intrusive, but she could still feel that surge in her panic levels, and she needed to know what his idea of a family was if he was going to throw around marriage proposals like baseball bats.

'I see them on occasion. We're all busy people.' He was frowning at her. 'I don't have a problem with my sisters, Lulu.'

'Maybe not, but you seem to think you have a responsibility to protect them despite the difficulties in your relationship, and I wonder if that's why you're talking about marriage to *me*.'

'Lulu, if I'm going to be a father I don't have much choice.'

So there it was. She hit out at him. 'You've been married before and it didn't last,' she said.

'I was a kid. I wanted some stability and normality.' He snorted. 'It went to hell in a hand basket, naturally. It couldn't ever have been anything other than a disaster. At that age it's hard to be tied down.'

'You weren't faithful to her?' Lulu didn't really want to know.

'She cheated on *me*.'

That brought her up short.

'But—but why?'

Maria had brought out the rest of their meal, but Alejandro remained where he was.

'Valentina married me to get away from her domineering father and then discovered she'd swapped one ranch for another.'

'You rescued her,' Lulu said dully as it all fell into place.

His sisters. His wife. *Her?*

'No, Lulu, I was nineteen and horny and I'd seen a lifetime of the havoc my father's indiscriminate whoring around had caused to our family. So I did the traditional thing and married her. But she liked the glamour, and I wasn't playing enough polo at the time to make my name. I was too busy saving this place from all the debt my father had drowned us in. So she slept with one of my teammates who *had* made his name.'

How any woman could exchange Alejandro for another man baffled Lulu.

'So there you have it, Lulu. The man who just proposed marriage to you. Quite a catch.'

She didn't know what to say.

'But, really, how unlucky could we be?' he went on.

Her eyes went up to meet his. She was not sure at first what he was referring to. As the penny dropped she realised he had referred to their situation in the same bored dismissive tone he'd used to impart the sorry story of his upbringing and early marriage.

Something primal stirred inside her. This wasn't a part of that. Everything in her rebelled against it.

This was real and special and he had no right to bring it down to the common denominator of those women who had failed him so fundamentally.

She wouldn't fail him.

Which was when Lulu realised she was in a lot deeper with him than she'd understood going into this conversation.

He carried the steaks over to the table. It all looked beautiful. There was even candlelight. But Lulu had never felt less like sitting down with him.

Alejandro might not have phobias to hide from, but he was carrying some serious damage from his parents. Yet he'd managed to get on in life and achieve so much in such a short amount of time. How? Where did he put the anger? The answer was in front of her. Into his work. Into the hours she'd seen him put in today. This was what he did. He *worked*.

She hid. He worked. What a pair they were.

A pregnant pair?

All of a sudden Lulu needed to sit down.

'What is it?'

Alejandro was at her side, all his masculine bravado in the face of his disturbing childhood recollections gone as he hunkered down beside her. He took the glass from her hand.

'I'm only twenty-three. You're a workaholic. This could be disastrous.'

Alejandro frowned. 'I shouldn't have told you all that. Lulu, it's in the past.' He cupped her face. 'That ship sank years ago—it's just wreckage floating past us.'

Us.

That was when it occurred to Lulu that this conversation had started off lightly enough, with her teasing him about a proposal he hadn't even made, and now somehow they'd both come round to the idea that it could be real.

She looked into Alejandro's eyes and saw her own amazement reflected back at her. Something inside her had soared over the last weeks, because he'd seen the worst of her and he hadn't run.

She thought of all the things he'd told her. She wouldn't run either.

Lulu came downstairs the next afternoon feeling confident that she looked her best in a backless raspberry silk dress worn over flowing white silk pants and a pair of thirties cream-and-black heels with perfect bows.

She knew from all Alejandro had told her that the match today, at the Campo de Buenos Aires, was one of the most important in the polo calendar. The dress code was 'cocktail', but there would be countless beautiful women and press photographers and she was nervous. She didn't want to be feeling like the odd one out. So she'd gone for glamour—a red lip and a light hand on the mascara—and teased her hair so that her curls were crisp but not overdone. She'd attached a matching silk rose to her hair with a clip instead of wearing a hat.

All in all she felt ready to face the international jet set and not disgrace herself.

Alejandro was in shirtsleeves and jeans. She knew he'd be changing into his gear at the Campo and afterwards into more formal wear for the reception.

Her breath, however, did catch as he came towards her, caught anew by his rugged looks.

'You'll be travelling separately from me, Lulu. I've got a car waiting for you now.'

'Separately? Why?'

'The press—paparazzi. With the guest list, two royal princes in attendance and a couple of half-dressed rock stars it will be wall-to-wall.'

'But they won't be interested in *me*.'

'Trust me on this, Lulu, you need to go in privately.'

'*Très bien,*' she said at last, moistening her lips and reaching up to brush the hair off his forehead. 'Well, when will I see you?'

'I'll find you. Don't worry—I'm sending Xavier with you. He won't leave your side.'

'Okay.' She wasn't sure if she was happy he was giving her a bodyguard, but she guessed she'd rather have someone to help her navigate the ground than go alone.

The last three weeks had been the happiest of her life. Alejandro had taken her with him wherever he went and, although she'd kept close to him, she had grown accustomed to the open spaces around her and was secure in the knowledge nothing was going to come cycloning out of that endless blue horizon to sweep her up.

If it did Alejandro would probably punch it.

The thought made her smile as she headed for the car.

The horse-riding lessons had developed into her doing a little gentle riding up and down the corral every day. He'd taken her about Luna Plateada in a Jeep, introduced her to the hands, to the gauchos, to the rhythms of the life they lived here.

She had seen that his heart was not so much with the *estancia* but with the horses and the breeding programme.

Besides the Criollos he had interests in a stud in the Caucasus, with Khaled Kitaev, where they were breeding mountain Kabardins.

She'd spent many nights lying beside him, listening to him musing over breed characteristics. She knew more about the oestrous cycles of mares than she really thought she ought to. But she liked the way he grew so passionate on the subject—as if it had his heart and soul in a way she suspected neither polo nor this ranch did.

The ranch was something he held in trust for the next generation.

It wasn't really about him.

Polo, she suspected, was his stress-breaker.

It was the horses that mattered—they were his passion.

As she was driven past the stables and they headed out for the highway Lulu pressed her hot cheek to the cold glass of the window and let the truth sink through her.

She was in love with him, and the only thing that mattered now was working out how to make this work.

CHAPTER FIFTEEN

As HE ATTACHED his gear Alejandro was only too aware of the crowds outside. He couldn't stop thinking about Lulu. Out there. Possibly in the sick bay. He blanked it and told himself she was in good hands with Xavier. If she was feeling in any way under pressure she would do what she needed to do. If he'd learned anything it was that Lulu was superb at self-care.

But he hadn't been parted from her for even a day since he'd brought her to the *estancia*, leaving aside the twenty-four hours he'd spent in Buenos Aires at the beginning of her visit, and it felt a little strange to be on his own again.

Weird.

He focused on what he needed to do, but in the back of his mind as he cruised the stable where his mounts were tethered he knew these last three weeks had been the best of his life.

When Khaled had rung and said he was getting married he'd thought his old friend was *loco*. But right now he understood that psychology. Keeping Lulu on a short leash appealed greatly, and putting a ring on her finger was the best way of ensuring that. She was definitely an old-fashioned girl. A wedding ring would have special properties for her. She wouldn't stray. She would stay with him. He could have her for ever.

Only experience told him that nothing lasted. Not mothers or wives. You thought you had something in your grasp, but if it didn't want to stay you had nothing.

The night after Lulu's confession in the stables he'd asked her over an alfresco dinner on the terrace how she managed at L'Oiseau Bleu, and he'd put the information she'd given him into practice.

'When I started, I had Gigi with me. We learned about the place together—how it works, what goes on—so there were no surprises.'

This he knew was key. Routine was everything for Lulu.

'There's a strict schedule for every show and that helps a lot. Also, you're in a team. I do have limitations, but nobody could link them to my anxiety condition.'

She'd looked so serious about this he had immediately wanted to confront anyone who questioned her over it.

'As it is, I've been offered solo roles so many times I can't count, and the money would be so much better.' She'd given a little Gallic shrug. '*Mais cela est impossible!* I feel more comfortable in the chorus line. Besides—' She'd broken off, suddenly looking a little shy.

'Besides…?'

'The solo roles are nude.'

'Nude?' Alejandro had put down his knife and fork. 'You mean you go on stage…?'

'Topless.'

'Naked,' he'd said at the same time.

Lulu had thrown her napkin at him. 'Don't be ridiculous—what kind of stage show would have naked women?'

Alejandro could have named several, but he hadn't been prepared to risk Lulu throwing something more substantial at him.

He'd cleared his throat. 'I was given to understand you all performed topless.'

'Not at all.'

She'd looked so cross his heart had stumbled. She'd told him once before that she wasn't topless on stage, and he realised he hadn't entirely believed her. He hadn't then—but he did now. Lulu didn't lie. She was almost painfully honest and that was part of why he'd fallen in love with her. She meant what she said.

A woman who meant what she said and did what she said. He waited to feel that old trapped feeling, as if the jaws of some mechanism were closing down on him.

He thought of his mother, railing against the hand life had dealt her. His father, flickering in and out of their lives, as insubstantial a male role model as you could imagine with his string of young girlfriends. His ex-wife, complaining about how he'd trapped her, and that moment of horror when he realised he'd married a woman startlingly like his mother.

He'd vowed he would never be like his father, and he'd held to that. Lulu was with him now because he wouldn't visit *his* childhood on any other kid. Especially a kid of his own.

Only that was just a part of the picture.

He knew now why he'd brought Lulu with him to Buenos Aires. Because she wouldn't do any of those things the people who had been supposed to love him had done.

She wouldn't cheat and lie and walk away.

Because she loved him.

She wouldn't be here, curled in his bed every night, if she didn't love him.

And that was when, like a herd of unbroken Criollos thundering across the plains of his barren heart, it all fell into place.

It wasn't until she saw the wives and girlfriends of the players being photographed with their significant others before the match that Lulu experienced the first drop of cold doubt.

Then, between chukkas, she saw Alejandro being photographed with two socialites, and when she asked questions of Xavier the poor guy tried to distract her by taking her to pet the ponies.

Honestly!

But she didn't feel confident enough to stalk across the ground, push those two girls onto their behinds and stick a passionate kiss on Alejandro—as well as sticking her heel into his foot!

Instead she stood with her glass of champagne and her smile, sat in her box during the match, decided what 'separate entrances' really meant and began to feel sick.

It all made a horrible kind of sense: if she wasn't pregnant, he didn't want their relationship to seem official in front of the world.

Lulu told herself not to be silly, not to jump to conclusions. But why else would he do this? Was he ashamed of her? Was it because she was a showgirl and he was a sixth generation du Crozier?

She set her chin mutinously. What was so hot about being descended from a horse-stealing profiteer anyway?

Only she lost her hold on her anger as Alejandro and his team thundered up and down the field. She caught her breath every time he swayed low in his saddle. She knew he wouldn't fall—she knew intellectually he was the best player on the field. But her heart still sat in her throat and she was relieved when the last goal was scored and the victory cup was filled with champagne.

'What do we do now?' she asked Xavier, who had been flirting with a very pretty blonde girl and now turned back to her with 'duty' written all over his face.

'It's all right,' she interrupted him as he began to say something about going to the marquee. 'Why don't you enjoy yourself here a little longer? I'll just pop off to the ladies'.'

Xavier didn't argue with her, and she made her way determinedly towards the sponsor's marquee.

The pitch was crowded, and there was a great deal of jostling, but she focused on her outcome—which was finding Alejandro.

She saw him with two of his teammates. They were laughing, and Alejandro had the cup under his arm.

It was as she raised her hand to catch his attention that a woman standing beside her with glorious sunshine-blonde hair turned to her and said, 'Don't even try, honey. There's a queue for Alejandro du Crozier and the competition is fierce.'

'Pardon?'

But the woman had already turned to her companion and forgotten about her.

Lulu blinked and swallowed.

'Lulu!' Alejandro had finally seen her and was shouldering his way towards her like the force of nature he was.

Somehow she'd forgotten in the last weeks who he was, his reputation, and the very public life he led.

The public life he'd sidelined her from.

Why?

What was wrong with her?

Why did that woman think she couldn't cut it with the competition?

She looked up at him and some of her distress must have been in her eyes, because he frowned. But then he caught her around the waist and lifted her with both hands. Instinctively she put her arms around his neck and then he was kissing her—deeply, passionately—and she kissed him back—furiously, possessively.

After almost a month with Alejandro she had massive skills in kissing!

As her heels touched the ground again a little light applause broke out around them.

Lulu didn't even care. She had her arm around him, and he was hot and sweaty, and he was hers.

'Come on,' he said, 'walk me to the showers.'

Twilight was gathering outside. People called out to him, but apart from lifting his hand to give a brief wave he ignored them, steered her off, away from the official crowd, towards the players' amenities.

Lulu was full of mixed emotions. She didn't understand what had gone down today but she knew it was crucial to whatever was between them.

'Alejandro, why did I have to arrive separately? Nobody knew who I was. One woman told me I didn't have a chance with you.'

'Que?' Anger rippled across that steady surface she depended on. 'What woman?'

'I don't know—some woman. Are there a lot of groupies?'

'Sí.' He stopped and pulled her in against him. 'But that doesn't affect us.'

'Well, it does if no one knows who I am.'

He frowned. 'It won't happen again.'

'It wouldn't have happened at all if you'd let me arrive with you, like a normal couple—like everyone else,' she finished, feeling she was whining but not knowing any other way to put it.

He studied her face. 'Look, I'll be honest with you. I arranged for you to enter privately because I was concerned you would have a panic attack. I didn't want to put you through that level of anxiety.'

She shook her head. 'But I wouldn't—I mean I thought you understood.'

'Understood *what*, Lulu?'

He looked faintly irritated. Or it might be that he was just tired. It had been a hard match, and he still had to shower and change and talk to the sponsors and the media and… And she was holding him up.

'This is what you do, isn't it? You fly around the world and play polo for six months of the year.'

'Sí.'

'So every time you play I'll have to be secreted away?'

He released a gusty sigh. 'Once we get you into a routine it won't be a big deal, but until then you need to be careful.'

'Why? Because I'll embarrass you?'

'Because, *mi chica loca*, I can't keep my mind on the match if I'm worrying about you.'

Lulu flinched. She knew enough Spanish now to know he'd called her his crazy girl. She tried not to let that get its teeth into her. 'You're right,' she said heavily. 'I didn't think of that.'

His expression softened and he framed her face with his hands, stroked her hair as if he needed to touch her.

'It will get better, Lulu. *You* will get better.'

She knew then, even if he hadn't faced it, that she couldn't fit into his lifestyle. Alejandro was operating on a timescale that ended with her getting better. She was never going to get better. Even if she hadn't discussed this with her therapist she would have known it on a gut level herself. Some things you just had to learn to live with and, where you could, embrace them.

Alejandro had made her comfortable within her limitations, but he was waiting for her to 'get better'.

Suddenly her path became terrifyingly clear. 'I'm going back to Paris. Tonight.'

'Hang on—what?' He looked genuinely thrown.

'The new season for our show starts up next week, I'd have to go by Monday anyway. You know I have a job.'

'I don't want you to go.' He spoke as if this were a fact. Not a request. He seemed to realise this, because he exhaled a breath and said more reasonably, 'Listen, I don't know where all this has come from, but I think you're having a reaction to the stress of the day—'

'No!' She exploded in a low roar, yanking herself free of him. 'You do *not* speak to me like that, Alejandro. I am *not* crazy—do you understand me? I came here with you to Buenos Aires because I was scared and I thought it was the right thing to do.'

She frowned, because that wasn't entirely true. She'd come because she'd wanted something with him, and for the last couple of weeks she'd thought she'd found it. Had it all been a fantasy? Cooked up by a combination of her tendency to cling to people who offered her support and her inexperience with men so she hadn't understood she was fooling herself?

'I thought it was the right thing to do,' she repeated. 'Instead we've just confused the issue.'

'I'm not confused, Lulu.'

'Well, I am! Do you know what a baby would mean for me? It would mean dismantling all the new stuff I've been putting in place to try and make my own life. It would mean no downsizing to a flat I can afford to pay for, no starting college, no career that I've been dreaming of. All the things I've been working so hard towards—to make myself independent—would be taken away.'

It all came pouring out, and that was when Lulu realised what she feared was not her ability to rise to this very grown-up challenge, but that she was going to lose her options.

That she would be handing over responsibility for her life to Alejandro and nothing about her would have changed.

'If feels like all my life I've been losing ground, inch by inch. I want my life to *open up*, Alejandro, not close down.'

She shut her eyes, because she knew how she sounded. Selfish. Self-centred. All the horrible things he'd once said she was.

'But I know one thing,' she whispered. 'If I'm pregnant I don't want to be making choices out of fear. Part of me wants you to wave a wand and make it all work—absolve me from being a bad person who feels angry and resentful that her life choices are being taken away from her. Again.'

It was the 'again' that silenced Alejandro when he would have argued with her.

He couldn't do it to her. If she felt trapped the last thing he should do was clang those bars shut.

A dark tide of bitterness came, moving up through him. He'd been blind. *Again.*

She gave him a sorrowful look. 'You're thirty-two. You've been married and divorced, you've carved out a successful career and you run a working *estancia*. There's nothing you can't do, Alejandro. And I've done what? Held down a chorus role in the Bluebirds. I'm not ready to have a baby,' she choked.

It was a relief to say it. It was also incredibly painful, because she knew now she was going home without him.

He placed a hand that was incredibly gentle on her shoulder, but his eyes—they looked dead. Her heart stuttered.

'I will phone you as soon as I have the results,' she said, making herself hold his eyes.

'I want to fly you back to Paris,' he said quietly in return.

She started. 'N-no. I can fly by myself.'

Let me be normal! she wanted to yell, until it splintered the air, but who was she railing against? Alejandro? Herself?

'You need someone to travel with you. Let me organise that, at least. I want you to feel safe.'

Lulu felt it like a punch to her chest.

After everything that had happened over the last few weeks he still saw her as crippled. Just like everyone else. She knew then that she was doing the right thing—no matter how much she was hurting.

'I am capable of boarding a flight alone,' she said, in a voice that felt wrung out with yelling, although neither of them had raised their voices.

He was being so appallingly reasonable—and quiet.

'Lulu—'

She knew the words that would stop him in his tracks

but it would hurt like razor blades bloodying her mouth to utter them.

'Don't you understand, Alejandro? *I don't want you.*'

She turned around and walked. Very fast. Very deliberately. She knew after those words that Alejandro would not follow.

CHAPTER SIXTEEN

IT HAD BEEN six weeks. Summer had turned to autumn and leaves rolled along the Paris street as Alejandro parked his hire car and looked up at the unexceptional six-storey building wedged between a laundromat and a thriving North African restaurant.

He checked the address. This was it.

Pocketing the car keys, he went inside and took the stairs up four flights.

He was ringing her bell when he realised this couldn't be the flat her parents had paid for.

Lulu was living within her own means.

He recognised that this wasn't going to be as easy as he'd thought.

If she'd put her plans into action she might be less inclined to give him a hearing. Plus, he was still angry with her. It burned more the closer he got to this moment, seeing her again, when he knew she damn well didn't want to see him.

Well, he wasn't giving her a choice. He knew Lulu. She'd only run and hide. The memory of her hunched over and trembling behind that nineteenth-century desk flashed unexpectedly to mind, but he shoved it aside. Thinking of Lulu small and fragile and vulnerable only got him so far. She wanted him to see her as strong. He'd treat her that way.

The sound of a dog barking preceded the door opening. She had at least four chains on it, which satisfied his desire for her to be safe but also had him wondering about the neighbourhood.

The door swung open and his pulse sped up.

It was Lulu. In soft blue leggings, a stripy pullover, and she was holding a fluffy black dog in her arms.

Her hair was longer. Her eyes looked bigger—as if she'd lost weight.

Or maybe it was because she was staring at him.

She was so beautiful.

All his anger fell away.

'Alejandro?'

She looked as if she was seeing a ghost and it occurred to him that he should have rung. But it hadn't been common sense that had seen him walk out of a sponsor's event in Connecticut and take a flight direct to Paris this morning. It had been the certainty that if he didn't claim her now she would never be his.

'Lulu.' His usual smooth charm with the female sex had deserted him and he was lost for words.

She looked so delicate—nothing like the determined and robust picture she'd built for him over the phone.

Because she'd rung him to confirm that she wasn't pregnant.

He'd had a moment when disappointment had bloomed so hard and fast in his chest he hadn't been able to speak.

She'd repeated his name and he'd found the appropriate words—it was good news…she must be relieved—and said he wanted to come and see her.

She hadn't spoken again, and it had been the longest moment, stretching between them across continents.

He had been in London, she here in Paris. Obviously in this depressing-looking little flat.

'I don't know if that's a good idea,' she'd said at last, in a small voice.

He hadn't pushed then, because he'd learned not to push. It was why he had never made an effort to be in his sisters' lives.

He'd kept thinking about what Lulu had said about loving his sisters, about trusting them. That was why a few weeks ago he'd invited the girls to join him in London. It had been a good weekend—catching up, sharing news. And he was currently drawing up a contract to give the girls equal shares in Luna Plateada. It was something long overdue.

'What are you doing here?' Lulu said now, her eyes fixed on his.

Good question. He should have been here six weeks ago. Instead he'd been touring with the team. Going to bed at night at ten, getting up before dawn, blocking what was standing in front of him now from his mind. He'd been gently mocked by a couple of his teammates and friends for eschewing the nightlife that went along with a tour. He'd had no interest in other women.

He was looking at the reason why.

'Are you free for dinner?'

She looked flummoxed. 'I have a show tonight, I'm not off until after eleven.'

No other man, then. He could feel the knot of tension he'd carried in his gut these past weeks easing.

Or at least not tonight. Tomorrow—who knew? Paris was a big city. He could imagine hundreds of worthy men lining up to take her out to dinner, to set aside the doubts and fears he'd held on to too long. One of those men would put a ring on her finger.

'I'll pick you up.'

'I don't know, Alejandro...' she said slowly.

'You're so busy with this new life of yours you can't date?'

She moistened her lips, widened her eyes slightly. 'Is this a date?'

'What else would it be?'

'You want to *date* me?'

'Indisputably.'

She hesitated. 'Just because you're in Paris tonight?'

He knew then he had a lot to prove. 'No, *amorcito*, I'm here because *you're* in Paris.'

* * *

It was bedlam.

The new girl from Australia, Romy, had pulled a hamstring in the last number and was in too much pain to perform the 'Little Egypt' set.

Anna, the *maîtresse de ballet*, was on her knees, begging Lulu to don transparent scarves and wiggle her way through the act.

'Those extra pounds on your hips can only help,' she wheedled.

'Those pounds you told me not four hours ago I was to get rid of or I'd be fined? *Those* pounds?' Lulu demanded.

Anna clambered off her knees, dusting them off. 'Well, maybe we can come to some sort of agreement.'

'Oui,' said Lulu crisply. 'A *signed* agreement, before I go on to tell you that the extra pounds are *my* business.'

'Wow, Lulu, what happened to you in Argentina?' asked Trixie.

'The mouse roars,' said another dancer, Leah. 'We should *all* get dumped by hot polo stars, girls.'

Lulu ignored them. All she could think about was what was awaiting her tonight, when the show was over.

He'd come for her.

When her period had made an appearance the day after she'd got back she'd cried and cried, and right up until Alejandro had appeared at her door this afternoon she hadn't really known why.

At first, as she'd gone about putting into practice all her plans, she hadn't been able to work out why she wasn't relieved. It meant all her old goals were still in place—nothing had been shifted. Nothing but her.

She'd changed. Her priorities were different. She no longer felt the need to prove herself because deep down she knew now that she would make a superlative mother. If only because she would love her baby. It wouldn't be easy, but nobody's life was easy, and if she had a little more to overcome than other people it would just make her stronger, more resilient.

She could actually *see* herself as a wife and mother, see herself occupying that next stage in life. And it didn't mean giving anything up.

She'd rung Alejandro and told him the no-baby news while he'd been on tour. There had been female voices in the background and he'd told her he was in a marquee, picking up an award. He hadn't sounded very interested in it—it had only been later that she'd learned from the newspapers that he'd picked up that award from royalty.

Then he'd asked to come and see her and she'd said no.

She'd thought he was being nice. Tidying up the loose ends.

So why was he here?

She faced herself in the mirror. Why would he want to be stuck with someone like her? She might be getting better, but she was never going to be completely without her irrational fears.

Only wasn't that falling back into her old patterns of thought? She'd learned that from him—learned to catch herself at it. Alejandro had given her a release from them when he'd talked to her about her father.

He'd also given her a tool to work with.

It was that new knowledge which acted as a powerful guidance system inside her. Her daily fear of constant collapse had receded and it was allowing her to see everything a lot more clearly.

She'd told her parents her plans at her first Sunday lunch back home, and as she'd suspected her mother had had a meltdown. But Jean-Luc had overridden those objections and told her he was proud of her, that they would step aside as she wished, although if she needed them they would always be there.

Which was when she'd flung her arms around Jean Luc's neck and told him she couldn't have a better stepfather if he was Gregory Peck.

The following weeks had passed in a blur of activity. She'd watched strangers traipse through her flat and she'd wandered through other people's until she'd found one in the next *arrondissement*. It took up half of her weekly income, but it had its own bathroom, which was a plus, although no courtyard or anywhere to sit in the sun.

Still, she wasn't home much, between working nights at L'Oiseau Bleu and college starting up, and her puppy Coco had to spend more time living at her parents. *She* seemed to live on the bus between college and the cabaret.

She told herself it was true independence, but knew it wasn't going to be easy.

Nothing worthwhile ever was.

So facing down Anna hadn't really been that difficult just now. It was thinking about Alejandro and what his appearance back in her life meant that made everything ache...

'Why don't you girls all mind your own business?' said Adele suddenly. 'Worry about your own love lives or lack thereof!' She reinforced this uncharacteristic show of support by leaning down and murmuring, 'I've got your back, Lu.'

That Adele should prove to be her ally wasn't so unexpected, Lulu guessed. Since she'd stopped worrying about people discovering her condition she'd developed a backbone and had been getting a lot of the respect she'd missed out on in the past.

'Thanks, Lulu, for helping out,' Romy said, hopping over on one leg and lowering herself into a chair. 'I just keep it to a figure eight, but make sure you only drop two scarves at a time—no more, or you'll run out...'

Lulu waited for more instructions, but Romy had stopped speaking.

In fact everyone was quiet.

She looked up and everything went haywire.

Alejandro had never been backstage at a theatre.

Up until the moment he'd stepped through the stage door he had pictured L'Oiseau Bleu as a girly joint.

He hadn't been far wrong.

The first person he ran into was a topless peacock, or so she appeared to be, who shrieked, clapped her arms over her breasts—and then changed her mind, asked if he was Alejandro du Crozier, and if so could he sign her…?

Then he slammed into a stagehand who told him to go around to the front of the building and approach the booking office. No members of the public were allowed backstage during a performance.

'We've got a nudity clause,' the guy said.

'I'm not interested in the nudity. I'm looking for Lulu Lachaille,' Alejandro told him.

'You'll have to speak to the manager—'

'Who is on her honeymoon,' Alejandro cut him off.

He could hear music. Knew that elsewhere in this place there was a show going on. He wanted to get to Lulu before she hit the stage, because he had this crazy, unrealistic idea that if he didn't he would have lost her.

He couldn't wait until eleven o'clock. He'd already waited six weeks.

'I mean the *assistant* manager,' the guy fired back, looking uneasy.

'Who is…?' Alejandro was ready to slice and dice this guy.

'Alejandro du Crozier!'

He turned around. The feather-clad blonde hip-swinging towards him was vaguely familiar.

'Susie. Susie Sayers.' She gave him a speculative sweep, from his boots to the curl of his overly long chestnut hair.

He remembered. Susie. The bridesmaid with the wandering hands.

'Where is she?' he demanded without preamble.

'Come this way, gorgeous. Follow Susie!'

He followed the bouncing ostrich feather tail down a corridor, and he heard the sound of shrill female voices before he saw the dancers.

A couple of naked women shrieked, and one or two just put their hands on their hips and watched him come in.

Then he saw her.

Or he thought he saw her.

Sitting at a mirror framed with glowing bulbs, applying powder to her already luminescent skin.

'Alejandro!' She dropped the brush and swivelled around in her chair.

He couldn't get over how she looked. She was wearing a rhinestone bikini, a long ostrich feather tail and towering heels.

She was a showgirl.

Until this moment he hadn't really believed it.

'What are you doing here?'

'I came to see the show.'

'Five minutes until Little Egypt.' The announcement came over the tannoy.

'That's me.' She shimmied out of her tail in front of him, and Alejandro was confronted by Lulu's very luscious, very familiar behind in a tiny sparkly G-string.

She was going on stage in *that*?

Like hell she was!

Lulu began attaching a skirt made of scarves, her hands working fast as she arranged them.

Alejandro relaxed slightly. That was better.

'Enjoy the show,' she said, and with an entirely un-Lulu-like taunt of a smile she slipped past him.

Alejandro turned around and was confronted by a roomful of semi-naked women, all looking him speculatively up and down.

'Ladies…' he said and, feeling ridiculously objectified, waded his way out of the dressing room to find out what Lulu was up to.

He found out from the wings of the stage. Against a set he assumed was supposed to resemble nineteenth-century Egypt, Lulu swayed and manipulated her hips to the snaky, seductive music.

Ridiculous as it was, he had never actually thought about Lulu being a dancer, but her talent was evident. He couldn't take his eyes off her.

The problem was he imagined every other man in the audience was in the same predicament.

As the scarves fell away his tension grew—until there she was, virtually naked behind a semi-transparent screen. Only he could see she was wearing a flesh-coloured bikini.

And as he looked around at the faces in the audience below Alejandro realised half of them were women.

When Lulu wrapped herself in a crimson robe and came out to centre stage there was a burst of thunderous applause and he watched her take a bow, as she must do every night. Alejandro joined in with the applause—and then it occurred to him that she *didn't* do this every night and he'd just seen something extraordinary.

Lulu had performed solo.

It was a different woman he escorted into an exclusive restaurant overlooking the Luxembourg Gardens.

His gaze dropped to her bottom, now encased in a fish-tailed dark purple cocktail dress, but somehow he could still see that strip of sparkles.

She had never looked more beautiful, with her skin luminescent against the coloured silk, cut modestly across her breasts, and her delicate shoulders bare beneath narrow straps.

As he seated himself opposite her Alejandro was very aware that this was how their relationship should have begun.

Dinner. Dancing. Him coming to Paris to see her again and again. Flying her down to his yacht in the Mediterranean. Looking at her through candlelight.

He drew her out on her college course, how she was juggling her two worlds, the new flat, how her parents were dealing with it, and soon her hesitant replies grew more fluid. She lost her self-consciousness and began to talk as he'd never really heard Lulu talk before. She didn't apologise for anything—she just enthused.

He'd missed her so much, and yet he knew the woman in front of him had needed that time.

'You haven't been seeing anyone since you got back?' With difficulty he kept the question neutral.

'I—I tried. I had lunch with a guy on my course.' She looked up. 'He's nice.'

'Nice?' Alejandro struggled with that concept and lost. He inhaled. 'How about me? What am I?'

'You're *you*,' she said in a quiet voice, 'and you haven't said what you thought of the show.'

'You performed solo.'

'Only under duress—but, yes, I did.' She moistened her lips. 'Nothing else has changed, Alejandro. I'm still seeing my therapist. I still sometimes can't leave the flat. On my scale I'm doing well, but my scale is much smaller than yours.'

He frowned, but was careful to keep his voice level. 'In what way?'

'When I rang you about not being pregnant you were collecting a trophy from the Prince of Wales!'

He shook his head slightly. 'And...?'

'That's your life. You're out there on the world stage and I'm... I'm on stage at L'Oiseau Bleu, still trying not to lose my lunch.'

He fingered the stem of his untouched champagne glass, his frustration building. 'I never hung our relationship on the idea that you would get better, Lulu,' he said slowly, choosing his words carefully, 'but I think *you* did.'

'What do you mean?'

'I think it's a convenient excuse for you. If you weren't "sick", as you call it, what other excuse would you use to not be with me?'

'I'm not making excuses.' She shifted in her seat, very pale now. Her mouth quivered.

'You have a kind of agoraphobia, and yet you climb on stage with the other Bluebirds every night of the week. You do it because it means so much to you. Yet you won't take the chance to have a relationship with me because I'm on the world stage? As far as I can see, Lulu, they're both stages. You choose which one you want to stand on.'

She was breathing fast. 'You're the one who won't accept me as I am.'

Alejandro held her eyes with his. He looked so incredibly calm, when she was breaking into a million pieces.

She willed him to tell her he *did* accept her. That he would move heaven and earth to be with her. And suddenly she was angry with him.

What right had he to do this to her? He should have left her alone. Instead he'd dragged her to dinner just to flay her alive.

'Can I give you an opinion you're not going to like?'

'No,' she said, in a small, tense voice.

'I think you've used your phobia in the past to keep men at arm's distance. I don't think you've allowed yourself to accept how truly frightening living with your father was.'

Lulu opened her mouth to disagree, to tell him he was way off base, only...

'You don't want to find yourself in that situation again, so somewhere inside yourself you're still that little girl, hiding away.'

She sat very still, as if he'd opened up Pandora's Box and what had jumped out was eyeing her. She found she couldn't move.

When he spoke again his voice had deepened. 'What I want to know is why me?'

She inhaled his warm, musky male scent and the answer was there before she'd even thought about it. *Because the moment I clapped eyes on you the backs of my knees went and that had never happened to me before.*

But that wasn't the only reason.

'You were so awful to me I didn't have any choice but to fight back,' she whispered.

'And you never fought back with your father, did you? You always ran away—like your mother told you to.'

She gave a slight nod, because to have done any more would have shattered her.

'So there we are. It's not fear that's holding you back, Lulu, its anger.'

The powerful wave of emotion that had been pushing its way through her body since he'd arrived on her doorstep that morning broke, and Lulu found herself scraping back her chair from the table.

Perhaps he said her name—she wasn't sure, because she was running across the restaurant. She knocked a waiter's arm and the tray he carried went smashing to the floor.

Heads turned…there was a flurry of activity around her…but Lulu couldn't stay.

'I'm sorry… I'm so sorry,' she muttered, and continued to push her way out of the restaurant.

And then she was out in the floodlit square, the autumn breeze cold on her bare arms. But there was no going back, and she ran down the street in her clumpy heels, her heart pounding.

'Lulu!'

Alejandro caught her before she could hail a taxi.

He turned her in his arms.

In that moment Lulu wanted to deny it. She wanted to shout at him that her phobias had nothing to do with her, that it was something outside of her. Something she couldn't control.

Her father.

She looked up into Alejandro's beautiful face, lined with concern for her, and knew he was right. She'd never got the chance to confront him.

'He never loved me!' she shouted, shoving Alejandro in the chest with both hands, unable even to shift him, which was hugely, crazily comforting. 'He was so full of anger he couldn't love anything. How can you say I'm like that? I'm *not*!' She stumbled back, hugging herself. 'I'm not like that, am I?'

And there it was—her greatest fear. She wasn't loveable. There was something intrinsically wrong with her.

The girl with the madman for a father.

The question was like a knife she'd put to her own throat.

'No,' he said in a hoarse voice, stepping up to her, laying that knife down. Offering his large body as both punching bag and shelter. 'You're not filled with anger, Lulu, you're *angry*. There's a difference.'

He put his arms around her and this time she didn't fight. This time she let him tighten his arms around her.

'You have a right to be angry, *amorcito*,' he said, his mouth warm against her temple.

She clung to him, not caring that they were in the middle of a public place, taking all the skin-on-skin contact she could get from him. And if a small part of her wondered where private, buttoned-up Lulu had got to, the rest of her knew.

Her family wouldn't recognise her.

Nobody would. Only Alejandro.

He had undone all her buttons from the very beginning. This was the last one.

'You *should* be angry,' he reiterated.

She clutched at him—not because she was frightened, but because she felt that she could.

She didn't have to hide her feelings any more.

'I was never allowed to be angry with my mother,' he told her, his mouth at her ear. 'That's why I know how you feel. And because of that I almost lost you. That morning when you told me you didn't want to see me again I was reacting to old anger, Lulu. And if we hadn't gone to the castle…if I'd flown off in the other direction…'

'But you didn't.' She framed his face with her hands. 'You stuck around. You made me face you. You made me faces my fears.'

'You don't have to be afraid any more, little Lulu,' he said, with infinite understanding.

And Lulu let herself unravel some more, and when he put her in a taxi with him and tucked her against him she began to feel maybe she didn't.

He took her back to her flat but they didn't stay there. He had understood she would want her little dog Coco with her—her *toutou*—and he was all they collected.

The staff at the Paris Ritz didn't blink an eye as Lulu, still in her cocktail dress, carried her small bichon in her arms across the lobby like a queen. Because this was Paris, and they understood the importance of companion animals, and Alejandro du Crozier was a rich and famous guest and he could do what he liked.

In his bedroom she turned in his arms and kissed him, stroked him with a fervour she had never shown before, and he wanted her so badly his body felt on fire.

Lying in his arms, Lulu just looked at him, with those big brown eyes full of all the sweetness and stubbornness, hopes and fears her heart harboured. And Alejandro saw himself reflected in them, and he knew then it really had been love at first sight.

He'd walked down that aisle, on that fateful flight from

Heathrow to Edinburgh, and all she'd had to do was lift those big eyes.

Sí, definitely hooked.

'I love you,' she said simply. 'You know I do.'

He did. He swallowed hard, because it seemed he'd waited his whole life to hear those words from this woman.

'I want a ring,' she said seriously. 'I'm not just moving in with you.'

'Naturally.'

And then he gathered her up in his arms and just held her, and a great peace came over him because she loved him.

Neither of them was trapped. It was the lack of love that made you feel trapped.

They loved one another enough to defeat anything that might stand in the way of them being together.

'And, Alejandro…?' Lulu said, hugging him back.

'Yes, my love?'

'I'm planning on a big fairytale wedding. We might need a castle too…'

* * * * *

A RING TO TAKE
HIS REVENGE

PIPPA ROSCOE

For my editor Sareeta.

Thank you for whipping this into shape and helping me to see the way to a better book.

May it be the first of many!

PROLOGUE

London...

ANTONIO ARCURI GESTURED for the petite brunette to slide into the limousine ahead of him. He might be accustomed to ushering women he'd only just met into his chauffeur-driven town car, but not when it was business. Never when it was business.

Yet there had been no other option. His morning meeting had run unacceptably late, and now he could neither cancel this last interview for a new PA nor be late for his meeting with the other two members of the Winners' Circle—the racing syndicate he co-owned.

Antonio had been waiting almost a year to see his closest friends Dimitri and Danyl, his brothers in more ways than blood could ever account for. So he had been forced to multi-task. And Antonio hated nothing more than having his hand forced.

So far, the brunette—Ms Guilham—had yet even to raise an eyebrow at the somewhat unusual relocation of their meeting, which boded well. The way that she struggled with the wayward hemline of her skirt as it rose up over toned, creamy thighs the moment she sat back on the plush leather seat did not. The hemline that when she was standing bordered on the overly conservative was now a sincerely unwanted distraction.

Settling into the seat beside her, Antonio studied Emma Guilham from the corner of his eye. She was petite. Beautiful, he conceded, then filed and discarded the fact. Whether a future PA of his was attractive or not was irrelevant. At least she had finally stopped fidgeting with her skirt.

The limousine pulled away from the dark underground parking area of his London office, emerged into pale wintry sunlight…and into busy central London traffic. He cursed silently and resisted the urge to glance at his watch. He knew what time it was and he was cutting it fine.

'Your driver should take St James's and then Pall Mall. Christmas and Regent Street don't mix well.'

She locked her hazel eyes on his and Antonio felt a sudden start in his chest. Her gaze held no desperate eagerness to please, no fevered excitement, nor the sensual assessment he often felt when women looked at him. He knew he was attractive and took full advantage of the fact—though never with his employees.

But, most importantly, there was no pretence in her eyes. And that was both unusual and—to him—invaluable.

Compared to the three other interviewees he'd met, she was, on paper, the least impressive. At barely twenty-two, Emma Guilham was young. But while the other candidates had varied in age from late twenties to early fifties, she currently seemed the least flappable. He didn't need to look at her CV. His quick mind recalled all the pertinent information and he proceeded with the interview for the position of his new PA.

'You graduated with your International Business

Studies degree from SOAS after attaining four A levels. You can type one hundred and twenty words per minute, you like travelling and reading,' he stated, somewhat disconcerted to see the hazel flecks in her eyes transition into sea-green foam. 'You are hardworking—a fact repeatedly attested to by the CFO of my London office, where you have been working full-time for the past few months, and part-time for the year before that. At the same time finishing your degree—another thing my CFO repeatedly emphasised.'

A quick nod of the head was Emma's only reaction, which drew a frown to his forehead. Usually candidates like to expound on their virtues when he raised the opportunity to do so. He left a second, a breath of space for her to speak, but she remained silent.

'The position is in New York. I deal in high-stakes, highly confidential business acquisition and I expect long hours, absolute focus and complete discretion. Both in business matters and personal. I am not always present in the New York office, but your presence will be required there full-time.'

'Of course.'

He continued to watch for the smallest change in expression. She had yet to display the excitement or even the badly supressed shock and awe that he had so irritatingly witnessed through the previous interviews.

'You don't seem to be engaging with this interview, Ms Guilham.' He had no patience for time-wasters. And he had no need for a 'yes' woman, but still. This was... unique.

'You have yet to ask me a question, Mr Arcuri,' she said, with no trace of accusation or offence in her tone. 'May I speak plainly?' she asked, and he gestured for her to do so with a swift swipe of his hand.

'Mr Arcuri, I have attended three preliminary interviews for this position—one with UK HR, one with North American HR, and one with your previous PA. I am under no illusions as to my limited experience in comparison to more seasoned applicants, and can only conclude that your willingness to squeeze me in to your "commute" is a gracious courtesy. It is one that I appreciate.'

At this, the brunette rapped on the window to talk to the driver.

'Left here, then second right,' she said, before turning her gaze back to him. 'I believe at this point your choice comes down to personality. And as far as you're concerned, as my future boss, I don't have one. You want someone to live and breathe Arcuri Enterprises? That I can do. You want someone to handle an international diary? I can do it with my eyes closed. You want someone to bar the way and dissolve anything that might prevent your valuable time from being spent as you wish? I'm the one you want. Anything else your background checks can uncover or you don't need to know. I want to work for you because you're the best. It's that simple.'

The limousine glided to a stop outside the grand building of the Asquith Club in London just as Antonio was digesting the rather impressive and somewhat surprising speech that had filled the car.

Ms Guilham smiled, not unkindly.

Antonio felt a small smile pull at the edges of his lips in response.

'I have one question, Ms Guilham.'

'Yes?'

'If you were stranded on a desert island and you were allowed one item, what would it be?'

Antonio had heard many different answers to the question over the years. Mozart's music, the complete works of Shakespeare, a piano. But he'd only ever heard *her* answer once before. It was the one he had given himself.

'A satellite phone.'

He nodded, betraying nothing.

'Mr Arcuri, thank you for the opportunity to speak with you. I shall look forward to hearing from HR and hope that you have an enjoyable lunch. I'll see myself back to the office.'

With that Emma Guilham left Antonio sitting in the car, feeling stunned for the first time in some while. And he wasn't the only one, considering the way his driver was currently watching Emma's departure with something like awe.

As Antonio exited the limousine and made his way to the private room at the Asquith where Dimitri Kyriakou and Danyl Nejem Al Arain waited, he forced his mind away from the way Ms Guilham's hips had swayed as she'd walked towards Piccadilly Circus tube station.

With ruthless efficiency he refocused his mind on the Winners' Circle.

The three men had met as students, and their friendship had been forged in the depths of their darkest moments. Through it all they had supported, commiserated and celebrated with each other. And when, after university, Antonio had needed capital to start his business, Dimitri, Danyl and his maternal grandfather had been his first investors. He had, of course, paid them back with interest, and in half the promised time. But he had never forgotten the debt he owed his friends.

Antonio knew in his heart, in his blood, that he wouldn't be here today without them. And they would say the same of him. And now, after a year, all three men—each of whom regularly featured in the newspapers as some of the greatest living business figures— would finally be together in the same room again.

As he made his way towards the table in the private dining area a small blonde was hastily leaving, casting him with a frowning glance as she passed.

'What did I miss?' Antonio asked, taking in the appearance of his friends.

Wrongful imprisonment had taken its toll on Dimitri, yet his powerful Greek features still turned the heads of any nearby female. And Danyl didn't need to rely on his royal status as Sheikh in line to the Terhren throne. Brooding intensity radiated from him—as Antonio's last assistant had remarked.

Only the might of the American legal system had put a halt to their quarterly meetings—the one immovable feature in Antonio's increasingly full diary. But within the year Dimitri's innocence had been realised and proclaimed, and now they were finally back together again.

'A proposition,' Dimitri replied in response to Antonio's question.

'In public? During the day? Gentlemen, you're putting my scandalous reputation to shame,' Antonio asserted.

'A *professional* proposition,' growled Danyl through gritted teeth.

'She—' nodding to the exit made by the blonde woman '—wants to race for the syndicate in the Hanley Cup,' Dimitri clarified.

'We have a jockey,' interjected Danyl.

'She says she can win all three races.'

Antonio was mildly intrigued. 'That's not been done since...'

'Since her father trained the horse and rider twenty years ago,' supplied Dimitri.

Antonio's mind raced through the implications. '*That* was Mason McAulty?'

A rather undignified grunt emerged from Danyl's direction.

Antonio considered the possibilities...the amount of the winning purse, the attention from the global press. News of their racing syndicate had ebbed and flowed over the years, but no one could argue with the level of their success. Founded shortly after their university days, it had been the perfect venture for three men who loved the high-stakes world of gambling, horseflesh and adrenaline.

Antonio had once been a serious contender for international-level polo, but that had been before Michael Steele's actions had all but destroyed his family. Biting back the familiar anger that was never far away from his thoughts of the man, Antonio forced his attention back to the proposition.

'Can she do it?' he asked.

Dimitri shrugged, but Danyl seemed to be giving it some thought.

'Most likely,' he eventually said.

'I'm in,' Antonio stated with an innately Italian shrug of his shoulders. If Mason McAulty managed it, the win would be incredible. If she failed... Well, was there any such thing as bad press? Antonio liked the edge that it would place them on. Hell, he practically *lived* on it.

'Why not?' Dimitri said, throwing his hat into the ring.

Danyl nodded almost reluctantly, his lips a grim line of determination. Antonio might not know the source of the furious look Danyl cast towards the exit Mason

Mcaulty had left through, but he very much hoped she knew that she was playing with fire.

'Whisky?' Dimitri queried as Antonio finally took his seat.

'Absolutely,' Antonio replied, relaxing back and drinking in the sight of his friends. 'It's good to have you back.'

'Say that again and I'll *know* you've gone soft,' came Dimitri's terse reply.

'If I wanted to listen to a bunch of women gossip, I could have stayed at home and visited the harem,' Danyl concluded.

Antonio scoffed. 'You don't have a harem. If you did we'd never see you.'

But instead of relishing the familiar bond he had with his two closest friends, Antonio found his mind returning to the woman he had just decided to make his new PA.

Emma Guilham...

CHAPTER ONE

Eighteen months later...

EMMA SWEPT THE long tendrils of dark hair back from her face and into a discreet neat bun with swift efficiency. Even had she not seen Antonio Arcuri's occasional frown when a few strands would escape the hold these pins had on her hair, she instinctively knew that this was what her ruthless boss wanted from her. Discretion, speed and efficiency.

As she checked her appearance in the ladies' bathroom at the New York office of Arcuri Enterprises, the shadowed silver insignia of the letters *A* and *E* conjoined in the corner of each large mirror snagged her attention and sent a thrill of satisfaction through her.

She had come so far from her mother's small but comfortable home on the fringes of Hampstead Heath. She thought back to the quite outrageous way she had been interviewed by Antonio in that limousine, inching its way through London's Christmas traffic. She had, in her mind, been brazen. But then Emma had honestly thought that she stood no chance of getting the job. With nothing to lose and everything to gain, she had simply spoken the truth.

She had meant every word she'd said, and had stuck

to each and every one of them in the last eighteen months. She had fought so hard to be here—to be in New York, to be Antonio Arcuri's PA. And she wouldn't let his wholly uncharacteristic, unscheduled and increasingly imminent arrival now put her off her stride.

Ever since the ping had sounded on her phone at one in the morning, alerting her to the fact that Antonio would be back from Italy and in the office in less than six hours, Emma had felt something akin to panic. Only she had assured herself she no longer *did* panic. Instead, Emma had launched herself out of bed, scanned his appointments and found nothing in his diary to warrant such an unexpected return. So, she had no idea what to expect from her brooding Italian boss.

She had begun to look forward to the times when Antonio was away from the office. Whether it was for his immovable meetings with the other members of the Winners' Circle syndicate, or his visits to his offices in London, Hong Kong and Italy, she relished the time when she only had to deal with him through the separation of email and the occasional video conference. She welcomed these reprieves from his presence. Because in reality, in the flesh, Antonio was simply... overwhelming.

It was more than his classic good-looks. His bitter-chocolate-coloured eyes, set against defined cheekbones and a determined jaw would be devastating enough on any man. Along with the smooth Italian tan that contrasted with the deep rich wine colour of lips that were almost cruelly sensual. Every inch of him was honed, powerful and predatory. But she knew that even all those attributes combined didn't matter. It was the vitality—the authority that resonated from his very being—that really called to her.

But she had learned to temper her attraction. Refused to allow it to interfere with her work. She was here to do a job—not to lust after her attractive boss. She refused to fall into the trap so many other women had fallen into. Besides, she had goals—places she wanted to see, things she desperately wanted to do—none of which included Antonio Arcuri.

The door to the large office bathroom slammed open and a string of women rushed in, each armed to the hilt with make-up bags. Emma watched them for a moment, producing the tools of femininity that were used to enhance and seduce, delicately applying a million products as she once had, at the age of seventeen, using them with a heavy hand to mask the ravages of chemotherapy.

But she forced the memory aside. It wasn't as if Antonio cared at all about her appearance. Just her ability. Emma smiled ruefully at the row of Arcuri's female staff. Antonio had that effect on women. But not her. She might find her boss devastatingly attractive, but she wasn't going to be distracted by him.

She wasn't going to be distracted by any man.

Settled behind her computer in the outer room of Antonio's top-floor office, she let a feeling of control and calm wash over her. This was her domain and she loved it.

The clean chrome lines made the CEO's office on the twenty-fourth floor of the Manhattan skyscraper more than she could ever have imagined. The glass-fronted building afforded a highly sought-after vista of Central Park, allowing incredible views of the famous skyline to be her daily backdrop. The decor screamed money and wealth. Even if she only borrowed it dur-

ing the day, before returning to her tiny apartment in
Brooklyn each night.

Coming to New York had been the first thing Emma
had been truly able to check off her Living List, after
five years of remission had finally signalled the end of
the terrible illness that had taken so much from her. And
even if she had stayed in her role as Antonio's personal
assistant for a little longer than she had originally intended, failing to tick off some of the other things on
her Living List since coming here...she chose to ignore
it. She was happy. And there was always time in the
future—in *her* future.

'Do you know why he's here?'

Emma looked up from her desk to find James, a very
nervous low-level exec, almost twitching with panic. He
swept his glasses off his face, revealing bleary eyes, and
cast her a look as other staff, equally nervous, watched
from the corridor.

Word of Antonio's impending arrival must have
spread like wildfire for, while it wasn't unusual to see
some of the Arcuri staff beavering away at this un-
godly hour of the morning, it was unusual to see *all*
of them. But that was the effect of Antonio Arcuri. He
didn't ask—he expected. He didn't demand—he simply didn't have to.

'Is he here yet?' James asked now, not waiting for
an answer to his first question.

'Mr Arcuri has business to attend to, nothing more,'
she said reassuringly, not really knowing if that was
true or not.

'It's just that... Well, given the current climate...'

'Arcuri Enterprises is strong enough to survive *any*
climate—current or otherwise,' Antonio's Italian-ac-
cented voice cut in harshly.

Emma hated the way he did that. Crept into rooms like a silent-footed panther. And she felt pity for poor James, who had turned from nervously pale to humiliated red with just one sentence from their boss, before fleeing the room.

Antonio turned on Emma. 'Why does everyone look as if they're about to get fired?' he demanded angrily.

Emma resisted the urge to sigh. He was clearly in *that* mood. A mood which made it easier for her to resist eating up the sight of his six-foot-plus powerful and lean frame.

'It is a little unusual for you to break your trip to Italy.'

'I need Danyl and Dimitri on a conference call immediately. And I need you to start a research file on Benjamin Bartlett. Everything and anything you can find on him and his company,' he said, throwing the last over his shoulder as he moved towards his office.

'I'll get the research team on it right away.'

'No,' Antonio said, pausing mid-stride. 'No one else is to know. I want you to handle it personally.'

With that, he stalked into his office, slamming the door behind him, and Emma sighed again. She closed the open folder on her desk concerning the Arcuri Foundation's charity gala—a project she had already invested much of her spare time in—knowing that she would have to take it home that evening. And as she dialled the numbers she knew by heart to get Dimitri and Danyl, she wondered just who Benjamin Bartlett was and why he was so important.

Antonio Arcuri willed the adrenaline coursing through his veins to subside. He discarded his suit jacket on the sofa and instead of taking a seat at his desk stalked towards the floor-to-ceiling windows fronting his office and flexed his hands.

He had decided to give the task of researching Benjamin Bartlett to Emma on the flight back here from his mother's house in Sorrento. He had been impressed with his calm, unflappable PA over the past eighteen months. Eighteen months in which he'd ruthlessly tamped down his initial and very much unwanted sensual interest in her from the moment she had stepped into the limousine on his way to the Asquith club in London.

Of course it helped that she dressed like the founding member of some religious organisation, and showed absolutely no interest in him whatsoever outside of their business interaction. He'd had PAs before who had raised their eyebrows and been uncomfortable handling some of his more indiscreet requests, such as fending off ex-lovers or acquiring suitable parting gifts. Despite what her conservative appearance suggested, Emma had handled each and every one without judgement or comment. The only thing she asked for was financial approval.

In short, Emma Guilham was *very* good at her job.

Which was exactly why he trusted her implicitly to handle the research on Bartlett. He couldn't risk news of his interest in the man leaking out before he'd had a chance to arrange a meeting with him. But it wasn't Bartlett himself that he was after. He could have taken or left his famous heritage brand, having no need to add it to his investment portfolio. No. It was the *other* potential investor that Antonio had in his sights. The investor that Antonio wanted to crush beneath his heel until no trace of him remained.

As he stood before the windows he didn't see a millimetre of the lush green sanctuary in the middle of New York's bustle. Antonio saw victory within his grasp.

Finally Antonio had the chance to bring Michael Steele to his knees. To cripple him completely, once and for all.

For so long he'd been nibbling away at the outskirts of Steele's business dealings. And each time Antonio took one more bite from the man's holdings he thought of his mother and sister. Of the shock and devastation Steele had wrought against his family with efficient ruthlessness. The subsequent pain that had nearly destroyed his mother, and the emotional scars that his young sister had turned against her own body until there had been almost nothing of her left.

Antonio had spent years clawing his way up the financial ladder...for this. The chance to destroy Michael Steele once and for all.

The buzz of the intercom cut through his thoughts and Emma's voice announced that she had Danyl and Dimitri on the line for him.

'What's wrong?' demanded Danyl.

Many would have been forgiven for thinking they heard anger in his voice, but Antonio knew better and identified concern.

'Nothing's wrong. In fact it's the exact opposite.'

'It must be...what?...six in the morning in New York?' queried Dimitri. 'Even *you* don't usually start until a bit later.'

'It's seven.'

'I feel sorry for your PA,' remarked Danyl. 'She just went into battle with my assistant to get me in on this call instead of calling the Terhren Secretary of State.'

'Don't feel sorry for her,' Antonio responded. 'Be impressed.'

'I am,' Danyl replied. 'Anyone who can put my assistant off state business is worth their weight in gold.'

'I have it. The way to take down Steele once and for all.'

Antonio didn't need to explain who he was talking about, nor why it was so important. Dimitri and Danyl knew what this meant to him—had meant ever since the age of sixteen.

'How?' asked Dimitri.

'I've been reliably informed that Benjamin Bartlett is looking for a healthy financial investment in his company. It would be Steele's last chance for financial security. He has the capital to invest, but not enough to survive without it.'

'And you plan to ensure that *you* win the investment,' stated Dimitri. 'Whatever you need—it's yours.'

Antonio smiled. 'That's not necessary. I can counter any investment offer he makes to Bartlett.'

'I've met Bartlett. I must say I'm surprised that he's looking for investment. He's always been financially stable.'

'You know him?' demanded Antonio. 'How?' he asked, his quick mind already working out how to use this to his advantage.

'He's a keen horseman. A regular feature on the international racing scene.'

Antonio frowned, scanning his usually perfect memory for any moment when he might have met the man amongst the numerous races they had attended as members of the Winners' Circle syndicate.

'He usually keeps to himself, though,' Danyl continued. 'Tends to stay away from the more *lively* areas that we enjoy. He'll probably be in Argentina for the first leg of the Hanley Cup. Do you know why he's looking for investment?'

'The why doesn't matter. I'll do anything to make sure that I win the investment and not Steele.'

Silence greeted his pronouncement. For a moment Antonio worried that the connection had been lost.

'Antonio, be careful. Desperation makes a man dangerous. I know this better than anyone,' Dimitri warned.

'I can handle the man.' Antonio practically growled down the phone.

'I wasn't talking about *him*.'

A knock on the door preceded Emma's appearance with the espresso he very much needed at that moment. Telling Dimitri and Danyl to hang on, he put the call on hold and waited for Emma to put the coffee on his desk and leave.

He was also buying time. Dimitri's warning hadn't fallen on deaf ears. But Antonio had spent years waiting for this day. He knew his mother would be saddened by his continued pursuit of revenge. She had pleaded with him over the years to move on. To put the hurt behind him—behind them all. But he couldn't.

As Emma retreated to her desk behind the door to his own office, he surprised himself by wondering if she would understand. There had been times when his usually conservative, cool-eyed assistant had shown a deeply hidden spark of defiance, something like the fight he felt at that moment. But as the door clicked closed he put that thought aside and resumed his call.

'That might not be the only problem that you face, Antonio,' said Danyl.

'Whatever it is, I can handle it.'

'I'm not so sure. Bartlett is notoriously moralistic. And your recent and very public exploits with a certain Swedish model might be a rather large putting off for him.'

An image of the blonde who had graced his bed for a number of months rushed into Antonio's mind. For the most part their encounter had run along the usual lines. Brief but sensually satisfying trysts whenever their diaries brought them together. Until she had started to ask for more. To ask for things he had told her wouldn't be part of their relationship. And when he had ended things she had quickly transitioned from a cool, poised and sophisticated companion into a raging, deeply resentful and incredibly publicly wounded lover.

'I can hardly be blamed for the fact she went to the press. I made her no promises—no lies were told. She knew the score and should have handled the end of our...interaction...with more finesse.'

'Whether or not she *should* have, she didn't. And Bartlett won't like it one bit. He has a strict morality clause for all his board members. And the last to break it two years ago is still looking for work, from what I hear.'

'What exactly are you saying, Danyl?'

'Well, you might need to take yourself off the market, so to speak.'

What? Shocked, Antonio didn't realise that the word had failed to escape his tightly clenched jaw.

'You've either shocked him into silence or you need to explain more clearly what you mean, Danyl,' Dimitri said, laughing.

'Marriage,' replied Danyl.

'Just because *you're* looking for a wife, it doesn't mean *I* have to.'

Everything within Antonio roared an absolute *no* at the idea. All the women he had encounters with knew the deal—even the Swedish model, though she'd seemed to forget it.

Short term, high hits of sensual pleasure were important to him. He was a virile male, after all, and not one to deny himself sexual satisfaction. But nothing more. He neither wanted nor needed the distraction of anything more permanent.

He washed away his distaste at the very idea of marriage with a hot, strong shot of espresso. He scanned his mind for any examples of a healthy, successful partnership and could not find one. Neither Dimitri nor Danyl had any particular fondness for the institution of marriage themselves, though for Danyl—being the future ruler of Terhren—it had become a considerably more pressing matter.

Their bachelor status was something that the press had latched on to more than once when covering the successes of their Winners' Circle racing syndicate. And it was certainly something that drew a wealth of beautiful women to their door. Was Antonio ready to consider closing that very door on the one thing aside from his business that he took *very* seriously?

'How bad is he really?' he asked his friends.

'That board member I mentioned…? He hadn't even had an affair. It was the rumour that Bartlett objected to.'

'Perhaps you don't have to…how do the Americans say it?…eat the whole hog—?'

'*Go*, Dimitri. It's *go* the whole hog,' interrupted Danyl.

'Please—we're talking about a wife, here. Can we leave out references to eating and hogs?'

'That's what I'm saying. Perhaps it doesn't have to be a wife.'

* * *

Emma had finished filing the quarterly reports, reassured countless staff members that, no, she didn't think Antonio's sudden appearance meant staffing cuts, and given consolatory smiles to a number of overly disappointed female employees who had failed to catch sight of Antonio before he'd locked himself in his office for most of the day. She had collated all the information she could on Benjamin Bartlett from initial online searches and saved it to Antonio's private drive, and finally settled down to eat the lunch she had missed three hours ago.

So, of course, as her mouth was full of avocado and bacon bagel, that was the precise moment Antonio Arcuri chose to appear before her desk. With a demand that took every ounce of her control not to choke on.

'Emma. I need you to find me a fiancée.'

Emma's usually focused and quick mind halted in its tracks. Of all the things she'd ever been asked by her notoriously difficult boss, this had to hit the top of the list.

'Do you have a particular person in mind? Or will anyone do?'

She had finally managed to swallow her mouthful around the shock that threatened to lock her throat in a seized position. And she was hopeful that her voice betrayed none of the sarcasm she felt so deeply, and instead projected only the smooth efficiency she knew Antonio prized so highly.

Emma loved being a personal assistant. She knew there were people who looked down on what they considered a lowly position. But, to Emma, the satisfaction of ensuring that her boss's day—his *life*—ran without stumbling blocks was important to her. She liked feeling indispensable. She liked knowing that she was part of something much bigger than she could ever achieve on her own.

And she liked fixing things.

If she was honest, it was because she knew how awful it was *not* to be able to fix something for herself. How scary and frustrating it could be. Whether it had been her breast cancer or the subsequent breakdown of her parents' marriage, she had been devastated by the sheer helplessness that she had felt at the time. And, whilst Emma might not have been able to fix the damage to her parents' marriage in the past, she could certainly help find Antonio a fiancée in the present.

Antonio pinned her with a gaze that would have removed a certain amount of testosterone from many of his male employees and likely increased the pheromones in the female ones.

'Was that sarcasm?'

'No,' Emma assured him, hoping the painful blush staining her cheeks wouldn't give her away. 'I simply wondered if you had your sights set on someone specific.'

'No,' he replied, frowning.

'So...' She battled on through the oddness of the situation. 'Do you have any parameters for this search? Wealth, previous marital status, level of attractiveness...?' She was desperately thinking of a polite way to say *bra size* when she registered with some surprise Antonio's confusion. He clearly hadn't thought this through.

'Reputation. She must be scandal-free.'

Emma fought to contain the rather un-ladylike snort that tickled her nose. It sounded as if he were looking to buy a prize heifer with an up-to-date vaccination history. Which made her wonder, horrified for a moment, whether the poor woman in question might in fact be required to present a full medical history.

'And I need her within two days.'

'Antonio, I'm not Amazon Prime. I can't just produce a…*a fiancée*,' she whispered harshly, fearing that she might be overheard, or even accused of some kind of highly salacious 'procurement' for her boss. 'Perhaps if you could explain the…the context, it might be slightly easier for me to…to understand what's needed.'

She knew she was stumbling over her words but, given his current mood, she clearly had to choose them wisely.

'I am about to set up a meeting with Benjamin Bartlett, who is touting for investment in his company. A company in which *I* must be the sole investor. And, being a notoriously moral man, Bartlett might be reluctant to involve himself with Arcuri Enterprises given…' He trailed off, circling his hands in a typically Italian gesture.

'Given your recent experience with Inga the Swedish—?'

'I know what she was, Ms Guilham,' Antonio cut in.

'Quite. So you need a beard?'

Antonio's hand went to the smooth planes of his chiselled jaw. 'A beard?'

'Not that kind of beard,' she said, suppressing the smile that toyed at the edges of her mouth. 'You need a fake fiancée to mask your previous indiscretions so that Bartlett will find you more palatable and therefore be more likely to welcome your investment.'

'In a nutshell, yes.'

'And am I to presume that all of this—' she said mirrored his Italian gesture '—needs to be kept under

wraps? No one is to know about this, as well as the research into Bartlett?'

He nodded his dark-haired head once. 'There is another party interested in investing with Bartlett. My
interest cannot get out to that person—or any other for
that matter.'

The darkness of the warning in his voice was something that Emma hadn't yet encountered in her boss.
And that in itself was enough to inform her that this
wasn't to be taken lightly.

Her quick mind filed the top-line notes of his request. 'Okay. I'm going to need to clear your schedule
tomorrow evening.'

This was why Emma was good, Antonio thought
to himself. Apart from the slight slip-up of her earlier
sarcasm, which he would happily put down to surprise,
when she took on a task she was efficient, direct and
held none of the self-doubt he had seen in staff twice
her age.

He knew her announcement of his change of plan
for tomorrow would be wholly and one hundred per
cent in line with her new-found task. A task that she
hadn't balked at, and had only posed pertinent questions on. Mostly.

'Done.'

'I'll have your blue tuxedo sent to the dry cleaners
and prepared for the gala.'

'What gala?' Antonio queried.

'The Arcuri Foundation's yearly charity gala. You
are usually in Italy during these two weeks, which is
why you are never sent an invitation.'

'We have a charity gala?'

For the first time in eighteen months Antonio was

surprised to see something like anger in Emma Guilham's eyes.

'Yes, we do.' She paused, once again masking her obvious feelings on the matter with her legendarily cool gaze. 'And it will be the perfect place for you to find a fiancée.'

CHAPTER TWO

ANTONIO HAD SPENT the last twenty-four hours going over the research files Emma had put together on Bartlett—and the other research she had provided.

If he found anything distasteful about looking at the pictures and brief biographies Emma had collated of several of the single female attendees of that evening's event, he ruthlessly forced it aside. He had but one goal. And tonight would be the first step in achieving it.

Emma buzzed on the intercom, interrupting his thoughts to announce that the car was there to take them to The Langsford Hotel. Although it was only a fifteen-minute walk from the office, and he'd been inclined to make that walk, Emma had swiftly denounced the idea, saying that it wouldn't 'do' to have the CEO of Arcuri Enterprises *walking* up to the red carpet in front of the world's press. After all, she had said, she was apparently now in the business of safeguarding his reputation.

He'd repressed a smile. He was beginning to enjoy these brief glimpses of a dry English humour that she had hidden from him until now. Pulling at the sleeves of the tuxedo's jacket to fit them to the lines of his arms and torso, he opened the door to his office—and stopped.

Emma was perched on the end of her desk, leaning over towards the phone and looking quite unlike any way he'd seen look before.

She was still adorned in her usual monotone colours of black and white, and the wide panels of her loose dress covered all but the faintest glimpses of her figure. But her dark hair was piled up on her head in thick twirls, revealing strands of gold and deep reds that he had not seen before. It framed her heart-shaped face perfectly, and a light dusting of make-up served to accentuate the hazel and green of her eyes. A nude gloss lent a sheen to her lips that sent a punch to his gut more powerful than any brighter, richer colour could have achieved.

She looked natural and fresh—and so very different from the women he usually spent his time with.

'Yes, don't worry. The waiters know what to do. But because Ms Cherie was a last-minute addition to the invitation list we couldn't have known her dietary requirements before. The kitchen staff always make three extra portions of each main, so just reassure her that a vegan option will be made available to her.'

Antonio watched as Emma hung up the phone, catching the unusual sight of a long, shapely, creamy calf.

'Vegan?'

Emma turned, clearly surprised to find him standing there.

'Enough of a crime to scratch her off the fiancée list?' she asked.

'Not yet,' Antonio said, forcing his libido under control.

During the day—in her usual office attire—she wasn't so much of a problem. But even though Emma was covered from head to toe, that glimpse of smooth marble-like skin was enough to snare his attention. And he suddenly understood why Victorian England had deemed ankles the most threatening thing to society since smallpox.

Shaking his head to rid his mind of inappropriate thoughts about his PA, he led the way to the elevator that would take them down to the limousine waiting for them in the underground car park.

In the confines of the metal box, with Emma beside him, Antonio realised that it was going to be a long night.

Emma couldn't wait for this night to be over. They hadn't even arrived at the gala and she was already exhausted. It had taken every waking minute she'd had, not only to put together her research on Bartlett and compile the dossiers on Antonio's prospective fiancées—not that most of them *knew* they were prospective fiancées—but also to ensure that the foundation's gala wasn't single-handedly ruined by the very man in charge of organising it in the first place.

Marcus Greenfeld was a fusty old man, with fusty old ideas about how to run a charity. And it made her mad. She'd caught sight of his opening speech on the photocopier on the twenty-third floor and realised that something had to be done.

She'd hastily rewritten the thing, told a bold-faced lie to Greenfeld's assistant that Antonio had wanted to take a look at it, and sent it off to the teleprompter before Greenfeld had even been able to think of questioning it. Or question the three extra invitations she'd had issued to fiancée options four, five and six.

Antonio might have told her what he needed in a fiancée but, honestly, the man's taste in women was so varied she couldn't tell which way he would go. Though option two—the vegan Ella Cherie—was looking increasingly less likely.

As the limo pulled up to The Langsford she remembered she had yet to tell Antonio about the other last-minute invitation.

'Dimitri will be here tonight,' she said as they slowed to a stop. 'Danyl was…unable to attend.'

'Well, he *is* running a country.'

Emma wasn't so sure. She'd heard angry words in the background when she was on the phone to his assistant. There had been something behind the bitterly shouted phrase, *'I wouldn't go back to that hotel if you paid me!'* that had made Emma concerned that her suggested location for the gala might be a mistake.

But there was nothing online other than praise for this exquisite, world-renowned hotel. A hotel she'd heard of even back in London, when she'd scoured the press reports of its grand opening. She might never be able to afford to stay in the amazing hotel herself, but that didn't mean that she couldn't experience it vicariously through work.

'Why?' Antonio asked, and Emma wondered briefly if she'd missed something.

'Why, what?'

'Why did you invite them?'

'I thought that you might need some independent advice on your choice.'

Antonio looked at her, but she was unable to divine his thoughts.

'Wingmen—I thought you might need wingmen,' she clarified.

'Emma,' he said, with censure heavy on his tongue. 'I have *never* needed a wingman.'

And the answering shivers that rippled through her body told her just how right he was.

As she did at most events Antonio attended for work, Emma stayed discreetly behind him during the initial introductions, her quietly whispered words prompting him with the names of the gala's guests and their partners. There had been times in the past when the additional information she provided had saved him from embarrassment—especially once when Antonio had nearly mistaken a man's mistress for his wife.

He was surprised to see so many recognisable faces. He could honestly say that he had never given this gala a first thought, let alone a second. If it didn't contribute to bringing Michael Steele down, it didn't matter to him. Marcus Greenfeld—the man Antonio had inherited along with the foundation he had secured for Arcuri Enterprises all those years ago—had never demanded anything of him and he liked it that way. Antonio had never taken to the man.

'Natasha.'

Emma's voice cut through his thoughts. He turned to find her welcoming the statuesque and considerably beautiful black woman making her way towards him.

'How lovely to see you again,' Emma said, kissing the woman on both cheeks.

The answering smile spoke of a friendship between the two and he instantly recognised the woman as fiancée option number one.

'Natasha—allow me to introduce you to Antonio Arcuri. Antonio—Natasha Eddings,' she said, gently proffering the woman to him like a gift, before swiftly disappearing to leave him alone with her.

Within minutes Antonio didn't have to bring to mind

Emma's handwritten scrawl on her brief bio—*This is my favourite*—to see why Natasha was Emma's choice. Natasha was articulate and intelligent, beautiful and, in short, practically perfect. But while she might meet *his* requirements, he had the odd impression that he did not meet hers.

'It would seem that my usual and widely reported charm might be falling a little flat this evening,' he remarked, testing his theory.

Natasha smiled apologetically. 'I'm sorry, Mr Arcuri. Emma did explain to me the delicate nature of your…interest,' she said, clearly searching for suitable phrasing.

A shiver of alarm passed through him quickly, but she pressed on.

'I assure you that I don't know why—only that you are looking for a fiancée—and no one will hear about it from me. I know that Emma has not spoken to anyone else of it. But…'

'You are perhaps involved with someone?' he offered, giving Natasha a way out.

'I am. Whoever you choose will be a lucky woman. I am sure of it. But I'm afraid I am not she.' Natasha smiled gently, smoothing any potentially ruffled feathers.

'Rest assured, Natasha, whoever he is,' he said, referring to her involvement, '*he* is the lucky one.'

The smile that lit her features was bright and spectacular.

'Thank you. May I offer a suggestion, Mr Arcuri?'

When he nodded his assent, she continued.

'Perhaps you don't have to be looking so far afield.'

With that, she disappeared into the crowd, leaving Antonio with a thought that was matched only by a growing suspicion on his part. But the clinking of glass interrupted his partially formed idea, sounding out the fact that the opening speech from Marcus Greenfeld was about to begin.

Having prepared himself for the most boring fifteen minutes of his life, Antonio was faintly surprised at the warm, heartfelt introduction given by the man as he clearly outlined the charity's main functions. Though his voice was slightly stilted, the words were full of compassion and drive—and were, in a sense, a call to arms.

Looking across the audience, he saw them resonate, and a ripple of emotion shuddered through each of the attendees that he, himself, was not immune to. The only thing preventing the speech from being truly inspirational was the man delivering it.

From the corner of his eye Antonio saw his CFO, David Grant, approach quietly, and they greeted each other with a fond nod of welcome.

'I have to say,' Antonio said in hushed tones, 'Greenfeld's doing much better than I remember.'

His CFO frowned, then smiled. 'Ah… I heard that it was down to you, but now I'm beginning to think that your PA has been sprinkling her magic fairy dust over his speech—as well as over this gala.'

Antonio was confused. What had Emma to do with all this?

David let out a gruff laugh. 'For the last two months Emma has been running interference with Greenfeld and doing everything possible to ensure this night is an unusual success. You're always out of the country for this event, but it's been growing steadily more boring and more dull each year. It was Emma's decision to move the gala to The Langsford and provide gift packages for the guests. Not to mention rewriting the speech. She's done wonders.'

Wonders, indeed. Antonio was about to voice his frustration at the fact that his perfect PA had effectively been moonlighting, but David's next words stopped him short.

'I suppose it's only natural, given her personal experience. Cancer research is one of the main focuses of the Arcuri Foundation, and that clearly makes her the perfect support for the event.'

Antonio stared at his CFO. Cancer? Emma had experienced cancer?

A roar sounded in his ears and it took him a moment to realise that it was the sound of the guests applauding.

Emma had watched Greenfeld's speech from the sidelines of the large entertainment suite at the top of The Langsford. She had pretended to be checking the gala's gift bags, ensuring that the male and female packages were all present and contained the small bottles of champagne a local winery had been happy to supply. Other companies had also lent their support, through handmade bracelets and perfume for the women, aftershave and cufflinks for the men.

She knew she'd thrown Antonio's name around as if it was currency, but it had been worth it. And if her boss took issue with it, then she would set him straight. Tonight the gala was predicted to raise more money in donations than the last two events put together.

Once again she was pushing something bigger than herself out into the world, and this time she could do some actual good. Funding would reach beyond the not so small world of Arcuri Enterprises and help people— *really* help people who desperately needed it. And for that...? Yes, for that she would go into battle with her boss if needed.

But as her hands had hovered over the blue and pink cloth gift bags Greenfeld's voice had projected her own words back to her, and she'd cursed the man for not being moved, for the barrier between his words and the emotions she felt in her chest. The man was simply not good enough at his job.

Still, Emma chided herself, she couldn't do *everything*. Tonight she should really be checking on how Antonio was getting on in his search.

Although she was pleased with the fiancée options she'd miraculously pulled from the gala at the last minute, she had noticed Natasha's departure from her conversation with Antonio with something horribly like relief. She liked Natasha. The bright, intelligent woman had been at several of the foundation's functions, but hadn't been able to help the awful sting of jealousy curling in her chest as she had seen them talk.

Antonio might be an unconscionable playboy, and she might have had to smooth the emotional waters for his ex-lovers, but she'd never had to see it personally. Through the hackneyed words of the international press that followed him almost constantly, she'd been able to see simply an incredibly attractive man who enjoyed beautiful women with good grace and no false promises.

And if she was foolish to wonder what it would be like to be one of those beautiful women, then that was her own look-out.

She had long given up on fantasies of being a beautiful blushing woman on the arm of a dashingly handsome man. Her experience with cancer had seen to that. It may have stolen her breasts—which she had been prepared for. But somehow it had been the prospect of nipple reconstruction that had truly defined its effect on her sense of self. Unwilling and emotionally unable to face yet another surgery, Emma had instead opted for medical tattoos. The tattooist had been kind and had worked wonders. The tattoos meant that she didn't look in the mirror and immediately see something missing. The implants she could handle, and the scars she could deal with, but that last thing had been the hardest.

And, beyond the fight she'd won against cancer, it wasn't just flesh and time that it had taken from her. It had stolen her parents' marriage, and it had stolen her sense of femininity. At seventeen she'd been a child, and now, at twenty-three, she had yet to feel like a woman. She was unable and unwilling to put herself out there and find someone she might trust her delicate sense of self to—trust, should the worst happen, that they'd be there for her on the other side.

Her eyes were drawn to Antonio's presence across the room. Standing almost a foot above most of the guests, he was never hard to find. And as she saw him laughing with fiancée option number four—one of the last-minute additions she had added just in case—she gave herself a little mental slap.

Putting her feelings back into a box, she went to check on the preparations for the gala meal.

Had anything ever been as annoying to him as this woman's laugh? *Ever?*

Antonio couldn't help but think not, as she pealed out another reel of hysteria at an inane observation that had fallen flat on his own ears.

He couldn't hold it against Emma. Amber—he couldn't keep thinking of her as option four—was fine. On paper. Two degrees...a board member at her mother's make-up company...daughter of an international diplomat. Tick, tick, tick. But in person...? She was a car crash. She was loud, there was that awful laugh, and then there was her appearance. Clearly she was a stunning woman, but as she nearly fell out of her tightly constricting dress he couldn't bring himself to feel anything other than distaste.

'So, you're into horseflesh? I love to have a flutter on the ponies occasionally. You're going to be in Buenos Aires for the first leg of the Hanley Cup next week?'

His noncommittal 'mmm' wasn't enough to put her off. But it did remind him of the need to check in with John—the trainer he had secured for the Winners' Circle from the staff his family had been forced to let go.

It had been both a gift and a curse to work with the gruff northern Englishman. Antonio was still unable to relinquish fully the stranglehold the past had on him even now, in the present. He wondered if Mason McAulty was still furiously adhering to the strict schedule she had set herself...

But his train of thought was interrupted as Amber placed a long-nailed hand on his forearm, and Antonio resisted the urge to flinch.

'Is it true that you have a *female* jockey riding your horse? How simply thrilling!'

Cue more laughter. Laughter that made him wonder what dry response Emma would have come up with.

Damn it.

Emma—the woman he had worked with for eighteen months and never known about her medical history. He wasn't so uncouth as to require one for members of his staff, and neither was he such an ass that he would have treated her any differently. But as his eyes raked over Amber and her figure-hugging outfit he suddenly realised what it was about Emma's figure that had always niggled at the back of his subconscious.

Breast implants. He hadn't initially noticed them—in fact had only just realised that they *were* implants. They weren't obvious—in reality they were incredibly subtle—and the disguising of them was clearly intended by her choice of wardrobe.

In an act of what could only be described as self-preservation, any time he had come near to considering his PA's *assets*, he had swerved sharply away. So, even as a man who considered himself a connoisseur of beautiful forms, perhaps he could be forgiven.

Assimilating this new information about Emma didn't make him think any less of her—only more. It added yet another layer of complexity to a woman who was beginning to take up far too much of his thoughts for a member of his staff.

'And that was when—'

'I'm sorry,' Antonio said insincerely, 'I've just seen someone I need to speak to.'

He left the blonde woman practically stamping her foot in his wake and went to find… Anything would be better than that.

Until he walked smack-bang into Marcus Greenfeld.

'Mr Arcuri,' he proclaimed, before Antonio could extricate himself from the situation. The man took off his greasy glasses and began rubbing them with his tie. 'Kind of you to come. Didn't have to, of course,' he said apologetically. 'I hope you don't mind the…the extravagance. But then, of course, it was your suggestion so, yes… Thank you. I—'

'You have done an amazing job.' The lie was giving the man far more credit than he was clearly due, but it was necessary to ensure that Emma's inspired intervention was fully felt. 'This evening's gala has garnered a huge amount of positivity,' he said, loudly enough for Emma to hear as she made her way over to the two of them.

Did he notice a slight blush on her cheeks?

'Mr Greenfeld... Mr Arcuri—the meal will be served shortly,' Emma informed them.

Antonio's hawk-like gaze raked over her—*all* of her. Even dressed in the clothes he now saw that she wore like armour, she outshone Amber like the north star.

'I was just telling Marcus how much I'm enjoying the gala. A truly wonderful event. And with that in mind I have decided to double the donations raised this evening. Marcus,' he said, turning back to the man, 'please be so good as to announce that before the meal starts. Let's see if it greases some wheels.' He tried not to look at the man's glasses as he spoke.

His statement signalled the end of the conversation, but Marcus Greenfeld still took an awkward moment to realise it was his cue to leave.

Emma was looking at him with huge round eyes. The same eyes that had first caught his attention in London. He needed to get his own eyes off his PA and on to the next fiancée option. He needed to keep his mind on track. He wasn't here for the charity—he was here to help secure the Bartlett deal.

'That's...that's wonderful, Antonio. Thank you so much.'

'You don't have to thank me. It's my charity, after all. Besides... It's good publicity.'

'I don't believe that,' she said, levelling him with a stare that saw far too much, and speaking in a voice that held too much optimism. 'I think you're doing it out of the kindness of your heart.'

'Don't paint any illusions about me, Emma. Trust me—there's very little good left in me.'

'Well, then. I'll just have to nurture that last little bit of goodness.'

As she slipped away into the throng of guests his errant mind wondered what else she might nurture and he cursed himself to hell and back.

When the guests started to make their way in a somewhat chaotic line through to where the meal was being served, he saw Dimitri peel off from a group of attractive women.

'Enjoying yourself?' Antonio asked as they stood back and watched the guests pile in for the meal.

'Absolutely. I wouldn't have missed this for the world,' Dimitri replied, full of laughter.

'I'm glad you find humour in this.'

'And in your purpose,' Dimitri responded, clinking his glass of champagne against Antonio's. 'So, anyone caught your eye yet?'

As Antonio scanned the guests at the gala, all decked in the kind of finery that suited their opulent surroundings, his eyes snagged on Emma once again.

'Emma shared the list of suitable candidates with me, and I must say, apart from that girl Amber, she's chosen wisely. Though if you're not overly taken with option one I'd be happy to take her off your hands.'

'*Che palle*, Dimitri.' Antonio cast Dimitri a dark look, but his friend only shrugged.

'*Ti?*' Dimitri queried in Greek.

'Natasha Eddings—"option one"—is not up for grabs. This isn't a cattle market, Dimitri. This is important. If Bartlett is even going to meet with me, then I need a fiancée to resolve any detrimental effects of my previous...assignations.'

'Is that what the kids are calling it these days?'

'Don't joke. This is a serious matter.'

'I know,' Dimitri said, his eyes shining with understanding. 'But, Antonio, you can't just stumble across a woman you've never met before, make her an offer to be your fake fiancée, expect her to have little or no ulterior expectations, and present her to Bartlett wrapped in a bow.'

Antonio bit back a curse. Dimitri was right. Urgency and necessity had made his usually quick and clever mind sluggish and slow. He saw the many flaws in his plan immediately.

What had he been thinking? He needed the deal, he needed to bring Steele to his knees, and he needed a fiancée who would understand and support him in it.

His eyes caught Emma, laughing with a member of the hotel's staff before stepping away through the glass doors to the balcony that wrapped around the outside of the hotel. She had done so much. He was impressed with how she'd multi-tasked, clearly making an unprecedented success of the event whilst never missing a beat in her day-to-day role. She was conscientious, bright and articulate. And above all she was professional. In short, she was perfect.

'Mum, it's...' Emma paused, pulling her mobile briefly away from her ear to check the screen for the time '... one a.m. in London. What are you doing up?'

'Oh, I got stuck into a painting and the next thing I knew it was midnight.'

As Emma looked out onto the famous New York skyline she imagined her mother in the brightly lit, airy loft of her home in Hampstead Heath. When her parents had divorced her father had been the one to leave, moving into a flat nearer to the school where he worked, but only round the corner from the home they had all once shared.

The divorce had signalled the end of the nightly fights that had become a regular feature of Emma's life—desperate and painful arguments her parents had thought she hadn't heard. The heart-wrenching accusations, the arguments over how differently to handle their sick daughter, and her father's confusion as to why Louise Guilham had changed beyond his recognition.

Emma had initially felt relief when they'd separated, and then guilt, knowing that her father still desperately loved her mother. His painful bewilderment at the transformation in his wife and child had cut Emma deeply, and prompted the awful thought that had it not been for her illness her mother might have somehow stayed with her husband, and she might have somehow found a way to keep them all together.

'Where's Mark?'

Emma liked her mum's partner. He made her happy, and he also gave her the space she needed to be creative at unsocial times. Emma knew better than most that when her mum 'got stuck into a painting' she could be gone for days. She loved her mum's paintings—her favourite one hung on the wall of her little Brooklyn flat—and still felt bad that her mother's work had been put on hold during her illness at a critical time in her mother's career.

'Asleep. I just wanted to know how the gala went.'

'It's still going, but it's going well. Antonio has offered to double the event's donations.'

'That's wonderful, darling.'

But even through her mother's happiness for her Emma could sense her distraction. She was probably staring at the painting critically right at that very moment.

Emma was about to ask when they might come over to visit her. Her mother and Mark hadn't made it out there yet, but that was okay, because she'd hardly had a spare moment since working for Antonio. But as if the very thought of him had conjured him from thin air, she felt rather than heard his presence behind her.

'Love you lots, but I'd better go.'

Emma hung up the call and put her mobile back in her purse. She gathered herself, knowing that her emotions were a little too close to the surface for her to face her boss just yet.

Adjusting her mind's eye back from her home in Hampstead to the beautiful night-time vista of famous skyscrapers silhouetted against the stars, she felt a cool breeze pass over her skin—and that was why she had goosebumps, Emma assured herself. Not because Antonio had come out here to find her.

He should be with the other guests sitting down for the meal. Perhaps he'd come to tell her that he'd found his perfect fiancée, she thought, uncharacteristically bitter.

She needed to pull herself together. Surely she could handle Antonio Arcuri's fiancée as well as she could handle him. But the thought of *handling* her boss gave rise to some very explicit images, and she had to push them aside as firmly as she placed a smile on her face and finally turned to see him.

He stood half in shadow, peering at her through bitter-chocolate-coloured eyes. There was something about the way he held himself. As if his body was restraining some kind of pressing energy. Energy she felt all the way on the other side of the balcony.

'Who was that?'

'What?'

'Who was on the phone that you love?' he asked, his Italian accent thick on the words.

Emma frowned at the personal nature of this conversation. She and Antonio didn't do personal. It was one of the things she liked and respected about him, and in her deepest heart she was thankful for it.

'My mother.'

'So there's no one at home waiting up for you? No boyfriend or otherwise?'

'No,' she replied, still confused.

'Then, Emma, I can see only one option before me. In order to secure the Bartlett deal I need *you*... *You* will be my fiancée.'

CHAPTER THREE

Huh... So *that* was what it was like to be proposed to.

It wasn't exactly how Emma had imagined it happening. Not even in her wildest imaginings. Though, if she was honest, Antonio Arcuri might have featured in some of her more fevered dreams—but never with such shocking words.

'In order to secure the Bartlett deal...'

'You will *be my fiancée.'*

While she might not have foreseen marriage in her future, if it *had* been to happen she would at least have hoped to be *asked.*

But why had he chosen her? Especially when he had a whole room full of perfectly suitable potential fiancées who were probably now picking the carbohydrates out of an exquisite three-course meal prepared by one of the finest chefs in New York.

She looked at him through the night gloom and saw something in his eyes. Something she had to look away from before it was transformed into pity.

'Who told you?'

'Who told me what?'

'Don't play games with me, Antonio. I'm not stupid.'

Anger ripped through her at an impossible speed. She'd wanted to start over. Start afresh in New York—

where people didn't know, didn't look at her as if she was an unexploded bomb waiting to go off. Yes, her work with the charity had naturally led to some astute observations by a colleague or two. But not Antonio. Because he hadn't known about her work with the charity.

'Is this because you feel sorry for me?'

'No!' he growled.

'I won't be used as some PR stunt to get what you want, Antonio. Playing on the sympathies of Bartlett with my "miraculous survival".'

'*Dio*, what kind of man do you take me for?' he demanded, clearly offended by the implication.

'The kind of man who would go to extreme lengths to acquire the perfect fake fiancée in order to pin down a business deal.'

'Well, I can hardly refute that claim. But my decision has nothing to do with your health and everything to do with the fact that you are a highly accomplished, educated woman who can move within my circles both with and without notice when necessary,' he stated, ticking her qualities off on each of his long, lean fingers. 'And, most importantly, you know that this will be solely a business arrangement. You will have no illusions of emotional investment that other women may mistake my offer to contain.'

'No, I don't have any illusions about the emotional investment behind your *"offer"*,' Emma replied, refusing to remove the sting from her tone.

Struggling to sort through the barrage of contrasting opinions he had bombarded her with, and against the wave of impatience he was sending her way, she turned out to the balcony.

He wanted *her* as his fiancée?

'I'm satisfied that you will not develop feelings for me and I will not develop feelings for you.'

A small sliver of hope curled in on itself deep within her. She should be pleased to hear that. She should want their relationship to be completely devoid of any possible emotional attachment, but somehow it still hurt.

'Why is this so important to you, Antonio?' she asked, hurt driving her to question her boss in a way she had never done before. 'You don't need the financial security of making the Bartlett investment, and you've never once cared about your...colourful reputation before. And surely if you want this deal badly enough you'll find a way to win against this other potential investor. What's really going on?'

He stared at her and said nothing for a moment. But then he spoke, as if realising that her agreement relied on full disclosure—or even part disclosure—and his next words shocked her.

'As I said before, it is not Bartlett that's important. It is the other man who might make investment in his company. Michael Steele is an evil man who cannot be allowed to succeed.'

Emma recognised the name, and knew that he had been the motivation behind some of Antonio's business dealings before.

'Why is Steele so important? Why go to such extreme lengths for a man who...?' She trailed off, not quite knowing who he was.

'A man who destroyed my mother and my sister's happiness—who changed their lives irrevocably and cruelly. This is Steele's last and final chance to gain financial security for himself. If he fails to win the Bartlett investment deal, he will lose his business. And I am determined to make that happen to the man...' He stopped, reluctance and anger warring for supremacy in his features. 'The man who is my father.'

Shock rippled across her skin and shivered through her body. Michael Steele was Antonio's father?

Antonio never talked about his family—had always valued his privacy above all else. She'd never once heard him mention his father—whose name he clearly no longer bore. But the darkness in his eyes and tone held so much anger and fury it crashed against her, pulled and pushed her away from Antonio like a tide.

It was unquestionable. And she couldn't help but wonder just how much his hatred of his father—something she simply couldn't comprehend—had driven him to this point.

'I will do anything to secure that investment, Emma. Anything. So if you have a price, name it. I will give it to you on a silver platter should you require it.'

Antonio would find himself a fiancée—whether it was her or someone else. But perhaps she could do something good with his offer. The thought raised hopes in her—some that she had discovered recently and some that she had long forgotten.

'What I want is for you to get rid of Marcus Greenfeld,' she practically growled. 'The man is incompetent and the foundation could be doing so much more. *You* could be doing so much more.'

'Is that it?' he demanded, his sensual mouth forming in a grim line of determination.

'Well, while we're at it, you can give each of my parents an all-inclusive holiday to wherever they want.'

'Done and done,' Antonio said, discarding her outrageous request as if it were nothing. 'You should know that as my fiancée you will be coming to Argentina for the Hanley Cup, once my meeting with Bartlett has been arranged.'

A rush of excitement swept across her skin. She'd always wanted to see the world. It was why she'd come to New York eighteen months ago.

'There will be a need to keep up this façade for a short while after the deal. Six months should be enough. So naturally you will accompany me on my visit to Hong Kong as well.'

As she thought through the future, to the trip to Buenos Aires and the trip to Hong Kong, the reality of what she was agreeing to dawned on her.

'And what about after Hong Kong? After six months when I'm no longer needed as your...your fake fiancée?'

'You'll be taken care of,' he announced.

She was sure he meant that. There was clearly no way she would be able to continue as his assistant once their 'engagement' was broken. She knew that he would provide her with a glowing reference and help secure her a future position, because he was that kind of boss. But she also knew—more than most—that the only person who could take care of her was herself.

No, she had never seen marriage or relationships in her future, but that didn't matter. Antonio wasn't offering her either. But there was something that scared her a little about being cut loose from her role as his assistant. And that, Emma realised, was the true price of what he was asking—her job. She had always meant to use this position as a stepping stone to other things. And maybe this was the not so gentle nudge that she needed.

Perhaps she could find work in Hong Kong? For a man she didn't find so frustratingly attractive. The trip to Argentina would be exciting too, and posing as his fiancée would be a way to help give her parents something too. Marcus Greenfeld would be removed and someone infinitely better, would replace him.

So, yes. Emma was prepared to cut her ties to Antonio once this was done.

'All I want is an appropriate reference.'

'Naturally,' he stated, as if they hadn't just bartered over the rules of their engagement.

Perhaps as his fiancée she would be able to tick off a few more things from her Living List. But she couldn't bring herself to ask for anything specifically for herself. After what she had faced, everything was a bonus. She didn't need anything more. Not really. The only thing she had ever wanted—could ever want—was for her body to feel like hers again. But not even the all-powerful Antonio Arcuri could do that.

'You have yourself a fiancée, Mr Arcuri.'

Finally, for the first time since Antonio had discovered that his father was after an investment in Bartlett's business, he felt the first taste of success on his tongue. Now all he had to do was get Bartlett to agree to a sit-down in Argentina.

His quick mind had already calculated the steps needed to accomplish that. But first he needed to reveal his new fiancée to the world.

He would, he realised, have to find a new PA. And, of course, ensure that Emma would have her pick when it came to choosing her next position. It was a thought that registered merely as an irritation alongside the satisfaction that Emma would be his. No, not *his*, he hastily affirmed. His pretend fiancée. For a business deal. Nothing more. He wouldn't risk *anything* interfering with his ultimate goal.

Another cool breeze brushed past them on the balcony and Emma shivered. He shrugged out of his jacket and placed it around her delicate shoulders. She accepted it without a word, clearly focused on her sudden and surprising 'promotion'.

Knowing they had to return to the gala, Antonio guided her through the balcony doors to the reception room. Even the dim event lighting was harsh on his eyes as they adjusted from the dark starlit night.

At the end of the room the doors were open and the gala guests were beginning to wander back through to the bar to continue with the night's agenda, hopefully having lined their stomachs in order to allow them to further enjoy themselves.

He judged that nearly thirty people were now filling the bar area, and decided that it would be enough.

'We should get ready to leave,' he said to Emma.

'The gala isn't set to finish for another two hours yet. I—'

'You can let the foundation's staff handle the rest. From what I've heard you've handled quite enough already. Besides, I have a feeling you're going to want to make a quick exit.'

'Why?'

He didn't give her time to think about it. He didn't give himself time to think about it. He had already decided his course of action should she say yes out on the balcony. He was about to ensure that the world knew about his new fiancée—in the quickest, most expedient way.

Antonio pulled her towards him, slipping his arms through the space between his jacket and her body. His hands met the curves he'd imagined to be there—the dip of her small waist, the arch of her back. They had a mind of their own as they swept across the silken material of her dress, sparking little bursts of electricity across his skin from the gentle friction. And his lips…

Emma felt the swift, determined crush of Antonio's mouth against hers. The shock of his hands against her waist, her back, startled a gasp from her. His tongue made swift work of the opportunity and plunged between her slightly parted lips.

Fire. Everything he did, every move he made, conjured up only that one word and that one sensation. It felt as if flames were licking across her skin, burning her from the outside in. For a shocking moment she thought her knees might buckle, and thrust out her hands to clutch the material of his shirt in her fists, anchoring them together even further.

As his tongue plunged more deeply into her mouth she felt as if her skin was a barrier—to him, to it, to what she wanted…

And then she heard the whistles. The cheers and the shouts grew louder, until she pulled back from Antonio's embrace and discovered they had a rather interested audience.

If Antonio had still been wearing his jacket she would have tried to hide in its lapels. She wanted the ground to swallow her up.

Until she realised that this public display was exactly what Antonio had wanted.

The stinging blush of embarrassment and shame painting her cheeks prickled and hurt. Of course he hadn't got carried away in the moment like she had. He had intended this. Was experienced in this. Antonio needed this and he needed her to play the part of doting fiancée—not naïve, out-of-her-depth PA.

She saw Dimitri come to the front of the crowd and

watched as a brief look of surprise was replaced with a surprisingly boyish grin.

'Permit me to be the first to congratulate you on your *now public* engagement,' Dimitri announced loudly, encouraging the already jubilant crowd into more cries of excitement and congratulation.

Within seconds mobile phone flashes were dusting them as if in strobe lighting. Antonio anchored her in place, pressed against his chest, smiling for all the world as if he were a newly engaged happy man, and Emma did her best to follow his lead.

After a minute Dimitri stepped forward to shake hands with Antonio, whispering that he hoped they both knew what they were doing through a fixed smile.

'Antonio is a very lucky man, Emma. But he is also a handful. So if you find yourself in need, you just call me.'

Dimitri pressed a kiss to Emma's cheek, and she couldn't help but smile back.

'Thank you, Mr Kyriakou.'

'Dimitri. Please,' he said, dipping his head low and studying her intently.

He didn't look at her in the way other men had once, but in a way that conveyed sincerity. And something slightly darker than his apparent good humour.

'I mean it, Emma. Anything. Just call.'

'Okay—that's enough. I don't need you putting off my fiancée at the very first step, thank you,' Antonio interrupted, with the kind of patience and affection only borne out of a long friendship.

'So,' Dimitri said, stepping back and rubbing his hands together. 'Would you like an impromptu engagement party? Or a highly skilful distraction so you can make a quick getaway?'

'A distraction, please, Dimitri. But nothing—'

'Nothing scandalous. Yeah, I got the memo,' he said with an eye-roll, disappearing into the crowd, calling for champagne and a dance with the most beautiful woman present in the room—aside from Emma, of course!

Antonio guided his assistant to the elevators, hoping that the kiss hadn't dulled her unflappable nature in the same way it had his. *Dio*, had he known that beneath that buttoned-up conservatively dressed professional there was a siren waiting to be unleashed, he might have given a second thought to making Emma his. His *fake fiancée*, an internal voice shouted in his mind.

He would have to keep such displays of public affection to a minimum if he were going to have a hope in hell of containing this situation. So he clung to the next step. Clung to what he knew needed to happen.

'Your passport. Is it still in the office?'

For a moment he thought she might not have heard, but then understanding dawned across her features.

'Yes.'

'And the change of clothes you usually keep there?'

'Yes,' she said, and her efficient swift nod did nothing to dislodge her perfectly placed hair, pinned at the base of her neck. His fingers wanted to reach out and pull that hair apart, feel it against his skin.

He forced himself to focus. 'Given the likely content of tomorrow's newspapers, and the public reaction to our announcement, it might be better if you do not return home this evening.'

Emma frowned, thinking through the suggestion. 'You think they know where I live? But I'm no one. How would they—?'

'You are not *no one*, Emma. You are now the soon-to-be Mrs Arcuri, and I don't think I need to remind you of the interest my considerable wealth brings.'

'And you wouldn't want a camp of reporters outside a tiny one-bed apartment in the deepest depths of Brooklyn?' she asked, with a trace of that British wry humour dancing across her words.

'I am not a snob, Emma.' He swung round to look at her, shocked that she might even think so until he saw the smile painting her pretty features as she turned her head up to his.

'Not going for the Prince and the Pauper angle?'

'I couldn't if I wanted to, Emma. I'm no prince, and I pay you considerably more than what a pauper has.'

Emma let out a huff of laughter as the lift doors opened onto the exquisite chequered foyer of The Langsford. She followed in Antonio's wake as they approached the reception desk. The words *penthouse suite* and *charge to my personal account* drifted through her mind as she watched the interaction, feeling oddly displaced.

It took her a moment to realise that he was organising for her to stay here, in this hotel. She was his assistant, the booking of hotels was usually her domain, and yet it felt… She couldn't find a word for what it felt like to see Antonio in action, catering to *her* needs.

As he led her away from the hustle of the concierge's desk towards a private elevator and presented her with a gold key card, he asked if there was anything she might need from her apartment. Anything that couldn't be purchased for her between now and Buenos Aires. There was no way he would let her go back to her apartment and deal with the gang of wolves that would be sure to be camped out on her doorstep, waiting for an interview.

Assuring him that there wasn't anything, Emma

stepped into the elevator and stopped. Antonio was staying in the foyer. He would either be going home or back
to the office, she realised. She felt that she should say
something, that there should be some conclusion to the
events that had just happened, but oddly she couldn't.

'I'll need you in the office tomorrow morning, to
pick up your laptop and passport and amend our travel
details before we fly to Argentina.'

She agreed just before the elevator doors closed
and she was taken upwards through the building. The
smooth, swift motion seeming to increase the swirling
in her stomach. What on earth had she just agreed to?

ARCURI OFF THE MARKET FOR GOOD?
BY ROANNA KING

Shock engagement of international
tycoon breaks hearts!

*Female socialites around the world woke to
breaking hearts this morning at the news that
international investment tycoon Antonio Arcuri
of Arcuri Enterprises is officially off the market.*

*The notorious and now presumably ex-play-
boy, often seen wining and dining a bevy of beau-
ties from models to heiresses, has been stolen
from our clutches by...his secretary!*

*Little is known of the Englishwoman Emma
Guilham, other than that she has been in his em-
ploy for eighteen months and that she has been
unavailable for comment.*

*Such a surprising turn of events must surely
form a suspicion that there will be another shock
announcement in just nine months' time. But,*

whatever the future holds for the happy couple,
this intrepid reporter is very much looking for-
ward to what is sure to be the future Mrs Arcuri's
grand unveiling in Buenos Aires!

Antonio had known the press fall-out would be big,
but Roanna King and her regular exposés on the private
lives of the rich and famous had made his engagement
sound torrid. That she had put the word *secretary* in
italics was bad enough, but the presumption that Emma
might be pregnant?

Antonio threw the newspaper across the small table
before him in disgust.

He checked his watch. His private jet had taken off
from a New York airport less than forty-five minutes
ago. Glancing across the narrow cabin now, he observed
Emma taking in the lavish decor of the Arcuri jet, and
hoped that it hadn't turned her head. She needed to be
ready for the call with Bartlett.

A thought which reminded him of the last phone call
he'd received on his almost constantly vibrating mobile
since the news of his engagement had broken.

No, he'd assured his mother, his PA was *not* pregnant.
Yes, he was sorry that he hadn't called to tell her himself. *Dio*, he cursed himself, he hadn't even thought to
warn her, to tell her. He'd been so focused on Bartlett
and his father that he hadn't realised how his engagement would look to his mother and sister.

As to his mother's question about when she might
meet her future daughter-in-law, he'd only been able to
put her off. *Would* they meet? he asked himself. He had
no doubt that the two women would get along fine. More
than fine, if he thought about it. His mother would appreciate the smooth efficiency and dry humour of the

small brunette. But it sat awkwardly with him, and he couldn't stop the words that Emma had said earlier that day about her own parents from ringing in his mind. *"I won't lie to them."*

She had been forced by the newspapers to contact her mother and father and explain the situation. He didn't like it—he didn't want anything jeopardising this deal—but he hadn't been able to refuse her request.

His own mother was a sentimental woman, who believed that love and happiness were a vital part of life and should be a vital part of her son's life. But he couldn't bring himself tell her that he had no room for such things. So, he'd lied to his mother and ignored the clenching in his gut. It was a sacrifice worth making, he assured himself, as finally Benjamin Bartlett had agreed to a phone call.

He had twenty minutes. Twenty minutes to convince Bartlett to come for a sit-down in Buenos Aires. Or all this would have been for nothing. Rather than allowing doubts to enter his mind, he should be using that driving force to push him forward. He would succeed. He had to.

Emma could feel impatience and expectation pouring from Antonio in waves. She tried to block it out and instead focus on the very strange and really quite wonderful experience of travelling in the company's private jet.

The limousine had taken them to the airport where, instead of queueing to get through Customs and Security, they had simply been looked over and then led up a set of stairs beside the plane.

Emma feared she might have been spoiled for ever.

She had ignored the way that the air stewardess had cast a disparaging look her way, seeming to take in her appearance and discard it as beneath her notice. It wasn't exactly Emma's fault that she was wearing yesterday's office clothes, having been unable to get back to her apartment and not yet having had the opportunity to buy new ones.

Still, she'd accepted the glass of chilled Prosecco the unnervingly beautiful woman had placed on the table in front of her.

The stewardess was clearly reserving her blood-red lipstick smiles for Antonio. Perhaps it was because of the article. She could hardly have missed the headline screaming about Emma and Antonio's shocking engagement on the newspaper beside the man in question. Not that it seemed to prevent the woman's bright gaze lingering on him as if she would like to consume him whole. Nor had it prevented the way her hand rested on his shoulder just a little bit too long to be appropriate.

Emma cursed the way her stomach dropped as she wondered whether they had perhaps enjoyed each other's company before. Jealousy wasn't part of their bargain and she wouldn't let it dim the fizz of excitement that was building as she adjusted to the realisation that they were actually going to Argentina.

Her Living List might be full of hopes and dreams, but they had been practically based on her income, on her finances. This deal with Antonio took her possibilities to a whole new level. As his PA she had only ever borrowed a taste of that elegance, but now she could experience it for herself. Perhaps for these six months she could enjoy all that Antonio had to offer. Well. Almost all. She knew she wouldn't have the one thing that her body refused to realise she *couldn't* have.

Antonio's phone started to vibrate noisily.

'I'm going to put it on speaker,' he said, leaving the

phone to jerk around on the table between them, as if this wasn't the one phone call he'd been waiting a week to receive. 'I'd like your opinion on Bartlett, given your research.'

She nodded, and he finally accepted the call.

'Mr Arcuri?' Bartlett's assistant was on the line.

'Yes.'

'Mr Bartlett for you. Hold, please.'

The line went silent for a moment.

'Arcuri! I hear congratulations are in order...'

Antonio froze at the American's cultured tones; for a second they had sounded so much like his father's. He muted the call momentarily, cleared his throat and then resumed the call, cursing at the fact that Emma had witnessed this errant chink in his defences.

'Thank you, Mr Bartlett, your congratulations are very welcome.'

'Am I to presume that your insistence to speak to me is down to the fact that you have uncovered the news that I am looking for investment?'

'Yes.'

'Then I would love to know your source. I was under the impression that it was a highly guarded secret.'

'A gentleman does not kiss and tell, Mr Bartlett.'

'I would hope that you have been kissing no one other than your fiancée, Mr Arcuri.'

'I assure you that is most definitely the case,' he said, trying to ignore the way Emma was watching him. 'As to how this information was uncovered—I assure you that it was not from any party related to *your* business.'

Antonio knew there was enough weight in his tone to indicate that the leak had come from the only other person involved in the negotiations. His father. It was exactly as Antonio had intended.

'I must say I am surprised,' Bartlett pressed, refusing to rise to the bait, 'that a man such as yourself—a man with a reputation for ruthlessness—would want to invest in *my* business.'

'You have a quite remarkable heritage brand, Mr Bartlett, one that any investor would be lucky to be involved with. And ever since I began my relationship with Emma I have been motivated to make more...holistic business decisions.'

'Your relationship is quite recent?'

'Emma has been with me for eighteen months, and during that time I have come to realise what a wonderful woman she is,' he said, this time unable *not* to look at the woman in question—unable to take his eyes from the faint blush that rose to her cheeks. 'She is kind, caring and compassionate, Mr Bartlett, and I am sure you will discover that yourself, should you choose to meet in Buenos Aires and discuss things further.'

There was a pause on the line.

'As you are aware that I am looking for investment, I am sure you are also aware that your father is the only other petitioner in the matter?'

'Surely whether I am aware or not is incidental? Having two people determined to win investment into your company can only be a good thing for you.'

'I appreciate that, Mr Arcuri, but I refuse to allow this to turn into a circus. I have my reasons for wanting to keep this investment opportunity quiet, and if I am to meet with you in Buenos Aires then I want your assurance that it will remain the case.'

'I promise you, Mr Bartlett, that no one will hear about this matter from me, or anyone connected with me.'

'Good. Then I look forward to meeting both you and

Ms Guilham in Argentina. But I warn you, Antonio, your father's offer is good. You'll have to do something pretty spectacular to rival it.'

Antonio let Bartlett's warning settle in his mind as he finished the call. He gathered his thoughts, and was curious as to what Emma had taken away from the conversation.

'So…?'

'I think you are going to have to work hard to win his approval,' she replied grimly.

Bartlett's warning was irrelevant, he told himself. Antonio had waited sixteen years for this. Sixteen years to take his father down for destroying his home and his family.

He would do *whatever* it took to ensure it.

CHAPTER FOUR

EMMA WAS ROUSED from her sleep as the limousine pulled up to The Excelsus hotel in Buenos Aires and she wished she had managed to stay awake. The view from the plane as it had descended into Argentina had promised a stunning and wonderful place that she'd only ever had an internet connection to. Having booked Antonio's travel itinerary there a number of times, Emma had been eager to see it for herself.

She'd been captivated by the tall, gleaming structures that reached into the sky, surrounded by a harbour of sand and sea, with twinkling with promise and excitement in the morning light, and she was sad that she had slept through the journey the waiting limousine had taken once they had made their way through the sleek airport hallways.

As she got out of the car, surprising both the driver and Antonio—clearly she had been expected to wait for the door to be opened for her—she was hit by an almost cold wind, the kind that she had come to expect from an English autumn. Remembering that Argentina's coldest winter months took place during June and August, the slight chill in the air made Emma nostalgic for home.

When Antonio failed to emerge from the car, she turned back to catch his gaze through the open door.

'I'm going on to the stables. You can go on in and rest up in our rooms if you like.'

But Emma didn't want to go to the hotel. She wanted to see Buenos Aires—wanted to see the grand entrance to the race course and the small lakes she had only seen in internet pictures.

'I'd like to see the stables,' she said, but the slight delay in the careless shrug of his response made her realise that she was imposing. That he might want this time to himself.

'By all means,' he said, gesturing her to return to the car.

She got back into the warm interior, thankful for the heat that softened the surprising chill still stinging her arms. The fresh air had wiped away the jetlag she hadn't so far been aware of. Having stayed awake during most of the flight, she had effectively worked through the night and arrived in Argentina late morning, with only two hours' time difference.

She settled back into the plush leather seat, desperately trying to ignore the proximity to her boss that shouldn't be affecting her the way it did.

Antonio's fierce gaze was locked on the scene outside the window, as if he was actively trying to ignore her presence. But he had agreed that she could accompany him to the stables, and Antonio was not a man who would have agreed had he really not wanted her there, she assured herself.

The car took a sweeping loop away from The Excelsus, and Emma was slightly disappointed to find that it pulled up again only a short while later. The stables were housed directly beside the hotel, and she vaguely remembered that being the reason Antonio preferred to stay there.

This time she waited for the driver to open her door, and a half relieved, half satisfied look crossed the man's features. She thanked him and then stood up to take in the incredible view as he went to open Antonio's door.

The grounds of the racetrack were long and rectangular, flat and surrounded by thin fencing. Off to the left the impressive stretch of the hotel building loomed over the edges of the race course, with thin lines of aqua-blue hinting at the infinity pools that were boasted by the hotel. In her mind she filled in the hundreds and thousands of people who would cover the stands and the balconies on race day, and the incredible noise they must make.

She heard the slam of the car door behind her, and turned to see Antonio stalking off towards a group of large white buildings with terracotta-coloured roofs that reminded her oddly of the American stables she had seen amongst the Winners' Circle holdings. She followed him through the fenced-off area, where there were more signs of life, people and horses emerging from corners and shadows as if they had previously been hidden from view.

She was two steps behind Antonio as he went deeper and deeper into the large central building.

To call it a barn would be wrong. The sheer size of it could have enveloped the whole apartment block she lived in back in Brooklyn. This structure had sleek lines, all glistening steel and chrome, and the expansive concrete floor was spotless and wet from where a young teenager further down was cleaning it. The smell of horse sweat and manure was barely discernible, and the only sound she could make out aside from Antonio's leather-soled footsteps was a hushed conversation coming from one of the stalls.

* * *

Antonio was so conscious of Emma's presence he almost missed the broad sound of John's northern English accent coming from the stalls where Veranchetti was currently housed. At sixteen and a half hands, the horse was glorious. Its black coat gleamed in the shafts of sunlight filtering through the window at the back of the stall.

As he neared, the voices became more distinct, and the feminine lilt of an Australian accent came to a halt.

'Antonio?' John's voice called out from inside. 'That you? Reckoned you'd have swung by before now.'

Only John could make the reproach sound like a greeting. Antonio caught Mason's eye as she made her way out of the stall. A brief nod was all she threw at him before heading off out of the building.

'How are you?' John asked, coming out from the stable.

'Good, John. I'm good.'

'I'll say,' John observed, watching as Emma stayed just behind Antonio. 'I take it this is the lass, then?'

Antonio felt himself on unsteady ground as he suddenly realised that he had failed to take into account yet another person he now had to add to his list of deception. John was the only member of his father's staff he'd stayed in contact with after he, his mother and sister had been forced to return to Italy.

It was a contact that he and the other members of the Winners' Circle syndicate had very much used to their advantage.

'Must say, I would've thought I'd not have to hear about it on Twitter.'

'Since when are *you* on Twitter?' Antonio asked, a smile playing at the edges of his mouth. 'John—allow

me to introduce you to Emma Guilham, my fiancée.'
The word felt strange on his tongue.

Emma came forward, having hesitated only slightly
when he'd said *fiancée*. 'Nice to meet you, John,' she
said warmly, reaching out to shake his hand.

'Oh, no, lass, I'm all mucky,' he said, wiping straw
and mud onto his already dirty jeans.

'Don't be silly. I'd hardly be a match for Antonio Arcuri if I was worried about a little dirt.'

John let out a bark of laughter, shook Emma's hand
and turned to Antonio, his eyes approving. 'I'm going
to like her. First one I've met of yours—and the last,
by all accounts.'

Something like guilt threatened to spark in Antonio's
gut, but Antonio pushed it aside. *Dio*, he couldn't let
her anywhere near his sister Cici. His sister would be
broken-hearted when it all came to nothing.

'How's V?' he asked, swiftly changing the focus of
the conversation.

'Veranchetti,' replied John, 'is doing fine. Survived
the trip over and has been acclimatising for a good
while now.'

'And McAulty?' Antonio asked.

From what he'd heard in the last eighteen months
she'd been doing everything she'd said she would—living and breathing the horses from the Winners' Circle
stable. John had been giving him, Dimitri and Danyl
weekly reports, and had voiced his positive opinion
and utter confidence in her on more than one occasion.

'She'll do.'

It was about as high a seal of approval as John would
ever give. And, from the way he was looking at Emma,
it seemed to be covering both of the women who had unexpectedly entered Antonio's life in very different ways.

Antonio had felt the calm of being inside a stable settle over him from the moment he'd come out of the wintry sun and moved into the shadows. But it was an odd calm. It always had been. The kind of calm that happened before a storm was about to hit and change everything.

He wondered if it was like Pavlov's dog—if in some way he'd always feel like this in a stable. It was the one place where he'd repeatedly sought refuge when things at home had got too much. When he'd wanted to take the first horse he saw and ride like hell away from his home, his father and all that entailed. It was the kind of calm that anticipated adrenalin…anticipated action and adventure.

It was the kind of calm he hadn't felt since being forced away from his home, his horses, and his once possible career as an international polo player.

As if John sensed the dark memories taking hold of Antonio, he led them from the quiet peace of the stable back out into the sunlight.

'Were the overnighters okay?' Antonio asked. It would have taken them a long time to get from America to Argentina, with several stops along the way.

'Yep—paperwork was all in place, and everything went well. You might want to check in with the folks from the Hanley Cup. They've got some things for you to sign.' John indicated over his shoulder to where there was a small office hidden amongst the larger buildings.

Antonio nodded his head, willingly taking the proffered escape from the stables and the threatening memories of his past.

Emma didn't know what she'd expected from the stables, but it hadn't been John. In the eighteen months she'd worked for Antonio she'd never had anything to do with the Winners' Circle. He'd handled all that himself. Oh, she'd been curious—but never enough to intrude on Antonio's personal endeavours.

John had watched Antonio walk off towards the office and now turned his attention back to her.

'I've known that one for a long time, Emma.'

'Is this the bit where you warn me off?' she said, half joking and half afraid of what he might say.

'No, lass. Reckon you know what you're getting yourself into. But that boy…he's just like a natural-born mustang. Wild and ready to bolt at any moment.'

Emma wanted John to stop. She was struggling enough to maintain the image of Antonio as her boss and now her fiancée. She wasn't sure she was ready to see him as the boy he'd once been.

'His da,' John continued, 'he were a hard man—no doubt. And he all but broke that boy. You've got him this far, Emma. Hold on to him. Even if he tries to bolt. He's worth it, lass.'

She didn't know what to say. She couldn't tell him the truth. That this engagement of—what?—less than twenty-four hours?—was just for show. Just for a business deal. The sincerity ringing from John's voice was irrefutable.

She smiled, knowing that she couldn't do anything but keep up the façade and not break an old man's heart. 'I'll do that, John. Or I'll try,' she said on a laugh, to lighten the tone.

To change the subject, she nodded back towards the stable.

'Is Veranchetti the horse Mason's going to ride in the Hanley Cup? I'm afraid I don't know much about it,' she said ruefully.

'Yup. They've got good a chance, I reckon.'

'It's an odd name—though I suppose they all have odd names.'

'Cici—his sister—named him after the hero of one of her favourite romance novels. Antonio didn't have the heart to say no,' he said, squinting in the sunlight, looking out at the course.

'Does Cici ride?'

'No, she was never that interested in the horses. But you don't want me raking up old ghosts, Ms Guilham.'

Whether John had purposely shied away from the past, or whether he'd noticed Antonio's return, she couldn't tell. Either way, his presence clearly sounded the end of their conversation.

'John's been telling me that Veranchetti's chances are good. I might even have to place my first ever bet!' she said brightly.

Antonio's dark glance told her that he didn't believe her, and as he said his goodbyes and ushered her back towards the limousine Emma felt horribly as if she'd been treading where she shouldn't have been…

The foyer of The Excelsus gleamed in the sunlight through the glass-fronted entrance. She resisted the temptation to shiver, which was more from the incredible luxury surrounding her than the temperature. Her low heels clicked on the marble flooring as they made their way towards the reception desk.

'Mr Arcuri!' A perfectly suited manager greeted Antonio and then turned his attention to Emma. 'And Ms Guilham. Welcome to The Excelsus.'

Momentarily startled that the manager had greeted her by name, Emma was wrong-footed.

The man pressed a sleek black folder and two black-coloured room cards across the desk towards her. 'Your belongings have been taken up to the suite. Would you like me to show me to your rooms, Mr Arcuri?'

'No, thank you, I am sure that everything will be in order,' Antonio responded, pausing only to pick up the folder and key cards before marching towards a discreet lift hidden behind steel panelling in the opposite direction from the more public elevators in the centre of the foyer.

Emma was left trailing behind, feeling once again unsettled in this environment. The excitement she had felt back in New York when she'd stayed at The Langsford was beginning to rise again. This was a glimpse of a lifestyle, experiences, that she couldn't have imagined putting on her Living List, and she was eager to see her room.

As she came to a halt beside Antonio the question she'd felt niggling at the back of her mind had clearly become apparent.

'Yes?' Antonio demanded, with a return of the autocratic boss she knew he could be, who for just a moment had been absent at the stables.

'How did he...?'

'Know your name? I would think that, just like John, *many* people now know your name. After all, to all intents and purposes, you are the future Mrs Arcuri.'

Emma remembered the press articles speculating on who she was, how she had managed to capture the notorious playboy, whether she might be carrying his child. She was thankful that she had managed to get hold of both her parents to let them know what was about to happen, but hated to think of them reading all the gossip and conjecture.

The discreet lift doors opened and Antonio entered,

waiting for Emma to do the same—but she couldn't. He was in there, taking up the whole space, dominating it. Some kind of self-preservation instinct kicked in, preventing her from joining him. Until Antonio reached out a hand, caught her by the wrist and pulled her right into hell with him.

The move had startled her so much she had fallen against him, found herself pressed against the hard planes of his chest, and the physical contact drew an almost instantaneous reaction from Emma, who had been trying desperately to forget the shocking kiss that had announced their engagement to the world.

He was looking down at her, his dark hawk-like eyes watchful, almost waiting...

'Capable of standing on your own two feet?'

Embarrassment painted her cheeks red as she disengaged her body from his. The lift was ascending with barely a jolt, and she put the flip of her stomach down to the ascent of nearly twenty floors in just seconds.

Coming to a halt, the lift opened onto a hallway with only two doors at opposite ends, and Emma slapped down her active imagination that had been expecting to walk straight out into a penthouse suite.

Not waiting for her, Antonio exited and made his way towards the door to her left. She followed, and as he swiped the key card and pressed his way forward into the suite she hovered by the door.

'Emma?'

'Yes? Oh, sorry. Now that you're safely settled in, I'll take my key and find my room,' she said, trying to look anywhere but at where her new fiancé was standing.

His silence drew her gaze like nothing else could have. He stood there, barely a hair out of place despite the flight and the visit to the stables, his head cocked to one side, and looked at her with something in his eyes she didn't want to name.

'This is your room, Emma.'

Shock kept her in place, hovering outside the door to the suite. She was pretty sure her jaw had dropped.

'That's not going to work, Antonio.'

'Of course it is. You're my fiancée—where else would you be staying?'

'Who's to say that I'm not the kind of fiancée who believes in…in waiting for the wedding night?'

Words like *sex* were dangerous at the best of times, but with him…? She cursed internally. She wasn't going to be able to do this.

'No one—and I mean *no one*—would believe that I would allow my fiancée to have her own set of rooms. We're on this path, Emma, and I will not let anything or anyone question that. This is going to have to be believable, so get used to it.'

He was standing in front of her now, so close, and strangely even more dominating than he had been in the lift.

Before she could take a breath, he continued, 'You have your company credit card?'

Her mind was spinning enough that she was not able to understand why that would matter, but she nodded.

'Good—perhaps if you look the part it will help you act the doting fiancée.'

She looked down in dismay at the sensible, albeit rumpled clothes she had worn on the plane. He was right. Not only did she need a whole wardrobe of clothes—those she hadn't been able to retrieve from her apartment before coming here—but she needed a particular style of clothing.

She scowled at him. *'No one,'* she said, echoing his earlier words, 'would believe you would settle for *doting.'*

The concierge at The Excelsus had arranged for a car to take her to the most exclusive mall in Buenos Aires, with the assurance that it had a wide selection of fashion stores from which she would be able to get everything that she needed.

In the years since her breast reconstruction Emma had taken to shopping for clothes online, enjoying the fact that she didn't need to expose her insecurities to anyone but the four walls of her bedroom. This, however, was daunting. But she knew Antonio was right. The level of sheer extravagance in even the daywear of the women in the hotel had been enough to convince Emma that if she needed to be Antonio's fiancée, on his arm at evening events and at the racetrack, she would need thick and very expensive armour to succeed.

Besides, millions of women around the world who'd had reconstructive surgery did this every day. So could she.

But now, standing in the fourth store she'd entered, she felt the drive and determination that had brought her there beginning to fade. It wasn't just a dress or two that she needed—it was an entire wardrobe. She knew that there were women who would kill to be left free in one of Argentina's hottest fashion districts holding a credit card without a limit, but right now it was all just a little too much.

Some of the shocking and outlandish creations she had seen on display were so far outside her comfort zone, and the sheer sensuality of the Argentinian designs were both tempting and frightening in contrast to the office-style respectability of the clothing she was used to wearing in New York. But this was getting silly. She had spent so long hiding her figure behind loose clothes and dark colours. Perhaps this was a chance to make the most of this opportunity—even if she did feel slightly out of her depth.

She took her courage in both hands and approached a saleswoman who had been eying her suspiciously. Briefly, in a no-nonsense way, Emma explained the situation.

Rather than cloying mawkish sympathy she had prepared herself for, she was surprised and oddly touched when instead the woman beamed, informing her that she would be utterly delighted to help.

Antonio had just exited a shop, with a present each for his sister and mother safely in transit to his hotel, when he'd caught a glimpse of Emma slipping into a store. He'd held back a moment, losing her briefly as she moved amongst the mannequins and rows of designer clothes. Then, curious to see how she was getting on, he hadn't been able to help himself as he followed her in, telling himself that he only meant to make sure that she chose clothing suitable for her new role.

He'd felt the vulnerability coming off her in waves when he'd discussed her need for a wardrobe, and had had an urge to reach out and comfort, to protect. The only other women in his life he'd ever felt like that about were his sister and his mother, and from them he understood only too well how important it was for a woman to feel beautiful in what she wore.

As he neared the back of the shop he was surprised by a high-pitched *coo* falling from the lips of a shop assistant. He turned just in time to see Emma twisting around to catch a glimpse of herself in the floor-to-ceiling mirror by the changing rooms.

Need and desire consumed him fiercely and unexpectedly the moment his eyes snared her. There she stood, in a strapless dress that hugged her perfect breasts and stomach, leaving her arms and shoulders bare while layers and layers of blood-red silk cascaded from her slim waist, looking almost as shocked as he felt.

He watched as she took in her own appearance, her eyes drawing upwards from where the dress fell at her bare feet all the way to the top, where she met his eyes in the reflection of the mirror.

In a second the shock in her gaze was shuttered. Her eyes narrowed and she spun round, looking at him accusingly. 'How did you find me?'

Affronted by the way the fire in her voice matched the temperament of the dress, he couldn't help the retort that fell from his lips. 'I don't have a tracker on your phone, if that's what you're implying.'

She scowled, and oddly Antonio felt—and resisted—the urge to laugh.

'I'm here by mere coincidence,' he concluded.

'You don't believe in coincidence.'

'No,' he said, feeling exasperation rise within him.

He really didn't, and in that moment he wondered what kind of game the gods responsible for their lives were playing. Because that was exactly how he felt right now. *Played*.

As her hands clutched instinctively at the skirts of the dress he remembered just for a moment the feeling of her skin beneath his palms, and he forced himself to turn away before he embarrassed them both. The almost painful shock of arousal had hit him hard, and he knew it had nothing to do with how much time had passed since he'd last been in bed with a woman.

He could almost *taste* desire as he made his way over to the seat beside the dressing room. He was some kind of masochist to stay, but he didn't have the will-power to leave.

A glass of champagne was left discreetly on the table beside the chair, and when he took a sip the bubbles scraped against his raw throat.

'It's not right,' Emma said, looking at him, and for a moment he forgot that she was speaking about the dress.

He felt his eyes narrow instinctively, and everything male in him roared that she was wrong.

Before sanity prevailed.

'Perhaps not. Try something else.'

It was a command. Uttered in a harsh tone. One that did not befit the dressing room, and Emma felt it down to her very soul.

Yet she didn't think that they agreed for the same reason. She had never chosen clothes to accentuate her breasts before. At least not since the surgery. Before that she had been seventeen and happy with her body. Had never suffered from the kinds of insecurities she'd seen in her friends as they judged themselves against each other, against impossible to achieve celebrity figures.

But afterwards? Yes. She had let her insecurities run her wardrobe.

The selection of clothes given to her by the lovely sales assistant here was impeccable. Some of them were rather more extreme than others, but she had begun to view it as a kind of shock therapy. The more ex-treme made the less outrageous palatable, when once she would have baulked at the whole lot.

Emma had known women—powerful, strong, inspiring women—who had embraced their bodies and their lives with vigour after chemotherapy. She had longed to find that sense of self, and now she was beginning to realise that the courage that had seen her battle fiercely with the chemo was still needed to battle her future.

Stepping back into the changing room, she fought the instinctive urge to run. Run from Antonio's assessing gaze...run from the desire. She wasn't foolish enough to try and hide from what it was that had sprung forth between them.

She undid the zip hidden in the side seam of the dress and it pooled around her feet. She stepped out of the delicate red silk and her body felt the lick as if of flames across her body. There was only a thin curtain of material separating her from Antonio. She knew it and so did he.

Her exposed skin feeling overly sensitive, she reached for the last dress the assistant had procured for her.

Having already chosen some incredible day clothes, she only had evening functions to cater for, and she cursed herself for leaving the best for last. It was her favourite dress of the selection, and she'd wanted to have this moment for herself. But outside sat Antonio, glass in hand, as if he were waiting for a show. Except rather than taking her clothes off she was putting them on.

Suddenly she wanted him thrown off balance as much as she was. She wanted him to be feeling just an ounce of what he was doing to *her*.

Standing in a thong and nothing else, she reached for the dress and stepped into the skirt. The fabric of the dress's blue silk was covered in a subtle lace flower pattern detail, with a figure-hugging bodice. It rubbed against her sensitive skin at the same time as the cool silk soothed. The sleeves were sheer, with the same lace detail covering her arms but leaving her décolletage bare. It covered even whilst it revealed and she silently thanked the shop assistant's perfect eye.

Before she stepped out into the dressing area she looked at herself in the mirror, feeling that same sense of shock she had experienced when she'd seen herself in the red dress moments ago.

Was that really her? Whilst her hair and minimal make-up were almost ordinary, the dress had called forth something within her. Something powerful and feminine… Things she'd always wanted to be but had never seemed to achieve. There was a blush to her cheeks, making more of her cheekbones than she was used to, and the glitter in her eyes shone like diamonds.

She pulled aside the curtain that separated her from Antonio and everything else faded away—the assistant, the shop…it all disappeared and only he came into focus.

And her lungs stopped working.

Because Antonio Arcuri, destroyer and saviour of global companies, was looking at her as if she were the only thing in the world and she nearly came undone.

CHAPTER FIVE

THREE DAYS OF trying to ignore the woman living and breathing in the same suite was driving Antonio insane. He was now thoroughly regretting the impulse he'd had to stay and see Emma's last outfit at the shop. Ever since that moment he'd been imagining what it would be like to peel her out of the silky dress and enjoy every delight her stunning figure had to offer.

But he couldn't. Emma was nothing like the women who graced his bed. The women who lived and played in his world—the women who had the hard edge needed to take his emotion-free entanglements. Emma didn't know how to play that game, and although she might hide it well she would break in his arena.

Besides—as he reminded himself for the hundredth time—there was far too much at stake.

He had done everything needed to ensure the meeting with Bartlett would be a success. He had orchestrated an irresistible deal the man would be insane to refuse. But he didn't like the silence from his father. Didn't trust it. The man must be up to something.

For the first time Antonio found himself wondering just how far he would go to get his revenge.

And the only answer in his heart was, *However far it took...*

It was gone eleven, and Emma had retired to her room almost an hour ago. In that time he'd pulled out all the files on Bartlett they had collated in the last week and turned the sumptuous living room into a practical office. The meeting with Bartlett was set for tomorrow evening—and the day of races that would commence the first leg of the Hanley Cup would start the following morning. Everything was lining up nicely… But he couldn't shake the feeling of an approaching storm.

As if he had summoned demons for Emma too, he heard sounds of distress coming from her room. Worried, he got up from the sofa and was halfway towards her door when he heard her scream. He rushed into her room, barely noticing as the door slammed back against the wall, probably leaving a dent, and took three strides to her bed.

She was tossing and turning, caught up in the cotton sheets, kicking out desperately. He could see the trails of tears on her cheeks. *Dio*, it must be some nightmare.

Remembering how his sister had suffered so badly from them in the year following their departure from the States, he sat down on the bed beside Emma's restless form and gently took hold of her arm.

'Emma…' he whispered. 'Emma, it's just a dream.'

She thrashed against his gentle hold and let out a whimper that struck his heart.

'Emma, come on. It's just a dream. You need to wake up.'

Her eyes sprang open, searching for focus. A shudder racked her body, and she gasped on an inhalation of much needed breath.

'You're okay. It was just a dream.'

But the hurt in her eyes told him he was wrong.

She looked so vulnerable, so in need of comfort, that

it took everything in him not to take her in his arms, to replace the fear in her eyes with want, with arousal. He wanted her to feel the same need, the same desire that burst into life against his skin when it met hers... something he knew could only be satiated by a touch, by a caress.

He cursed himself to hell and back. He couldn't take advantage of her. Not now...not like this. *Not ever*, he warned himself.

Emma took in Antonio's presence. The light filtering through from the living room cast his face in night-time shadows, so much more welcome than her awful dream. For a moment—just a moment—she thought he might reach for her. Might kiss her as she so desperately wanted to be kissed. But seconds passed and he didn't. He held himself back.

She nodded. Resting her hand on his where it held her arm. 'I'm okay. It's okay. I'll be through in a min-ute. I just need...a minute.'

As Antonio left her room she willed the fierce beat-ing of her heart to slow. Her fingers brushed away the traces of the nightmare from her eyes and she realised that the tears she had thought contained by the dream had escaped.

She moved to the en suite bathroom, passing the wardrobe full of the clothes they had bought two days ago with an accusatory glance, as if they could be held responsible for causing old fears to surface. The fear that the cancer would come for her again, just when she was beginning to hope that she could reclaim her sense of self, reclaim the sense of her body.

She splashed water on her hot cheeks, finally shak-ing off the hold of her terror. Wide awake, and not ready even to consider going back to bed, she pulled on the hotel's silk robe and padded into the living area of the suite on bare feet.

She took in the devastation caused by Antonio's preparation for the meeting with Bartlett with a rueful smile.

'I am very glad you don't usually work like this. I'd have the cleaners quitting on me each and every day if you did.'

He looked up from the papers he held in his hands, his hawk-like gaze refusing to be distracted by her attempt at small talk.

'Nightmare?'

'Yes. Clearly,' she replied.

She was surprised to see his chiselled features soften.

'My sister used to get them regularly. Would you like some tea?'

'Because I'm English?' Emma asked, holding on to the warm offer like a lifeline.

'Yes. Clearly.'

She smiled as he gave her words back to her.

'What would you have given your sister?'

'Well…' he said, as if searching his memory. But she knew that the answer would immediately be on his lips. 'She was thirteen at the time, but a little limoncello didn't hurt her one bit. Not that this hotel has limoncello stocked in the suite's bar. But there is whisky?'

'I'll take the whisky. Thank you.'

As she watched him step behind the corner bar that edged one side of the suite she took in his powerful appearance. Even three days of solid work, constantly sorting through all the figures and research data that they'd been able to put together, hadn't put a dark hair out of place. Dressed in his suit trousers and a shirt, sleeves rolled back on strong tanned forearms, he was mouth-wateringly handsome.

The brief glimmer of concern in his eyes as he had woken her from her nightmare had been devastatingly tempting, and not for the first time Emma wondered what it would be like to rely on that power, that compassion. A compassion he was yet to show, however, in any of his business dealings.

She turned away from the temptation of his presence and stepped towards the windows that looked out over the stands of the race course. In just a few days they would be full of spectators, sound and chaos. But at that moment they seemed peaceful and quiet. She pressed her hand against the glass and allowed it to leach away some of the fevered heat she reluctantly attributed to the man behind her.

As he approached, a glass of whisky in each hand, she became horribly conscious that she was only wearing a silk negligée and the robe. The cool, delicate touch of the fabric did nothing to ease the prickles of heat racing across her skin at the mere sight of his reflection. Her mind, torn between the horror of her nightmare and the ecstasy of Antonio's proximity, warred between her hurt and her heart...

Her heart should know better. But it didn't. Her heart wanted him to put those damn glasses down and take her in his arms.

Schooling her features, calming the erratic beating of her pulse, she watched as he waited for her to turn, clearly knowing that she had seen him in the reflection in the window.

'My sister never really wanted to talk about her fears, but in the end she saw that it helped.'

Desperate to hold on to any thread that took her away

from her desires, and also curious, given how little she knew about his past and his family, she turned and accepted the glass he offered her.

He moved back to the beautiful sofa and cleared some of the paper from it, making room for her on the opposite end, a safe distance away from his presence.

'How long did she have nightmares for?'

For a brief moment Emma wondered if Antonio would choose to ignore her question, but after a small sigh he started to talk.

'They carried on for a year after my parents' divorce.'

His eyes turned dark, consuming the golden flecks she sometimes saw there.

'It was public and very messy. In order to reduce the settlement, my father paraded my mother's affair through the courts and the international press. He had the divorce granted in Italy, where people are still notoriously moralistic about such things. Had we been in North America, it might have been different. But whatever continent he might have chosen, it didn't seem to affect the press interest.'

He shrugged—such an Italian gesture of dismissiveness for clearly such a painful thing. Emma could only guess at the depths of the emotions he was struggling with.

'How old were you?'

'I was sixteen, but Cici was only thirteen. Without Michael's financial support my mother couldn't stay in America. Her father offered to help, but only if we came back to Italy. So we left.'

'That must have been hard.'

Emma knew what it was like to have her entire world change at such a young age. It had dripped onto her experiences like rain falling through leaves. Each tear-shaped drop hitting another aspect of her life. It could not have been much different for Antonio, his sister and his mother.

'It was. Everything we knew—friends, school, staff. That's where John worked. In my father's stable.'

'You had a *stable*?'

Emma had known that he must have had money growing up—he had some mannerisms that only financial security could give—but the idea of having a stable was almost inconceivable for a girl who'd had a struggling artist mother and a state school teacher father.

Antonio smiled ruefully. 'The full American package. Stables, private education, piano recitals—for Cici, not me. I was on track to be a member of the American polo team. But… I left that behind too.'

She let the silence fall, not wanting to interrupt the hold of his memories. Her heart reached out to the boy who had lost his dream.

'Cici struggled with it more. Losing her friends. And, even though he's an evil bastard, she suffered from the loss of her father too.'

Emma couldn't help but notice how he referred to his sister's pain, but not his own. *Her* father, not his. As if Antonio had cut him out of his vocabulary as determinedly as his father had cut them from his life.

She took a sip of her whisky. His was neat, but he'd added ice to hers which she was thankful for. The ice-cool liquid took the edge off the warmth of the rich Irish blend.

'Cici needed stability in that year, and I worked very hard to give it to her.'

'What about your mother?'

A small smile graced his lips. 'She was—*is*—a beautiful Italian socialite with little education and less work experience. Her father was rich, but bad financial investments had stolen much of his wealth by the time we returned to Italy. He gave us what he could, but I wanted Cici to stay in private education. In order to do that I needed to work after school.'

'And what about you?'

'I,' he said with mock sincerity, 'am an academic genius.'

And she wished he hadn't said it. The playful mask he wore was just as alluring as the truth behind it.

'I didn't need private education. I got my scholarship to NYU...met Dimitri and Danyl. They became my family, each of us having experienced our own hardships. There we were, foreign students, not unaccustomed to America, but perhaps our differences forged our friendship as much as our similarities. We worked hard and played harder. It was at university where we first conceived the Winners' Circle syndicate. My interest in horses had never faded and it was matched by Dimitri's and Danyl's. It was they, along with a small investment from my grandfather, who helped me start Arcuri Enterprises. Within two years I had paid them all back with interest, and bought my mother and sister a house—a *home*—in Italy. Dimitri and Danyl helped me ensure that they would be okay.'

'You protected them. Your sister and mother.'

She cursed her foolish heart for unfurling beneath the warmth of his words as he spoke of his friends, his family. And finally she began to understand Antonio's determination to secure the Bartlett deal. He wanted revenge—that much was clear. He wanted to hurt his father in the only way that he knew how.

But Emma couldn't help the feeling growing within

her that he might not like what he found once he'd achieved it.

'Yes,' he said simply, in relation to her earlier statement, as if it was the only way it could have been.

'It must have been a hard responsibility to bear,' Emma observed.

'I would do it again and again.'

'Where are they now?'

This time his smile broadened fully and her heart nearly stopped at the sight. It illuminated his dark features with light and pleasure, and in that moment she was thankful that he wasn't like this all the time. It would be...devastating.

'A beautiful estate in Sorrento, on the Amalfi coast, with olive trees and lemon groves.'

His simple words conjured a million images in her mind, and she could almost smell a hint of citrus in the air about them.

'And your sister?'

'No more nightmares.'

'Nothing more to fear,' Emma said, her own nerves beginning to twist at the way the conversation was going.

'No.'

'And what is *your* fear, Antonio?'

Emma didn't know what gave her the courage to ask. Perhaps it was the darkness outside, or the intimacy created by the only light in the living room dusting them with a warm, gentle golden glow.

But even in that soft lighting she saw his features grow dark. Something bitter entered the air, and the determination that had hung around Antonio since he'd come back to the New York office and asked her to research Benjamin Bartlett returned.

'That my father will never pay for what he did to my mother and sister.'

And for what he did to you, Emma added silently as the ripple of his words sent icy shivers through her body.

She took another sip of the cool whisky, trying to forestall the question she knew was next on Antonio's lips.

'And what is yours, Emma?'

Antonio watched Emma pull the thin silk robe around her shoulders, covering and protecting herself from the memory of her nightmare. He wished for a moment that she hadn't. The way the soft material had opened just slightly at the V of her chest, the smooth creamy skin thinly veiled, had been his only anchor—his only tie in the storm of emotions that had surfaced beneath his stark words as he'd recounted his past.

He heard the chink of ice in her glass, drawing him back to the present as she rested it between her palms as she might hold a hot drink.

'Well, I suppose the nightmare started in pretty much the usual way—I was being attacked by zombie cats.'

He couldn't help but laugh. 'Zombie cats is usual?'

'Well, hyper real, at least. They were attacking me, and I was managing to escape, but they were keeping me from something. And then I realised that they were keeping me from getting to a doctor's appointment. I was waiting for new test results.' She took a shaky breath. 'The cancer had come back.'

Shivers covered his forearms. He couldn't even begin to imagine that kind of fear. 'What was it like?'

'Horrible,' she said simply, without malice or anger, or any of the kind of emotions he would have projected onto the situation.

He wasn't sure about continuing to ask, but he felt that she needed to talk about it, and he trusted her enough to tell him to stop if he caused too much pain.

'How old were you when you got ill?'

'Seventeen.'

Antonio cursed. It fell from his mouth without thought or he would have held it back, but Emma only smiled her gentle small smile.

'What surprised me was how utterly practical it all was. The diagnosis was shocking, terrible, but there was a chain of events to follow—things to be done and so much to organise. After a few days the diagnosis became a fact. Just a fact. A hurdle—a thing to overcome. All the stress and worry about A levels, about boys, about who was better friends with who...the things that had seemed so important in my day-to-day life...suddenly just seemed so small in comparison.'

'Weren't you angry?' he asked.

'Yes...and no. There wasn't really time to be angry. There was the operation, and then the chemo. And through it all I just felt that I couldn't let the anger take hold. I felt that my anger would feed the cancer, some-how. It's so very different for each person it happens to. Some people are able to use anger to fight it, to give them energy. But I didn't want anything else eating away at me. If I clung to being positive, if I held to the determination that I would beat it, then I knew I would win. I would take back my life.'

She took a breath and he marvelled at her strength.

'I had to put my A levels on hold during the treat-ment. I had a double mastectomy, then chemotherapy followed by breast reconstruction. Some women choose to have the reconstruction immediately following a mas-tectomy, but after speaking to my doctors I wanted to make sure that the cancer was completely gone before moving forward. And at that point I really didn't want another operation.'

Antonio saw the fierceness in her gaze as she spoke. The fire he had only seen glimpses of before was there now, shining in her eyes, burning in flushed cheeks, and it was glorious. He relished her strength and determination, allowed it to feed him too.

'It took about a year, all in all. And by that time, although supportive, my friends had moved on...found relationships, started university, gone travelling around the world. None of which I begrudged for a second. But I felt out of step. Just a little behind. Like this thing had happened to me and no one else. But that wasn't quite true.'

'What do you mean?' he asked.

'One of the hardest things was telling other people. I felt as if I had to manage their emotions, their reactions. I'd find myself reassuring *them* that I would be okay. That it would all be fine. More often than not it was just—' she shrugged '—awkward.'

She took another sip of her drink and a little shiver rippled across her skin as she swallowed the oaky alcohol.

'I had a boyfriend at the time,' she revealed, swirling the ice cubes around her empty glass. 'He was a...a sweet boy. But I think telling him was the hardest. Because the look in his eyes...' She shook her head against the memory. 'It was fear, guilt, anger... Fear of what might happen, guilt that he didn't want this, that it wasn't what he'd signed up for, and anger that this had happened to him. Yes, clearly it was happening to me, but it was something that he might have to deal with.'

'He left you?' Antonio asked, hearing the growl vibrating in his own words. The sheer anger and fury swept up in him by her simple words shocked him.

'No. We'd only been dating—if you could even call it that—for a few months. It wasn't serious, and it probably wouldn't have lasted much longer. So I let him go. He argued with me. I could see that he wanted to do the right thing. But I needed to focus on me, on my fight, not on ensuring that he was okay.

'I was determined to ensure that the cancer cells didn't multiply and spread—didn't affect things outside of my body. It's so hard not to let cancer become everything around you. Everything you see. Family.... Friends. Cancer is a thief if you let it be. It doesn't just take lives, it takes body parts, time, experiences, relationships…

'My parents' marriage broke down soon after my treatment,' she confided. 'They're much happier now, and that's great. But nothing was the same after the cancer. My home, my parents…my body. Everything had changed.'

'I'm sorry.' Even as he said it, he knew the words to be inefficient, wrong…too little.

'Don't be sorry,' she said, a flash of anger sparking in her eyes. 'Don't apologise. Because cancer shouldn't be excused. It's not a thing to pardon or to forgive. It is not a thing to be normalised. You don't get to apologise for cancer. You can help fight it. Help beat it. Help those who *do* fight against it. But *never* apologise for it. There's funding for research and new technologies… that's why charity foundations are so important. That's why *yours* could be so much more.'

Antonio held the weight of her gaze, held the weight of her accusation. He knew she was right.

She seemed to gather herself before him. 'I'm sorry,' she said.

'Don't be. You're right. I should have been more involved. I should have made the time to attend the yearly galas. And you're absolutely right about getting rid of Greenfeld. I've already put motions in place that will remove him from his position. After the success of the gala—which was mainly down to you—the board supports my decision and we're already considering other options. Once this deal is done, I promise you it's the first thing on my list when we return to New York.'

Emma smiled—almost as if she had a secret.

'What?' he asked, suddenly incurably curious about her—everything and anything about her. He wanted to know it all.

'I have a list too.'

Emma couldn't believe that she was telling him about her list. During chemo she had heard people talk about their bucket lists, and had felt overwhelmingly sad that the supposition was at the end there would be death, not life.

'It's my Living List. My mum helped me to make it,' she said, smiling at the memory of being in her parents' sitting room, pen and paper in her hands, as her mother and father encouraged her to write down everything she wanted to do when it was all over.

'What's on the list?' he asked, drawing her from her memory.

She looked at him and realised how their bodies had shifted position on the sofa. Somehow during their conversation she had turned towards him, her back against the armrest, her legs stretched out. If she moved an inch her feet would be in his lap. And Antonio had turned towards her, mirroring her position, one leg bent, anchored over the other.

It was beguiling, having Antonio Arcuri's full attention. The low light from the small lamp on the table beside him shaded half his features, highlighting the cut of his cheekbones, the hollows of his throat...a throat she wanted to run her fingers over, her tongue...

But it was the look in his eyes as he asked the question. Curiosity and something else. Something almost pleasurable.

She felt heat swirl in her stomach and, desperate to dampen this quickening attraction for her boss, she focused on his question.

'A whole lot of things—big and small.'

'What's the biggest?'

'Only a man would ask that first,' she joked, and appreciated the humour that was returned to her in his eyes. 'Okay—I think the biggest would be that I want to see the sun rise over a desert and set over the Mediterranean.'

'In one day?' Antonio asked, his surprise almost funny.

'Not necessarily. I'm not fussy. Just a sunrise. Just a sunset. But, yes, deserts, sea views... I want to see the world. I'm really looking forward to Hong Kong,' she confided.

'I know the perfect place to take you.'

'Where?'

'It's a surprise. But you'll like it,' he assured her, and that thrill of excitement began to unwind throughout her body and across her skin. 'The smallest?' he pressed.

'Ah. The smallest I *have* achieved. I wanted to eat a stack of American pancakes with crispy bacon and maple syrup. It was *divine*.'

He laughed as she groaned with remembered pleasure. 'What else?'

And once again Emma's thoughts went to the one thing that she hadn't been able to write on the list in front of her parents. She was sure that her mother would have understood, but writing *losing my virginity* had just seemed more than a little uncomfortable.

But it was about so much more than simply having sex. At the time, Emma had been approaching her reconstructive surgery with the same practicality that had pushed her through the other areas of treatment.

Now, when she looked in the mirror she just saw shapes. The shapes that had been taken away and then put back on her body. It was hard for her to see her breasts, her body, as her own. To own them, to glory in them. She had a good figure—she knew that. But somehow she had never felt able to exalt in it. To see it as her *own*.

'You didn't ask me to help you achieve anything on your list,' Antonio stated when she didn't answer his question.

'When?'

'When I offered you whatever you wanted.'

'No,' she said. She hadn't. 'These are things *I* want to achieve Antonio. *I* want to make them happen. Asking you to do them for me…kind of feels like cheating.'

He let that lie between them, and the silence was consumed whole by the tension and crackle of attraction on the air between them.

Antonio's declaration to dedicate more time and energy to the charity had been almost fierce. And Emma found herself wondering what it would be like to have that dedication and power directed at her. As a woman. As someone or something beautiful.

She couldn't help but study him once again in the half-light of the room, seeing the way it illuminated his masculine beauty. She could lie to herself and pretend to think that it was her wayward thoughts about her virginity that had conjured her attraction to him by association—not the curve of his almost cruelly sensual lips, the feel of his eyes on her body. She could blame it on the new and surprising intimacy that had been created between them in these last few hours and not on the way his direct gaze, eagle-eyed and intense, seemed to reach into her and kick up her pulse.

But she wouldn't.

She had always found Antonio powerfully attractive. Had always felt prickles of awareness when he was nearby. He was as tempting as the devil.

Those gold flecks had returned to his eyes, surfing the waves of molten chocolate that seemed to radiate…heat. And desire. It became a tangible thing, and she could almost taste it on the air. She felt every single inch of her skin where the silk robe rested against it, felt the smooth material of the sofa beneath her calf muscle. She felt the space between them that seemed at once so small, yet almost insurmountable.

She willed her breath to become silent, knowing that she couldn't give in to the temptation burning between them, reluctant to let sound or action break this strange hold.

But sanity prevailed. Yes, she'd seen more to her handsome boss than she could have imagined. The grief and pain of his childhood had called to something within her. But she couldn't get involved with him. Because for all his promises she couldn't rely on anyone if the worst was to happen. Because it never lasted. Not really. People left, people changed, people wanted other things… And in the end the only person Emma could rely upon was herself.

She looked about the room, finally severing the connection that had formed between them. And then, lifting up a stack of papers, she asked him about Bartlett—a line of questioning that Antonio seemed equally relieved to take up.

'Bartlett's company is a fourth generation, family-owned heritage business and—'

'No, I didn't mean his company. Who is *he*? What makes him tick?'

Antonio paused for a moment, as if he honestly hadn't given it much consideration. He picked up the files and she shook her head, a gentle laugh falling from her lips.

'Antonio…' She couldn't help chuckling as she gently reprimanded him. 'He is the father of two children, Mandy and James, both are at university, both studying business. Mandy, by the way, certainly seems to be enjoying it thoroughly from her Instagram account—'

'You follow her Instagram account?'

'Yes, you asked me to research Bartlett, so I did.'

He nodded, as if slightly surprised. 'How did you get all this?'

'Bartlett's PA—Anna—used to work for someone who does a lot of business with the boss of your London office. We know each other quite well. She helped with some of the information, but she wouldn't cross any lines. Perhaps you should take a look at the notes in the blue folder. They're a bit more personal than business facts.'

But the word *personal* brought back memories of the earlier moment they had shared.

Realising that she had lost his concentration, Emma

felt a wave of tiredness sweep over her, and as Antonio took up several of the documents in the blue folder she decided to leave him to it and return to her room. This time hoping not to avoid her nightmares but dreams of her handsome boss.

CHAPTER SIX

THE NEXT DAY, by the time Antonio returned to the suite, he was physically exhausted. He'd been down to the stables to see John and V, but John had practically thrown him out because his 'state of mind' was affecting the horses. So he'd spent two hours in the gym, pushing himself hard.

Anything to force his shockingly one-track mind away from Emma Guilham and back to the meeting they had with Bartlett in a little over an hour. He had tried to pretend that the intimacy they'd shared the night before didn't mean anything. He'd tried to ignore the strands of desire that had woven between them before she had shifted the subject away from the personal and back on to Bartlett. But he hadn't quite managed to achieve it.

John was right. Antonio had to get his mind in order—had to shelve these thoughts and put them back in the box he never opened. He needed to get Bartlett to choose him, because if he didn't his father would go unchecked. Michael Steele would live his life without ever feeling what his mother felt…his sister felt. The painful sting of humiliation, the acute devastation when everything changed beyond recognition…the realisation that the very fabric of life could not be trusted.

And Antonio needed that—needed Michael to feel that.

He walked into his room and pulled his sweat-soaked T-shirt over his head, discarding it as he crossed into the bathroom. Turning on the scalding hot spray of water, he pushed the rest of his clothes from his body and tried very hard not to imagine Emma doing the same. Before she covered that irresistible body in the dress he'd bought for her that morning.

He hadn't been able to help himself. The clothing she'd purchased on their first day in Buenos Aires was perfectly adequate. But he didn't want 'adequate' for her. After last night, he wanted to see her in colours. Because that was what he had seen when she had talked about her experience with cancer.

He didn't want her to hide her figure behind the blacks and whites she usually wore. He could only guess that she hadn't quite come to accept her body. She hadn't said as much, but he had read between the lines. And he knew exactly how damaging that could be to a woman. To anyone.

And it was a crime—because Emma was simply stunning. So that morning, when he'd been out buying the last thing that would make this 'engagement' seem real, he'd passed a shop window and stopped in his tracks, realising at once that the dress on the mannequin was perfect.

The moment he'd seen it Antonio had wondered what Emma's curves would look like beneath the material— what the silk would reveal or conceal, what sound would it make running across her satin-smooth skin. How the colour would look against the pale cream tones of her bare arms…

The rush of his thoughts sent his body's blood south, shockingly fast, and Antonio gritted his teeth in an effort to keep himself under control and switched the shower from hot to icy cold.

And he knew—*knew* with one hundred per cent clarity—that he could not treat Emma with the same detachment that he used to handle the other women in his life. She wasn't like the women he usually took to bed. The ones who knew that he wouldn't offer them anything more.

He could no longer fool himself that it was because he was putting off anything deeper until after he had brought his father to his knees. He was self-aware enough to know that he didn't trust something as dangerous as love. It was a tool used by those more powerful, wielded to hurt, to harm.

It was as if Emma's honesty had lifted the lid on his ability to lie to himself. He knew that he had avoided anything emotional because of the power it had to be used against him. And he would never be victim to it again. But somehow Emma had managed to sneak beneath the armour he wore around his heart. To bring forth truths from his lips that he'd never shared with anyone other than Dimitri and Danyl.

And whilst everything in him wanted to run, to push her away, to save her from the darkness that threatened to consume him as he went further down his path of revenge, he knew that he wouldn't. That what he was about to do would only bind them together further.

He shut off the shower, dried himself and dressed quickly. He caught his reflection in the mirror. The perfectly tailored suit of dark blue cashmere wool matched his mood. On the bedside table was the small box that he had obtained before going to the gym.

He had thought he would simply go to the shop, make the purchase and leave. But, surprising himself, he had pored over the selection, discarding the more traditional cuts and colours and focusing instead on finding something that was unique and utterly… *Emma*. Not the PA he had spent eighteen months working with, but the woman who had hidden fire within her—the one who in fits and bursts had shown herself to be empowered… incredible, even.

He grabbed the box in his fist, then forced himself to relax his grip, hating what that said about him and his hopes for her reaction as he stalked through the suite. The tight leash on his emotions stretched taut, he called out to Emma, but didn't hear a reply.

He knocked on the door to her room, forcing himself to make it gentle and not pound on it as his heart was pounding within his chest. When there was still no answer he pushed gently on the door, ignoring the voice in his head that told him to turn back.

Smaller than his, though not by much, the room stretched out before him in rich, bold contemporary colours of black, grey and red. Emma had pushed back the curtains, revealing the night-time sky that trespassed over the race course as dusk beat a hasty retreat. Or perhaps it was Antonio who was trespassing…

He turned towards the bathroom, where he could hear the clicking of her heels on marble flooring. He was about to turn around and leave when the bathroom door opened and in walked Emma…

And his breath caught in his lungs.

She was incredible. So beautiful, so strong and powerful.

And he hated the thought that she didn't realise it.

From her feet, the deep, rich burnt orange silk bled upwards into lighter tones of amber and yellow, no less bold, but bright and eye-catching. The dress lay over her chest in a deep V, revealing the valley between her breasts. It clung to a waist that couldn't be broader than the span of his hand. It flared out from there and hung all the way to the floor.

But it wasn't until she stepped further into the room, when the high split revealed perfectly toned legs that went on for miles, that the breath that had been balled up in his chest finally escaped on an inaudible *whoosh*.

The moment she had seen the dress that had been delivered to the suite a few hours earlier her heart had almost stopped. She'd been surprised that her first reaction hadn't been instant refusal, hadn't been the thought that she could never wear such a revealing creation, but instead she was struck by how it reminded her of one of her mother's paintings. It had the same colours of the first piece her mother had produced after Emma had returned home from her last hospital stay.

There was no way that Antonio could have known about the painting, let alone the impact of the dress. But as she'd lifted the delicate material from the white box it had arrived in, and seen the way the rich golden colours shimmered in the light, she had known that she couldn't *not* wear it.

So she had put it on, and stared at herself in the mirror. Simply stared. Bold and bright, the smooth silk hugged curves she had never put on display before. For all her words the night before about being positive, about embracing the future and all it had to offer, she realised that perhaps she had left *this* behind. Allowed it to be swallowed up. That when she had thought her battle with cancer over in fact she had to continue to fight each day, to take back the things she had lost.

More than her breasts and her parents' marriage, her sensuality, her sense of self as a woman.

But now Antonio was looking at her in a way she couldn't decipher.

'How do I look?'

'Amazing,' he said without pause. 'But there's something missing.'

He reached into his trouser pocket and produced a small blue velvet box.

With trembling hands she took it from his palm, trying to avoid the zip and zing of electricity that passed between them. She laughed a little as she struggled with the little metal clasp on the box. But the moment her gaze caught the ring inside she stopped. Everything stopped.

It was a beautiful green sapphire, encased in rose gold. The precious stone was surrounded by tiny diamonds which continued the whole way around the band. It stole her breath—and in some part the walls around her heart.

'It's perfect,' she whispered as she slipped it onto her finger. She couldn't let him do it for her, it would mean too much.

'I'm pleased,' he said, holding her eyes with the same sincerity she had felt from him the night before. 'No matter what happens, I want you to keep it.'

'I…' She was speechless. 'I can't, Antonio. I don't deserve it.'

'It's not about deserve, or need. I want you to have it.'

Emma didn't know what to say. And if, somewhere deep down, there was a single tendril of sadness that this wasn't real, then that was her own fault. She'd known what she was getting into when she'd agreed to this deal. And just because she was emotional about it, it didn't change a thing.

Oh, but she wished she could.

By the time that they left the suite Emma was thankful for the reminder that their relationship was purely a business arrangement.

By the time they got to the lobby Emma had put away the childish hurt and pulled her armour back into place.

By the time the limousine arrived at the restaurant where they were to meet Bartlett, Emma was ready to do battle and slay dragons to help Antonio secure investment in Bartlett's company.

She had felt the hurt emanating from Antonio the night before as he'd told her of his childhood. She could see how important it was to him and wanted to gift him something of what he'd given her... The ability to reach for what it was that she wanted.

The lounge area of the famous Amore por la Comida restaurant spread out before them, coloured in rich amethyst hues set off perfectly by the golden twinkling stars piercing the night sky that could be seen from the windows surrounding all sides of the bar and seating areas.

The impeccably mannered head waiter was about to show them to the table when Emma felt Antonio stiffen beside her. A shiver rippled through his body like a shock wave, and she looked about them to see what might have caused it.

Coming towards them was a tall suited man she had never met before. There was something vaguely familiar about him, but she was forced to turn away from the frigid glare in his crystal blue eyes.

Instinctively she knew that this was Michael Steele, Antonio's father, and she couldn't help the way her hand slipped into the crook of Antonio's arm, as if trying to hold on to him, support him, give him something to warm the air that had suddenly cooled about them.

Antonio should have known. And perhaps deep down he had. Because his father's appearance didn't surprise him as much as it should have. He felt the drive of renewed determination fuel him. Indignation was but a second thought.

'Antonio,' Michael said as he drew close to them. 'I'd say that it's good to see you, but we both know that would be a lie.'

The charming, almost warm, smooth voice sharpened the harshness of his words.

'Why are you here?'

Antonio knew from bitter experience that the less he said to his father the better. He wondered whether Michael would have the gall to admit that he was here, at this exact place and time, because of his meeting with Bartlett. Clearly Michael had his informants, just as Antonio had his.

A cold smile graced lips that should be as familiar to Antonio as his own. In the three years since he'd last seen his father Michael Steele had grown in his mind to monstrous proportions. Instead, all he saw was an old man before him. But Antonio knew that appearances were deceiving and his whole body was on guard.

'Well, I heard rumours about the notorious Winners' Circle syndicate trying to win the hat-trick at the Hanley Cup. Surely that's a feat worth watching? If it succeeds. It would be such a shame if you were to fall at the first hurdle, so to speak. And, of course, it's a chance to catch up with old friends.'

Antonio bit back a curse. The man had absolutely no

interest in the Winners' Circle, and his allusion to 'old friends' could only mean Bartlett.

'I'm surprised you have any friends left, Michael.'

Anger had made him weak and he hadn't been able to prevent the snide comment falling from his lips.

'Come, now. There's no need to resort to childish swipes at your father.' Michael Steele barely allowed time for the reproach to strike before picking up yet another thread of venom. 'And this must be your *convenient* fiancée.'

The dismissive gesture of Michael's hands irritated him less than the fact that his father didn't even bother looking at Emma, let alone acknowledging her in any other way than by reference. Fury scoured him inside out, coursed through his veins. Antonio had long since stopped caring about the painful barbs Michael might throw in his direction, but he would not countenance any rudeness towards Emma.

'Her name is Emma. And you'll afford her the respect she deserves.'

'Respect? For a PA who miraculously becomes your fiancée when you so desperately need your reputation intact? How much did she charge you? I bet she's worth every penny of that green sapphire on her finger.'

His father's ice-cool eyes turned white-hot in a second and Antonio wanted to reach out and grab the man by the throat. But that was exactly what his father wanted. To cause a scene. To create a scandal that would make *him* look like the victim. Just the way he had done with his mother during the divorce.

Antonio had spent years studying his father's playbook, and he would not allow himself to rise to the taunt.

'Priceless,' he replied to his father's taunt.

'What?' he heard his father ask in confusion.

'Emma,' he stated, turning to her, locking his gaze with hers as if it were the only thread he could tie himself to amongst the seething emotions that were threatening to drown him.

She didn't show shock, fear or resentment—just curiosity, as if she too wanted to know what he meant.

'She is priceless. She is everything I didn't realise I needed.'

He watched as her eyes widened in surprise at his words, and hated it that he'd said them for his father—hated that he'd somehow tainted the sentiment.

'And I will not let you diminish her or hurt her. Take swipes at me, old man, or my company, but stay the hell away from her,' he growled.

For a second he saw shock in his father's eyes, but he rallied quickly.

'You think you can go up against me and win?' he snarled.

That was the voice he remembered from his childhood. The one that had haunted his sister's dreams and fuelled his own need for revenge.

'You have been nothing more than a pest, sniffing around my cast-offs. Once I win this investment with Bartlett, be assured the next business I'm coming after, *son*, is yours.'

'That's where you're wrong, *Father.* You won't win this deal with Bartlett. You've overplayed your hand and you're desperate. I can see it. And soon so will everyone else.'

Antonio unclenched his white-knuckled fist and forced himself to relax. He placed his hand on the small of Emma's back and guided her before him. He was thankful when she began to pick her way through the tables towards the head waiter, whose face betrayed no indication of hearing the conversation he must have heard.

Electricity crackled where his hand touched the almost indecently low back of her dress, but that wasn't what disturbed him. He realised that she was trembling—just slightly, not visibly—but he could feel it ripple over the soft, smooth acres of skin beneath his fingertips and he couldn't help himself.

He needed it—he needed *her*. He needed to wipe away that horrible encounter with his father. For her. For himself. He pulled her back, spinning her into him, and reached for what he so desperately wanted.

As his lips crashed down on hers he took advantage of the surprise she clearly felt, once again. How, after only one kiss, the taste and feel of her could be so familiar to him, he couldn't grasp. But his hand flew out to her cheek, holding her for his kiss, feeling her skin cool beneath the warmth of his fingers. He felt the wild flutter of her pulse beneath his palm, and satisfaction thrummed through him as it kept time with his own frantic heartbeat.

His tongue delved deeply into her mouth, relishing the way hers met and matched its every move. He didn't care that they were in a restaurant—didn't care that his father might still be watching. This wasn't for anyone else but them.

Starbursts of arousal and need crept up his spine, flaring and burning away the bitter taste of anger and resentment. And the moment her hand came up to his neck, pulling him to her as strongly as he wanted to pull her to him, he felt satisfaction, ownership, possession. A silent, primal roar sounded in his mind. *Mine*, it cried.

The realisation was startling, and enough for him to break the sensual hold that forged them together.

He drew back from their embrace, staring into eyes that were wide and dark with a desire that matched his own. Emma was breathing quickly, her cheeks flushed, and through the knowledge and the feeling of pleasure that he had done that to her, that he had caused her to feel that way, was a question ringing loudly in his mind.

Just what the hell had she done to him?

The head waiter cleared his throat discreetly and resumed his pathway towards the table where Benjamin Bartlett stood, waiting for them.

If she had known what Antonio had planned to do she would have stopped him. But, whether he'd noticed or not, the encounter with his father had unnerved her. Despite what Antonio had told her the previous night, his description of his father's cruel, ruthless behaviour, Emma had wondered if there was some reason, some explanation for his father's actions. She had thought he'd spoken with the hurt of an abandoned son, and now Emma felt terrible—as if that belief had somehow betrayed Antonio.

Because what she had seen in Michael Steele's eyes, heard in his voice, had convinced her that he was a horrible man, with no conscience nor regard for others. She understood, now, Antonio's need for revenge. Could feel it barely restrained beneath the surface of his skin. The power of it was dark, and she wished so much that he would turn away from it—even though she knew he wouldn't.

But that kiss had momentarily short-circuited her brain. Words of reassurance and support had fled beneath the sensual onslaught of his lips, and the wicked way they had demanded arousal and pleasure from her body had made her quiver with need. A need that went unsatisfied now he'd pulled away from her, leaving her wanting and shaking with desires she had never experienced before.

Realising that he had done that in public, in the middle of the restaurant full of nearly one hundred people, frustrated and angered her. But she needed to put aside that anger, because Benjamin Bartlett was there, standing at their table, waiting for them and looking decidedly uncomfortable.

And Emma was there to help Antonio win him over. Not because of the deal, and not because she was his convenient fiancée, but because she wanted to help *him*. Help him put his past to rest the way he was beginning to do for her.

She forced a smile to her lips, joy to her eyes, and took the hand Bartlett extended to her.

'Ms Guilham. It's lovely to meet you,' he said, his American accent more cultured than she had remembered from the call on the plane to Buenos Aires.

Unlike Michael Steele, Benjamin Bartlett seemed softer somehow, despite his height and lean stature. In some ways he was more like Antonio than Michael. Even though, at that precise moment in time, she could hardly say that there was anything soft about Antonio at all. In fact he seemed almost reluctant, as if still locked into an unconscious battle with his father.

'Likewise, Mr Bartlett. I hope we haven't kept you long?'

'Not at all.'

He waved them away, as if they hadn't just stood there in the middle of the restaurant kissing and instead had merely been a little delayed. And she realised then that what had made Bartlett awkward hadn't been the kiss, but the fact that he had clearly witnessed the interaction between Antonio and his father.

'I meant to ask,' Emma said as they took their seats, reaching for a conversation that she hoped would start them on potentially neutral ground, 'how is Anna's grandson? He wasn't very well the last time we spoke.'

A smile painted Bartlett's features. 'He's doing well, thank you for asking.'

Bartlett turned to Antonio, who hadn't been able to conceal his momentary confusion.

'My PA's grandson had appendicitis, and she had to stay home to care for him last week.' Turning back to Emma, he continued, 'She wanted me to pass on her congratulations. And I'd like to add mine to that,' he said, gesturing to Emma's hand.

The heavy weight of the beautiful green sapphire suddenly felt tight around her finger.

'I must admit I did wonder who it would take to make this reckless playboy settle down,' he said, but a smile took some of the sting out of his words. 'I don't believe he could have done any better.'

Emma forced some heat into her smile as guilt nibbled at her stomach. *Lying.* She was uncomfortable with lying.

'Thank you, Mr Bartlett.'

'Benjamin—please call me Benjamin,' he said, taking his seat and gesturing to them both to do the same. 'I hope you'll forgive us for talking business over our meal?'

'Of course. Antonio's very passionate about your company and I can't help but be intrigued.'

'Oh, really?' Bartlett asked.

'I have a great deal of respect for what you have

achieved,' Antonio stated, finally picking up the thread of the pitch he'd worked on non-stop for almost a week.

Phrases that Emma had heard him muttering to himself over the last few days ebbed and flowed in the conversation. They ordered drinks and food, and between the starters and the end of dessert Emma marvelled at how Antonio used his carefully constructed words to weave a spell that she was sure Benjamin Bartlett was falling under.

Each line of his pitch was carefully orchestrated, bent and moulded to the positive, outlining how Arcuri Enterprises could support, aid, help the company to grow, rather than muscle in and take over. It was skilful, almost surgical in its precision.

The warmth of Bartlett's interaction with her was very different from the careful assessment he was giving Antonio. Whilst Bartlett might be congenial, he was still a fierce businessman who was choosing his investor wisely.

'You clearly know a lot about my business, Antonio.'

'I use my research well.'

'And what does your research say about me?' Bartlett asked—and the query not one made out of vanity.

'That you are a traditional businessman who believes in keeping things the way they are. You don't like change, and you fight vehemently for your company, your brand and its continued success. You don't believe that a business deal should be done until the second bottle of whisky has been opened, and as we're in a restaurant, not a bar, and you have refused a drink with your coffee, I can tell that you haven't yet made up your mind about who is best to support you financially through the next successful stage of your business.'

Bartlett gave a surprised chuckle. 'And how did you know about the whisky?'

Antonio looked to Emma, who leaned in and said conspiratorially, 'Us PAs have our secrets, Mr Bartlett. Do allow us to keep them.'

'Ah... Of course. That is as it should be,' he replied with another warm smile.

Emma laid her fork down, defeated after less than half of the exquisite chocolate dessert she had ordered. In truth, she had neither eaten nor tasted much of the meal they had shared. Her nerves had been wound tight for Antonio. *Because* of him.

'Arcuri, it has certainly been an interesting evening. I thank you for the work you have clearly put into making this pitch, and I hope you will understand if I take this under consideration until next week. I have shareholders—many of whom see your father as a very good option.'

It was a phrase Antonio had expected, but one that was none the less unwelcome. Whether Bartlett had said it to garner a better deal from him, or whether it was the truth didn't really matter.

Yes, he'd seen desperation in his father's words and actions, but it was Dimitri's phrase that ran through his mind as he left the restaurant with Emma. That desperation made people dangerous. And he knew in that moment that he would go to any length, any extreme, to bring his father to his knees.

CHAPTER SEVEN

BY THE TIME they entered the reception area of their hotel, Antonio's thoughts were no longer on Bartlett *or* his father. Something which, at one point he'd thought almost unimaginable. But that had been before they'd come to Argentina—before Emma had worn the dress he'd chosen for her, and before he'd kissed her in a crowded restaurant and wanted the whole world to burn with him.

So instead of planning his next step he was still tasting her on his tongue. Instead of feeling the black plastic key card in his fingers he was feeling her skin beneath the palm of his hand. And there was nothing he could do to relieve the ache in his chest.

Not just because Emma wasn't like the women he usually spent his nights with—women who agreed to his unemotional demands. He saw in her all the goodness, all the soft, delicate parts of her life that had come together like a silk tapestry—one that he should admire and leave untouched. She deserved someone better than him. Someone who wasn't focused on a path straight to hell...someone who wouldn't drag her there with him.

He slid the key card into the slot beside the door and walked into the suite. When he'd left earlier that night, with Emma wearing his ring, on his way to meet Bartlett, he'd imagined that when he returned he'd feel...different. That he'd feel the thrill of satisfaction at ensuring his father's destruction. That somehow meeting Bartlett would have eased the adrenaline he'd felt rushing through him for over a week—would have settled the raging beast within him.

But he didn't and it hadn't.

Instead a different kind of heat burned within him—one that made him feel just as restless and just as dangerous. He stalked over to the bar area, poured two whiskies—one over ice for Emma—and after a second thought added two ice cubes to his own, hoping to cool the fervour of his libido. In his heart, he hoped that she would refuse the drink, that she would bid him goodnight and leave him alone with his new demons.

But she didn't.

Emma closed the door behind her, turning her back momentarily on the man who had come to mean so much to her. She was buying herself time. She knew it. Had known it since before their meal with Bartlett—since the moment Antonio's lips had crashed down onto hers. Perhaps even since the previous night.

It was as if her skin was feeding off the strange tension that had been summoned by their bodies' wants and desires in the car journey back from the restaurant. The silence that had fallen between them only seemed to place a spotlight on it, illuminating what she wasn't naïve enough to dismiss.

But was she brave enough to ask—demand for herself what her body wanted?

Looking at Antonio now, standing before the large windows, his broad shoulders and lean hips accentuated by the smooth planes of his suit, staring out at the stars, she knew that it had always been going to come to this.

He had coaxed from her body things she had never imagined. He had made her feel sexy, wanted and desirable. And Emma didn't want to let go of it—didn't want to sever the strange thread that bound them together.

Her cancer had struck at a time when she had been inexperienced, and nothing and no one had tempted her since.

Until now.

And if some part of her warned that this wasn't just about claiming her body, that it was much more to do with her heart, then she ruthlessly forced that thought aside. She wanted to strike through that invisible wish on her Living List. The one that she'd never had the courage to write down, but now had the courage to ask for.

'Antonio—'

'No.'

'I haven't—'

'You don't have to say it, Emma. You *shouldn't* say it. Shouldn't ask it of me. You should go to bed.'

His tone was dark and heavy—rough like bitter coffee and as tempting as sin.

'You don't know what I'm going to ask,' she assured him…assured herself.

He turned, then. Pinned her with his hawk-like gaze. She knew it was meant to intimidate, but instead it served only to enflame.

'Really? I am a man very well versed in feminine desire, Emma. A woman does not…*you* do not need to put into words what I see in your eyes. What your body is crying out for.'

Embarrassment stung her cheeks. She had thought

that he might be as surprised as she was to find herself asking for such a thing. But he had known. Had seen it in her. Had everyone else?

But she refused to be ashamed of it. She held his gaze, used it to empower her. She felt herself stand tall against the onslaught of his presence.

'You asked me what I wanted, Antonio. Back at the gala. And yesterday you said that I had not asked anything for myself. So now I'm asking. I want *you*. This night. Just one night,' she said, leaving the rest of her thoughts unspoken.

She wanted to feel cherished…wanted to love her body. Wanted *him* to love her body.

'Do you know what you're asking, Emma?'

'Yes.'

'Do you really? A no-strings affair? Just sex? You are too innocent to know the consequences of your request.'

'I'm not going to lie and tell you that I'm experienced, because I'm not,' she said, taking a step towards his forbidding frame. 'I'm not going to lie and tell you that I'm not terrified, because I am. But I know what I want. And now I'm asking you for it. Just one night, Antonio.'

She was only asking for one night because she knew instinctively that she couldn't risk anything more. Yes, she might be inexperienced, but she knew that much.

'Emma—'

It was a plea from his lips. One that she couldn't allow herself to listen to.

She took the final step towards him, closing the distance between them. Looking up at him, standing chest to chest, she saw his lips hovering so close to her own. It was intoxicating. She'd never tasted need, actually *tasted* it on her tongue, but she knew that it would be nothing like the taste of him, his true self. Without the masks, the fakery of performance.

Her chest rose, trying to contain the beating of her heart, pushing against the silk that cleaved in a V to her breasts, as if inviting his gaze, begging for his touch. She had never felt like this. Had never felt the power of desire rushing over her skin, making her bold, making her needy.

'You said I could have anything I wanted. Please… please don't make me—' The word *beg* stuck in her throat.

She reached up, her hand cold against the hot skin of his clenched jaw. He hadn't moved a muscle, but she felt emotion swirling within him with the force of a storm. He was almost vibrating with it.

Their breathing was harsh and it echoed within the silence of the suite. Antonio's eyes were a molten mixture of fury and desire, matching her own. She allowed the heat from his body to lap against hers like a tide, threatening to overtake her and knock her down. Her mouth was inches away from his. But she wanted him to make that last move. She wanted it, needed it—needed him to prove that it wasn't just *her* in this. That he was as weak as she in this moment.

And suddenly his lips were on hers, almost punishingly. His arm snaked around her back, holding her against the onslaught of passion that was so much stronger than a tide. For a moment she basked in that power, in the feel of him encompassing her completely. She allowed it to happen to her, to shock her as his tongue demanded entrance and his body commanded surrender. Then she came to life under the sheer level of need that was binding them together.

She pushed back against the kiss, opened herself to

him. Tongue clashed against tongue, teeth nipped at lips. Her hands unclasped from his shoulders and ran down the shirt covering his chest. She pushed with one and pulled with the other, desperate to feel *more*. His hands wound their way into her hair, and she thought she might have heard a groan as he sank his hands into the sleek knot and sent the pins flying, leaving her dark auburn hair to cascade down her back.

He started to walk her backwards and she felt his strong thighs against hers in an almost erotic slide. The slit of the silk skirt parted, allowing her bare legs access to the rich material of his trousers, making her feel naked against him.

As if he, too, was thinking the same thing, one of his hands left her hair, trailed over the naked V left by the silk around her chest, down to her waist. His hand flared to span it for just a moment, before lowering even further down, skating over her hip before his fingertips traced their way to the cut in the skirt and slipped through to the bare skin of her thigh.

Emma gasped as his hand wrapped around her bottom, bringing her thigh up, allowing him to step fully between her legs, and gasped again as she felt the hard ridge of his arousal at her core. It was a promise. It was a threat.

He pulled back from their kiss, gazing down on her as if warning her that this was the point of no return, failing to realise that she'd crossed that bridge a long time back. As if her body was completely his now, her hips pressed forward against his, desperate to feel him deeper, *needing* to feel him deeper.

They came up against the arm of the sofa and he guided her back, perching her there.

'Had you asked any other man, Emma, he would

have taken you to a bed covered with roses,' he ground out against her lips, unaware that that she wouldn't have wanted that. Simply because it wouldn't have been *him*. 'Had you asked any other man, he would have showered you with gifts and seduced you with words,' he continued, unaware that he had given her the greatest of gifts, offering her words of truth instead of lies, and that it meant so much more.

'I am not that man,' he said, as if answering her thoughts. 'But,' he said, with a fierce sincerity that pinned her heart, 'I will stop at any point. Know that. You are in control here, Emma. This is your decision. If you want me to—'

She cut off his words with a kiss of her own—just as powerful, just as impassioned as any of those he had given her.

As if the last barrier had been broken, a flood of need passed between them in that kiss. His hands ran the length of her chest and breasts, down once again to the silky slit in the dress. She nearly cried out as his hands caressed the soft skin of her thighs, as his hands found the thin piece of material holding her thong together and pulled, tearing the string as if it were nothing and tossing it aside. He brought his hands down around her bottom and lifted her up against him, the material of his trousers pressed against her core, shocking her and setting a fire within her.

He stepped back, and the loss of heat from where his body had pressed against hers allowed the cool air of the room to raise goosebumps on her arms. At least that was what she told herself as she shivered against his touch. His fingers found the slick wet heat of her core, at first gently running over her clitoris, bringing an unbidden cry from her mouth.

She thought she heard him curse, but she couldn't tell. The sensations he was wringing from her body were overwhelming. She might not know what to do, but her body moved instinctively, her legs opening to his hand as his fingers mirrored his tongue as he kissed her, pushing into her, delving further and deeper. Her body arched back over his powerful arm of its own volition, pulling her away from his kiss.

Need rose deep within her, yearning, demanding something that she couldn't fathom. Her breath became gasps, and she felt unable to contain all the emotions, all the sensations within her. She cried out, his wicked sensuality bringing forth even more want, and found herself begging, pleading for something she couldn't quite name.

She barely noticed him settle between her legs, but the moment his tongue pressed against her core, wet heat against wet heat, a wildness was wrenched from her and she came apart in an explosion of white fire-bursts. Stars dusted the back of her eyelids and she fell into an abyss.

Antonio watched as Emma's orgasm spilled waves of shivers across her skin, flushing her cheeks with pleasure, and he was speechless. He had never seen anything so beautiful, tasted anything so sweet, experienced anything so humbling as this moment.

But as she opened her eyes, and he saw wonder and awe painted in them, he knew it wasn't enough for him to know these things. She must too.

'Do you trust me?' he asked.

'Yes,' she said simply.

He gently reached for the shoulder straps of her dress. Emma stiffened.

He knew that she was scared, embarrassed…he couldn't even begin to imagine what else she might be feeling. But he wanted to help give her back her body. He wanted her to appreciate it as it should be appreciated.

He moved slowly and gently, allowing her to get used to the idea. He pushed aside the thin straps of silk and bared her to him. He could see that she was struggling, but all he saw was perfection. Beautiful and powerful. Her breasts bore faint scars from the surgeon's knife, and as he pressed open-mouthed kisses to her skin he marvelled at the tattoos that had skilfully created nipples and areolas.

He brought his hands round to cup her breasts and nearly groaned out loud at their rightness. They felt heavy as they spilled into his hands. His thumb ran gently over her skin, and her answering shudder as it did so almost brought a smile to his lips as he bent forward and took one breast into his mouth. He laved her breasts with his tongue, first one, then the other. Emma hung her head back, pressing them further into his mouth, and he returned the favour as he pressed his groin into hers, bringing her back to him with a piercing need that nailed them both.

The sensations Emma felt were foreign and strange. She wanted his touch so much, and frustration, resentment and sadness warred in her chest. She hated it that her nipples were no longer there. This was the bit in her treasured romance books that she always skipped over. How the hero would touch, kiss and tease the heroine's nipples until they became taut and tight. She missed that feeling with an ache so deep. She hated it that her body would never be able to do that.

She had feared so much that this would hurt even more in practice than in thought. But she had been wrong. Antonio had caressed and kissed her breasts, rather than avoiding them, had touched her so much that she wasn't sure she could take it any more.

Her hands went to the silk straps of the dress. She wanted to turn away.

'Don't hide from me, Emma. You're so brave and so very strong,' he said between each kiss and caress of her breasts. 'You said that what you wanted most was this…but this isn't about me.'

She wanted to tell him that he was wrong, but in the deepest part of her she knew that he was right.

'This is about you. You've had the courage to ask for what you want…it's time to *take* what you want. It's time to stop hiding in the shadows and step into the light. You're beautiful. So beautiful, Emma…'

She hated it that his words stirred her heart, felt tears forming at the edges of her eyes, betraying her.

'I want you to say it,' he told her.

She turned her head away from him. The words were locked in a throat tight with emotion. She didn't want to say it, but Antonio asked again. Not angry, not frustrated, but with understanding and compassion shining from his eyes.

'I'm beautiful…' she whispered.

'Again, Emma,' he commanded.

'I'm beautiful,' she said, this time with a little more strength. 'I *am* beautiful,' she said, finally allowing belief to make the words strong.

Antonio scooped her up from where she was perched on the arm of the sofa and carried her through to the bedroom. And when her head rested on his chest he shook away the thought that it felt as if it had always been there.

He gently laid her on the bed, watching her eyes slowly focus on him where he stood over her, still dazed from her own empowerment and her orgasm. And even though he was so ready to take her, so ready to find his own release, he wanted her to be with him, wanted her to feel everything that he felt.

If this was his one stolen moment, then he would make it count.

Antonio's hands left her chest to pull at the edges of his shirt. Impatient to feel her skin against his, he ripped the shirt apart, sending buttons flying across the room, watching as Emma's eyes widened in both shock and arousal.

As his hands went to the waistband of his trousers, hers found the zip at the side of her dress.

'Stop,' he commanded. Her eyes found his, her cheeks painted red with desire and perhaps just a trace of embarrassment. He leaned forward. 'That's for me to do, Emma. That's *my* pleasure.'

He leaned back and brought down the zip on his trousers, relishing every second as she watched him slowly push them off his legs. He watched her restless legs, sliding up and down against each other as if the friction might get close to the pleasure he could administer.

He smiled knowingly, stepping forward, pressing her thighs apart and bringing the palm of his hand to rest at her centre.

Emma jerked her hips against the contact of his hot palm between her legs. There was nothing but the autumnal silk of the dress between his skin and hers, slick and ready.

He sat on the bed next to her, reaching around to her side and slowly, ever so slowly, releasing the dress's zip from its casing, drawing it down to where it ended at the top of her hip. His hands swept under the material, feeling their way across her stomach and up to her breasts. He moved one hand down in between her legs and parted her there with his fingers.

As her hips rose off the bed to meet his hand he swept the burnt orange silk from beneath her, moved it up above her waist with his other hand. He brought her breast to his mouth and whipped the material over her head as he savoured her breasts, relishing each cry that fell from Emma's lips.

He gathered the dress in his fist and threw the crumpled silk onto the floor, then leaned back and took her small dainty feet in his hands. He stroked the insides of her feet and placed them apart, moving in between her legs. As his hands caressed their way up her calves, over her knees and up her thighs, Emma sighed, watching his hands work their way up over her hips towards her breasts, her spine arching off the bed, pressing them into his palms.

For what seemed like hours he stayed there, caressing, licking, tasting all that she had to offer. Watching her both lose herself and find herself in the passion they were creating together.

Reluctant to leave the soft satin of her skin, he leaned towards the bedside table and took protection, tearing off the foil and positioning the latex over himself. Her small hands came over his as he rolled the condom over his length, her fingers wrapping around his erection, smoothing down to the base.

Before she could chip any more away from the last

shreds of his will power he picked up one of her hands, whilst positioning himself at her slick core.

He looked at her, silently begging her... For refusal or acceptance, he didn't know any more. Her hands slid around him, clasping his hips and gently pulling him towards her, sealing their fate.

As he slowly pushed himself between her thighs he kissed the inside of her palm and entered her so carefully it was almost torture. But it wasn't torture at all. It was bliss. She was so wet, so ready for him, and he sank deep into the tight, wet heat of her, allowing her body to shift and make room for him entirely.

Never before had he felt so deeply connected, so deeply *with* someone. And something inside him shifted. Something he couldn't allow to take hold.

He inched forward just a little more, and Emma's eyes widened and locked on to his.

He waited for her to acclimatise to him, and when he saw that she had he withdrew and plunged back into her, deep and hard. Her cries of pleasure rang out in the room, urging him on, into her again and again. An incredible sensation was stretching throughout his body, taking a firm hold on his chest and what lay hidden there beneath his ribs, and he knew—*knew* that this wasn't just sex.

His cries soon joined hers and he grasped her wrists, holding them above her head, staring down into her eyes. He couldn't hold back any more—he couldn't hold *anything* back any more.

Sensing that she was on the brink of her second orgasm, feeling the tightening of her muscles around him, hearing that special, perfect pitch of her voice, he thrust into her one last time, and they fell together even more deeply over the edge than ever before.

* * *

Antonio woke in a panic. His heart pounded in his chest, a cold sweat gathered on his brow, and his head was filled with thoughts of his father cruelly ripping him from Emma's sleep-fuelled embrace.

It took him a moment to place himself. A thing that had never happened to Antonio before in his life. Not when he, his mother and sister had been wrenched from America and sent back to Italy…not in any of the numerous hotel rooms where he had spent countless nights for his business.

But the fear didn't recede. Unaccountably, Antonio couldn't shake the feeling that something awful was on the horizon—waiting to crash down and blow everything to smithereens.

Emma turned beside him, the smooth sleek line of her spine exposed where he had pulled the sheets back from their stranglehold around his chest. He needed to move, needed to leave the safe haven of her bed, was reluctant to somehow infect her with his thoughts.

He grabbed his trousers from where he'd thrown them off only hours before and padded his way through to the living room, gently closing the door on the passion and emotion of earlier hours.

He forced his legs into the trousers and fastened the zip and the button around his waist. Signs of their lovemaking were everywhere. Discarded clothes, rumpled paper and documents from the Bartlett deal neither of them had seen in the urgency of their need.

He paced the room. Back and forth. And still couldn't shake the feeling of impending doom. His father had something. Something that Antonio didn't. Something on Bartlett, he decided. He was too self-assured for a man on the brink of destruction. That was what had bothered him most about his father. Yes, he'd seen desperation—but he'd also seen triumph.

And then he did something he'd never thought himself capable of.

He found his mobile phone amongst the chaos of the room and pulled up the number of Arcuri Enterprises' private investigator.

Not caring what time it would be in America, he spoke quietly and efficiently, outlining his need for the man to dig up anything and everything he might be able to find on Bartlett, or his family. Only days ago Emma had pointed out that Bartlett's daughter was something of a party girl. She might be on to something.

If Antonio felt any guilt then he forced such a feeling aside, bringing to mind instead that horrible confrontation with his father. The only way to fight a monster was to become one himself. His father would pay for what he'd done. And if that meant reducing himself to his father's level, ruining his soul, Antonio was willing to do so.

CHAPTER EIGHT

CLASH OF THE TYCOON TITANS!
BY ROANNA KING

Arcuri vs Steele, son against father, who will win?

It would seem that Antonio Arcuri's shock engagement was just the beginning. The business world is holding its breath as father and son pitch for the same deal! Sources close to the tycoons have suggested a last-ditch battle of wills.

For years Arcuri has nipped at the edges of Steele's business dealings, and is now pulling out all the stops to slash and burn with his legendary ruthlessness—his father, no less.

And while women around the world are still mourning the loss of this international bachelor, men are salivating, placing bets on who will draw first—and last—blood.

With so much on the line for these two men, it will certainly be a clash of the tycoon titans!

DIMITRI'S GREEK-ACCENTED VOICE rose above the hum of the crowds as he read the article out loud, clearly just for the hell of it.

'At least they didn't mention Bartlett by name,' he noted.

'I doubt very much that it was by mistake or from some inherent sense of propriety. This has the stink of my father all over it,' Antonio growled.

'He must be desperate if he's willing to risk such exposure, given how notoriously private Bartlett is,' Danyl reflected, looking out at the race course from the balcony of the hospitality suite set aside for the Winners' Circle.

Discreet servers had placed trays of delicate food there, none of which was appealing to Antonio at that moment. He shifted his sunglasses back over his eyes.

Danyl turned in his seat beside him, pinning him with a powerful gaze. 'You have something to hide?'

'No,' came Antonio's terse reply.

Danyl gave a spectacularly *un*-regal grunt in response, and placed a Bloody Mary on the table in front of him. 'Hair of the horse that bit you, so to speak.'

Antonio ignored them both and took a mouthful of the thick, spicy tomato juice.

'Virgin?' queried Dimitri as Danyl rolled his eyes.

The sting of tabasco sauce caught Antonio in the back of the throat and he forced himself to swallow the drink through a throat thick with convulsions.

'For God's sake, Dimitri.'

The sounds of the crowd and the announcements over the Tannoy drifted up from the race course below.

'Did anyone see Mason this morning?' Antonio asked, when in truth his mind had been searching for Emma. Emma whom he'd left sleeping in the hotel room while he'd sneaked out like a thief.

'John was guarding her like a dog. He wouldn't let anyone near her this morning. Said something about not letting us "psych her out".'

'Us or you, Danyl?' Dimitri asked. 'You still haven't said how you know her.'

'I still haven't said that I *do* know her.'

Antonio let the sounds of his friend's light-hearted squabble fall over him as he tried to block out the memory of Emma's sighs of pleasure that still, even now, thickened his blood.

He clenched a fist, trying to regain control of his errant body. He couldn't believe what madness had overtaken them last night. He'd promised her only one night, but now he wondered if he could keep that promise. It wouldn't last—it couldn't. He would only end up hurting her, letting her down, drawing her deeper into his own need for revenge.

'You might want to put that glass down, Antonio,' Dimitri said, his words cutting through the emotional fog that was surrounding him.

'Mmm?'

'The glass. If you carry on, it might just crack.'

Antonio looked down to see white knuckles encasing thin glass and put the drink back on the table. Danyl was looking at him with a raised eyebrow, wry curiosity painting his features.

'Dare I ask how the Bartlett deal is going?'

'Actually, our meeting went very well. Even after my father made his surprise guest appearance.'

Concerned silence met his statement. Danyl and Dimitri were watching and waiting for the explanation they knew he would give them. They alone knew the depths of his hatred for his father, the true extent of which he hadn't been able to confess to Emma.

They greeted his account with an anger and fury that matched his own. And Michael Steele's treatment of Emma was high on their list of his crimes.

'Are you sure you want to go that way?' Dimitri asked when Antonio confessed the action he had directed his PI to.

'If there's anything to find you can be sure that Michael will have already discovered it, and he will plan to use it to his advantage.'

'And are you willing to do the same? To use blackmail to get what it is that you want?'

A commotion at the paddock drew their attention and prevented Antonio from needing to answer Dimitri's question. As Antonio recognised Mason's colours and Veranchetti's proud stance he forced all other thoughts from his mind.

Emma wove her way through the throng of people in the stands towards the stairs to the hospitality suite, where she knew Antonio and his friends—the Winners' Circle syndicate—would be. The day was beautiful, despite the bad weather forecasted for later. It was strange to think that there could be anything like rain on the horizon when the air, despite being stirred up by the spectators, was calm and the sun was strong.

She felt a laugh rise within her chest and stifled it. Here she was, in a sea of people, and no one was looking at her because of what she lacked. She was invisible. And yet she felt as if she knew a secret that no one else did.

Throughout the night she had reached for Antonio, had felt him reach for her, and they had teased and taunted each other to completion more times than she could believe. Those precious hours were a montage of sensation and feeling, always with the heat of Antonio beside her, over her, behind her. It was as if her body had craved that warmth, needed it to come alive again.

She felt re-made—re-worked in a way she couldn't have expected. It was as if an old ache around her heart had lessened and she felt lighter than she had done in years.

She had woken alone and hadn't been surprised, realising that on some level she must have heard him leave. A web of nerves had tightened around her stomach. How would they be the next time they encountered each other?

No, she thought now, pressing a hand against her belly to quell the butterflies. She wouldn't be embarrassed about last night. They were adults. And what they had shared was incredible. Antonio had made her see herself in a way she had never done before and that was something more precious than she ever could have realised.

She felt strong and, yes, even a little giddy. Last night she had seen him, Antonio Arcuri, as needy and as aroused as her. She had met him as an equal and nothing would take that away. And to be his equal—not his PA, and not his fake fiancée? It thrilled her.

Was this what love was? *Desire*, she hastily corrected herself. A high that made her feel powerful, strong? She relished that feeling and all of a sudden her chest was fit to burst. Excitement swept through her as she began to climb the steps towards the balconies bordering the race course.

Her heart pulsed within her chest and she wondered how anyone could live like this, in this constant state of awareness and excitement. Would it go away? Would it dim over time? Did she want it to?

For so long, so many years, she had wanted to feel this way. Wanted to own herself, to feel cherished and desired. Somehow, despite her optimism and determination to experience all that life had to offer, she had let herself hide from the one thing that she had truly wanted.

Here she was, on the brink of having it all, and suddenly she felt the fear that it could all be taken away. And that was when she knew just how much she had sacrificed—just how much she had pushed deep down within her, ignoring the wants and desires that she craved.

This man—hell-bent on revenge, but capable of the tenderness of last night—had stolen her heart. The goodness in him that she could see made those feelings even more powerful. She wanted him to win the Bartlett deal against his father. Not because of the hatred that Antonio felt for him, but to put an end to it so that Antonio could move on.

Even from this high up Antonio could imagine—could remember—the feeling of sitting on top of a powerful horse pawing at the ground with shod hoofs, the flex of the animal's muscles beneath the saddle, the creaking of leather, the way a horse would lift and shift beneath him. The thrilling rush of adrenaline that would pound through both him and the horse together, as one. That moment just before the horse would pull back, ready to launch itself forward, ready to catapult into a gallop and leave just about everything behind.

At one point in his life riding had meant freedom—escape from a father who had made his and his mother's and sister's lives a misery. In the end, he realised, he'd not escaped anything.

As the noise picked up around the grounds, mixing with incoherent announcements from the Tannoy, Antonio battled with the past and the present. Somehow he knew that it was all rooted in the events of the night before. Bartlett, his father, Emma, business, passion... All of it was making him feel as if he were on some precipice, and he couldn't tell whether he was about to be saved or doomed.

The shrill of the bell signalling the start of the race cut through the stands as the barriers on the starting gate opened and the horses leapt forward.

For just a moment the breath caught in his lungs.

But it wasn't because of the race.

He felt her presence behind him, as she stepped out on to the balcony that jutted out over the course below. He teased himself, holding himself back from the moment when he would turn and look at Emma. A test of sorts. One that he failed.

She was dressed in a white sleeveless top with dark blue flowing trousers. Her thick dark hair swirled around her. She raised her hand to catch at the strands, sweeping them back from her face as she looked down at the horses, rather than at him.

His heart thumped painfully in his chest as tension ran through the crowd on a ripple that reached all the way to the balcony. Urgency filled the air, and the noise created by the people reached higher towards a crescendo that, just for a moment, he thought might never find its peak.

And still he could not take his eyes from the woman who had come to stand beside him. He felt her on his skin, through the layers of his clothes, over the hours since they had shared a bed. The bed he wanted to take her back to and never leave.

Suddenly her body sprang into action. Both arms were raised and she was punching into the air, her cry of surprise matched only by the furious yells of the two men beside him. A fist thumped on his back—Dimitri, lost in his excitement. And Danyl was staring deep into the winner's gate, as if not really sure he had seen Mason McAulty lead Veranchetti to victory.

Antonio hadn't. All he'd seen was Emma. And he shuddered as a cold bead of sweat trickled down his spine.

He watched with an unwarranted anger unfurling in his stomach, seeing Danyl and Dimitri sweep Emma up into swift, joyous embraces. The small balcony suddenly seemed overly full as waiters descended with bottles of champagne and hands reached over the balcony walls to offer congratulations and cheers of success.

A possessive streak he hadn't realised he owned coursed through his body. If he'd noticed the flash of the cameras, he couldn't say. If he'd told himself it was for appearances' sake, rather than the desperate need to feel her lips against his, it would have been a lie.

He pulled her to him—a move that was becoming increasingly familiar and ever more welcome—until he was an inch…a breath…away from a kiss that he already knew would enflame the burning furnaces of his desire. Something that would have the power to take away the painfully fierce anger boiling in his chest as he thought of his father, as he thought of his own actions.

He teased them both, watching the hazel flecks of her eyes dissolve into sea-green depths. Over the din, the shouts and cries of the crowd around them, he heard her gasp, saw the moment surprise sizzled into expectation and want, and pushed the moment further. To when nothing else could be seen, heard or felt—when it was just the two of them.

When he could make her realise that this wasn't for the press, for Bartlett, for anyone else other than him and her.

And then he took what he so desperately wanted.

* * *

Emma felt her hand creep up towards Antonio's neck, pulling him deeper, forging them together with tongue and teeth. She laved his tongue with her own, brought the thumb of her other hand to the corner of his mouth, relishing the sensual power she wielded now, daring him to taste her. Taste more of her.

She gave no thought to anyone around them, no feeling for the concern as to where this might lead, and it thrilled as much as terrified her. She matched his almost desperate movements with her own, taking everything he had to give and offering her all in return.

He had turned her into a wanton woman and she shamelessly claimed him for the world to see. She wanted to imprint herself on him, wanted to eradicate the memory of all who had come before her. Wanted to be the only thing he needed.

'That's enough, you two,' Dimitri called out, bringing Emma crashing back to the present.

She slowly pulled back, satisfaction stretching through her to see Antonio Arcuri as dazed and shocked as she felt.

'No,' she whispered, for his ears only. 'It's not enough,' she said with a gentle shake of her head—before she turned a beaming smile on Antonio's friend and relinquished her hold on Antonio to accept a glass of champagne .

'Gentlemen. Congratulations,' she said, in a surprisingly steady voice.

Three hours later and the promised storm had bruised the sky a deep purple, but for all its bluster it had still failed to break. The wind was whipping up the leaves around the trees that lined the streets below, reminding

Antonio of the crowds of people surrounding the winner's gate earlier. The press had burst upon them in a hail of flashbulbs, firing questions about the next two races, to be carefully deflected by three men who knew better than to engage with the paparazzi.

Mason McAulty, the female jockey whose name was now on everyone's lips, had been discreetly spirited away by John, moved on to prepare for the next race in Ireland almost before her feet had left Veranchetti's stirrups.

Danyl, who had watched her go with the same frantic energy of the storm, had barely commented on the win—as if both relieved and concerned by it—and had simply stalked through the halls of The Excelsus towards the private function room that had been prepared for the closing event of the Hanley Cup's first leg.

It was a glamorous affair, attended by royal dignitaries, international syndicates, horse breeders and owners. Models hung from arms like accessories, but none took Antonio's notice. A waiter passed by with a tray full of the finest champagne, but even the promise of cool nutty flavours and frothy light bubbles wasn't enough to disguise the taste of Emma still on Antonio's tongue.

It was addictive. He wanted more. And he *never* wanted more.

He made his way over to the bar, looking for a drink that would succeed in refocusing his tastebuds. Bartlett would be there to celebrate the Winners' Circle's success, although he was still to confirm whether he would choose his father or him. But Antonio knew. He would be chosen in the end. He was now sure of it.

Dimitri was at the bar, his brooding presence enough to create a wide berth around him, clear of people. Danyl was still looking out over the race course through the windows as the first drops of promised rain slung themselves against the glass. In contrast to the gloss and sheen of revelry that dusted the other guests, the members of the Winners' Circle seemed consumed by their own demons.

Dimitri reached behind the bar, ignoring the frown from the barman busy with another customer, grabbed a glass and poured Antonio a drink from the bottle of obscenely expensive whisky beside him. Dimitri threw an impressive stack of pesos onto the bar, which mollified the barman.

'Why does this feel like a wake rather than a victory?' Dimitri demanded. 'Come on—we're celebrating!'

Antonio cast a glance in Dimitri's direction. There was a light in his eyes that Antonio hadn't seen for far too long. 'What is it?'

Dimitri's gaze was fierce. 'They got him! The SEC have finally brought civil charges against Manos,' he said, spitting out the name of his half-brother, 'and my name is finally and completely cleared.'

'Now, *that* I can drink to,' Danyl said, and he leaned over and poured himself a large helping of whisky.

'It's been a long time coming,' Antonio added, 'but well worth the wait.' He savoured the burn of the alcohol in his throat.

'I'm sorry that I can't stay for longer,' said Danyl. 'I have to fly home. My mother has been talking about brides and babies again.'

Dimitri choked on his drink. 'Nothing, and I mean *nothing*, would tempt me into taking a bride, let alone having a baby,' he said, slamming his glass down on the bar. 'But it seems that the same cannot be said for Antonio.'

He felt the weight of both men's gazes on him. 'It's

just for show. Bartlett needed reassurance to get him to the table—Emma offered that.'

He saw Dimitri's eyes lock onto something over his shoulder. 'I don't think that's the only kind of enticement she's offering,' Dimitri replied.

Antonio's stomach clenched even before he had seen her—awaiting, expecting, the punch to the gut he had begun to experience each time he caught sight of her. The hair on his neck prickled as he forced himself not to immediately turn towards the entrance to the bar. Holding off the moment for as long as possible…both punishment and penance.

'You bloody fool,' Danyl said.

'What?' Antonio asked.

'You've slept with her,' Dimitri accused.

Finally lifting the leash on his body, Antonio turned to watch her enter the room. She was wearing the midnight-blue lace dress he'd seen her try on in the dressing room the other day. It wrapped around her skin as if it had been painted on, and yet there was nothing indecent about it. Only the reaction it had caused in him.

Because although he was an experienced man, and he'd had his fair share of women, nothing he'd seen until that moment had made him want to back a woman into the nearest room, throw out any people in the near vicinity and rip the clothing from her body.

And Antonio had the unnerving suspicion that she knew it too. She was taunting him in that dress, making him want to take back his promise from only hours before…the promise that they could only ever have one night. Because right then he wanted to live that night over and over and over again.

He watched her walk over to Bartlett, rather than avoiding the man as he himself had done so far. He nearly flinched when she laid her hand on his arm, offering him a smile that was both familiar and pleased. When she whispered something in his ear, eliciting a fond reaction from Bartlett, Antonio nearly broke a wisdom tooth because his jaw was clenched so hard.

'She's making some powerful friends, Arcuri,' Dimitri warned. 'You'd better watch out.'

Antonio couldn't take his eyes off her as she turned in their direction and wove through the tables dotted between them. And she held his gaze for all she was worth, right until she stopped barely a foot away from him. Then she turned her amazing smile on his companions.

'Gentlemen,' Emma said by way of introduction, 'how far into the celebrations are we? Starting gate or halfway?'

'A little bit of both. Emma, I must say, you look ravishing!'

'Why, thank you, Dimitri. As always, you look devastatingly handsome.'

'Careful—if you carry on being so charming I might have to steal you away from Antonio myself.'

She laughed, and laughed even more when she heard Antonio's answering growl. If she'd ever wondered what it might feel like to be the centre of his world... Well... She was beginning to feel it now.

'What's your poison, Emma?' Dimitri asked, and for all the outward brooding she had seen in him from across the bar when she'd first entered, there was something almost kind in his eyes.

She took in their glasses, and the outrageously expensive bottle of whisky, but decided against the heady amber liquid she now associated with dark nights and deep secrets.

'Prosecco, please.'

The barman nodded, and placed a full flute on the bar.

She turned to Danyl. 'Your Highness,' she said, with a small bow of her head, knowing from experience that anything more overt would rankle. For someone who held such a public position, the Sheikh of Terhren was a deeply private man.

'My assistant wishes to pass on his congratulations and his immense relief,' said Danyl. 'He is very much looking forward to a time when he no longer has to do battle with you. You have knocked his considerable confidence in his own abilities.'

She knew it was flattery, gentle and teasing, and it felt so good to be amongst Antonio's friends. It wasn't often that she saw this side of her fiancé—her *boss*—she hastily corrected herself. Though she couldn't really say that he was her boss any more. Last night had put an end to that and replaced stern reminders of her place with delicate strands of hope. Hope that this could be so much more.

She turned to greet Antonio and the words stuck in her throat. He looked so sexy, so powerful. He hadn't changed, as she had, and was still dressed in the same dark trousers and shirt open at the collar that he had been wearing earlier that day. But where before there had only been traces of stubble, now a dark shadow covered the planes of his cheeks and strong jawline and her fingers itched to reach out, to touch the deliciously rough edges.

She didn't have to wonder what he thought of the dress. It was all there in his eyes. It was the same struggle she'd had when she'd looked in the mirror before coming to the bar. Was this the right thing to do? Was she brave enough to take what she wanted and damn the consequences?

Looking at Antonio in that moment, she felt a smile pull at the edge of her lips. One that found a quick answer.

He leaned in and bent his mouth to her ear. The warmth of his breath threw cold shivers down her back as his words reached her.

'You're going to pay for wearing this dress later,' he warned darkly.

'Is that a promise?' she enquired innocently, while the devil in her danced.

'Oh, so much more than a promise, Emma,' he said, before returning to the circle of his friends.

Something like relief spread through her chest. It was all going to be okay. Dimitri pressed her glass into her hand and drew back to make room for her at the bar. No, she decided, it was going to be more than okay.

Antonio watched Emma chat happily with two of the world's most powerful men and wondered how she could ever have doubted herself. The promise he'd made to her, warning her that it would only ever be one night, was turning to ash, leaving only the taste of anticipation on his tongue. He wanted her. He would have her. Tonight.

And suddenly it seemed that it was all possible. That he'd get the Bartlett deal, that he would wreak his revenge on his father, that he might even get to keep Emma for a while. He could certainly make her happy—perhaps help her tick off some more of the things on her Living List.

Pleasure uncoiled in his chest—a different kind from what he was used to. This wasn't the thrill of the chase, or the knowledge that he had won some kind of challenge. It was the kind of pleasure he'd experienced only a few times as a child at being given something… Something precious…a gift without strings. And he wanted to unwrap that present. Right now.

Some hours later Emma was making her way back to the bar from the bathroom when the concierge found her.

'Ms Guilham, there is a package for Mr Arcuri at reception. We didn't want to interrupt him.'

Emma looked in Antonio's direction, and seeing him surrounded by his friends, laughing with a lightness she hadn't seen from him for quite some time, she understood the concierge's quandary.

'Are you happy for me to sign for it?' she asked, and when he agreed she followed him out of the bar and through the much quieter halls to Reception.

The sudden silence of the corridor made her feelings of happiness seem so much bigger, so much harder to contain. She had enjoyed talking to his friends, the feeling of being amongst them. The bond they shared was so clear and so strong it was a wonder to her. And she questioned for the first time whether perhaps it was *she* who had caused the distance between her and her friends from school, that perhaps *she* had kept that distance.

Emma decided that enough was enough. No more hiding when there was so much joy, so much of this indescribable feeling to experience.

The concierge reached behind the desk and produced a thin manila envelope, along with an electronic pad for her to sign on receipt.

She gently pulled the envelope open and, seeing the name 'Bartlett' on the cover sheet of the papers in neat handwritten capitals, didn't think anything of it. Not for a moment did she consider that it was something she shouldn't see.

But as she pulled out the documents inside the folder she realised just how wrong she had been.

CHAPTER NINE

ANTONIO HAD STARTED to wonder where Emma had got to about an hour ago. Danyl had left—he was returning to Terhren—and Dimitri had turned his attentions to a rather beautiful Iranian woman.

Antonio had no intention of blocking his pursuit. Ever since Dimitri's imprisonment a cloud had hung about him. And the news of his half-brother's involvement in his imprisonment had not done as much as he'd thought to lighten it.

Unease started to nibble at the edges of the excitement he'd felt earlier in the evening. It wasn't like Emma simply to disappear. He knew he hadn't missed her amongst the glittering, bejewelled guests at the Hanley Cup's closing party. He had lost that sense of her. That he could feel her presence should have been warning enough. But the fact that he couldn't...

He made his way back to the suite, his heart pounding, aware that something must be terribly wrong. Which was perhaps why he was not surprised to find the rooms shrouded in darkness when he entered.

Emma stood in front of the huge windows, illuminated by the bursts of lightning that fired through the night sky. The storm that had been promised was finally breaking.

His gaze caught a glimpse of the private investigator's dossier on the side table—open. And that was the moment he knew that everything he thought he might have had, everything that had made him feel so much hope, was about to slip through his fingers. Not just the Bartlett deal, but Emma too.

In the time it took for another burst of lightning to burn through the night-time sky he realised suddenly just how much she had come to mean to him—how much he wanted her to be his. And not just until after the deal…after Hong Kong. He wanted to show her the world. He wanted to help her achieve everything on her Living List. He wanted to make her his for ever.

But then he saw her bags, packed and waiting by the door to her room, and knew he'd been foolish to allow himself to think such thoughts. He could never have her—not whilst seeking his father's punishment. He could never have her and still do the things that needed to be done—to become a monster to catch a monster. But it didn't stop him from wanting to try.

'What is this?'

Her voice cut through the silence. The question echoed in the burst of thunder that rolled across the race course outside.

'Emma—'

'What *is* it?' she demanded, her voice suddenly more powerful and commanding than the elements raging beyond the windows.

'It's a file I requested to be compiled on Bartlett.'

'Do you not think that you offered the best deal to Bartlett?' she asked.

'Yes.'

'Do you not think that you deserve to win this contract on your own merit?'

'Yes,' he growled, his anger, his fear, all working to meet her tone.

'Then explain to me what *that* is.'

'It's insurance.'

'Insurance?' she spat.

He had never heard her tone so dark, so angry, and he hated that he had made it so. Hated that he had tainted her in any way because of his need for revenge.

'That isn't insurance. That is the complete and abject desecration of a person, Antonio. Your PI has dug up dirt on Mandy Bartlett and—what? You were going to use it to blackmail Bartlett into letting you invest in his company?'

He met her accusations with silence. There were no shields to protect him from the truth of her words.

'Is this because of what I said the other night? Because I followed her on social media and saw that she was young and foolish?'

The heartbreak in Emma's voice was too much for him to bear. But he simply couldn't tell her that she was wrong.

'Did it give you a lead to where your PI should look?'

'Yes,' he said, the word drawn from the very depths of his soul.

She turned her back to him and finally he glanced at the open folder—pictures of a young student spilled from it. Snapshots of a small blonde partying with her friends. And while one or two showed a happy, fun-loving girl, a few he could see peeking out beneath showed that she had started to experiment with drugs, that images of her scantily clad, showed her in poses that were highly salacious.

The thought of sharing them with the girl's father turned his stomach.

But the accusation, the pressure of the weight in Emma's eyes made him angry. Angry that his father had forced him to this—angry at himself. So he turned that anger and used it against Emma.

'It's hypocrisy. That *I* needed *you* to make me seem more palatable to Bartlett when his daughter is—'

'Stop,' Emma commanded, her hand coming up between them to accentuate her words unconsciously. 'Stop right there. It's *not* hypocritical to hold to a moralistic lifestyle while another human being chooses not to. This is a young girl taking a bad path. Those frozen snapshots aren't the whole picture of who she is and what she will be. Though they will be the *only* picture if you give them to her father.'

She was almost out of breath. She desperately wanted him to see what he was doing, to see where he was going. It was a path she wasn't sure he was going to come back from.

'Mandy Bartlett is a young girl making mistakes and hopefully she will learn from them. What she is *not*, Antonio, is a pawn to be used in a sick game between you and your father.'

'It is not a sick game, Emma. My father deserves to burn in hell for what he did.'

'Because he left you? Antonio, I realise that it must have—'

'No!' he roared. 'This isn't about him leaving, nor blackening my mother's name, nor forcing us to leave our home. *Dio*, we could have handled that. But Cici… She had more than just nightmares after the divorce,' he said, his voice hoarse with the emotion he had bottled up for years.

* * *

As if it were yesterday he remembered his mother's frantic phone call from Italy, just six months into his time in New York, begging him to come home immediately. She had been incoherent, and the only thing he'd managed to gather was that Cici was in hospital.

Nothing—*nothing*—had ever made him feel so terrified as those seven hours on the private jet Danyl had secured for him.

Until he'd seen the sight of his sister's small, impossibly emaciated frame. The doctors had explained that she must have been hiding it for years.

Antonio had known *exactly* how long she'd been hiding her eating disorder from them. At sixteen she'd weighed less than she had at thirteen, when Michael had changed their lives for ever.

And he'd not known. He'd not seen it.

His mother had been as truly shocked as he, and together they'd spent the next two weeks not leaving her side. The sounds of his sister's sobs had cut him deeply. He just hadn't been able to comprehend the negative sense of self coming from his once fun-loving, happy sister.

She had taken all the hurt and all the pain of her father's rejection, of being cut off from her friends and the life she had once known, and turned it in on herself. And he'd felt…angry and furious. He had known exactly who was to blame and had vowed to have his revenge.

Antonio hadn't realised that he'd been speaking—saying the words of his mind out loud to Emma in the suite—until he felt the rawness in his throat, saw the gathering tears framing her eyes.

She crossed the distance between them in quick

strides and wrapped her arms around him. Her body gave warmth and life to his that had turned so cold. She pressed kisses to his neck, pulling his mouth to hers, and he greedily consumed what she had to offer.

This kiss was so different from those that had passed between them before. Not one borne of a selfish need for satisfaction, of the infernal heat of their desires, but one of warmth, of comfort, of support and the one thing he could not bring himself to name.

He sought out the areas of her skin not concealed by the lace fabric of the dress. He needed to feel her beneath him, to take every comfort she was offering and more. In their kiss he tasted the salty sweetness of her tears, evidence of her grief for him and perhaps even of his own.

'I'm sorry,' she whispered against his lips. 'So sorry that you and Cici had to go through that.'

And he felt it down in the darkest part of his heart— her words beginning to shine a soft light on a place he'd thought unreachable. The place he'd thought irrevocably damaged by his father, by shock and fear for his sister.

Emma's heart had wrenched open at the sight of Antonio in such pain. He was on a precipice—one foot on land and one hovering above an abyss. Her only thought at that very moment was to comfort, to love the man she knew he could be—the man torn apart by a sense of injustice, the man who was devastated by the consequences of the careless actions of his father.

Her hands traced the lines of his strong jaw. His skin was cold to her touch, as if his memories had leached the warmth from his body. She imbued her kisses with every emotion she felt for him, desperate to show him that love had the power to heal. Not with words. Antonio wasn't ready for words. But with actions, deeds.

For just a moment he seemed simply unable to accept what she had to offer, and she wondered if she might not be able to reach him. Then, on a deep shudder, as if a barrier had fallen down and crumbled through his body, she felt his hands on her body. Touching, caressing, pulling her towards him.

Soft warmth turned to molten heat and threatened to consume them both whole.

Pulling him gently within her embrace, she walked them backwards towards her room, sidestepping the bags she'd placed there only an hour before. She drew him further, feeding him with need and desire and the love she felt for him.

Her hand went to her hair, releasing the pins that held it in place, allowing it to tumble down around her shoulders and arms. She found the discreet zip hidden at her side and pulled it down, peeling the lacy fabric from her skin.

His gaze seared her as she stood before him but she bore it, stood tall and proud beneath it. Wearing only panties and her heels, she felt no sense of the self-consciousness she had experienced the first time they had come together. There wasn't even a thought to her breasts or her femininity. There was only her need for him, her love for him, and it felt more powerful than anything she had experienced before. She revelled in the way his gaze ravaged her body—not just one part, not just *that* part, but all of her. As if he were seeing her for the very first time.

But he seemed struck still by the storm of emotion she read in his eyes. Not unsure, but unmoving. So she crossed to him, her hands going to the buttons of his shirt, undoing them so that she could feel the warmth and heat of his powerful chest. She marvelled at the light but rough dusting of hair beneath her fingers, at the way his heart raged beneath her hand. She followed the hollowed dips to the waistband of his trousers and unbuckled their fastening.

Throughout all of it he had yet to move, as if he were simply incapable of it. But tension and energy pulsed beneath his skin, begging for release, demanding it.

She left the trousers open and returned to his chest, pushing the shirt from his body, relishing the way he shivered beneath her touch, warmed beneath her kisses. But still he held himself back from her in a vice-like grip of control.

He was so glorious. Standing shirtless in her room. Her fingers traced the span of his upper arms, the defined muscles of his torso, the tense muscle offering such power and protection. She wanted to feel his arms about her, wanted to be in his embrace.

And suddenly, as if he'd heard her need, her desire, Antonio swept his arms around her, holding her to him as his open-mouthed kisses plunged the hollows of her neck. Electric currents matched only by the lightning crashing outside the windows licked up her spine and across her exposed skin.

In the space of a heartbeat he had taken control—or lost it. Emma couldn't really be sure. He devoured her with his touch, fed on her as a starving man would his first meal. He walked her back to the bed and came down on it with her, not once breaking the contact of his lips.

His hands and mouth worshipped her body, exploring every inch of her. She kicked off her shoes, leaving only the small thong covering her modesty. His hands gently pressed her thighs apart and he pressed hot wet

kisses against the material. Her own answering wet-
ness was no longer an embarrassment, simply a declaration of her desires and needs. He teased her through
the fabric, making her desperate to remove this last
barrier between them.

She groaned—or he did. Their united need was no
longer distinguishable. Her hips bucked off the mattress,
her body making its own demands while her mind and
heart simply loved.

With swift movements he removed his clothing and
shoes and leaned over her, his arms coming to rest either side of her face, holding her, cherishing her there.
He pressed the length of his body over hers, the weight
comforting, enticing, and elicited a restlessness from
her body that was almost fevered.

His erection pressed against her abdomen and she
sneaked a hand between them, taking hold of the length
of him, exploring him with her fingers. His skin was
smooth and hot, his arousal powerful, as she stroked
teasing shudders of pleasure from him.

His gaze found hers in the darkness of the room and
no words were necessary. He removed her thong—not
quickly, or urgently, but slowly, pulling the lace slowly
down each thigh, his hands sweeping it further, over
her ankles, taking his time. Not to allow her fears to be
allayed, but her desires to be inflamed.

He came back over her, gold flecks shining in the hot
molten lava churning in his eyes. It seemed for a moment as if he wanted to say something, as if the words
had somehow caught in his throat. But she didn't need
words.

She reached for him then, her hands coming to his
back, urging him to her, urging him into her, and as he
entered her she felt him fill all the empty spaces she

hadn't realised she had until she'd met him. Until she'd seen the man beneath the outer layer he wore about him like armour. Until she'd seen the man he could be.

He pressed deeper, further into her, filling her from the inside out as if they were no longer two people but one. And then there was no room for thought, only sensation. The slick slide of him within her was teasing dizzying need and arousal from her. Pushing her closer and closer to the edge of that same precipice she had sensed him upon.

Lost. He was lost. Antonio was drowning in a sea of emotion and sensation. Emma had cast a spell over him, soothing long-held hurts and filling the spaces with *her*. She was all he could see, all he could feel.

He plunged into her, wringing a cry from her lips, answering the one made by his soul, no longer wanting to think, no longer wanting to hurt. He took her mouth with his, exalting in the sweetness of her, his tongue mirroring his body's actions. He consumed the breath she exhaled, not wanting even that to escape his reach.

Sensation and need became overwhelming as he drove them again and again towards the edge of their release and pulled back. Desperate to stay in this state of bliss, desperate to hold back from the moment it would all come crashing down.

He teased and taunted, wringing pleasure from them both in equal measure. Sweat slicked his brow and hers. The room was filled with the gasps and sighs of exquisite arousal as time suspended its march as if just for them, giving them the simple gift of each other.

But soon need became a palpable thing and he could no longer hold back. He drove them both to the brink, holding them there on the edge. He could taste it on his tongue, in his throat, and hear it in the desperate cries falling from Emma's perfect lips.

With one final thrust he plunged them into the abyss, the joint feeling of their completion sending them into a spin he was sure would never stop.

Antonio woke from the sleep he hadn't realised had fallen over him. He knew before he had even opened his eyes that Emma wasn't with him. It was as if his body had become so attuned to her presence that he no longer needed sight.

And he didn't want to move. Didn't want this moment to happen. Because despite what had just passed between them he knew there was only one outcome—could only ever have been one outcome.

Reluctantly he left the bed, making his way to a bathroom wet with condensation from a shower he hadn't heard Emma take. He couldn't look at himself in the mirror as he stepped beneath the hot spray of water, shutting off the voice that called him a coward in his mind. Whether because of what he would do or couldn't do he didn't know.

Drying himself with a towel, he grabbed his discarded trousers and thrust his legs into them. The fact that only twenty-four hours earlier he had done the same, taken the same action, wasn't lost on him.

The night before he had been about to make a decision that would turn the tide in his battle against his father, no matter the cost. And now he knew instinctively that he would be asked to make the same decision again.

He walked through to the living area of the hotel suite, sidestepping Emma's bags, still packed from hours before. If his heart ached to see them there, he forced it aside.

Emma was sitting on the sofa, illuminated only by the light of dawn breaking over Buenos Aires through the windows. He tried to force a smile to his lips, but couldn't. There wasn't one answering his gaze as she caught sight of his presence.

Antonio was surprised to find that he no longer felt the sting and heat of anger. There was only resignation and sadness for something that was yet to pass. The kind of prescient ache that met inevitability.

'Are you going to use this?' she asked, holding the dossier on Mandy Bartlett.

Emma's heart was torn in two as he stood there, bisected by the shadows of the sunrise. Half in shade, half in light. She wondered which side he would choose. She had asked him the one question she wasn't sure she was ready for him to answer, but knew that she needed hear it.

'If I have to,' he said, and his words made her want to weep.

'Really? You'd destroy this man's family, just like your father did, to get what you want?'

'He deserves it, Emma.'

'Michael might—but does Benjamin Bartlett? Does Mandy?'

She hoped that she could make him see. Before he did something that would change him for ever.

'I will do *whatever* it takes. You already know that.'

She was surprised to hear softness in his voice—not anger, not fury, but gentleness, as if he were preparing her for news she didn't want to hear.

But she wasn't done fighting yet.

'No, I know you, Antonio. I have seen the person beyond the bitter hatred of your father, beyond the fear of the damage done to your sister. I've seen the love you have for her and your mother, the love you have for Dimitri and Danyl. I have seen the man you think you are not, and he is amazing. But if you do this,' she said, hoping against all hope, 'if you use this dossier you will destroy the goodness in you.'

She hated it that she was almost pleading now.

'You don't need to stoop to this level, Antonio. You're better than that. You could win the deal without it. I know it… I know it because I love you.'

Antonio's hand flew up between them, as if warding off her words.

'Don't say that, Emma.'

'Why not? It's the truth. I love you. I can see the man that you are beneath this path of revenge you're on.' She just hated it that he couldn't see it for himself.

'Emma, please—'

'No. You've shown me that all this time I've been hiding. You told me as much last night, when we were together. But it wasn't just my body that I was hiding. And you know that. You knew it then and you know it now. I was hiding from reaching for what I really wanted.'

No longer could Emma hold back the words and thoughts that had been forming, slowly shaping in her mind and heart.

'All this time, all these years, despite my Living List, despite the things I wanted to achieve—events and experiences that are almost meaningless in themselves— what I was really hiding from was love. And now that I *am* reaching for it, asking for it—asking to be loved by you and asking you to be worthy of that—you refuse?' she demanded.

She knew that he felt something for her—possibly even met her love with his own. Whether he would choose that instead of his need for revenge she really wasn't sure. But she knew that their love wouldn't survive if he chose wrong.

'I told you when we first made this deal, Emma, that emotions weren't going to be involved. They *can't* be involved.'

'But emotions are the one thing that's been driving you this whole time!' she cried.

'I can't afford to let my father get away with it. He is a villain, Emma.'

'But are you willing to *become* him to get what you want? Are you willing to become a villain yourself?'

'Emma, if *I* found this, then I guarantee you that my father will have.'

For the first time Emma heard something like desperation enter his voice.

'Then help Bartlett find a way through it,' she said, hoping that Antonio would find a way through his need for revenge. 'Show him the kindness that your father never showed to your mother or you or your sister.'

'I just can't take that risk. I *need* to do this.'

The despair in his voice nearly broke her. Nearly sent her running to this man who had stolen her heart like a thief. But she couldn't—no, she *wouldn't*.

'Then you do it without me.'

She made her way towards the cases by the door, but his words stopped her mid stride.

'It wouldn't have really mattered, though, would it?' he said, his words icy cold and ruthlessly quiet.

'What are you talking about?' she asked, turning towards him, confused at the change in his tone.

'Whether you had discovered this or not. You wouldn't have trusted me—trusted *this*—so you're leaving before you find out.'

'I—'

He didn't let her finish. 'Just like you did to that scared seventeen-year-old boy who might have battled through his fears for you. It's just another excuse to stop yourself from taking a chance.'

Emma felt the blood drain from her face, sucked into the vortex of ice running through her core. *Fear.* She felt fear.

'What is it, Emma? You think we're all going to leave? That we're not strong enough to stick it out with you?'

Antonio's words cut her, chipped away at the frigid centre of her. She hated him then. Hated it that his words were unearthing her deepest fears. The fears she barely allowed herself to admit to owning. The fears that held a mirror up to herself while she threw her accusations at him.

Of course she was scared! She was terrified. Terrified of him using the information in the dossier and even more scared of what it would mean if he *didn't*.

Because then she'd have to stay—really invest—wouldn't she? Not just some giddy, excited fantasy feeling such as she'd been enjoying these last few hours. But the harder stuff—the things that would make her or break her. In that moment she was on the precipice. The edge of a giant cliff-face. One that meant she would have to finally place her trust in someone not to hurt her. Not to leave.

Had she done that? Had she really let her seventeen-year-old boyfriend go without giving him a chance? Was she doing the same again with Antonio?

Her head ached and her mind swam, and in that moment she clung to the only thing she had in front of her.

'You want me to give *what* a chance? Your deal? The

role of fake fiancée? Or could we actually be more than that, Antonio?' she demanded.

It was as if they had become prize fighters, each taking the most painful chunk out of the other.

'There's just six days until the final meeting.'

It seemed neither was willing to admit just how far they'd come, just how much they meant to each other.

She shook her head, her heart breaking into a thousand pieces, the hurt magnified by each fracture, as if punctured by the shards of itself.

'If you can come up with this,' she said, gesturing to the documents that had torn them apart, 'then you can come up with an excuse as to where I am for Bartlett. But, Antonio,' she said—her last warning, her last hope, 'I'm telling you. There's no coming back from this. If you do this you'll be worse than your father. Because you *know* what you're doing, what you're risking, and just how many people you're hurting.'

Antonio didn't move while she retrieved her bags from the doorway to her bedroom. He didn't react to the kiss she placed on his cold cheek and he didn't say a word as she closed the door to the suite behind her.

Emma knew that it was the last time she would see Antonio. Oh, she was sure she would see pictures of him—might even happen upon him in person. But that person wouldn't be the man she had fallen in love with. If he did this—if he used that folder—she would never see that man again.

CHAPTER TEN

ANTONIO HEARD THE pounding on his New York penthouse apartment door and honestly couldn't tell if it was real or the manifestation of his hangover. Each strike followed the words that had been turning over and over in his mind since he last saw Emma.

You'll be worse than your father.

They had become a mantra, a taunt, a final threat hovering over him. One that he couldn't escape. Because he couldn't help feeling that Emma might be right. That in seeking his revenge he would actually be *worse* than his father.

The thought scoured him from the inside out, carved away at the deep ache in his chest.

Reluctant to open his eyes, he turned over and promptly fell onto the floor. The sofa. He'd been on the sofa.

He heard the door swing open and a pair of expensive black leather shoes came to stand very, *very* close to his head. He heard a string of Greek swearing, fit to turn the air blue, and the shoes disappeared. Antonio groaned, knowing that he'd sunk pretty low this time.

He'd been back in New York for two days since returning from Argentina, and in that time he'd answered none of the phone calls from his office, despite the rising panic in his CFO's tone. Instead he'd done nothing but drink and stare at the dossier on a woman he'd never met, might never meet, but who had come to represent the final blow to his relationship with Emma.

Antonio mustered the energy to roll onto his back, every muscle and brain cell protesting. Apart from his heart. His heart relished it, clearly deeming him worthy of such extreme levels of—

Ice-cold water crashed down on his head, the shock making him inhale quickly and deeply, taking half of the liquid into his lungs. He lurched up and bent over, choking and ready to kill Dimitri, holding a now empty jug.

'I've seen you in some pretty bad states, but this is just pitiful.'

'Get out.'

'No.' Dimitri held out a hand and hauled Antonio off the floor.

'Coffee,' was all about Antonio could manage to get out of his mouth.

'Shower,' Dimitri commanded.

It took a moment, but Antonio finally got himself off the floor and made his way through to the kitchen of his apartment, to find Dimitri manhandling a miniature saucepan on the stove.

'Did I fall through the rabbit hole?'

'It's called a *briki*. For an Italian, your coffee equipment is woefully lacking. It's a disgrace.'

'And you just *happened* to have this in your pocket?' Antonio asked, even the image of his friend with a *briki* in his pocket failing to raise a smile to his lips.

Dimitri looked affronted. 'Last year—Christmas. I didn't know what to get you. Emma suggested something that would make you more human in the mornings. It was in the back of your cupboard.'

'And the coffee? It doesn't look like it takes ground beans.'

'That I *did* bring with me.'

Antonio leant back on the kitchen counter that he rarely used and waited as Dimitri poured thick dark liquid into two small coffee cups.

'What are you doing here?' Antonio demanded, thankful that Dimitri ignored the hostility in his tone.

'You didn't answer your phone.'

'What's happened? Is everything okay?'

Panic rose in his chest, filling up the spaces and making it impossible to breathe. Had things got so bad that he had turned his back on his friends? Had something happened to Emma? For just a moment he felt the sliver of guilt as sharp as a chef's knife.

'Well, Danyl's trade negotiations are hanging by a thread, but he'll fix that. My father's company is on the brink, but *I'll* fix that. What are *you* going to do?'

Antonio cursed.

'You really messed this one up,' Dimitri said, casting an angry glance in his direction. 'And Emma is too good a person to mess with. So get in the shower. You smell like self-pity and alcohol and I don't like it. Be quick.'

Antonio forced himself under the hot water jets of his powerful shower. But it did nothing to remove the taint of dark grime he felt on his skin—had felt ever since seeing the photos of Mandy Bartlett his PI had dug up…ever since Emma had walked away from him.

Antonio decided to leave his hair wet. Although he was feeling much better, rubbing his head didn't seem that appealing. He entered his kitchen to find Dimitri poring over the images in the folder on Mandy Bartlett, and felt oddly furious that yet another person had seen them.

'Damaging stuff.'

'Yes,' Antonio practically growled, feeling oddly proprietorial over the contents of the folder...over Mandy's downward descent.

'Girl needs some sense knocked into her.'

'She needs help, Dimitri.'

'Yeah. Not sure her father will give it to her if he gets hold of these, though,' Dimitri mused. 'So Emma's gone, then?'

'Yes.'

'A shame. I like her.'

Antonio felt himself bristle.

'Don't be stupid—not in *that* way. So you can put the caveman back in the box.'

Antonio took a sip of the rich, peaty coffee, almost scalding his tongue in the process. He wasn't sure whether he was ready to hear what Dimitri had to say, but he knew Dimitri would say it anyway.

'Look, I know how much this deal means to you. I know your need for revenge, Antonio—trust me,' said Dimitri. 'I really do. And I will support whatever decision you make. Because you're my brother. You're my family. I don't believe those people who say you can't pick your family because I can and I have. You and Danyl—you're it. Whatever you choose to do with Bartlett is your own matter. I'm not here about the deal. I'm here about *her*.'

And finally all the resistance, all the avoidance that he'd practised since Emma had left him in the hotel suite in Argentina, dropped away.

'She held a mirror up to me, Dimitri. And I didn't like what I saw,' he admitted finally. The ache in his chest was opening up into a river of pain. 'The horror in her face...the betrayal... I don't think I can come back from that.'

'We all have to face the darkest parts of ourselves at some point, Antonio.'

There was no judgement in Dimitri's eyes, but in a way it only served to enrich the last memories he had of Emma and all the emotion he had seen in *her* eyes.

'Do you love her?'

'Yes. I do,' he replied—without thought, without pause.

He'd known it when he'd gone to the hotel suite that last night in Buenos Aires—known it as he'd allowed her to walk away from him. Had known it because it had hurt more than any other single thing in his life.

She had offered him everything. Love, acceptance, a way forward—a way other than the path of his revenge—and he had refused it all. He had refused *her*.

'Then you do what it takes, Antonio.'

'Even if that means letting go of the feud I have with my father?'

Emma pulled the cotton robe around her shoulders as she sank into her mother's sofa in the small house in Hampstead Heath. She had flown back into London four days ago and had slept for practically all of them, as if her body's learned response to trauma—emotional or physical—was rest.

So much had changed since she'd last left this house. Not only for her, but for her mother. Her old bedroom was now the spill-over storage area for Mark's hobby— his cars. Spare bits of machinery, cases of tools, several worn, torn and oil-stained clothes hung over the corners of barely held together boxes.

She was surprised to find that it didn't upset her. She was glad that her mother had found Mark—a kind man who loved her deeply. How could she begrudge her mother the very thing she wanted for herself? But every time she thought of Antonio her heart ached a little more. She knew that she was feeling grief—grief for him, for herself. But even through that pain, the exhaustion and the upset, she knew that she should get up every day and fight for the future she had once closed herself off from.

The sitting room was still just how she'd remembered it. Books lining two sides of the room, paintings framing the windows on the front wall, and covering the back wall completely, as if they were puzzle pieces, separated by only the thinnest of gaps of wall. It felt familiar—but not as soothing as it had once been.

Her mother entered the room, her jeans and loose shirt covered in mismatched blotches of cast-off paint, thin lines from where she had cleaned the pallet knife she used against her thighs.

Louise Guilham was beautiful. Emma had inherited her mother's thick dark hair and slender form. But it wasn't her physical appearance that made her beautiful. It was her happiness in following her dream of painting, in her love for Mark. It glowed from her skin and Emma felt sallow and shadowed in comparison.

She mustered a smile as her mother looked momentarily confused to find Emma curled up on the sofa at five in the afternoon, a robe wrapped around clothes she had slept in, not having had the energy to change. That was her mother's way when she was locked into a painting. The world could descend into Armageddon and she'd still be considering which colour to put where.

'Would you like a cup of tea?' Louise asked.

'I don't suppose you have any whisky?' Emma replied, memories of a conversation with Antonio so very close to the surface of her thoughts.

Her mother raised an eyebrow, but disappeared into the kitchen, returning with two glasses full of ice and amber.

'Do you want to talk about it?' she asked Emma, pressing the glass into her hands and taking a seat beside her on the old, battered but comfortable sofa.

Emma turned, resting her back against the sofa's arm, stretching out her legs. Her mother took Emma's feet in her hands and put them on her lap, passing soothing strokes over her bare skin as she had once done so many times when Emma had been ill.

Over the last four days, between hours of sleep, Emma had unfolded the story of her and Antonio, opening her heart and her mind to the mother she wouldn't hide a thing from—ever. But now Emma felt the stirrings of the question she had always wanted to ask and never had the courage to.

Until now.

'Not about Antonio, no. But I want to talk to you about Dad.'

'Oh? Okay.'

Mark hovered in the doorway. He must have heard Emma's question, and now he sent them both a gentle smile. He announced that he was '*just going to pop to the pub*', and left them alone, free to talk openly.

Yet another thing for which she was grateful to Mark.

'Mum, was it my fault that you and Dad split up? Was it because I got ill?'

'Oh, Em,' her mother said. 'How long have you thought that?'

'Since it happened,' Emma admitted guiltily.

'Oh, my love. No. No, it wasn't your fault at all— and neither was it because of the cancer,' she said, both sincerity and sadness in her voice.

Her mother's attention drifted to the window and she sighed.

'Your father and I met and married when we were very young. We loved each other greatly. And when you came along we loved you even more. But unlike some couples who are able to grow together, grow *up* together, we just…*didn't*,' she said, with a small shrug of her shoulders.

'So you stayed together because I got sick? That's even worse,' Emma said, guilt piercing her already fractured heart.

'No, sweetheart, we stayed together because we loved *you*,' her mother said, her voice and tone adamant and powerful. 'And that love was a strong, beautiful amazing thing that saw us all through the darkest of times. Neither me nor your father would change a day of it.'

Emma felt a huge weight lift from her chest as the fear that had been holding her back for so long left and was replaced with the truth in her mother's words.

Looking back, it was as if the memories that she had always shied away from had been freshly painted over, dusted in fine golden light, showing her different images. Where once she had felt guilt and sadness, she now felt strength and light. Seeing the way that they had stayed together as a gift.

And in that moment she realised that Antonio had been right. She *had* been running away from him. Consumed by her own fears, she had run away from her feelings. She had not stayed with Antonio when he had most needed her. Worse, she had done the very thing she had always been scared that someone would do to her.

'Oh, Mum…' Emma couldn't help the cry falling

from her lips. 'I left him…' she said, tears trembling at the edges of her eyes.

Her mother laid a reassuring hand on her legs. 'From what you told me, Emma, he had a decision to make and he had to make it by himself.'

'Mum, I love you. So, so very much. But I have to go.'

Antonio resisted the urge to place a finger between his collar and his neck in an attempt to loosen the feeling of a noose tightening around him. He could not— *would* not—show any sign of weakness in front of his father *or* Bartlett.

They were in the boardroom at Bartlett's sleek offices, just a few blocks over from Antonio's own office. That he was being forced to breathe the same air as his father angered him. But he had to let that anger go. Bartlett had promised a decision today, after final pitches from himself and Michael Steele, in a move that was both highly unusual and had taken on the air of a courtroom with closing arguments.

His father had blustered through his determined statements—more of the same kind of financial arguments that had been printed in the world's international press over the last week. About how Michael's age and experience gave more weight to his investment and the promise that he could best his son financially.

Which he couldn't.

But apparently the more he said it, the more Michael thought Bartlett would believe it. Michael had also made asinine suggestions as to Antonio's scandalous reputation and the damage it would do to Bartlett's company—in spite of his recent, perhaps even *conve-*

nient engagement—and once again Antonio's anger that his father should involve Emma in this had been swift.

But just as swift was the recrimination that he had brought Emma into it himself.

Antonio took a moment, after his father had finished, and Bartlett turned his attention to him. He checked his feelings, checked his decision and felt at peace. Possibly for the first time in years.

'So much has been said about the strength, might and determination that got my father here,' Antonio began. 'About how he's the right man to invest in your company and see it into the future. But I disagree. And not just because I don't believe him for a second.'

He pushed the threads of anger aside, holding on to the purpose of his intention for the meeting. Holding on to the memory, the realisation of what Emma had shown him.

'It's not very often that business deals come down to right and wrong. You're a man of strong morals, Mr Bartlett,' he said, holding the older man's gaze, needing him to see the truth of the words he was about to say. 'And if I'm honest—*truly* honest—I can't say the same of myself.'

He saw the shock on Bartlett's face, heard the small gasp that spoke of his confusion at a man appearing to sabotage his own pitch.

'I came after this deal not because I want to invest in your company, Mr Bartlett, but because I want my father not to.'

He didn't have to look at his father to know that he was practically vibrating with glee—he could feel it in the air, the drop in temperature from Bartlett's end of the room matching the raised heat from his father's.

'And in order to do that I betrayed and treated badly

a woman of such high integrity that she would put us all to shame. She certainly put *me* to shame,' he admitted, feeling the words ring true in his heart. 'She showed me that I was reaching only for revenge when what I should have been reaching for was to be *better* than him— better than my father. A better man for myself and the woman I love. I did and still do want to invest in your company, Mr Bartlett. But not at the price of my morals or my heart. And I should warn you that if you choose my father, you'll be selling your soul to the devil. Make your decision, Benjamin. And once you have—whatever it is—there is a matter I'd like to discuss with you. One that I'd like to help with, if you'll let me.'

With that, Antonio got up from his chair and turned—expecting to leave, expecting to walk out into the sunshine of a New York summer, expecting to track down Emma wherever she might be and beg her forgiveness.

But it seemed she had other ideas.

Emma was standing in the doorway of the boardroom, and his first thought was how truly amazing she looked.

Her eyes shone, and her hair was loose around her shoulders—it was the first time he'd seen it so during the day, outside of the nights of passion they had shared. She was dressed in a brightly coloured dress that hugged her chest and waist, flared about her legs, and a simply outrageous and uncharacteristically Emma pair of high heels encased her feet.

But it was exactly how he'd always imagined her. Bright, feminine, sensual and powerful.

'How much did you hear?' he asked, walking towards her, hoping that she wasn't a figment of his fevered imagination.

'Everything,' she said, allowing him to guide her away from the office.

He couldn't take his eyes from her—couldn't bring himself to say another word until they were free from the office, the deal, his father. He wanted to leave it all behind him.

Well, not *all*. He had meant what he'd said to Bartlett. Once the deal was made—whether Bartlett chose him or not—Antonio wanted to speak to the man about his daughter. He either knew and wasn't sure how to proceed, or he didn't know and would need help and support to get through to her. But Antonio wouldn't allow the situation with Mandy Bartlett to go unchecked.

They emerged from the office onto the sidewalk and, still without a word, he took her hand and led her as quickly as her heels would allow across the road, towards the lower entrance of Central Park. He wanted life, greenery and peace to be the background of their next conversation. Not the high-rise hustle and bustle of Manhattan.

Walking away from the summer crowds of tourists gathering around the ice-cream sellers and busking musicians, Antonio drew them towards the quieter pathways, dappled with leafy shade and cool breeze. But when he got where he'd wanted to be he suddenly found himself unsure. What if she didn't want him? What if his decision hadn't made any difference to her feelings?

In the end it seemed that Emma found her courage before he did. She stopped, gently pulling on his arm, turning her towards him.

'Antonio, I'm so sorry that I left you,' she said. 'I never—'

'Don't be sorry,' he interrupted, hating it that she felt an ounce of sadness or regret about the actions that had forced him to confront his feelings in a way that nothing else had. 'I needed to see the true depths of the darkness I was about to fall into before I could reach for you, before I could reach for the light.'

He paused, hoping that she understood his words, took them into her as deeply as he meant them.

'I want to be worthy of you, Emma. I want to be better than him. I am now and will continue to be. Whether you'll do me the honour of becoming my wife or not. I know you will—'

'Wait,' she said, throwing up a hand between them. 'What?' she asked.

He cursed, realising that he'd blundered over the most important thing he'd ever asked in his life. The first time they had done this it had been for the deal. This time he wanted it to be a moment that she cherished, that she remembered, might even tell their children about one day.

'Emma, I love you. So very much,' he said, digging into his pocket for the small box he'd arranged to have sent over from the shop in Buenos Aires. 'I know you heard what I said in the room with Bartlett and my father—but I want you to hear it now. Here, without them present, not for show or for a deal, but for *you*. For years I've shied away from love, from meaningful relationships, because I thought that love was a destructive, harmful thing. Something my father used against my mother—something that left my sister destroyed when it was withdrawn from her. And something that left me with my own scars. But that wasn't true. You showed me, that last night in Argentina and in so many ways preceding it, that love is a healing, powerful, amazing thing. I know now that what my father did wasn't borne of love. And no matter what happens—whether you say yes or not—I want you to know that I love you, and I will love you every single day for the rest of my life if you will let me.'

He got down on one knee, drawing the curious gazes of some of the few people passing by. And it was then that Emma truly knew the power of their love as it washed over them both from his words, his eyes, his heart.

'Emma Guilham,' he said, taking her hand in his, 'would you do me the incredible honour of being my wife?' he asked, sending her heart soaring higher than she had ever felt.

She couldn't help the laugh that escaped her lips, but she too had words she wanted to share. Things she wanted him to understand so that they could move ahead with all the love and security she knew they would both feel.

She gently tugged at him, attempting to pull him up from where he knelt. And she laughed again when he shook his head and refused, drawing even more attention from the people passing.

'If you won't stand then I shall have to come down to you,' she taunted.

'So be it. I will not move until I've had your answer,' he said, a stubborn determination filling his words in a blissful promise that she wouldn't have thought him capable of when she'd first met him.

So she did as she had said and took to her knees, facing him, holding her gaze with his and, just like Antonio, not caring of the attention they were drawing.

'For so long I thought myself strong, capable—no,' she said as he tried to interrupt her, knowing that he would contradict her words, but knowing too that she needed to say them. 'I was, am and will continue to be a survivor. But for all the promise and hope put into that list I made as a seventeen-year-old, I never had the courage to ask for the things that I truly wanted. Self-acceptance, self-love and ultimately true love itself. Antonio, you showed me that my scars are beautiful, you taught me to reach for the things I was too scared and too unwilling to admit to myself that I wanted, and you proved to me that doing so, whether successful or not, was the real gift. You showed me that it was okay— more than that, *vital* for me to put my whole self out into the world. And I love you for it, and I will love you for it until my last breath. So, yes, Antonio Arcuri, I *will* marry you.'

The moment the words had left her mouth Antonio pulled Emma to him in a kiss that she would never forget. It was full of the taste of love, passion and everything in between. It was full of light, laughter and finally, the knowledge that they would live happily ever after.

EPILOGUE

One year later...

ARCURI WELCOMES THE
BIRTH OF HIS SON!
BY ROANNA KING

International tycoon announces the
birth of a beautiful baby boy!

*Hearts across the world might have burned with
envy at the pictures of Antonio Arcuri's wedding
only four months ago. The shocking speed not only
of his engagement to Emma Guilham—his one-time
PA—but his subsequent marriage raised more than
a few eyebrows amongst our hallowed readership.*

*One could argue that the reason for this was
the soon-to-follow birth of their son, little Luca
Arcuri. But that would be an argument from a
harder heart than mine.*

*Because it's clear to see the love shining in the
eyes of this proud papa, and I can only wish them
luck in their future endeavours.*

*So let me be the first to congratulate you, Mr
Arcuri, on the wonderful birth of your son.*

EMMA ENTERED THE large open-plan living room of their house in Sorrento, with her gorgeous son Luca cradled in her arms, to find Antonio talking to himself.

'*"Harder heart than mine..."*' he muttered angrily. '*"Let me be the first..."* Really, how dare she?'

Antonio threw yet another one of Roanna King's articles into the bin.

Emma laughed—something she did so very much these days—and crossed the room to pull him into a kiss that wasn't nearly as deep as she'd like, but perfectly respectable given there were three of them squashed into each other's arms.

'How dare who?'

'Mmm?' he asked, as he took in the sight of his wife and child. 'I've forgotten—not important.'

And he meant it. All he had ever wanted was here in this room.

So much had changed in the year since he had discovered Bartlett wanted investment in his company—since he'd demanded that Emma find him a fiancée. At the time he'd thought that what he'd wanted was revenge, to destroy his father. But things hadn't quite turned out that way.

Soon after his *second* proposal to Emma, Benjamin Bartlett had got in touch. Apparently Michael Steele had tried to use the information about his daughter against him, but instead of buckling to the demands he'd made Bartlett had stuck to his instincts, turned to Antonio instead, and together they had worked to help Mandy Bartlett weather the storm that Michael Steele had launched upon the poor girl.

Sometimes Antonio very much wished that he'd found a way to avoid that for Bartlett and his family, but Antonio was beginning to realise that accepting the consequences of one's actions was an important part of the healing process.

Bartlett's shares had wobbled for a few days under the negative press, but with Antonio's investment they'd soon recovered. With Antonio, Emma and her father's support, Mandy Bartlett had gone into rehab and ended up finishing her degree and passing with high honours, and the Bartletts were now a firm fixture in their social calendar.

And as for Michael Steele—it hadn't taken long for the press to turn against the man. Once they'd discovered that it had been *he* who had leaked the dossier about Mandy's troubles, and there had been the suggestion—though unproved and unsupported—that it had been in retaliation for a rejected business venture, it had sickened the international press.

Hounded and stalked by their fury that he could abuse such an innocent young girl, Michael had found his existing business associates driving as far from him as possible. The man had become a financial and social pariah—though Antonio had been surprised to discover that it hadn't felt as good as he'd thought. It had been a period that had been difficult for Antonio, when he'd realised just how far he had nearly sunk himself. But Emma had helped him through with patient love, sweet comfort and reassurance.

Shortly after Antonio had made good on his first promise to Emma, and the Bartletts had been present, alongside Dimitri and Danyl, to toast Emma's new role as head of the Arcuri Foundation—celebrations that had gone on long into the night, full of joy, laughter and hope for the future.

Despite their busy schedule, they had already ticked off several of the things on Emma's Living List. Even

now, standing in their home in Sorrento, he remembered
the exquisite joy in Emma's eyes as they'd shared a sunrise over the Terhren desert, and the happiness shining
just as bright when they'd seen the sun set over the Mediterranean, surrounded by their closest friends, Danyl
and Dimitri, and their respective families.

'Where are you?' Emma asked, and smiled as she
passed his son to him.

'Right here, where I should be,' replied Antonio,
drawing his thoughts away from the past and holding
their precious son to his chest.

He watched Emma, stepping over the changing mat
and the stacks of muslins, nappies and other little things
he'd never thought to find such joy in, as she went to
the mirror that covered almost the entire length of one
wall. He watched her as she checked her hair and her
brightly coloured dress. He never tired of seeing her in
autumn colours, and he was sure that he hadn't seen
her wear black since Buenos Aires.

He gently put his sleeping son in the small bassi-
nette beside the sofa, already missing the soft, gentle
comfort of having him in his arms, and walked to his
wife, unable to resist the urge to hold her, touch her. He
wondered if he ever would.

He pressed a starburst of kisses along the beautiful
length of her neck, knowing Emma would understand
the gesture and the silent, sensual request behind it.

Emma playfully slapped his arms away from her.
'You know we don't have time, Antonio. Danyl and
Dimitri will be here with their families in little over
two hours, and Danyl's protection services always make
such a drama about the whole thing—they'll be at the
door in twenty minutes.'

'Having a sheikh as a friend has both its perks and its curses,' Antonio growled.

That each of the Winners' Circle had found happiness and love within the space of such a short time was still a marvel to all three men. But those were stories for another time. For now, Antonio's only thought was of his wife, and just what he could do with twenty little minutes.

A wicked smile crept across his face, and Emma soon discovered that twenty minutes could be just as pleasurable as a lifetime.

* * * * *

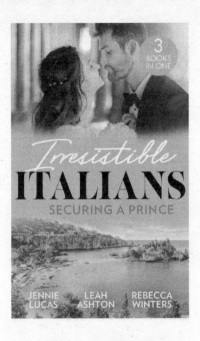

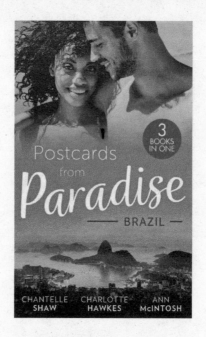

MILLS & BOON

MODERN

Power and Passion

Prepare to be swept off your feet by sophisticated, sexy and seductive heroes, in some of the world's most glamourous and romantic locations, where power and passion collide.

JOIN US ON SOCIAL MEDIA!

Stay up to date with our latest releases, author news and gossip, special offers and discounts, and all the behind-the-scenes action from Mills & Boon...

 @millsandboon

 @millsandboonuk

 facebook.com/millsandboon

 @millsandboonuk

It might just be true love...

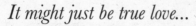